21ST CENTURY DEAD

21ST CENTURY DEAD

A ZOMBIE ANTHOLOGY

Edited by Christopher Golden

ST. MARTIN'S GRIFFIN
NEW YORK

21ST CENTURY DEAD. Copyright © 2012 by Christopher Golden. All rights reserved. Printed in the United States of America. For information, address St. Martin's Press, 175 Fifth Avenue, New York, N.Y. 10010.

www.stmartins.com

ISBN 978-0-312-60584-1 (trade paperback)
ISBN 978-1-250-01591-4 (e-book)

First Edition: July 2012

10 9 8 7 6 5 4 3 2 1

COPYRIGHT ACKNOWLEDGMENTS

CONTENTS

Contents

21ST
CENTURY
DEAD

ZOMBIES ARE GOOD FOR YOU

AN INTRODUCTION

Christopher Golden

A COUPLE OF YEARS AGO, I set out to examine the zombie craze through a different sort of lens. Tales of the walking dead have been around since long before Lazarus, populating the folklore of many regions of the world in one form or another. But in the early years of the twenty-first century, zombies experienced an incredible surge in pop culture popularity. George Romero had laid the groundwork decades earlier, with *Night of the Living Dead* and its sequels, but this was something far beyond what Romero accomplished. Many will point their fingers at one thing or another—a particular novel or film or comic book—as the spark that lit the fuse on the current explosion of zombie love, but such attributions never ring true to me. Pop culture hasn't embraced zombies because of *The Walking Dead* . . . it's embraced *The Walking Dead* because it's a damn fine drama (in comic book and in television form) *about* zombies.

I put together my first zombie anthology, *The New Dead,* to explore this phenomenon. I believed then, and am firmly convinced now, that all the chatter about people getting bored with vampires and simply needing a new monster is off base. Perhaps there is an element of that in the surge of zombie popularity, but if so, it's only because most modern pop culture vampires are not at all frightening, and people need something to *fear.*

The twenty-first century has so many fears. Some are old, filtered through a contemporary sensibility, and some are quite new. Our governments involve us in wars few want or believe in, partly because it's so hard to ferret out the individual jihadists who are our true enemies. We have orthodox wars in an unorthodox time. We fear the political and personal corruption that is eating away at our

1

culture. The Internet and twenty-four-hour news channels barrage us with tales of stolen or murdered children, nations crumbling, drug wars, parental neglect, natural disasters, and the erosion of honor, nobility, and personal responsibility in a million small ways.

We fear death, of course, and what comes afterward, and one of the ways in which we process that fear is by approaching our darkest wonderings from an oblique angle. In the twenty-first century, zombie stories have become one of those processing tools, not just for our fear of death but for fear in general. We live in a post–9/11 world, where the prospect of disaster feels far less like fiction and more like imminent possibility. When an earthquake and tsunami combine to take eighteen thousand lives in Japan, or an earthquake in Haiti kills over *three hundred thousand,* entering the list of the top five natural disasters on record, we are as horrified as ever, but perhaps not quite as shocked as we might have been, once upon a time.

The ground, you see, has become unstable beneath our feet. Not just the earth itself but the foundations of our world culture have become unreliable. Surely humanity has always been painfully aware of the ephemeral nature of life, and past centuries have had their share of disease and disaster, but in this century we are constantly reminded of the horrors the world has to offer, all day long and in close-up.

And yet we live and laugh and love. We hope for bright futures for our children and embrace our individual passions and cultural pastimes. With so much horror around us, it is imperative that we process our fears, and I have no doubt that zombie literature, film, and television are among the ways in which we do so.

The variety of stories in *The New Dead* pleased me greatly.

In *21st Century Dead* you'll find nineteen brilliant tales of death and resurrection. Some are down-and-dirty zombie stories, excellent examples of the form, whose intent is a punch in the gut, to entertain, to horrify . . . or perhaps all three. Others have a different purpose, helping us to examine and process our fears about a variety of issues, from drugs to religion to reality television. They explore dark futures, and dark hearts, plumbing the depths of love, loss, and neglect.

And some even give us hope.

I am fascinated by the variety of stories created by the stellar array of authors whose work is represented herein, and I hope you will share that fascination.

Now, read on.

You'll thank me later.

BITERS

Mark Morris

THE GUARD ON THE GATE stared at Mrs. Keppler's pass for a long time. He stared at it for *so* long, his face stern beneath his peaked cap, that Fleur began to get nervous. When the guard went back into his little hut, Fleur felt sure it was to call for reinforcements. She knew she'd done nothing wrong, and she was pretty sure that neither her friends nor Mrs. Keppler had done anything wrong, either, but the sense of guilt and crawling dread persisted just the same.

Maybe it was the research facility that gave her these feelings. It was like a prison, all high steel fences and barbed wire and clanging gates. In that sense, it was like a smaller version of the compound in which they all lived. But the difference with the compound was that you couldn't *see* the fences, not on a day-to-day basis anyway. And the guard uniforms were different here, gray and more formal than the faded brown combat fatigues that her brother Elliott and the rest of the perimeter security team wore. She saw the guard in the gray uniform speaking into a telephone and casting glances in their direction. Finally he put the phone down and marched stiffly across to the open door of the yellow school bus, where Mrs. Keppler was patiently waiting. Fleur was so relieved to see a smile break across the guard's face that her breath emerged in a gasp.

"That's all fine, madam," he said. "You have clearance to proceed."

Mrs. Keppler thanked him and the doors of the school bus concertinaed shut. The huge gates creaked slowly inward and Mr. Medcalf, their driver, drove through the widening gap.

Inside the facility, which looked to Fleur like nothing more than a mass of giant concrete building blocks stuck haphazardly together, more gray-uniformed men were pointing and waving their arms. Following their directions, Mr. Medcalf drove around to a car park at the back, where a squat, bald man whose brown suit matched the color of his bristling mustache directed them with fussy hand movements into a designated space.

"Welcome to the Moorbank Research Facility," the man said when they had disembarked. "I understand you're here to participate in the Infant Care Program?"

Mrs. Keppler, a tiny, owlish woman, who to Fleur and her friends seemed ageless, said, "Yes, that's right."

"Excellent." Raising his voice slightly to address the class, the man said, "My name is Mr. Letts. I'm the assigned facilitator for your visit here today. I'll be escorting you to the Crèche, explaining the procedure, and answering any questions you may have. Can I ask that you stick close together at all times and follow my instructions? We don't want anyone getting lost now, do we?"

He bared his small white teeth in a grin, which instantly tightened to an exasperated grimace when a hand shot up.

"Yes, Joseph," Mrs. Keppler said.

"Sir, miss, I was wondering, are the betweeners allowed to walk around inside?"

A few of his classmates sniggered at the babyish phrase. In her sweet and patient voice, Mrs. Keppler said, "Of course not, Joseph. We won't be in any danger. Isn't that right, Mr. Letts?"

"Oh, absolutely," Mr. Letts agreed. "Security is paramount here at Moorbank."

He led them across the car park, toward a pair of large glass doors beneath a curved metal awning. Next to the doors, inset into a recess in the wall, was a dark glass panel. The pressure of Mr. Letts's hand on the panel activated a crisscrossing network of glowing red lasers, which drew murmurs of appreciation from the children. After the lasers had scanned Mr. Letts's handprint, a series of clunks announced that the locks sealing the doors had disengaged, allowing their guide to lead them inside.

"It smells funny," whispered Millie to Fleur, before clenching her teeth as her words echoed around the high-ceilinged lobby.

Her voice clearly didn't carry as far as the girls had thought, because the only person who answered was Alistair Knott, who stooped to push his freckled face between the girls' heads to murmur, "That's the chemicals they use to keep the biters fresh."

Millie pulled an "eeew" face and shuddered violently enough to rattle her beaded dreadlocks, but Fleur just rolled her eyes. As Mr. Letts led them along a series of featureless corridors and up numerous flights of stairs, Fleur recalled Mrs. Keppler telling them in their history lessons that although people had started turning into what Alistair had called "biters" before Fleur and her classmates were born, it wasn't really all *that* long ago—only thirty or forty years. It was long enough, Mrs. Keppler had said, for the world to have changed from the way it had been at the beginning of the twenty-first century, and for the living to have become sufficiently organized that their lives weren't a daily battle for survival. However, it was not *really* long enough for the older generations, who remembered how things used to be, to have fully come to terms with the situation, or for scientists to have found a cure for the R1 virus.

The *R* in R1 stood for Reanimation. Mrs. Keppler had told them that, too, though Fleur, like most kids, had known that since she could remember. It was a word she heard almost daily. It was what politicians and newsreaders called those with the virus: the Reanimated. Most people, like Elliott and Fleur's mum, Jacqui, just called them R1s, though sometimes Elliott called them "reamers." Jacqui didn't like him using that word, though; she said it was "derogatory," which Fleur thought meant that it was kind of a swearword, though she wasn't sure why. Most little kids called the R1s "betweeners" because they were neither one thing nor the other. And there were other words for them, too, slang words like *biters* and *decoms* and loads of others.

What people never seemed to say, though, not directly anyway, was that the R1s were *dead*. It was like it was a taboo subject. It was like admitting something that was dark and forbidden. On TV, R1s were always described as "sufferers" or "victims" or "the infected." Fleur knew that scientists had been searching for a cure for the R1 virus for years, and she thought the reason why no one ever actually said the R1s were dead was that you couldn't cure death, and therefore that would mean the scientists had been wasting their time. When Fleur had asked Jacqui what the Reanimated were reanimated *from,* her mum had mumbled something about it being a "gray area."

And when Fleur had pushed her to explain further, Jacqui had gotten angry and said she didn't want to talk about it.

The facility was such a maze of corridors, staircases, and numbered doors that the novelty of being inside it quickly paled. Fleur tried to imagine what might lie behind the doors. Offices? Laboratories? Cells for the inmates? If so, they must be empty or soundproofed, because, despite walking for what seemed miles, she and her classmates did not encounter another soul, living or otherwise, on their journey. Plus, they heard nothing but their own clomping feet and Mr. Letts's occasional barked orders to stay together.

When their guide finally turned and held up a hand, Fleur initially thought it was to reprimand those children who had begun to moan about their aching feet. Then Mr. Letts turned to a keypad and tapped in a code, whereupon the door beside it unsealed with a magnified wheeze. He marched inside without explanation, leaving Mrs. Keppler to usher the children after him.

Entering shoulder to shoulder with Millie, Fleur found herself in a white oblong room twice as big as her sitting room at home. Despite its size, however, it was spartan, but for a desk, chair, and computer tucked into an alcove in the left-hand wall. The most notable thing about the room was that almost the entire wall behind Mr. Letts, who had turned to face the children filing through the door, was composed of black glass. It reminded Fleur so much of a cinema screen that she half expected Mr. Letts to tell them to sit down in cross-legged rows to watch a film about the history and function of the facility.

He didn't, however. He simply stood, hands clasped in front of him, until they were all quiet. Then he said, "This is the observation and monitoring room for the Crèche here at Moorlands. Behind me is the Crèche itself, which I'm sure you are all eager to see. However, before I reveal it, I need to prepare you as much as I'm able for what you're about to experience. I also want to talk for a few minutes about the Infant Care Program in general. Before I start, can I ask how many of you have seen photographs or news footage of the Reanimated?"

Almost all the children raised their hands.

"And how many of you have seen the Reanimated in the flesh?"

All but two of the hands went down.

Mr. Letts fixed Ray Downey, who still had his hand up, with a penetrating stare. "Would you care to tell us about your experience?"

Now that he had been put on the spot, Ray's smug expression slipped into one of nervousness. As if justifying himself, he said, "I was with my friend Jim Brewster. We were on our bikes one day and we heard all this shouting 'round the back of Hampson's store, so we went down to take a look. The biter was this old guy who must have gotten sick somewhere nearby and hadn't been reported in time. Mr. Hampson and some other men were holding him off with poles. Then the cops . . . er, the police came and they caught the biter in a net and took him away in a van." Almost reluctantly he added, "It was pretty cool."

"Cool," repeated Mr. Letts tersely. "Is that what you really thought?"

Ray Downey shrugged.

Pursing his lips disapprovingly, Mr. Letts turned to John Caine, the other boy with his hand up. "What about you?"

John's blond fringe twitched as he blinked it out of his eyes. His voice was so low and muffled that it sounded as if his throat were trying to hold it back. "My dad took me to see the perimeter when I was six. We didn't go very close. We parked on a hill looking down on it. When we were there we saw an R1 come up to the fence. A woman."

"And how did that make you feel?"

John frowned in embarrassment or resentment. "Scared," he admitted.

"Why?"

"Because she made a horrible noise. And her skin was all sort of . . . blue and purple." As if the memory had enlivened him, the rest of his words emerged in a rush that threatened to descend into incoherence. "There was this look on her face. Blank, but like something had taken her over, as if she was a person but not really a person, as if she had turned into something *awful.* . . ." He ended with a coughing gasp, as if he'd run out of breath, and then in the same low, muffled voice with which he'd started his account he added, "It gave me nightmares."

Mr. Letts nodded as if in approval. "Thank you. That is closer to the response I was looking for." Clasping his hands again, he said, "The point is that a firsthand encounter with an R1 is far more debilitating and disturbing than any amount of photographs or news footage can ever convey. The reason for this is that the Reanimated don't give off the subtle human signals we're used to, and which we subconsciously pick up on all the time; and so, denied of that input, and coupled with their alarming appearance, our minds automatically recoil from them. It finds them repugnant, it finds them *wrong,* and therefore something to be avoided."

He paused, allowing his words to sink in. Then he said, "That, I'm afraid, is something that you're all going to have to accept and put aside in this instance. As I'm sure you have been informed, the Infant Care Program has been designed and formulated with a number of objectives in mind. First, it is to give young people like yourselves prolonged exposure to R1 sufferers—but exposure which, if you behave responsibly, will not result in the slightest risk or injury to either yourselves or those around you.

"Now, some of you may be wondering *why* exposure to the Reanimated is considered such a valid and valuable exercise. The simple answer is that it will both enable you to understand and come to terms with those afflicted by the virus, and also hopefully allay some of the fears and prejudices you perhaps have about them. R1 is part of our world now, and despite ongoing research it is unlikely to disappear in any of our immediate futures. The more understanding and acceptance we therefore have of its effects and of those afflicted by it, the better it will be for all concerned in the long term. After all, it is likely that some of you will be working with, or in close proximity to, R1 sufferers once you leave school and venture into the world of employment. It is therefore best to be prepared—and the Infant Care Program is an invaluable step toward that state of preparation."

Warming to his subject, he continued. "A further reason why the program itself has been implemented is to give young people a chance to temporarily assume what is in effect a considerable amount of personal responsibility. This may seem daunting, even frightening, at first, but we in the program hope that ultimately you will come to look upon this next week as both a challenge and an opportunity to show just *how* mature and resourceful you can be. Before I talk about the specifics of your assignments, let me dispel some of the rumors about R1."

He raised a finger, as if about to accuse them of starting the rumors themselves. And then, as forcefully as if resuming an argument, he said, "Yes, R1 *is* a virus, but it could only be contracted by living beings such as yourselves if your blood and/or other bodily fluids were to become mingled with that of an R1 sufferer. R1 is not—I repeat *not*—an airborne virus. Neither can it be contracted simply by touching the flesh of a sufferer—however, we will issue you a plentiful supply of disposable gloves as an extra precaution against physical contact.

"In the unlikely event that you *should* get scratched or bitten by your assigned R1 infant during the course of the program, the important thing to remember is, firstly, not to panic, and secondly, to seek immediate medical attention. Although we are still some way from finding a cure for the virus, we have discovered a vaccine that can eradicate R1 cells in the early stages of infection. Evidence has shown that patients treated with this vaccine within the first ninety minutes of infectious contact have a 98.7 percent recovery rate. However, there is *no need whatsoever* for you to become involved in any situation where there is even the remotest risk of infection. The R1 infant assigned to you should remain muzzled at all times, and as long as you adhere to the necessary precautions you will be fine."

Alistair Knott raised a hand. Mr. Letts frowned. "Yes?"

"What about feeding time?" Alistair asked. "Won't we have to take the muzzles off then?"

"Not at all," Mr. Letts replied curtly. "We will issue you more than enough disposable feeding tubes, which you attach to the front of the muzzle. I will demonstrate how in a few minutes."

As if Alistair's question had emboldened the rest of the class, Millie now raised her hand. "What about the smell?" she said. "My mum says she doesn't want an R1 in the house because they stink."

Mr. Letts looked momentarily outraged, but a huff of exasperation downgraded the expression into a scowl. Acidly he said, "The facility's inmates do not smell. Like all R1 sufferers, it's true that their bodies have succumbed to a limited amount of physical corruption—a process which is subsequently arrested by what we call the 'R1 barrier,' which incidentally we still do not fully understand—but all of our test subjects have been treated with a combination of chemicals which negates the more unpleasant effects of bodily decomposition." He glanced at Mrs. Keppler. "Well, if there are no more questions, I think it's time for you to become acquainted with your charges."

For the first time Fleur felt jittery with nerves as the class lined up, each to be presented with a metal tag bearing a four-digit number. When that was done, Mr. Letts crossed unhurriedly to a narrow door tucked between the edge of the glass screen and the adjoining wall and tapped out a code on a keypad. The effect of his action, as he stepped back, was twofold. The lights flickered on in the Crèche, transforming the black screen into a viewing window, and the door unlocked with a series of clicks.

As she shuffled forward behind a dozen of her classmates, Fleur glanced almost unwillingly at the room beyond the glass. She was just in time to see rows of evenly spaced incubators made of opaque plastic the color of sour milk before she was through the door and among them.

The first thing that struck her about the Crèche was its stillness. The incubators were so silent that they might have been occupied by dead meat, or nothing at all. The stillness seemed to reach out and stifle the combined sound of almost thirty thirteen-year-olds—the rustle of clothing, the squeak of rubber soles on vinyl flooring, the soft rasp of respiration that was trying not to escalate beyond nervousness. When Mr. Letts, who had slipped into the room at the back of the group, spoke, it made them all jump.

"Some of you may be experiencing a sense of disquiet, perhaps even anxiety or distress, about now. Am I right?"

As if on cue, one of the girls—Fleur thought it might have been Lottie Travis—failed to curtail a sob. Around her, she became aware of heads nodding slowly, and then of her own joining in.

"That's a perfectly natural reaction," Mr. Letts said in an almost kindly voice. "Living babies are a bundle of instincts. As human beings we're used to them moving almost constantly, even in repose—but the R1 infants, as you will see, are a different case entirely. Their only instinct is to feed, but they seem to know—or at least their bodies do—that there is little point transferring energy and resources into limbs that do not respond in an efficient manner. Therefore, they remain motionless as they wait to be fed. Having lived almost all their short lives in the facility, they have become creatures of habit. They feed three times a day and they expel waste products once a day. The advantage of this for you is that as long as you administer to these routine requirements, you will find the R1 infants simple to maintain. If, however, you deny them their sustenance for any length of time then they will do what normal infants do. Can you guess what that is?"

Fleur put up her hand. "Cry?"

"Exactly," replied Mr. Letts. "Though it is a cry you will never have heard before, and almost certainly will never want to hear again."

Behind her, Fleur heard another sob tear itself loose from Lottie. There was a prolonged shuffle and bump as Mrs. Keppler led the girl through the crowd and out of the room, and then Mr. Letts said, "Time to match you up, I think."

Gesturing toward the incubators, he told them to search for the ones that matched the numbers on their tags. Fleur looked at hers as her classmates shifted around her like restless cattle. After a few seconds, several of her peers—Ray Downey, Alistair Knott, Tina Payne—broke away from the huddled group and began to move tentatively among the rows of tiny plastic boxes.

"What's *your* number?" Millie asked almost fearfully, as if one of the tags might prove the equivalent of a short straw.

"It's 4206," Fleur replied.

"Mine's 9733. Let's look together, shall we?"

The numbers on the incubators seemed random, as if this were a treasure hunt or a puzzle, but Fleur supposed they must adhere to *some* system somewhere. Like Millie, she tried to focus on the numbers stamped on the ends of the plastic boxes rather than on their contents, which remained nothing but darkish blurs on the periphery of her vision. It took her several minutes, but at last she spotted the number that matched the one on her tag.

"It's here," she said, suddenly breathless.

"What have you got?" asked Millie. "A girl or a boy?"

"I daren't look," Fleur replied.

"I'll look for you then, shall I?" Millie moved up beside her. After a few seconds, she quietly said, "It's a boy."

Fleur felt as though she were having to override a physical restraint in order to raise her head. She managed it at last, blinking to focus her gaze. The baby in the incubator was lying on its back with its arms upraised in a crucifix position. It looked not dead but as if it was pretending to be, which was somehow worse. Its eyes were dark glints in its mottled, bluish face, and its chest, which should have been rising and falling, was as still as a lump of clay and not dissimilar in texture.

"He's cute," Millie said, not at all convincingly. "What are you going to call him?"

Fleur's thoughts felt as heavy as wet cement. She blurted out the first and only thing that came to mind.

"Andrew," she said. "After my dad."

"So this is it, is it?"

Elliott peered into the portable crib, which Fleur had put on the kitchen table. As always, he looked tired and grubby after a long shift spent patrolling the perimeter, his hair peppered with the dust that kicked up from the scrubland. He was twenty, lean and muscular, often difficult to predict emotionally. Sometimes he was broody, uncommunicative; at other times he was easygoing, quick to smile. Fleur loved her brother, but she couldn't say that she fully understood his quicksilver personality. Needless to say, most of her friends found him mysterious, and so had a massive crush on him.

"He's a he, not an it," she said.

Elliott snorted. "Has Mum seen it?"

"Not yet. She's at Aunty Valerie's."

"Course," said Elliott, raising his eyebrows. "It's Friday. I lose track in my job." He opened the fridge, took out a bottle of soda, and opened it with a crack and a hiss. Dropping his weight into a wooden chair with a groan, he took a swig, then gave her a shrewd, sidelong look. "She won't like having it in the house, you know. She hates those things."

Fleur felt irritably defensive. "He can't help how he is."

Elliott shrugged. "Even so."

As Fleur prepared the baby's feed, the silence stretched between them. It was a silence redolent of bad memories and unspoken grief. The reason why Elliott was a perimeter guard was that their father had been one before him. Seven years ago, when Fleur was six and Elliott thirteen, Andy McMillan had been on patrol when a section of faulty fencing in his quadrant had collapsed, allowing a group of at least two dozen R1s to swarm into the compound. In the ensuing melee, Andy had suffered multiple bites—so many that the virus had taken hold quickly. Jacqui was the only one who had seen her husband in the hospital, raging and inhuman. And it was she, alone and traumatized, who had had to make the terrible decision that faced all R1 sufferers' next of kin—to allow their loved ones to live on in a contained, controlled environment or to give the order to bring their suffering to a swift and humane end.

Fleur had been too young to fully appreciate Jacqui's anguish over the decision, but Elliott's reaction and the subsequent screeching arguments between Fleur's mother and brother were scarred into her memory. Elliott had accused Jacqui of murdering their father. Jacqui had retaliated by saying that she had only been carrying out Andy's wishes, that he had made it abundantly clear that if the worst ever happened, the last thing he would want would be for his family to see him reduced to the state of a slavering, mindless animal.

Eventually, of course, the raw wounds had closed up and the arguments had subsided. But they had never properly healed. There had been so much venom released during the endless round of accusations and counteraccusations, so much anger and hatred and hurt expelled and absorbed by both sides, that there would always be a tenderness there, a weak spot. Jacqui and Elliott loved each other, relied on each other, looked out for each other—but there still existed an underlying tension between them, a sense that if, for whatever reason, circumstances should ever force the wound to reopen, then all the old venom and more besides would come gushing out anew.

It was Elliott who eventually broke the silence. "That stuff smells disgusting."

Fleur couldn't disagree. She had emptied one of the sachets of powdered meal, which they had each been given before leaving the facility, into a bowl and was now adding hot water, as instructed. The stench that rose from the reddish paste was like the most rancid dog food imaginable. Holding her breath and screwing up her eyes, she nodded at a silvery rucksack emblazoned with the Moorlands logo, which was leaning against a table leg. "Get a feeding tube out of the pack, will you?"

Elliott stretched out a leg, hooked the pack with his foot, and pulled it to him. He rummaged through its contents and extracted a short length of corrugated tubing with a metal screw attachment at one end and a funnel at the other.

"I'm guessing you mean one of these," he said, handing it to her.

She took it from him. "Thanks."

He watched as she screwed the tube into a circular aperture at the front of the visorlike muzzle that was fastened securely around the lower half of the baby's face.

"Fucking grotesque," Elliott said with a bleak laugh. "Now it looks like an elephant fetus."

Ignoring her brother, Fleur mixed cold water into the thick, foul-smelling gruel and then began to spoon it into the funnellike end of the feeding tube. After a moment the baby's black eyes widened, its limbs began to twitch and squirm, and it began to eat with a muffled, wet, gnashing sound.

"Oh, that is totally gross," Elliott said almost delightedly, rocking back in his chair.

Fleur shot him a disapproving look. "He needs to eat, Elliott."

Elliott sat forward again abruptly, his eyes narrowing. "Why does he? I mean, why does *it*?"

"Because it's a school project," Fleur said. "I have to look after him. Do you want me to fail for being a bad mother?"

Elliott shrugged. "Who's going to know?"

Fleur pointed at a thin metal bracelet around the baby's right wrist. "That monitors his physical state—his metabolism and stuff. They'd know if I didn't look after him properly."

Elliott peered at the bracelet. "I could probably fix that."

"Don't you dare!" said Fleur. "I want to do this properly."

"Why?"

"I just do, that's all."

Elliott pulled a face. "Well, I think it's sick. Looking after those things, keeping them alive . . ."

"They're test subjects," said Fleur. "Without live subjects we'd never find a cure for the R1 virus."

"That's what you're doing now, is it?" taunted Elliott. "Vital medical research?"

Before Fleur could reply, there was the rattle of a key in the lock and the front door opened, admitting a brief roar of traffic noise.

Fleur tensed as her mother's footsteps approached the kitchen. She'd wanted to get the first feed over and done with before Jacqui arrived home. As it was, her mother appeared in the kitchen doorway with her face screwed into an expression of repugnance.

"What's that awful smell?" she said.

"It's the baby's feed," said Fleur nervously. "Sorry, Mum. It does pong a bit."

Jacqui put down her bags and sloughed off her threadbare coat as she walked across the room. She'd become thinner over the last few years, though not in a healthy way. She looked haggard and pale, her green eyes too large for her once elfin face, her almost-black hair tied back in a lifeless ponytail. Fleur felt her guts squirm as her mother examined the feeding infant, the repugnance on her face hardening into something more deep-rooted.

"How was Aunt Valerie?" Fleur asked, to break the silence.

"Same as always." With barely a pause, Jacqui asked, "Where are you going to keep it?"

"In my room," Fleur said.

"It'll stink the place out."

"It doesn't smell. Only its food does. It'll be finished in a minute." She avoided Elliott's eye as she spoke, aware that she, too, was now referring to the baby not as "he" but "it"—compromising her principles to avoid conflict.

To her surprise, her mum said, "Poor creature."

Elliott made a noncommittal sound that could have been an acknowledgment of her comment or a rebuttal of it.

"I thought you hated the R1s," Fleur said tentatively.

"I hate the virus," Jacqui said. "And when people get infected, the virus is all they become." She nodded at the baby. "It doesn't mean I don't grieve for the people the virus wipes out, the ones who once occupied the flesh—or in this case the one who never even got a chance to become a person."

"You don't think the real person is still in there somewhere then?"

said Fleur. "And that if they find a cure those people will come back?"

All sorts of emotions chased themselves across Jacqui's face. "I want to believe," she said eventually. "But I don't know if I can."

"Ricky Jackson's dad took his back. Said he and Ricky's mum couldn't stand having it in the house. So did Lottie Travis's mum—she said it was giving Lottie nightmares. But did you hear about Tina Payne?" Millie's brown eyes were wide.

Fleur shook her head.

"Get this," Millie said, and lowered her voice to a dramatic murmur. "Her dad came home drunk, and the baby was crying 'cause Tina wasn't feeding it properly. So he took it outside and dumped it headfirst in the bin and buried it under some rubbish and didn't tell anyone. It was there two days before Tina went out and heard it crying."

"That's awful," said Fleur. "Was it all right?"

Millie's shrug sent her dreadlocks swaying and clinking. "S'pose. They don't die, do they, even if you don't feed them? You have to cut off their heads or burn them to kill them."

Fleur tried to imagine being upside down in a bin full of stinking rubbish for two days. The thought of it made her feel sick. "Do they feel pain or distress, do you think?"

Millie pulled a face. "Don't think so. Don't think they feel anything really."

"Must be awful," said Fleur.

Millie nodded. "Yeah, I'd rather be dead than . . ." Then she realized what she was saying and clenched her teeth in apology. "Hey, sorry, I didn't mean . . ."

Fleur waved a hand as though wafting a fly. "It's okay. So how did you find out all this stuff anyway?"

Millie dipped her hand into the pocket of her shorts and extracted a wafer-thin rectangle with a burnished steel finish. "Smartfone 4.5," she said. "Gossip Central. You should get one. Then we could talk all the time."

"I wish," said Fleur, trying not to look envious. "But we can't afford it. We've only got Elliott's wage coming in. Mum's got a 2.5, but she doesn't let me use it."

"Bummer," said Millie, then her eyes brightened. "Hey, I might be getting a new 5.1 for Christmas. If I do, you can have this one."

"Thanks," said Fleur, but she knew that even with the best network deal she could find, she would still never be able to afford to actually use the damn thing.

That was the only drawback about coming to Millie's—sometimes her best friend forgot, or simply didn't realize, how tight money was for Fleur and her family. That was why she hadn't seen Millie for the whole of the half-term holiday—she couldn't afford the bus fare and it was too far to walk. Ordinarily Fleur might have cycled around on her rickety old bone shaker, but with Andrew to look after she hadn't been able to. So she had been stuck at home all week with nothing to do except feed and change the baby, read books, and do household chores for Mum.

Now, however, it was Friday, which Mum always spent with Dad's sister, Aunt Valerie. Jacqui passed Millie's house on the way to Valerie's, so Fleur had persuaded Mum to drop her off en route and pick her up again on the way home.

The house Millie lived in was big, with apple trees in the front garden and a huge backyard with a swimming pool. Beyond the yard was a meadow, and beyond that was woodland. If you walked straight through the woods for about four hours, Millie's fifteen-year-old brother, Will, had told them, you would come to the perimeter. He had been there with his friends several times and said it was "jazz" and that they should do it sometime. However, the girls preferred to stay close to civilization—to the pool and the computer and Millie's mum's homemade peanut cookies.

Today had been the warmest day of the holiday. The girls had been for a swim and were now sitting on the wooden seat that encircled the largest of the ancient fruit trees in the front garden. Their backs were resting against gnarled bark that had been worn smooth by the pressure of many such backs over the years. Sunlight winking through the leaves overhead formed a moving pattern of light and dark on their bare legs.

"Can't wait to give the stupid thing back," Millie said. "Only three days to go now." She waved her clenched fists in the air and made a muted cheering sound.

Fleur glanced at Andrew, lying like a dead weight in his portable crib a few meters away. He seemed unaffected by the sunlight shining directly onto his tiny, mottled, blue-gray body.

"It hasn't been so bad," Fleur said. "In fact, it's been quite easy."

"Yeah, but I dread waiting for mine to shit every day," said Millie. "It stinks like . . . rotting fish or something. Doesn't it make you gag?"

"I've gotten used to it," Fleur said. "I hold my breath."

"But it's the look of it," said Millie, pulling a face. "It's *green*. And *slimy*."

Fleur grinned and was about to reply when a howl of pain from behind the house sliced through the drowsy afternoon air. This was followed by several people shouting at once, their voices shrill with panic.

"That's Will," Millie said, jumping to her feet.

She ran toward the path that led around the side of the house. Fleur glanced at Andrew, lying motionless in his crib, decided he'd be fine, and went after her.

The backyard was full of boys in swimming shorts. They were crowding around Will, whose dark-skinned shoulders were gleaming with water or sweat. Will was holding up his right hand, and so shocked was Fleur to see his bottom lip trembling and tears pouring down his face that she didn't notice the blood at first. Then she saw the cut on the pad of his upraised index finger, from which blood was trickling into his clenched fist. Fleur was confused. It didn't look bad enough to warrant all this fuss.

"What happened?" Millie shouted. "What happened?"

One of the boys glanced behind him and Fleur followed his gaze. On the stone flags a couple of meters from the edge of the pool was the portable crib that she assumed contained the R1 baby assigned to Millie, a girl whom Millie had named Rose.

"We were playing chicken," the boy said, his voice tight and high with the knowledge that they had made a terrible decision, a decision from which there was no going back. "It was Ryan's idea."

"It wasn't my fault!" a boy who must have been Ryan protested.

"Never mind whose fault it was," Millie shouted. "What's chicken? What do you mean?"

All at once Fleur knew exactly what they meant. Calmly but urgently she said, "They were daring each other to stick their fingers in

Rose's feeding hole. Only Will didn't pull his finger out quickly enough and he got bit."

Millie's eyes widened in horror. "You idiot!" she screeched at her brother. "You stupid idiot!"

Will was blubbing like a baby, tears and snot pouring down his face. "I'm gonna get the virus," he wailed. "I'm gonna become a biter."

"No, you're not," Fleur said firmly. "If you get treatment within the first ninety minutes they can stop the infection."

"Really?" Will said, his teary eyes stretched wide with desperate hope.

Turning to Millie, Fleur said, "He needs to go to hospital. Is your mum—"

But Millie was already wheeling toward the house. "Mum!" she screamed. "Mum!"

"He'll be fine, Mum," Millie said softly. "You'll see."

Millie's mum, Clara, had once been a model. To Fleur, her mahogany-colored skin seemed to glow, as if with some inner light. She had thickened a little around the waist since her modeling days, but even now, in her forties, she was a breathtakingly beautiful woman. At this moment, however, she looked wretched, her finely boned face taut with worry, her hands quivering as they twisted a tear-dampened handkerchief into smaller and smaller knots.

Fleur was sitting on the other side of Clara, in a plastic chair against the wall of the waiting area outside a pair of sealed, gray double doors. Above the doors was a sign that read:

R1 INFECTION AREA
RESEARCH AND TREATMENT
AUTHORIZED PERSONNEL ONLY

"Millie's right, Mrs. Hawkes," Fleur said reassuringly. "The man at the Moorlands Facility told us they have these drugs called . . ." She wrinkled her nose as she struggled to remember. "Antinecrotics, which block and kill off the R1 cells. They're like virtually a hundred percent effective."

Clara Hawkes nodded vaguely, but she shot a venomous glance

toward Andrew, who was lying silent and still in his crib on the seat next to Fleur. "I don't know why they let you girls *have* those damn things in the first place. I always said this project was a bad idea."

Fleur stayed silent. She knew it wasn't the right time to say that the babies weren't to blame, and that the situation had occurred purely as a result of Will's stupidity. Clara had insisted that Millie leave Rose behind at the house, even though she would need feeding again in an hour or so. At first, Fleur had thought Clara was going to tell her that she couldn't bring Andrew, either, but Millie's mum had been so preoccupied with her panic-stricken son that she had made no comment when Fleur placed Andrew's crib on the middle seat in the back of the car.

They had been at the hospital now for over an hour, waiting for news. The bearded doctor who had spoken to them when they first arrived had told them that Will would be treated immediately, but that they would have to monitor him for a while until they were sure that all traces of the infection had been eradicated.

"How long will it be before you know for sure?" Clara had asked.

"It depends entirely on Will's response to treatment," the doctor had replied smoothly. "Based on past experience, it could be anything between one and six hours."

In the seventy minutes or so since their arrival, a couple of white-coated doctors had entered the Infection area, having first tapped entry codes onto a keypad on the wall, but no one had come out. Fleur looked at her watch. It was almost 3:50 P.M. Her mum wasn't due to pick her up until six, but if nothing happened within the next hour she'd have to call her and tell her what was happening. She looked at Andrew lying in his crib. She couldn't say she felt any particular affection for the boy, but she no longer felt the anxiety and repugnance she had experienced in the presence of the R1 infants a week ago. In that respect, she supposed, the project *had* been a success, whatever Millie's mum thought. She looked around as the double doors to the Infection area hummed, clicked, and then began to open as someone pushed them from the other side. The person who emerged was the last one she expected to see.

"Mum!" she gasped.

Jacqui froze, a look of horror on her face. It was the expression of someone who has been caught red-handed, someone who has no-where to hide. As if reading her daughter's mind, Jacqui blurted out the question that was on Fleur's lips: "What are *you* doing here?"

"We were . . ." Fleur said, trying to pull her jumbled thoughts together. "I mean . . . Will got bit . . . Millie's brother, I mean." She frowned. "Why aren't you at Aunt Valerie's?"

For a moment Jacqui looked trapped—then her shoulders slumped. "Oh well, I suppose it had to come out sooner or later," she said.

"What did?" asked Fleur.

Jacqui gave her a strange look—a sad, resigned look that made Fleur's stomach clench.

Then, quietly, she said, "We need to talk."

Sitting hunched over, as if weighed down by a burden of unspoken revelations, Jacqui reached out and took Fleur's hands. She drew a long breath into her lungs and slowly expelled it, and then she said, "I lied. Your father's not dead."

The instant Jacqui said the words, Fleur knew she should have been expecting them. Yet, they hit her like a bolt of lightning. She jerked in her seat; her mind reeled; her world flipped upside down. She gripped her mother's hands hard to stop herself from falling, and from somewhere faraway she heard her own small voice asking, "So why did you say that he was?"

Jacqui sighed and slumped lower in her seat, as if she had been inflated by nothing but secrets and regret for the past seven years and it was all now leaking out of her.

"Because he wanted me to. Because he couldn't bear the thought of you seeing him like . . . like that." Her voice dropped to a whisper. "But *I* couldn't bear to let him go. I knew there was research going on. I knew that scientists and doctors were trying to find a cure for the virus. And if I'd given the order for your dad to . . . to be dispatched and then they'd found a cure . . ." She shook her head. "I would never have forgiven myself."

Fleur didn't know how to feel. Didn't know whether to be angry or happy, horrified or betrayed. "We could have helped you," she said, "Elliott and me."

Jacqui shook her head. "It wouldn't have been fair on you. You were just a little girl. I thought a clean break . . ."

Fleur said quietly, "But you let Elliott think . . . you let him *say* all those terrible things to you."

"It was the best way," insisted Jacqui. "The *only* way."

Another short silence, as if the conversation were too big or too painful to be handled in anything other than bite-size chunks.

Eventually Fleur said, "And what about now? Will you tell Elliott now?"

"Will you?" countered Jacqui.

Fleur shook her head. "I don't know. I don't know what to do. I don't know what to *think*."

"You don't have to decide anything yet. Why don't you just . . . get used to the idea first?"

Fleur let her gaze slide past Millie and Clara, sitting a dozen or so meters away, to the gray doors beyond them. "Is Dad in there?"

Jacqui nodded.

"So you come here every Friday? You don't go to Aunt Valerie's at all?"

"I see your aunt Valerie in the mornings," said Jacqui. "We have lunch and then I come here. Valerie used to come with me at first, but she found it too upsetting. Now it's just me."

"What do they do to him in there?" Fleur asked. Anger sparked in her and she welcomed it, grasped it. It was a real emotion, something to anchor herself to. "Do they *experiment* on him?"

"No!" Jacqui's denial was loud enough to make Millie and Clara turn their heads. Controlling herself, she said, "No, I wouldn't allow that. They try to cure him, that's all. Anything new they discover, any breakthroughs they make, your dad's one of the first to benefit from it."

"So he's a test subject," said Fleur.

"You make it sound bad. It's not bad. They're trying to make him better. They're not hurting him. I make sure of that. He has a good life . . . for what it is."

Another silence. Fleur felt sick and hollow. She was finding it all hard to digest. Finally she said, "Have they made any progress?"

Jacqui didn't answer immediately. And then hesitantly she said, "I think so . . . yes."

"I want to see him," said Fleur.

Jacqui looked alarmed. "I don't know if that's a good idea."

24

"He's my dad. I want to see him. You can't tell me he's alive and then not let me see him."

Now Jacqui looked anguished, torn. "I'm not being mean," she said. "I just . . . I don't want you upset, that's all."

"I can handle it," said Fleur stubbornly. "I'm old enough." She paused and then said with quiet conviction, "I want to see my dad."

Jacqui stared at her for what seemed to Fleur a long time. She stared at her as if she had never seen Fleur properly before, as if she had not noticed until now how quickly her little girl had grown up.

Then she gave a short, decisive nod. "Okay," she said. "Come with me."

She stood up and walked back toward the gray doors. Fleur picked up Andrew's crib and followed her. As they passed Millie and Clara, Millie half reached out. "Hey, you okay?"

"Fine," said Fleur, giving Millie no more than a glance. She could see that her best friend was brimming with questions, but she averted her gaze, unwilling to give Millie any encouragement to ask them right now. Instead, Fleur watched Jacqui stab a code number into the keypad on the wall, and then she followed her through the gray doors.

Dr. Beesley had hair growing out of his nose. Fleur couldn't stop staring at it. She felt not quite real. She felt as if this were a dream, or as if her thoughts were floating like balloons a few meters above her head. She shifted her gaze to Dr. Beesley's plump, wet lips in the hope that if she saw the shape of the words he was forming, she would find it easier to concentrate on them.

"We think there has been some definite progress," he was saying to Jacqui. "Thanks to the new drug treatment, Andy's aggression levels are considerably reduced, and he seems far more responsive to his surroundings and to both auditory and visual stimuli. Dr. Craig informs me that you were there when they played the music this morning?"

Jacqui nodded. "Yes. It seemed to me as if Andy was listening to it. Aware of it, at least."

Dr. Beesley nodded. "And he's the same with voices. He no longer automatically identifies a human voice as simply the location of a potential food source. When we talk to him he appears to listen.

Sometimes I swear he understands every word I'm saying." He chuckled at his own joke, then asked, "Did he establish eye contact with you this morning?"

"No, I . . . no," Jacqui said.

"Well, hopefully that will come. There have been brief indications of it already. Nothing conclusive, but we remain cautiously optimistic—as ever." Finally, Dr. Beesley turned his attention to Fleur. "So you've come to see your father, little lady?"

Fleur frowned and for a fleeting moment considered telling the doctor that she was thirteen, not six. Instead, she nodded.

"Very good. First contact with an infected loved one is never anything less than an emotional experience, but if you're prepared for that, I'm sure Andy will benefit from your visit."

"He might not," muttered Jacqui.

Dr. Beesley frowned. "I'm sorry?"

"Fleur found out about Andy by accident. Until twenty minutes ago she thought he was dead." Jacqui took a deep breath. "Now she insists on seeing him, though personally I'm worried how Andy might react. He never wanted his children to see him . . . well, you know. . . ."

"I see," said Dr. Beesley slowly. "Well, the decision is yours to make. I would offer advice, but such encounters are entirely unpredictable. All I can recommend is that if Andy *does* start to show signs of distress, it might be best to beat a hasty retreat."

"We will," said Jacqui decisively.

"Could I see my dad now, please?" said Fleur.

A little taken aback at her directness, Dr. Beesley said, "Er . . . yes, of course. This way."

He led Fleur and Jacqui along several corridors until they came to one that had a gate stretching from wall to wall and floor to ceiling. A six-digit code punched into yet another wall-mounted keypad opened the gate. Beyond were closed, numbered doors not unlike the ones at the Moorlands Facility. Dr. Beesley led them around the corner and halted outside door number 5.13. Another keypad, another entry code, and the door clicked open.

With a sweep of his arm, Dr. Beesley invited Jacqui and Fleur to precede him into the room. Not knowing quite what to expect, Fleur allowed Jacqui to go first, and then followed, moving with a lopsided lurch because Andrew's crib, which she was carrying by the handles, kept bumping against her thigh.

She found herself in what amounted to a smaller version of the Crèche at the Moorlands Facility. The anteroom was narrow, rectangular. A nurses' monitoring station, currently unoccupied, was tucked up against the left-hand wall. Directly before them, opposite the door through which they had entered, was another wall made of what appeared to be thick, transparent Perspex. The white-walled room beyond that was twice the size of this one, simply furnished with a bed and a chair, both of which were bolted to the floor. There was a man lying on the bed, arms by his sides, unmoving. Fleur could see him only in profile, but she gasped in recognition.

"Dad!"

He was thinner than she remembered him, and his skin had the same mottled, blue-gray hue of all R1 sufferers. Dr. Beesley appeared from behind her and indicated a small metal grille on the wall above a pair of buttons. "You can speak to him if you like. Just press this button here."

Fleur didn't move. All at once she felt uncertain, a little overwhelmed by the situation. Unable to tear her eyes from the motionless figure, she was only half aware of her mum stepping across to the grille and thumbing the button.

"Andy." Jacqui's amplified voice made Fleur jump. "There's someone here to see you."

To Fleur's consternation, the figure on the bed stirred. Her father's leg twitched slightly; his fingers moved like worms probing blindly for the light. He looked like Frankenstein's monster coming alive in some of the old movies she'd seen.

"Say hello to your dad, Fleur," Jacqui said softly. "Don't be shy."

Fleur licked her lips. She put down Andrew's crib and moved across to stand beside her mum. She felt as if she were floating, drifting. Jacqui, her thumb still on the Talk button, smiled encouragingly.

Fleur bent her head toward the grille. Her mouth was dry. She licked her lips again. Finally, she croaked, "Hello, Dad. It's me. It's Fleur."

Slowly, like an old man waking from a deep sleep, her father rose from the bed. First of all he sat up, and then he turned, his legs swinging clumsily over the side of the mattress, his feet brushing the floor.

Fleur stepped back, unable to stifle a small, involuntary bleat of distress. Viewing her dad full-on for the first time, she saw that his face was slack, expressionless, his mouth hanging open, his eyes blank and staring. There seemed to be nothing at all of the father she remembered in there. No life, no personality. He seemed nothing but a walking lump of dead flesh, a receptacle for the virus that animated him. He dropped his weight forward onto his feet, swayed for a moment, and then clumped heavily toward them.

Fleur took another step back and then felt a hand—her mum's—in the small of her back.

"It's all right," Jacqui said soothingly. "Don't be scared."

Fleur braced herself, then stepped forward. Her dad shuffled right up to the Perspex wall, so close that if he had been breathing, a mist of condensation would have formed on its transparent surface.

"Talk to him," Jacqui whispered. "Go on."

Fleur didn't know what to say. Then, hesitantly, she muttered, "I know you didn't want me to come here, Dad, but it isn't Mum's fault, so don't blame her. I kind of found out about you by accident, and I made her bring me. I'm thirteen now and . . . and I've missed you, Dad. I've missed you a lot." Suddenly she felt emotion welling inside her and did her best to swallow it down. After a few seconds she continued. "I know you're sick, but it isn't your fault, and you shouldn't be ashamed. The people here are trying to make you better. They say you're doing really well."

She wasn't sure her words were getting through. Certainly there was no change of expression on her dad's face. But suddenly his eyes flickered and slid to the left, making Jacqui gasp.

"He's looking at the baby," she hissed. "Show it to him."

Fleur turned, to find that Dr. Beesley had already picked up the crib and was handing it to her. She took it from him and turned with it in her arms, presenting it to her dad like an offering.

"He's not mine," she said. "I'm looking after him for a week, as part of a school project. He's sick like you, Dad, but everyone's working really hard to come up with a cure to make you both better."

Her dad continued to stare at the baby. He seemed mesmerized by it. Then, slowly, his gaze shifted. His pale, bloodshot eyes rolled up and all at once he was staring at Fleur. Staring *right* at her.

Behind her, Fleur heard Jacqui whisper, "I don't believe it. He's looking at you. Oh, Fleur, *he knows who you are.*"

Fleur continued to stare into her father's eyes, their faces—separated by the Perspex wall—less than a meter apart. She smiled. "Hello, Dad," she said softly. "Remember me?"

Moving as if in slow motion, Andy raised his right hand and pressed it, palm forward, against the transparent wall. Lowering the crib to the ground, Fleur echoed his action, raising her left hand and placing it against his, so that they were separated by nothing more than the thickness of the barrier between them.

Suddenly Jacqui let out a gasp, and Dr. Beesley, his voice hushed with wonder, said, "Oh my God. Would you look at that."

Fleur *was* looking at it. She couldn't tear her gaze away from it, in fact. As the single tear brimmed from her father's eye and trickled slowly down his mottled cheek, she didn't know whether to laugh or cry.

WHY MOTHERS LET THEIR BABIES WATCH TELEVISION

A JUST-SO HORROR STORY

Chelsea Cain

THIS, O MY BEST BELOVED, is a story—a new story, a terrible, terrible story, of a mother's love for her baby.

This baby was cruel, O my Best Beloved, always hungry, always crying. Back when the world was wild, in 2001, in a house in Spokane, Washington, the mother, kind, tired mother, wanted some peace and quiet.

"Please go to sleep, baby," the mother said.

"I will not!" shouted the baby—always hungry, always pooping—and then the baby began to scream. The scream was so loud that it frightened the salmon, who all swam back to the ocean, and startled the eagles, who fell from the sky. So the mother—always giving, always changing diapers—shook the baby, she shook and shook her until the baby's head was loose—her bad baby—always hungry, always yelling.

And after ever so many shakes, the baby was dead.

Off ran Mother, kind, frantic mother—always giving, always making dinner—she buried the baby in the backyard under the apple tree.

She had to!

Then the mother slept. She was so tired she slept for three days and three nights. And the salmon returned and the eagles flew in the sky.

But after three days and nights, that baby—that bad baby, always hungry, always spitting up—was hungrier still.

Up jumped Baby from her shallow grave, her skin pearly and bruised, sloughing off, revealing rotting muscle meat underneath, maggots and beetles in her eyes. Fast ran Baby—still hungry, still crying—into the house, flies following her. She ran to her mother's room.

"Feed me!" the baby howled.

The baby was already gnawing at the cat, holding it by the neck, its throat torn open, blood and cat hair around the baby's mouth.

O my Best Beloved, imagine the mother's surprise.

Up jumped Mother—always anxious, always vacuuming—from the bed. She caught the baby and wrapped her in a garbage bag and tied the garbage bag with rope and then she drove down the cul-de-sac, down the highway, past the big-box stores, to the bridge, and she tossed that bad baby overboard into the river.

She had to!

Off drove Mother—kind, loving mother—over the bridge, past the big-box stores, down the highway, up the cul-de-sac, all the way home, where she took a Valium and turned on daytime television until her head stopped pounding.

Then she rested.

Law & Order was on.

She watched ever so many episodes.

Night came.

Up jumped Baby—hungrier still, always with a diaper rash, never satisfied, never happy—from her watery grave. Her flesh half eaten by fish, eels in her eyes, she ran up the riverbank, over the bridge, past the big-box stores, down the highway, up the cul-de-sac, flies following her.

"Feed me!" she yelled. She had no manners then, and she has no manners now, and she never will have any manners.

Up jumped Mother, halfway to the kitchen, halfway to the butcher knife, but then she paused.

Something was different.

Baby was quiet. Baby—hungry baby, always kicking, always clawing—was still. Baby was watching the television set. Baby was good.

Mother—always singing, always reading *Goodnight Moon,* never complaining—patted Baby's slimy fontanelle.

The house was quiet.

And that, O my Best Beloved, is why mothers let their babies watch television to this day.

CAROUSEL

Orson Scott Card

CYRIL'S RELATIONSHIP with his wife really went downhill after she died. Though, if he was honest with himself—something he generally tried, with some success, to avoid—things hadn't been going all that well while Alice was alive. Everything he did seemed to irritate her, and when he didn't do anything at all, that irritated her, too.

"It's not your fault," Alice explained to him. "You try, I can see that you try, but you just . . . you're just wrong about everything. Not *very* wrong. Not oblivious or negligent or unconcerned. Just a little bit mistaken."

"About what? Tell me and I'll get better."

"About what people want, who they are, what they need."

"What do you need?" Cyril asked.

"I need you to stop asking what I need," she said. "I need you to know. The children need you to know. You never know."

"Because you won't tell me."

"See?" she said. "You have to make it my fault. Why should people always have to tell you, Cyril? It's like you go through life in a well-meaning fog. You can't help it. Nobody blames you."

But she blamed him. He knew that. He tried to get better, to notice more. To remember. But there was that note of impatience—in her voice, the children's voices, his boss's voice. As if they were thinking, *I'm having to* explain *this to you?*

Then Alice was hit by a car driven by a resurrected Han Dynasty Chinese man who had no business behind the wheel—he plowed into a crowd on a bustling sidewalk and then got out and walked away as nonchalantly as if he had successfully parallel parked a large car in a small space. It was the most annoying thing about the dead—how they thought killing total strangers was no big deal, as long as they didn't mean to do it. And since the crowd had only two living people in it, the number of deaths was actually quite low. Alice's death barely rose to the level of a statistic, in the greater scheme of things.

She was thoughtful enough to clean up and change clothes before she came home that night—resurrection restored every body part to where it should be at the peak of mature health, but it did nothing for the wardrobe. Still, the change in her attitude was immediate. She didn't even try to start dinner.

"What's for dinner, Mom?" asked Delia.

"Whatever your father fixes," said Alice.

"Am I fixing dinner?" asked Cyril. He liked to cook, but it usually took some planning and he wasn't sure what Alice would let him use to put together a meal.

"Go out to eat, have cold cereal, I really don't care," said Alice.

This was not like her. Alice controlled everybody's diet scrupulously, which was why she almost never allowed Cyril to cook. He realized at once what it meant, and the kids weren't far behind.

"Oh, Mom," said Roland softly. "You're not dead, are you?"

"Yes." She sighed. "But don't worry, it only hurt for about a minute while I bled out."

"Did the resurrection feel good?" asked Delia, always curious.

"The angel was right there, breathed in my mouth—very sweet. A bit of a tingle everywhere. But really not such a great feeling that it's worth dying for, so you shouldn't be in a hurry to join me, dear."

"So you won't be eating with us," said Cyril.

She shook her head a little, eyes closed. "'Dead' means I don't eat, Cyril. Everyone knows that the dead don't eat. We don't breathe except so we can talk. We don't drink, and if we do, it's just to keep company with the living, and the liquids all evaporate from our skins so we also don't pee. We also don't want sex anymore, Cyril. Not with each other and not with you."

She had never mentioned sex in front of the children before, except for the talk with Delia when she turned ten, and that was all about time-of-the-month things. If Delia had any idea what sex was,

Cyril didn't think she got it from her mother. So the children blanched and recoiled when she mentioned it.

"Oh, don't be such big babies, you know your father and I had sex or you wouldn't look so much like him. Which is fine for you, Roland, your father's a good-looking man, in his way. But a bit of a drag for you, Delia, with that jaw. And the resurrection won't fix that. Resurrection isn't cosmetic surgery. Which is really unfair, when you think about it. People who are genetically retarded or crippled or sick have their DNA repaired to some optimum state, but girls with overly mannish features or tiny breasts, or huge ones, for that matter, their DNA is left completely alone, they're stuck like that for eternity."

"Thanks, Mom," said Delia. "I love having my confidence destroyed once again, and I haven't even begun doing my homework yet."

"So you aren't going to eat with us?" asked Roland.

"Oh, of course I'll sit at the table with you," said Alice. "For the company."

In the event, Cyril got out everything in the fridge that looked like it might go on a sandwich and everybody made their own. Except Alice, of course. She just sat at the table and made comments, without even a pause to take a bite or chew.

"The way I see it," said Alice, "is that it's all poop. Nothing you're putting on sandwiches even looks appetizing anymore, because I see that poopiness of it all. You're going to eat it and digest it and poop it out. The nutrients will decay and eventually end up in some farmer's field where it will become more future poop, which he'll harvest and it'll get processed into a more poopable state, so you can heat it or freeze it or thaw it or whatever, chew it up or drink it, and then turn it into poop again. Life is poop."

"Mom," said Delia. "It's usually Roland who makes us sick while we're eating."

"I thought you'd want to hear my new perspective as a postliving person." She sounded miffed.

"Please speak more respectfully to your mother," said Cyril to Delia.

"Cyril, really," said Alice. "I don't need you to protect me from

Delia's snippy comments. It's not going to kill me to hear her judgmentalness directed at the woman who gave birth to her."

"Feel free to criticize your mother's defecatory comments," said Cyril. "Or ignore them, as you choose."

"I know, Dad," said Delia. There was that familiar hint of eye rolling in her tone of voice. Once again, Cyril must have guessed wrong about what to say, or to leave unsaid. He had never really gotten it right when Alice was alive, and now that she was dead and resurrected, he'd have no chance, because he was no longer dealing with a wife, or even, strictly speaking, a woman. She was a visitor with a key to the house.

Within a few weeks, Cyril had found himself remembering the awful night of Alice's death as a particularly lovely time, because she actually sat with them during dinner and wasn't trying to lead the children off into some kind of utterly bizarre activity.

She showed up at any hour of the day and expected to be able to take Delia or Roland with her on whatever adventure she'd gotten into her head to try with them.

"No, Alice, you may not take Roland out of school so he can go scuba diving with you."

"It's really not your place to say what I can or cannot do," said Alice.

"The law is clear, Alice—when you die you become, in a word, deceased. You no longer have any custody over the children. Thousands of years of legal precedent make that clear. Not to mention tons of recent case law in which the resurrected are found to be unfit parents in every case."

"Aren't you lucky that the dead can't get angry," said Alice.

"I suppose that I am," said Cyril. "But I'm not dead, and I was furious when I found you practically forcing Roland to walk along the top of a very high fence."

"It's exhilarating," said Alice.

"He was terrified."

"Oh, Cyril, are you really going to let a child's fears—"

"He was right to be terrified. He could have broken his neck."

"And would it have been such a tragedy if he did?" asked Alice. "I was run over by a car and I turned out okay."

"You think you're okay?" asked Cyril.

Alice held up her hands and twisted her wrists as if to prove that her parts worked.

"Here's how I know you're not okay, Alice," said Cyril. "You keep trying to put the kids in high-risk situations. You're trying to kill them, Alice."

"Don't think of it as death. I'm not dead. How is it death?"

"How can I put this kindly?" said Cyril—who by this point had actually stopped trying to be kind. "You're dead to *me*."

"Just because I'm no longer available for empty reproductive gestures does not mean I'm not here for you, Cyril."

"I'm going to get a restraining order if you don't stop taking the kids on dangerous activities. You don't have any guardianship rights over these children."

"My fingerprints say I'm still their mother!"

"Alice, when you were their mother, you wanted them to relish every stage of their life. Now you're trying to get them to skip all the rest of the stages."

"You can't manipulate me with guilt," said Alice. "I'm beyond human emotions and needs."

"Then why do you still need the children with you?"

"I'm their mother."

"You *were* their mother," said Cyril.

"I was and I am," said Alice.

"Alice, I may have been a disappointment as a husband."

"And as a father, Cyril. The children are often disappointed in you."

"But I meet a basic minimum, Alice. I'm alive. I'm human. Of their species. I want them to be alive. I'd like them to live to adulthood, to marry, to have children."

Alice shook her head incredulously. "Go outside and look at the street, Cyril. Hundreds of people lie down and sleep in the streets or on the lawns every night, because the world has *no* shortage of people."

"Just because you've lost all your biological imperatives doesn't mean that the rest of us don't have them."

"Cyril, your reasoning is backward. The children will be much happier without biological imperatives."

"So you admit you're trying to kill them."

"I'm trying to awaken them from the slumber of mortality."

"I don't want to awaken them from that slumber," said Cyril sharply. "If it's a dream, then let them finish the dream and come out of it in their own time."

"When someone you love is living in a nightmare," said Alice, "you wake them up."

"Alice," said Cyril, "you're the nightmare."

"Your wife is a nightmare? Your children's mother?"

"You're a reanimated dead woman."

"Resurrected," said Alice. "An angel breathed into my mouth."

"The angel should have minded its damn business," said Cyril.

"You always wanted me dead," said Alice.

"I never *wanted* you dead until after you *were* dead and you wouldn't go away."

"You're a bitter failure, Cyril, and yet you cling to this miserable life and insist that the children cling to it, too. It's a form of child abuse. Of child exploitation."

"Go away, Alice. Go enjoy your death somewhere else."

"My eternal life, you mean."

"Whatever."

But in the end, Alice won. First she talked Delia into jumping from a bridge without actually attaching any bungee cords to her feet. Once again Cyril had no chance to grieve, because Alice brought Delia by to tell Roland how great death and resurrection were. Delia was fully grown. A woman, but in a retailored version of her dress that fit her larger, womanly body.

"The soul is never a child," said Alice. "What did you expect?"

"I expected her to take a few more years to grow into this body," said Cyril.

"Think of it as skipping ahead a few grades," said Alice, barely able to conceal her gloating.

If Cyril had thought resurrected Alice was awful, resurrected Delia was unbearable. His love for his daughter had become, without his realizing it, far stronger and deeper than his lingering affection for his wife. So he could not help but grieve for the young girl cut off in her prime. While the snippy, smart-mouthed woman of the same name, who thought she had a right to dwell in his house and follow him around, mocking him constantly—she was a stranger.

How can you grieve for people who just won't go away? How can you grieve for a daughter whose grown-up dead-and-resurrected self ridicules your mourning? "Oh, did Daddy lose his widdow baby?"

There was nothing to do but say an occasional silent prayer—which they mocked when they noticed him doing it. Only Cyril was never quite sure what he was praying for. Please get rid of all the dead? Please unresurrect them? Would God even hear that prayer?

Roland died of a sudden attack of influenza a few months later. "You can't blame me for it, this time," said Alice.

"You know you were sneaking him out into the cold weather specifically so he'd catch cold. The dying was a predictable result. You're a murderer, Alice. You should be in hell."

Alice smiled even more benignly. "I forgive you for that."

"I'll never forgive you for taking away my children."

"Now you're unencumbered. I thought that's what you secretly wished for."

"Thanks for telling me my deepest wishes," said Cyril. "They were so deep I never knew they existed."

"Come with us, Father," said Roland.

"In due time, I'll go where I can find what I need," said Cyril. "*You* don't need me.

Roland was so tall. Cyril's heart ached to see him. *My little boy,* he thought. But he could not say it. Roland's gentle pity on him was harder to bear than Delia's open scorn.

They would not go. They talked about it, but sheer inertia kept anyone from changing. Finally it dawned on Cyril. Just because he was the only predead resident of the house did not bind him to it. His life had been stripped away from him; why was he clinging to the house that used to hold it?

For the shower, the toilet, the bathroom sink; for the refrigerator, the microwave, the kitchen table; for the roof, the bed, place to store his clothes. The burden and blessing of modern life. Unlike the resurrected, if Cyril was going to eat, he had to work; if he was going to work, he had to look presentable. For his health he needed shelter from weather, a safe place to sleep.

The resurrected people that used to love him did not need this place, but would not leave; he needed the place, but could not bear these people who made it impossible for him to truly grieve the terrible losses he had suffered.

Job had it all wrong, thought Cyril. Having lost his wife and children, it was better to lose all his other possessions and live in an ashpit, covered in boils. Then, at least, everyone could see and understand what had happened to him. His friends might have been wretched comforters, but at least they understood that he was in need of comfort.

Just because he had to store his food and clothing there, and return there to wash himself and sleep, did not mean he had to *live* there, to pass waking hours there, listening to his dead wife explain his inadequacies to him, or his dead daughter agree with her, or his dead son pity him.

Cyril took to leaving work as soon as he could, and sometimes when he couldn't, just walking out of the building, knowing he was putting his already somewhat pitiful career in jeopardy. He would walk the streets, delaying the commute home as long as possible. He thought of joining his wife and children in death and resurrection, but he had seen how death stripped them of all desire, and even though his current malaise came from the frustration of his deepest desires, he did not want to part with them. Desire was what defined him, he understood that, and to give them up was to lose himself, as his wife and children were lost.

Bitterly, Cyril remembered the Bible school of his childhood. Lose your soul to find it? Yes, the dead had certainly done that. Lost soul, self, and all, but whatever they had found, it wasn't really life. Life was about hunger and need and finding ways to satisfy them. Nature red in tooth and claw, yes, but hadn't the human race found ways to create islands of peace in the midst of nature? Lives in which terror was so rare that people paid money to go to amusement parks and horror movies in order to remember what terror felt like.

This life was even more peaceful, even less lonely, wasn't it? When he walked the streets, he was jostled by thousands and thousands of the resurrected, who crowded every street as they went about their meaningless existence, not even curious, but moving for the sake of moving, or so it seemed to him; pursuing various amusements because they remembered that this was a thing that human beings did, and not because they desired amusement.

They crowded the streets so that traffic barely moved, yet they provided no boost to the economy. Needing nothing, they bought nothing. They had no money, because they had no desires and therefore nothing to work for. They were the sclerosis of commerce. *Get out of my way*, thought Cyril, over and over. And then: *Do what you want. I'm not going anywhere, either.*

He was living like the dead, he recognized that. His life was as empty as theirs. But underneath his despair and loneliness and ennui, he was seething with resentment. Since God obviously existed after all, since it was hard to imagine how else one might explain the sudden resurrection of all who had ever lived, what did he *mean* by it? What were they supposed to *do* with this gift that preserved life eternally while robbing it of any sort of joy or pleasure?

So, Cyril was ironically receptive when he found the uptown mansion with a sign on the door that said:

God's Anteroom

Nobody used the word "anteroom" anymore, but the idea rather appealed to him. So he went up the short walk and climbed the stoop and opened the front door and stepped inside.

It was a good-size foyer, which he assumed had been formed by tearing out a wall and combining the front parlor with the original vestibule. The space was completely filled by a small merry-go-round. As far as Cyril could see, no doors or stairs led out of the room except the front door, which he had just come through.

"Hello?" His voice didn't echo—the room wasn't big enough for that. It just fell into the space, flat and dull. He thought of calling again, louder, but instead stepped up onto the carousel.

It was small. Only two concentric circles of animals to ride, the outer one with seven, the inner one with three, plus a single one-person bench shaped like the Disney version of a throne, molded in smooth, rounded lines of hard plastic pretending to be upholstery.

Cyril thought of sitting there, since it required no effort. But he thought better of it, and walked around the carousel, touching each animal in turn. Chinese dragon, zebra, tiger, horse, hippopotamus, rhinoceros, giant mouse. Porpoise, eagle, bear. All extravagantly detailed and finely hand painted—there was nothing sloppy or faded or seedy, about the thing. In fact, he could truly say that the carousel was a work of art, a small, finely crafted version of a mass entertainment.

He had never known there was such a thing as a boutique carousel. Who would ever come to ride such a thing? And what would they pay? Part of the pleasure of full-size carousels was the fact that they were so crowded and public. Here in this room, the carousel looked beautiful and sad at the same time. Too small for the real purpose of a carousel—a place where people could display themselves to one another, while enjoying the mild pleasure of moving up and down on a faux beast. Yet, too large for the room, crowded, almost as if this were a place where beautiful things were stored while awaiting a chance for display in a much larger space.

Cyril sat on the hippopotamus.

"Would you like me to make it go?" asked a woman's voice.

Cyril had thought he was alone. He looked around, startled, a little embarrassed, beginning the movement of getting back off the hippo, yet stopping himself because the voice had not challenged him, but rather offered to serve him.

Then he saw her through the grillwork of the faux ticket booth in a space that must have been a coat closet when the house was first built. How did she get in or out? The booth had no door.

Her appearance of youth and health led him to assume she was dead and resurrected.

"I can't really afford . . ." he began.

"It's free," she said.

"Hard to stay in business at those rates," said Cyril.

"It's not a business," she said.

Then what is it? he wanted to ask. But instead he answered, "Then yes, I'd like to ride."

Silently the carousel slipped into movement without a lurch; had he not been paying attention, Cyril would not have been able to say when movement began.

The silence did not last long, for what would a carousel be without music? No calliope, though—what accompanied this carousel sounded like a quartet of instruments. Cello, oboe, horn, and harpsichord, Cyril thought, without any effort to sort out the sounds. Each instrument was so distinctive that it was impossible not to catalog them. They played sedate music in three-four time, as suited a carousel or skating rink, yet the music was also haunting in a modal, folk-songish way.

Cyril let the carousel carry him around and around. The movement did not have the rapid sweep of a full-size carousel but rather the dizzying tightness of spin of a children's hand-pushed merry-go-round. He had to close his eyes now and then to keep from becoming light-headed or getting a slight headache from the room, which kept slipping past his vision.

It did not occur to him to ask her to slow it down, or stop. He simply clung to the pole and let it move him and the hippo up and down.

Because the music was so gentle, the machinery so silent, the distance from him to the ticket booth so slight even when he was on the far side of the room, Cyril felt it possible—no, obligatory—to say something after a while. "How long does the ride last?" he asked.

"As long as you want," she said.

"That could be forever," he said.

"If you like," she said.

He chuckled. "Do you get overtime?"

"No," she said. "Just time."

"Too bad," he said. Then he remembered that she was dead, and neither payment nor time would mean very much to her.

"Do you read?" he asked. "Or do you have a DVD player in there?"

"What?" she asked.

"To pass the time. Between patrons. While the customers are riding. It can't be thrilling to watch me go around and around."

"It actually is," she said. "Just a little."

Liar, thought Cyril. Nothing was thrilling to the dead.

"You're not dead yet," she said.

"No," he answered, wanting to add, *What gave me away?* but keeping his silence. He knew what gave him away. He had asked questions. He was curious. He had bothered to ride at all. He had closed his eyes to forestall nausea. So many signs of life.

"So you can't ride forever."

"I suppose not," said Cyril. "Eventually I have to sleep."

"And eat," she said. "And urinate."

"Doesn't look like you have a restroom, either," said Cyril.

"We do," she said.

"Where?" He looked for a door.

"It has an outside entrance."

"Don't the homeless trash the place?" he asked.

"I don't mind cleaning it up," she said.

"So you do it all? Run the carousel, clean the restrooms?"

"That's all there is," she said. "It isn't hard."

"It isn't interesting, either."

"Interesting enough," she said. "I don't get bored."

Of course not. You have to have something else you want to be doing before you really feel bored.

"Where are you from?" asked Cyril, because talking was better than not talking. He wanted to ask her to stop the carousel, because he really was getting just a little sick now, but if he stopped, she might insist that he go. And if he got off, yet was allowed to stay, where would he stand while he talked to her?

"I died here as a little girl. My mother gave birth to me on the voyage."

"Immigrants," said Cyril.

"Isn't everyone?" she answered.

"So you never grew up."

"I'm up," she said, "but you're right, without growing into it. I was very sick, my mother wiping my brow, crying. And then I was full-grown, and had this strange language at my lips, and there were all these buildings and people and nothing to do."

"So you found a job."

"I came through the door and found the ticket booth standing open. I knew it was called a ticket booth as soon as I saw it, though I never saw a ticket booth before in my life. I could read the signs, too, and the letters, though they weren't in the language I learned as a baby. I turned on the carousel and it went around and I like to watch it, so I stayed."

"So nobody hired you."

"Nobody's told me to go," she said. "The machinery isn't complicated. I can make it go backward, too, but nobody likes that, so I don't even offer anymore."

"Can you make it go slower?"

"That's the slowest setting," she said. "It can go at two faster speeds. Do you want to see?"

"No," he said quickly, though for a moment he wanted to say yes, just to find out what it would feel like.

"No one likes that, either, though people still ask. The living ones throw up sometimes, at the faster speeds."

"Sometimes the resurrected come to ride?"

"Sometimes they come with the living ones. A dead mother and her living children. That sort of thing."

"How do you like it?" he asked.

"Well enough," she said, "or I wouldn't stay."

He realized she must have thought he meant how she liked her job, or watching the carousel.

"I meant, how do you like resurrection?"

"I don't know," she said. "I don't have a choice, so I don't think about it."

"When you were dying, what did you want?"

"I wanted my mother not to cry. I wanted to sleep. I wanted to feel better."

"Do you feel better now?" asked Cyril.

"I don't know," she said. "I suppose so. My mother isn't crying anymore. I found her after I resurrected. She didn't know me, but I knew *her*. She was just as I remember her, only not so sad. She and I didn't talk long. There wasn't much to say. She said that she wept for me until her husband made her stop so he could bury me. She wouldn't move away, because she would have to leave my grave behind, so they lived their whole lives nearby, and raised eleven other children and sent them out into the world, but she never forgot me."

The story made Cyril want to weep for his own dead children, even though they were alive again, after a fashion. "She must have been glad to see you," he said.

"She didn't know me. It was her baby that she wanted to see."

"I know," said Cyril. "My wife got my children to die and they came back like you. Grown-up. I miss the children that I lost." And then he did cry, just a couple of sobs, before he got control of himself.

"I'm sorry," he said. "I haven't been able to cry till now. Because they're still there."

"I know," she said. "I'm glad to see you cry."

He didn't even ask why. He knew: her mother, being resurrected, had not cried. The woman needed to see a living person cry for a dead child.

Needed. How could she *need* anything?

"What's your name?" asked Cyril.

"Dorcas," she said.

"Not a common name anymore," said Cyril.

"It's from the Bible. I never studied the Bible when I was alive. I was too young to read. But I came back knowing how to read. And the whole Bible is in my memory. So is everything. It's all there, every book. I can either remember them as if I had already read them, or I can close my eyes and read them again, or I can close my eyes and see the whole story play out in front of my eyes. And yet I never do. It's enough just to know what's in all the books."

"All of them? All the books ever written?"

"I don't know if it's all of them. But I've never thought of a book that I haven't read. If one book mentions another book, I've already read it. I know how they all end. I suppose it must be more fun to read if you don't already know every scene and every word."

"No worse than the carousel," said Cyril. "It just goes around and around."

"But the face of the person riding it changes," she said. "And I don't always know what they're going to say before they say it."

"So you're curious."

"No," she said. "I don't really care. It just passes the time."

Cyril rode in silence for a while.

"Why do you think he did it?" he finally asked.

"Who?" she asked. Then, "Oh, you mean the resurrection. Why did God, you know."

"This is God's Anteroom, right? So it seems appropriate to wonder. Why now. Why everybody all at once. Why children came back as adults."

"Everybody gets their perfect body," she said. "And knowledge. Everything's fair. God must be fair."

Cyril pondered that. He couldn't even argue with it. Very even-handed. He couldn't feel that he had been singled out for some kind of torment. Many people had suffered worse. When his children had

46

died, he was still able to talk to them. It had to feel much worse if they were simply gone.

"Maybe this is a good thing," said Cyril.

"Nobody believes that," she said.

"No," said Cyril. "I can't imagine that they do. When you wish— when your child dies, or your wife. Or husband, or whatever—you don't really think of *how* they'd come back. You want them back just as they were. But then what? Then they'd just die again, later, under other circumstances."

"At least they'd have had a life in between," said Dorcas.

Cyril smiled. "You're not the ordinary dead person," he said. "You have opinions. You have regrets."

"What can I regret? What did I ever do wrong?" she asked. "No, I'm just pissed off."

Cyril laughed aloud. "You can't be angry. My wife is dead, and she's never angry."

"So I'm not angry. But I know that it's wrong. It's supposed to make us happy and it doesn't, so it's wrong, and wrongness feels . . ."

"Wrong," Cyril prompted.

"And that's as close as I can come to being angry," said Dorcas. "You too?"

"Oh, I can feel anger! I don't have to be 'close,' I've got the real thing. Pissed off, that's what I feel. Resentful. Spiteful. Whining. Self-pitying. And I don't mind admitting it. My wife and children were resurrected and they'll live forever and they seem perfectly content. But you're not content."

"I'm content," she said. "What else is there to be? I'm pissed off, but I'm content."

"I wish this really were God's Anteroom," said Cyril. "I'd be asking the secretary to make me an appointment."

"You want to talk to God?"

"I want to file a complaint," said Cyril. "It doesn't have to be, like, an interview with God himself. I'm sure he's busy."

"Not really," said the voice of a man.

Cyril looked at the inner row, where a handsome young man sat on the throne. "You're God?" Cyril asked.

"You don't like the resurrection," said God.

"You know everything, right?" asked Cyril.

"Yes," said God. "Everybody hates this. They prayed for it, they wanted it, but when they got it, they complained, just like you."

"I never asked for this."

"But you would have," said God, "as soon as somebody died."

"I wouldn't have asked for *this*," said Cyril. "But what do you care?"

"I'm not resurrected," said God. "Not like them. I still care about things."

"Why didn't you let *them* care, then?" asked Cyril.

"Billions of people on Earth again, healthy and strong, and I should make them *care*? Think of the wars. Think of the crimes. I didn't bring them back to turn the world into hell."

"What is it, if it isn't hell?" asked Cyril.

"Purgatory," said Dorcas.

"Limbo," Cyril suggested back.

"Neither one exists," said God. "I tried them for a while, but nobody liked them, either. Listen, it's not really my fault. Once a soul exists, it can never be erased. Annihilated. I found them, I had to do something with them. I thought this world was a good way to use them. Let them have a life. Do things, feel things."

"That worked fine," said Cyril. "It was going fine till you did *this*." He gestured toward Dorcas.

"But there were so many complaints," said God. "Everybody hated death, but what else could I do? Do you have any idea how many souls I have that still haven't been born?"

"So cycle through them all. Reincarnation, let them go around and around."

"It's a long time between turns," said God. "Since the supply of souls is infinite."

"You didn't mention infinite," said Cyril. "I thought you just meant there were a lot of us."

"Infinite is kind of a lot," said God.

"To *me* it is," said Cyril. "I thought that to you—"

"I know, this whole resurrection didn't work out like I hoped. Nothing does. I should never have taken responsibility for the souls I found."

"Can't you just . . . put some of us back?"

"Oh no, I can't do that," said God, shaking his head vehemently.

"Never that. It's—once you've had a body, once you've been part of creation, to take you back out of it—you'd remember all the power, and you'd feel the loss of it—like no suffering. Worst thing in the world. And it never ends."

"So you're saying it's hell."

"Yes," said God. "There's no fire, no sulfur and all that. Just endless agony over the loss of . . . of everything. I can't do that to any of the souls. I *like* you. All of you. I hate it when you're unhappy."

"We're unhappy," said Cyril.

"No," said God. "You're sad, but you're not really suffering."

Cyril was in tears again. "Yes I am."

"Suck it up," said God. "It can be a hell of a lot worse than this."

"You're not really God," said Cyril.

"I'm the guy in charge," said God. "What is that, if not God? But no, there's no omnipotent transcendental being who lives outside of time. No unmoved mover. That's just stupid anyway. The things people say about me. I know you can't help it. I'm doing my best, just like most of you. And I keep trying to make you happy. This is the best I've done so far."

"It's not very good," said Cyril.

"I know," said God. "But it's the best so far."

Dorcas spoke up from the ticket booth. "But I never really *had* a life."

God sighed. "I know."

"Look," said Cyril. "Maybe this really is the best. But do you have to have everybody *stay* here? On Earth, I mean? Can't you, like, create more worlds?"

"But people want to *see* their loved ones," said God.

"Right," said Cyril. "We've seen them. Now move them along and let the living go on with our lives."

"So maybe a couple of conversations with the dead and they move on," said God, apparently thinking about it. "What about you, Dorcas?"

"Whatever," she said. "I'm dead, what do I care?"

"You care," said God. "Not the cares of the body. But you have the caring of a soul. It's a different kind of desire, but you all have it, and it never goes away."

"My wife and children don't care about anything," said Cyril.

49

"They care about you."

"I wish," said Cyril.

"Why do you think they haven't left? They see you're unhappy."

"I'm unhappy because they won't go," said Cyril.

"Why haven't you told them that? They'd go if you did."

Cyril said nothing. He had nothing to say.

"You don't want them to go," said Dorcas.

"I want my children back," Cyril said. "I want my wife to love me."

"I can't make people love other people," said God. "Then it wouldn't be love."

"You really have a limited skill set," said Cyril.

"I really try not to do special favors," said God. "I try to set up rules and then follow them equally for everybody. It seems more fair that way."

"By definition," said Dorcas, "that's what fairness *is*. But who says fairness is always good?"

God shrugged. "Oh, I don't know. I wish I did. But I'll give it a shot, how about that? Maybe I can eventually fix this thing. Maybe the next thing will be a little better. And maybe I'll never get it right. Who knows?"

And he was gone.

So was Dorcas.

Cyril got off the hippo. He was dizzy and had to cling to the pole. The carousel wasn't going to stop. So he waited until he had a stretch of open floor and leaped off.

He stumbled, lurched against a wall, slid down, and lay on the floor. The quartet stopped playing. The carousel slowed down and stopped. Apparently it automatically knew when there were no passengers.

A baby cried.

Cyril walked to the ticket window and looked in. On the floor sat a toddler, a little girl, surrounded by a pile of women's clothing. The toddler looked up at him. "Cyril," she said in her baby voice.

"Do you remember being a grown-up?" Cyril asked her.

The little girl looked puzzled.

"How do I get in there?"

"Hungry!" said the little girl, and she cried again.

Cyril saw a door handle inside the ticket booth and eventually figured out where the door was in the outside wall. He got it open. He picked up little Dorcas and wrapped her in the dress she had been wearing. God was giving her a life.

Cyril carried her out of God's Anteroom and down the stoop. The crowds were gone. Just a few cars, with only the living inside them. Some of them were stopped, the drivers just sitting there. Some of them were crying. Some just had their eyes closed. But eventually somebody honked at somebody else and the cars in the middle of the road started going again.

Cyril took a cab home and carried the baby inside. Alice and Delia and Roland were gone. There was food in the fridge. Cyril got out the old high chair and fed Dorcas. When she was done, he set her in the living room and went in search of toys and clothes. He mentally talked to Alice as he did: *So it's stupid to keep children's clothes and toys when we're never going to have more children, is it? Well, I never said it, but I always thought it, Alice: just because* you *decided not to have any more babies doesn't mean* I *would never have any.*

He got Dorcas dressed and she played with the toys until she fell asleep on the living-room carpet. Then Cyril lay on the floor beside her and wept for his children and the wife he had loved far more than she loved him, and for the lost life; yet, he also wept for joy, that God had actually listened to him, and given him this child, and given Dorcas the life she had longed for.

He wondered a little where God had sent the other souls, and he wondered if he should tell anybody about his conversation with God, but then he decided it was all none of his business. He had a job the next day, and he'd have to arrange for day care, and buy food that was more appropriate for the baby. And diapers. He definitely needed those.

He slept, and dreamed that he was on the carousel again, dizzy, but moving forward, and he didn't mind at all that he would never get anywhere, because it was all about the ride.

REALITY BITES

S. G. Browne

"WELCOME TO *REANIMATION REWIND,* the TV show that keeps you up-to-date on all of your favorite zombie reality programs. I'm Zach Taylor."

Zach Taylor, the living Ken-doll host of *Reanimation Rewind,* flashes an unnaturally white, blinding smile on the fifty-inch, flat-screen television, which is mounted to the wall in the office of Paul Silverman, vice president of production at ZTV Studios in Holly-wood.

"And I'm Megan Richards." The camera cuts to the cohost of *Re-animation Rewind,* the Barbie to Zach's Ken, who displays her own custom dental work. "Whether it's *Zombie Apprentice, Dancing with the Undead,* or *The Real Zombies of Beverly Hills,* we've got it all for you right here. So if you've got an appetite for the undead, get ready to dig in."

"That's right, Megan," says Zach. "Today, our show includes clips from *Survivor Zombie, The Reanimated Jersey Shore,* and *The Amazing Zombie Race,* where this week the remaining zombie and human teams are in New York City, racing from upper Manhattan to Coney Island. Trust us when we tell you that you're not going to want to miss that one."

"I can't wait," says Megan. "But first we kick things off with a clip from the most popular reality show on television: *The Z Factor . . .*"

Evan Carter, an independent producer, hits the Mute button as the screen is filled with the image of a female zombie with a missing eye and no lips. She's standing on a stage under bright lights, attempting to eat a microphone, her face in danger of sliding off her skull, as Simon Cowell unleashes some unheard criticism.

"This is what I'm talking about," says Carter, pointing at the television. "It's all retreads. Reboots. All these shows are doing is putting a new product in old packaging."

"That's the way it works," says Paul Silverman, sitting behind his island of a desk in his ocean of an office, a view of downtown Los Angeles floating in the background behind him. "You know as well as I do the entertainment industry doesn't want original. They want safe. They want marketable. They want a proven commodity."

"I know, I know," says Carter. "Giving Hollywood an original idea is like giving a four-year-old boy a prostitute. Neither one of them knows what to do with it."

"Truer words have never been spoken."

On the flat-screen television, the female zombie deep-throats the microphone and her lower jaw snaps off.

Silverman lets out a bark of laughter. "It may not be inspired, but let's face it, you can't beat the ratings."

"That's what I'm here to talk to you about." Carter sits down in one of the red leather wingback chairs opposite Silverman's desk. "I believe I have an idea for a show that *can* beat them."

Silverman leans back in his chair, hands clasped behind his head. "Talk to me."

"What are the most-watched zombie reality shows on television right now?" says Carter.

Silverman nods toward the television, where a clip from *The Reanimated Jersey Shore* shows four guidos in bathing suits scrambling out of the hot tub to get away from their naked, decomposing female zombie housemate, who has fallen into the water. "In addition to this one and *The Z Factor,* you'd have to include *Undead Idol* and *Zombie Fear Factor.*"

"None of which ZTV Studios created or produced," says Carter.

"Are you trying to put me in a bad mood?"

"Just doing some scene setting."

"How about you just get to the plot."

"Come on," says Carter. "How long have we known each other?"

"Too long," says Silverman with a smile.

"Would I ever bring something to you that wasn't worth your time?"

Silverman checks his watch. "I'm listening."

"Okay," says Carter. "In spite of everyone's preconceived pop-culture notions of zombies being these single-minded eating machines feasting on human flesh, what we have are a bunch of harmless, mindless corpses stumbling around, acting like they're still alive while they gradually decompose."

"Not exactly *The Walking Dead*."

"Right. People were expecting the apocalypse. Hordes of flesh-eating ghouls. Chaos and mass hysteria. Instead what they got was this." Carter motions toward the television, where a zombie fails the immunity challenge for his team on *Zombie Survivor* when his rectal cavity bursts open.

"Where is this leading?" asks Silverman.

Carter leans forward in his chair. "What if we could give the people what they were expecting? Something none of these other shows can offer? Something people didn't know they wanted until we showed it to them?"

"Keep going."

Carter stands up and walks around the office, which also contains a wet bar and a private bathroom. "I'm talking about reinvention. Reanimating the reanimated. Not just giving the public something new but revolutionizing the reality genre."

"This is television we're talking about," says Silverman. "People want something they can understand. Something that doesn't force them to think. They don't want clever and smart. That's why shows like *Arrested Zombie Development* get canceled."

On a clip from *The Amazing Zombie Race,* a walking corpse of unidentified gender staggers into the middle of Fifth Avenue in Manhattan and gets nailed by a bus.

"Besides," says Silverman, "how, exactly, do you reinvent mindless, living corpses? Whether you put them in a Jacuzzi, on an island, or in a hot-air balloon, they're still mindless, living corpses."

Carter stops in front of Silverman's desk. "What if they weren't mindless?"

Silverman removes his hands from behind his head and sits up in his chair. "I'm listening."

"What we have now are shows with different situations, different scenarios, but they're all interchangeable. They're all dealing with brainless casts and mindless contestants."

"Just like all of the old reality shows."

"Exactly," says Carter. "So what if we had a show where the zombies weren't all doing the same thing?"

"Such as?"

Carter puts both hands on Silverman's desk and leans forward. "What if we had a zombie that could talk?"

Silverman looks at Carter for several moments, then bursts out laughing. He keeps laughing until he realizes Carter's not kidding. "You're serious?"

Carter nods. "Never more so."

"Zombies can't talk," says Silverman. "It's impossible."

"That depends on your concept of what's impossible," says Carter. "We didn't think it was possible to fly. Or to walk on the moon. Or to clone DNA. And before the dead started walking, we thought that was impossible, too. Now they're starring on reality television shows."

"But the living dead don't have functioning respiratory systems," says Silverman. "They can't talk. From what we know, they can't even think."

Carter waves an arm toward the flat-screen, where a clip from *Dancing with the Undead* shows a professional male dancer performing a salsa with a female zombie as the entire flesh of one of her arms peels off like a glove. "None of *them* can think."

Silverman looks at the television, then back at Carter. "What are you getting at here?"

"What would you say if I told you I could get you a zombie that could not only talk, but that could also rationalize?"

"I'd say you need to lay off the inhalants for a while."

Carter smiles. "Hold on a sec."

Carter walks out of the office and comes back a moment later with a pale, limp-haired young man wearing wire-rimmed glasses, baggy pants, and a long-sleeved shirt buttoned at the wrists.

"This is Ted." Carter closes the door as Ted takes a seat in one of the leather chairs.

Ted nods at Silverman. "Pleasure to meet you, sir."

"Who the hell is this?" says Silverman, sitting behind his desk, looking from Carter to Ted and back again.

"Meet the star of your new zombie reality show," says Carter.

Ted sits in his chair, wearing a nervous smile.

"Is this some kind of a joke?" says Silverman.

"No joke." Carter motions toward his client. "Ted here is a living corpse who has somehow managed to maintain his cognitive functions."

Silverman looks Ted up and down. "I don't buy it. You look too good to be a zombie."

"I figured that would be your initial reaction," says Carter. "Ted, show the man."

Ted stands up and unbuttons his left sleeve, then pulls back the sleeve to reveal an open, bloodless incision running from his wrist to his elbow.

"Ted committed suicide in his bathtub," says Carter as Ted unbuttons the sleeve on his right arm to reveal a matching wound. "He woke up the next morning to discover he was a zombie."

Silverman gives Ted a dubious look. "You killed yourself?"

"It's a little embarrassing to talk about," says Ted. "Not just the suicide thing, but it took awhile to come to terms with the fact that I was a reanimated corpse. I mean, nothing can really prepare you for the shock, you know?"

"Denial is the first stage to acceptance," says Carter.

"Wait a minute," says Silverman. "How long are we talking about here? When did you commit suicide?"

"It's been almost a month."

"A month?" says Silverman. "That's ridiculous. If you've been dead a month, then how come you're not bloating or starting to liquefy? You weren't even embalmed."

Ted glances at Carter, who puts a single index finger to his lips.

"I've got a friend with connections in the mortuary business who gets me industrial-strength formaldehyde," says Ted. "It helps to keep my decomposition to a crawl."

"Aren't you worried about him outing you?" asks Silverman.

"He doesn't know what it's for," says Ted. "I mean, who would think I was using it for myself?"

"Fair point," says Silverman.

"Besides," says Carter, "once Ted's on television, it'll be a nonissue."

"Don't get ahead of yourself," says Silverman. "I haven't said yes to anything yet."

"What do you need from us to convince you?" asks Carter.

"A death certificate would be a start," says Silverman.

Carter nods. "I'm sure that can be arranged."

Silverman stares at the twin incisions on Ted's arms. "Presuming you're telling the truth, why did you want to commit suicide?"

"I'm an accountant," says Ted. "What woman in Hollywood wants to date an accountant, let alone have sex with one? Especially one who looks like me?"

"All valid points," says Carter.

Silverman rubs his chin. "I still don't believe it. It has to be a trick. You're just wearing makeup. No one could be dead nearly a month and look as good as you."

"No makeup," says Carter. "See for yourself."

Silverman gets up and goes around his desk and touches the incision on Ted's left arm, the wound opening beneath his finger.

"Christ!" He pulls his hand back. "You're as cold as my ex-wife."

"Room temperature, actually," says Ted.

"No pulse or heartbeat, either," says Carter. "See for yourself."

Silverman puts his fingers on Ted's left wrist for about ten seconds, then he feels the right wrist before placing his fingers on Ted's neck. "Incredible," he says. "I wouldn't have thought it was possible. How did this happen?"

"I'm guessing he's some sort of genetic anomaly," says Carter. "One of a kind. Or at least one of a very small and unique group."

Silverman leans forward and sniffs Ted. "Why don't you smell like a zombie?"

"I wear a lot of cologne and deodorant."

"That works?"

Ted shrugs. "It seems to do the trick."

Silverman sits down on the edge of his desk. "I'm still having trouble wrapping my brain around this, but for the sake of argument, let's say you're a zombie. So what's the pitch?"

"*A Zombie's Life,*" says Carter. "We follow Ted around documentary-style to see what it's like to be a zombie. We see the world through his eyes. What he has to deal with. How people react to him. Show the humanity of the living dead. The challenges of being a reanimated corpse in modern-day society."

"I like it," says Silverman. "Keep going."

"Another idea is a show similar to *Punk'd*," says Carter. "Only we would use Ted here as an apparent normal human, and when the unsuspecting victim realizes Ted's a zombie, hilarity ensues."

"Not bad," says Silverman. "There's nothing else like it on television right now. But it seems a little derivative."

"There's also *Cadaver Camp*," says Carter, "where Ted tries to teach other zombies how to talk and act like him."

"That one has promise," says Silverman. "What else?"

"Tell him about *Zombie Gigolo*," says Ted.

"*Zombie Gigolo?*" asks Silverman.

"It's kind of like the concept behind *The Bachelor*," says Carter. "Only this one's all about sex."

Silverman nods. "Tell me more."

"There are hundreds of necrophiliacs and corpse fetishists out there who would love the chance to have sex with an honest-to-God living zombie," says Carter. "Check the online forums and what's trending on Twitter. The research bears it out. And I'm guessing with the right marketing we could top the ratings for *The Z Factor* and *Undead Idol* combined."

"I like it." Silverman looks Ted up and down. "We'd have to spiff him up a bit, though. Give him a makeover. Colored contacts or some hip glasses and a new haircut. Maybe a personal trainer."

"We'd make him irresistible," says Carter. "The Brad Pitt of zombies."

"And we'd have to prove he's a zombie in order to make the show work."

"Not a problem," says Carter. "We have a physician verify he's dead. Get that death certificate you mentioned. Run a disclaimer before the show. Take him out for public appearances and get him on *The Today Show* and Letterman. Maybe even get him a guest spot on a couple of your shows and help boost their ratings."

"Great ideas," says Silverman. "But how long can we run with this? What happens when he starts to decompose? I'd imagine the effects of his formaldehyde treatments can only last so long."

Ted and Carter exchange glances.

"What?" asks Silverman.

Carter puts a hand on Ted's shoulder. "What if I told you he doesn't have to decompose?"

"What are we talking about here?" says Silverman. "Botox injections? Plastic surgery? Organ transplants?"

"Not exactly," says Carter.

"Then what?"

Carter looks at Ted, who clears his throat.

"Well, the first day I reanimated, I didn't eat. As you can imagine, I didn't have much of an appetite. Just spent most of my day curled up on the couch in shock."

Silverman nods. "I'm listening."

"But when I finally got some food in my stomach, it didn't stay there long. Less than five minutes after eating a ham sandwich, it came right back up. Violently. Like a volcano."

"That would have made for good television," says Carter. "Maybe we can get that in the first episode."

Silverman holds up one hand to Carter and points to Ted with the other hand. "Then what happened?"

"I figured it was just nerves," says Ted. "My stomach rejecting food because I was so upset. But it happened again and again. Every time I'd eat, no matter what it was, I'd throw it back up almost immediately after I finished. And I was starting to smell, which didn't help matters."

"How long did this go on?" asks Silverman.

"Until I found something I could eat that didn't upset my stomach," says Ted. "As it turns out, that same something keeps me looking like I'm still alive."

"I'm not following you," says Silverman. "I thought you said your friend supplied you with formaldehyde to keep you fresh."

"I do have a friend who gets me formaldehyde," says Ted. "But that's just a backup plan. In case I need it."

"A backup plan for what?" asks Silverman.

"What Ted's saying," says Carter, "is that he keeps from decomposing by eating human flesh."

Silverman looks at them, then lets out a nervous laugh. When he realizes that neither Ted nor Carter is laughing with him, his smile vanishes. "What the fuck are you talking about?"

"Well, in spite of the fact that I was dead, something had awakened inside of me, this hunger I'd never known before," says Ted. "So three days after reanimating, I finally went outside."

"Three days," says Carter. "It kind of has a biblical feel to it, right?"

"I went out at night," says Ted. "After midnight, just in case people noticed I wasn't, you know, normal, and I stumbled upon this young prostitute on Hollywood Boulevard who said she was just making some extra money until she landed an acting role."

Carter smiles. "I've heard that one before."

"Anyway, as soon as I saw her, I knew I had to eat her," says Ted. "So I told her I was a talent agent and convinced her to go back to my place under the pretense of giving her a private audition."

"Only she was more like the late-night snack," says Carter.

Silverman just stares at him.

"It was a lot easier than I thought it would be," says Ted. "She was a little chewy, but I kept her down. Fed on her for more than a week. Eventually I realized I didn't smell anymore. By the time I finished her, I discovered that I'd somehow managed to reverse the process of decomposition. I look better now than I did when I reanimated."

Silverman suddenly realizes he's standing in front of a flesh-eating corpse and slowly backs away.

"So what do you think?" says Carter.

Keeping his eye on Ted, Silverman casually raises one hand and gestures for Carter to join him over at the wet bar. "I think I need a drink."

Carter turns to Ted. "Sit tight."

"Sure thing."

Silverman leads Carter over to the bar and pours himself a glass of scotch from the decanter. "Where did you find him?"

"I caught him eating a waitress in an alley out behind the In-N-Out Burger on Sunset Boulevard," says Carter. "Another aspiring actress. We got to talking, I gave him my card, and the next thing you know, here we are."

Silverman gulps down half his drink. "Jesus Christ."

"Is there a problem?"

"Is there a problem?" whispers Silverman. "I'll tell you the fucking problem. There's a zombie in my office who eats humans, and *you* brought him in here."

"Oh, come on," says Carter. "Look at him. He's harmless."

They both look over at Ted, who smiles and waves back at them.

Silverman takes another drink. "What the hell am I supposed to do with him?"

"You sign him, that's what you do."

"Sign him? Are you . . ." he starts to shout, then lowers his voice. "Are you crazy?"

"You're crazy if you don't sign him," says Carter. "Look, I could have gone to a dozen other studios, two dozen other studios, but I brought him to you because we have a history together. And if you don't sign him, I guarantee you someone else will."

Silverman looks over at Ted, who is fingering the incision on his left arm.

"Listen to me," says Carter. "I'm giving you the opportunity to be the front-runner on this one. You can set the standard. Have the number-one zombie reality show on television. Blow all of the other shows out of the water."

"I don't know," says Silverman.

"What's not to know? This is a moment of truth. It's only a matter of time before another Ted comes along, another genetic anomaly, and another and another, a new generation of reanimated corpses who can talk and think and who eat human flesh. And before you know it, they'll all be starring in their own reality television programs."

"You think so?"

"I know so," says Carter. "We're on the cusp of a new era in reality television and I'm offering you the chance to blaze a new trail of undead glory. Something unlike anything anyone has ever done. And you never know. If it turns out there's only one Ted, then you'll have the only show of its kind on television."

Silverman takes another drink of his scotch, thinking it over. "Okay. I'm not agreeing to anything, but let's say for the sake of argument I sign him. How in the hell am I going to keep him from decomposing? He eats people, for Christ's sake."

"Feed him fresh cadavers. Homeless people. Interns," says Carter. "Better yet, feed him all of the reality show rejects who never make it past the auditions. Or maybe that could be the show. Think about it. Our own version of *American Idol*, only when someone fails the audition, they get eaten by a zombie."

"That would definitely add a certain edginess," say Silverman.

"Exactly," says Carter. "And think about it. A zombie eating a human being on television? Imagine the ratings."

Silverman starts nodding, then catches himself. "Jesus, what am I thinking? This is insane."

"No. What's insane is letting an opportunity like this pass you by." Carter points at the flat-screen television, where reanimated corpses stumble out of a closet on *Zombie Hoarders*. "Do you want to keep producing shows like this? Crap that everyone can see on any other channel? Shows that never get more than a 2.5 rating?"

Silverman watches the television for several moments, not responding.

"You know as well as I do that if you pass on this and I take Ted to one of the major networks, they'd jump at the chance to sign him," says Carter. "And you can bet that Showtime, AMC, and HBO would be all over him like maggots on a festering corpse."

"I could have done without the imagery," says Silverman.

On *Zombie Hoarders*, a female zombie stares into the camera, her eyes vacant. No sign of intelligence. No spark of conscience. Silverman looks from the mindless zombie on the television to the sentient zombie sitting in his office.

"How do I know he can deliver the goods?" asks Silverman.

"What do you mean?"

"I mean if I'm going to commit to this, I'm not comfortable investing in him as the next big thing unless I see him in action."

"What do you suggest?"

Silverman swirls his drink for several moments, then hits the intercom button on the phone at the bar. "Ashley, can you come into my office?"

"Be right there, Mr. Silverman."

"Who's Ashley?" says Carter.

"She's an intern," says Silverman. "Hey, Ted?"

Ted stands up. "Yes sir?"

"If you don't mind, I'd like to see what you're capable of doing," says Silverman. "Can you do me a favor and go wait in the bathroom?"

"Sure thing," says Ted.

"The bathroom?" says Carter.

"Tile floors," says Silverman. "Easier cleanup. Plus I just had new carpeting put in."

A moment after Ted closes the bathroom door, Ashley, a young blonde, enters the office. "You wanted to see me, Mr. Silverman?"

"Yes. Could you please take my suit to the dry cleaners? It's hanging on the back of the bathroom door."

"Absolutely, Mr. Silverman. Is there anything else?"

"No, that's all for now."

As Ashley approaches the bathroom, Carter leans toward Silverman, and says under his breath, "Won't you get into trouble for this?"

"I'll let the lawyers handle it," says Silverman. "Besides, she always forgets that I don't like whipped cream on my mochas."

Ashley reaches the bathroom and opens the door. "Oh, I'm sorry. I didn't realize anyone was—"

A hand grabs her by the hair and yanks her inside. She lets out a scream that cuts off almost immediately, then she's on the floor, visible only from the knees down, the rest of her body obscured behind the partially closed door, her legs kicking and scrabbling on the tile. The only sounds are strangled gurgling and smothered grunting.

When Silverman and Carter reach the bathroom, Ashley's legs are still moving but there's not much fight left in them. Silverman pushes the door open to get a better look and sees Ashley on the ground, her eyes wide open and blood pumping from a gash in her throat, her hands flailing uselessly at Ted, who crouches over her, tearing into her abdomen with his hands and teeth.

"Good God," says Silverman.

"I have a feeling God's not really paying attention at the moment," says Carter.

They watch Ted continue to tear into Ashley, his face covered with her blood as he chews on her flesh and motorboats her intestines.

"I've got to hand it to him," says Silverman. "He's got great technique. And I like his enthusiasm."

"I told you," says Carter. "The kid's a natural."

Silverman nods. "He's got a bright future. Though we're going to have to beef up our liability insurance."

They continue to watch Ted in silence as he devours Ashley the intern, then Silverman closes the bathroom door and walks back over to the bar.

"So what do you think?" says Carter. "Do we have a deal?"

"That first idea you mentioned," says Silverman as he grabs the decanter of scotch. "The one about following him around documentary-style?"

"*A Zombie's Life,*" says Carter.

Silverman refills his glass, then pours another glass for Carter and hands it to him. "What do you think about calling it *Reality Bites?*"

THE DROP

Stephen Susco

THE GIRL I MURDERED last December returned this morning, a few minutes after midnight, pounding on my apartment door. And I mean *pounding*—with a force and a will that should have been rendered entirely impossible by eleven months of decalcification and decomposition.

Eleven months. Six days. Two hours. Death just hadn't taken root.

Maybe my parents were right after all—maybe I *can't* do anything properly.

The blows jolted me from a kind of sleep-mode-reverie that had been conjured by the rhythmic motion of the countdown timer on my preferred mirror site. I'd been staring at the screen for hours, as if the pot might boil early under my withering stare. Like the fifty-million-plus other Cynapse addicts around the world, I'd been waiting for The Drop. Ten hours a day playing the damn game simply wasn't enough. No, us 'Napsacks were more than willing to sacrifice even more of our valuable time aimlessly ticking the days off our calendars, imagining the bliss to come as we suffocated the useless moments separating us from our next fix—the mythological "Revenant Patch."

It took a few seconds—most likely, *more* than a few—for my addled brain to register the aural impulse. I turned from the screen, freed momentarily from its hypnosis-inducing pulse, and faced the dark, brick-encased stairwell. Unsure if I'd imagined it. The storm had rolled in, a biblical downpour. The thunder had been rattling the windows of my loft for hours. It could have been a charge from

67

a particularly low cloud. Surely no one would be out on the streets tonight, not in this weather, especially not in this part of town—

The pounding, again. More insistent.

It's her. You know it's her.

Impossible. I'd ended her.

But who else *could* it be?

The visitors had trickled to a stop shortly after the murder. A few caring friends had found their efforts were in vain, and quickly realized—or was it rationalized?—that they had far better things to do. More numerous were the sympathy chicks with their late-night texts, casually fumbled queries inquiring as to the current state of my well-being, yearning for a greater moon of despair to come into their orbit to blot out the sweltering heat of their own unavoidable truths.

Most of these, naturally, I'd accepted—hungry for the pull of a new celestial gravity, however fleeting. Seeking solace in even the palest reflection, the most vacuous echo of what had vanished long ago from my own night sky. A momentary flash of light, of heat, in a world of desolation. A passing comet to recall a brilliant star, now absent.

Brilliant star, bullshit. She was a black hole. A crushing vortex.

The pounding had stopped. Even without the blackout curtains I'd had put in to quell the stifling summer heat, the windows would have appeared dark. The dim bulb of my desk lamp—installed at the insistence of my ophthalmologist—illuminated only the far corner of the factory loft. Anyone outside—anyone but *her*—would assume no one was in. Had they gone?

There was only one way to be sure. I pressed the button on the video intercom by the top of the stairs. The screen brightened to life.

Apparently I hadn't installed the camera in the right place—the LCD image was blurred by the rain, rendering useless the extra money I'd paid to ensure a crystalline 1080p view of any unwelcome intruders.

But in this case, I didn't need the heightened clarity. Even the most ephemeral image, as from the vestiges of our most inebriated and pharmacologically enhanced moments together, was enough. The vague outline of her body was enough: shoulders perpetually slumped, shielding herself from a constant psychic onslaught, rain-drenched hair draping limply across those Eeyore-inspired shoulders—long, now, a far cry from her more familiar, asymmetrical bob—the penetrating gaze that, in spite of the way her body trembled in the December rain, remained defiantly fixed on the lens of the camera.

She knew I was watching. And she knew I would come.

Eleven months dead. And knock-knock-knocking at my chamber door.

I was halfway down the stairs before I realized I was in motion. Reaching for the dead bolt before I could even question why.

You don't let the dead in. Never *let them back, not after—*

I'd scrubbed her memory. Deleted the e-mails, the photos, the mix lists. The boiler in the basement had consumed her old headshots, the chicken-scrawl notes she'd leave on the pillow, in the refrigerator, taped to the rearview. Rendering them to ash that I'd carried to the roof and spilled out across the city. Wishing I could somehow do the same to the residue of those same immutable images on display in my brain.

You slaughtered her. And then you picked the bones clean.

Yet, there she stood, the thick steel door no longer between us.

No. Look again. That's a dead girl standing before you—

Undeniably alive. Lazarus risen.

NO. A rotting corpse. A shambling, stinking, festering, rotten—

She raised a hand. Palm down, fingers limp. Her eyes entreating.

They need permission to enter, don't they? The dead, the vamps—

And I took it. God help me, I took her hand, her pale skin cold as ice.

She melted into me. Sobbing into my neck. Making it wet with her tears.

Not tears. Rotten flesh. Stale blood. Ichor and pus. Anything but flesh, vital blood, a beating heart. Anything but alive, again.

I felt the warmth of her breath on my neck. Indisputable proof of resurrection.

And in the wake of that singular sensation, I was damned. . . .

The things she'd left behind—her clothes, toiletries, books—these sheddings had been further victims of my rampage. Chalk it up to collateral damage. Or a weak resistance to physical association. Her tea was listed among the ranks of the dead, that horrible yerba maté she always quaffed, with just a touch of stevia, from a ridiculous hollowed gourd she'd had shipped from Argentina—a bonus item, most likely, added as a token of thanks for contributing to one of those ridiculous microloan scams. She always did have a soft spot.

Where the worms first took root. Where the flies deposited their larva—

I found a bag of the maté smashed under the lower platter of my Ikea lazy Susan—a piece of her that had become trapped in my life, like an irritating length of gristle wedged between teeth, the remnant of a meal that simply can't be shaken free. This lucky survivor had been torn open, the twigs inside turned dry and brittle, speckled with more-fortunate stowaways—a few stale, scablike corn flakes, and the remnants of an ancient bag of brown rice.

Mindy didn't seem to mind. She'd already gulped down half the French press, even without a sweetener to cut the acerbic edge. Her color had returned. But she gripped the teacup so tightly that I was worried it might shatter, and rip into her palms.

Nothing to bleed. Nothing but the powder of desiccated blood—

"The Drop. It was The Drop."

It had taken an hour for her to speak. Most of that time I'd spent staring at the cup in her hands. Waiting for it to burst. It was easier than risking a look at those *(dead, glassy, cataract-ridden)* violet-tinged eyes. Because then, if I'd caught her looking back, I would have had to speak. To ask why she'd come. A question that would have been patently absurd, in the long shadow of the last thing I'd ever said to her.

No, not said—written. To have spoken would have risked a response.

It wasn't even a year, and still the exact words remain elusive. But the intent, I'm certain that couldn't have been clearer. That, I remember. *"Don't,"* I believe was the subject line of the e-mail. *"Don't"* was also the beginning of every sentence in the body of the message. *Don't write. Don't call. Don't think of me. Don't think, if we ever pass each other on the street, that I will—*

Don't be alive to me. Please. Just die.

She defied death that night. By pounding on my door. By speaking first.

"The Drop. It was The Drop."

I could feel her eyes. Waiting for mine. I considered remaining like that forever: just staring at that fucking teacup. Immovable as a statue. Lifeless.

And then we'd have switched places. Dead to life. Alive to dead.

Join us—we are legion—

But instead I raised my head, as slowly as I dared. Seeking clues, wanting to understand how this had happened. There was twice the duct tape on her priceless Keds high-tops as there'd been before. And more vibrant oil droppings—deep-crimson and canary-yellow splotches punching through the pitch black of the sneaker fabric.

Death had brought about few changes, it seemed.

Higher, still: formless men's worker jeans clung to her skinny legs in clumps, knees scuffed and torn, the denim drying unevenly along with the leggings she wore underneath. Even higher: the ridiculous hoodie she knew I fucking hated, over the tour shirt of the band I knew *she* fucking hated.

So. She hadn't planned the trip.

I should have reasoned this earlier, when I hung her raincoat—*his* raincoat—on the hook in the landing. She never would have worn that deliberately.

Guess I've always been a little slow. Even more since Cynapse started taking up most of my mental RAM . . .

A memory of our first fight abruptly ripped back into my thoughts—another unwelcome, undead abomination I'd staked through the heart, now clawing its way from the sodden earth. She'd said the wrong thing—or maybe it was the right thing, that I simply didn't want to hear. I'd stormed out, wasted a few hours downing pints of weak beer at Solley's before staggering into the campus computer center. Late shift paid double, and the place was always deserted. I drunkenly flipped off the undergrad who gave me the stink eye for being twenty minutes late. He said something about filing a complaint. Kept him from theater rehearsal, or something. Put off his backstage blow job for a spell. I couldn't have cared less. They wouldn't fire me—no one else would work until 4:00 A.M.

The outer doors opened only once that night. It was Mindy, in pigtails, knee socks, and a pleated schoolgirl skirt that ended well above her scarred, knobby knees. An apology on her lips. A key card to the lock for the seminar room down the hall in her hands.

She knew how to work it. How to pull the strings.

And she damn well knew what she could have worn on that night. Our first night together in eleven months, six days, and two hours. But that's not the way her mind was working. Which meant she was desperate. And had nowhere else to go.

Or—she knew *exactly* where to go. Where there was someone who would always take her in, in spite of vitriolic promises of rejection drunkenly tapped out on a crummy Dell keyboard.

"The Drop. It was The Drop."

I crossed the River Styx. My eyes met hers.

"What about The Drop?" I mumbled.

"Connor. The Drop . . . took him."

"Took him *where*?" It was a sarcastic response. But she sat there and reasoned it out, brow furrowed, legs jittering, as if her old calculus professor had just popped out of the bedroom and offered her a million dollars if she could calculate the differential equation that determined the rate at which her tea was cooling toward room temperature, in Celsius.

"Away. It took him away."

At this point I glanced at the digital wall clock. I remember this action clearly, because my eyes had previously been glued to the damn thing all day—until the moment Mindy had knocked on my door. From that point I'd forgotten I even owned a clock, or that time even existed and could be measured—

. . . Eleven months six days two hours

It was almost 1:30 A.M. Another hour and a half until The Drop. There was a clear logic to the idea of releasing the Revenant Patch simultaneously around the globe—at the stroke of midnight, naturally, in the Seattle home office of Cynapse. They didn't want the basement trollers to get on the boards early, and poison what would surely be an overwhelming flood of orgasmic reviews. The Socioheads had studied how many prospective buyers always seek out negative commentary first, diving to the single-digit one-star reviews and giving them extraordinary weight even in the face of a majority of five-stars. "Sympathetic dissonance," I'd heard it called. And the corporate bean counters had surely listened. Playing it safe, in spite of the fact that most of the current subscribers had most likely already preordered.

There was an article in the *Wall Street Journal* about how the 'Napsacks farther north, up the Atlantic seaboard and into Quebec, were panicking about a nor'easter that was rolling in. They'd lose their minds if there were power outages. Colleges across the country had even canceled classes the next day, making The Drop a de facto national holiday.

The game itself was something of a cipher, a long and unusual reach from your typical MMORPG: instead of elves, orcs, warriors, and wizards, players adopted the elusive persona of a disembodied spirit—not in the supernatural sense but rather in the *technological*. No specific definition had been supplied by the game's creator— ambiguity was a good part of the charm—but collectively the players had deduced that they were adopting the roles of an advanced alien race that had somehow survived a cataclysmic astral event by converting their essence to a raw energy state.

Yeah, we'd all heard that before—at least, anyone who'd ever read a few sci-fi novels or seen any given *Star Trek* variant. But it was the execution that drove the concept. When you first signed up, it took ten hours of tests—psychological, intellectual, and symbolic—for the system to determine the foundational attributes of your avatar. *Ten hours*. That element alone exponentially multiplied the odds of Cynapse's predicted failure upon launch.

Naturally, the doomsayers—the game's competitors, mostly— were wrong. Subscription numbers raced upward at record speeds, hitting record levels. So they simply raised their voices, like haruspices who had masterfully surveyed the entrails and summarily judged the Cynapse empire a stillbirth. They predicted that the ten-hour ordeal would create a massive backlash in the face of what the game had to offer—a landscape of abstract puzzles, each with its own unique set of rules (and physics, for the ones presented in 3-D), waiting to be solved in a kind of massively cooperative group session. Why would gamers want to join thousands of others in what amounted to hundreds of hours of, say, the folding of brilliantly colored cylindrical tubes in order to properly align an ever-shifting chromatic resonance field for a purpose that remained undefined?

Every geek knows this old chestnut: Ken Olsen, cofounder and CEO of the legendary DEC computer company (the second largest for a time, behind IBM), famously pronounced, at a 1977 meeting of the World Future Society in Boston, that there was "no reason for any individual to have a computer in his home." Though somewhat erroneous when taken out of context, the lesson should have been crystal clear—in the realm of technology, one should always, at least outwardly, embrace all ventures with the enthusiasm and optimism of a child. Especially if one has far to fall.

And Cynapse's competitors fell very, very far. Memberships to their own digital realms plummeted. The converts were simply too numerous. And a ticket to Cynapse produced a level of commitment previously unseen. With World of Warcraft, the last of the titans to topple, the average player could be expected to dedicate twenty hours a week to gameplay—enough to certify it as a second career.

The average Cynapse player logged in twice that much. There was room for little else. Especially other games. It was a phenomenon. A revolution.

And everyone wanted to know what lay at the core—what connected all the thousands of seemingly unrelated modules. Books had been written; online referendums of professionals and civilians had been held ad nauseam. Some had theorized that Cynapse was an institutionally founded protein-folding project, a method of utilizing the computing and intellectual powers of the masses to achieve scientific breakthroughs—like the one pioneered at Stanford, which uploaded data-chewing screen-saver software to transform your PC into a passive supercomputer participant, one tiny gear of a much greater collective think tank. Or the more "active" breeds such as Foldit, out of the University of Washington, which in 2011 announced that gamers had solved in three weeks a mystery that had baffled scientists for over a decade—the structure of a protease molecule with the ability to hamper the proliferation of the AIDS virus.

Another popular theory was that the engine beneath the surface was no more unique than any other successful commercial venture—a fortuitous marriage of capitalism and concept with an adept illusionist at the center, weaving a rich tapestry of mystery to conceal, for as long as possible, that there was in fact no Great Answer holding everything together. No chewy core to be uncovered, for all the licking in the world. Much like a certain ever-so-popular TV series, trumpeted for years as the height of innovation, yet revealed in post-conclusion hindsight as nothing more than a vacuous experiment of narrative misdirection and manipulation—an attraction no more ingenious than a laser pointer used to wear out a particularly energetic kitten.

All the deduction, the scrutiny, proved to be a fruitless exercise. The purpose of the game remained inscrutable, a fact that didn't deter the ever-growing throng of enthusiastic 'Napsacks. Whether they were oblivious of the enigma or compelled by the surety of inevitable Revelation was an irrelevant data point. The ranks swelled. The world's average BMI ratio skyrocketed. Centuries of man-hours were logged in seconds.

And just when the soothsayers, having learned nothing from history (as usual), decided Cynapse had nothing left to surprise its audience—they announced the end of the game.

Rule 1 of any commercial venture: you *never* announce the end of the game. Not unless the game is already dying. And especially if it's the most popular game in recorded history.

The announcement of the Revenant Patch was accompanied by a surprisingly strongly worded promise from the usually taciturn game developers: *All Will Be Revealed.*

The public reaction had been akin to that of a flock of prepubescent boys to a cheerleading competition held in high wind.

Many of the holdouts—the noncommittal, the skeptical yet curious—bought a ticket to the final show. The servers were pushed beyond capacity. Governmental agencies fretted over the potential toppling of the 'Net itself and the societal disruption that could result.

But society held—and 'Napsack society held its collective breath.

Waiting for midnight, Seattle time.

Ninety minutes away.

"Away. It took him away."

"The Drop hasn't happened yet." I almost choked on the words, instinctively avoiding using her name. As if speaking it would summon her in a more fully realized fashion than the one sitting across from me, clutching her cup as if it were the wrong edge of a cliff the rest of her body was clinging to.

"He was QA. Got it a week in advance."

QA. Quality Assurance. In this case, game testers. The last line of defense.

The bastard had done it. Connor was obsessed with Cynapse from the beginning, always swearing he'd find a way to penetrate the Dyson Sphere of silence the company had built around the identities of the personnel involved in its development. Back then it seemed like every moment of his day, every free moment of awareness, he'd dedicated to hammering away at the Cynapse shield, using every connection and resource available to him. I remember being bewildered, when it happened, that he even had the time or the inclination to steal Mindy away from me.

"How'd he find a way in?"

"I don't know. He didn't tell me the details. He just quit his job and . . . started locking his door." She shivered. I refilled her tea. It didn't seem to help.

"He'd stopped coming to bed, and I knew he couldn't stay up all night. I waited until after three. The monitors were on, I could see the glow under the door. But his typing, that constant typing had finally *stopped*. . . ."

She hesitated again. Her eyes glazing, moving up over my shoulder. To my computer. There was nothing to see—just the countdown clock, inexorably moving closer to zero.

"Mindy?"

Her focus returned, her eyes immediately locking on to mine. I'd said it, I'd spoken her name, and in that transgression an unspoken bond passed between us.

Now there was no turning back.

"I picked the lock. It wasn't hard. Just took a paper clip. He was sitting in front of his monitors, hunched over, like he was awake and thinking or something, but . . . he wasn't. His eyes were open. And there was water on the floor. Below his chair. It was coming from his mouth. And that wasn't even . . ."

"What did you *see?*"

I regretted the words instantly. They revealed that I cared only about getting a glimpse, an early peek at The Drop. They betrayed the depth of my craving.

Her eyes knew it. And forgave me.

"They were filled with . . . fluid."

"He *drooled* on the screen?"

"What was on them *moved* like fluid. Like water on the surface of a deep pool. Like there was something down below, something rising up."

I didn't understand, but pressed on. "What did you do?"

"I thought something was wrong—like he'd had a stroke or something. I moved forward, just a step. And the screens just switched off. By themselves. And there was—"

Mindy glazed over again. This time it wasn't my computer, or the wall clock, or her tea upon which her eyes settled. They drifted up, ever so slowly, toward the ceiling. As if in a great effort to recall the specifics of a memory she'd tried to stuff away in the dusty corners of her mind—

. . . Anything but alive again . . .

"Mindy?" Her eyes kept rolling. Ever higher. Turning to whites.

I grabbed her shoulders. Shook her. She felt flimsy, somehow. Diaphanous. But her focus returned, and she continued as if she'd never paused.

"They saw me. They *saw* me."

I didn't press her—there was no point. It was shock. I'd seen it before, when my best friend in fourth grade, Bobby Doyle, sliced off the tip of his index finger, fooling around with the industrial paper cutter they've long since banned from use. I sat with him in the nurse's office, waiting for the ambulance to arrive, as he gently stroked the severed hunk of flesh in his palm and sang it Christmas songs.

Funny thing, shock.

"Did you talk to Connor about it, when he woke up?"

"He *was* awake. When the screens went off, I couldn't see anything—not right away. But then there was this . . . glimmer. Like a firefly. Like two. He'd turned around and he was just staring at me. His eyes, they were so . . . *wrong*.

"I went back to the bedroom. And this time, *I* locked the door. The next day when I came home from work, there were holes in his door, places where the screws had broken through. They were dead bolts. Five of them. He'd put them on backward, on the door instead of the frame. . . ."

She wobbled again. I put a hand on her leg. My pinky slid into one of the rips in the fabric and I felt the soft tension of the leggings underneath. A year ago the sensation would have made me rock hard in under a second. But not now. Something wasn't right here.

"When was this?"

"A week ago. Maybe longer. I haven't seen him since, except from outside."

"Outside?"

"There's no bathroom in that room. It's just a walk-in closet he uses as an office. And the window doesn't open—"

"Maybe he came out when you were at work?"

"I stopped going. I used sick days. I even slept on the floor, right next to the door. He never left."

I wasn't sure how to parse the next question flashing in my queue. There isn't a polite way to phrase, *Did you* smell *anything?* But she read my mind.

"He was typing, at first. So I knew he hadn't . . . and then, when the typing stopped, I heard the creak of his chair. He'd just *jerk* around every few minutes. Like he was having a seizure."

"What did you mean about seeing him outside?"

"I waited until it was dark, and went to the roof. Climbed down the fire escape. He'd painted the windows, but I could see inside. . . ."

That's when the tears started again. And in her eyes I could finally see the only thing I'd never seen there before, in all the time we'd been together: *pain.*

Something I'd never been able to elicit, no matter how hard I'd tried.

"I saw the wires. The *new* wires."

Funny thing, shock.

"Do you want to call the police?" For a moment she looked bewildered. Then she shook her head, and put the teacup down, rubbing away the indentations it left in her hand.

"I need you."

The static returned to my brain. How dare she. How dare she—

. . . *Stake in her heart aim for the brain fucking walking undead* . . .

"I need you to come. To come and see."

We went down the street to Solley's. They'd closed, but the occasional taxi driver knew enough to fly by on the off chance that an overenthusiast would wake up in the alley and need a late-night ride home. Easy to help yourself to a generous tip, from those types. But the alley was as abandoned as the bar—and the streets. I figured the drivers somehow knew this—imagine the sixth sense a guy could cultivate slinging fares in this city—because after fifteen minutes of no cabs, I tried calling. No one picked up at 411. No way to reach Dispatch.

We could have gone back to my place. But that would have brought Mindy back to a dangerous proximity to my bedroom—and I'd already fought that battle that night. So we trudged through the rain to the light-rail station a half mile deeper into the Dead Zone of downtown. It, too, was deserted. Two A.M. on a Thursday. The bars at the safe end of the city would still be open. I assumed it was the rain. And maybe The Drop.

There, at least, I was correct.

The train arrived right on time—to the very minute. Naturally, it was fully automated. The axiom holds: remove the possibility of human error from the equation, and generally the equation sings.

I think, therefore I am.

I am, therefore I fuck up.

QED.

All the cars were deserted, and I led Mindy to seats in the front. Maybe it was an instinctive attempt at consoling her—a symbolic and quietly desperate gesture to give the impression that we were in any way, shape, or form in control of this ride. As if we could, at any point, grab the reins and be in charge of our destiny.

Our *destiny. As if the past year had never occurred. As if I could wipe it clean, the same way I'd tried to wipe the memory of her clean.*

And look how well that *had gone.*

She settled back, and under the awful, energy-efficient LED lighting I could finally see the dark blotches under her eyes, the beginnings of wrinkles at the corners of her mouth. Too many cigarettes. Not enough sleep.

I almost nodded off myself, in the somnambulant rocking of the car. No, it wasn't that, was it? It was her. It was the fact that now that I'd touched her, I couldn't stop. My fingers stayed on her leg, caressing that exposed patch of nylon. She needed my comfort. She needed to know I was there.

Yeah. Sure.

The abrupt twitch of her body brought me back to attention. It was a sudden, jerking motion, so quick that I might not have noticed had the soles of her high-tops not *slammed* against the bottom of the seat when it happened.

Her eyes were drifting again. No, not drifting—*reeling* in their sockets.

Then she grabbed my leg. Squeezing with a strength that didn't seem possible.

I snatched at her wrist, startled—and the fugue ended as quickly as it had come, her muscles relaxing their grip. She looked down, saw my hand in hers. Her body shuddered in relief.

So I didn't let go. I couldn't.

And I didn't notice the pinpricks in my jeans until they started bleeding. Five, count 'em, tiny spots of red. Her fingernails, chewed down to nubs, must have punched right through. That's what I thought then, and that's why I didn't look.

I didn't look. So I didn't see.

We made it to Connor's just before two thirty. Only a half hour left until The Drop. It was all I'd thought about for months, ever since the announcement of the Revenant Patch. But Cynapse was the furthest thing from my mind as I rode up the elevator with Mindy.

I was going to *Connor's* place. I was going there to *help* him.

Because Mindy needed me.

There had never been an explanation, from either of them. Not that I'd given her a chance. Maybe I'd secretly hoped that she'd have seen through my e-mail . . .

. . . Don't look back the sun has set don't you ever look back . . .

Seen through the hurt and seen with clarity that my words were nothing more than yet another childish and desperate ploy to get her attention, to elicit a response. How do they always describe those mismanaged suicides? A "cry for help."

Jesus. Is that all it was?

But Connor—between us had risen an ocean of silence. A million images from our childhood friendship, suddenly drowned in the bleakest of seas. He went dark on Facebook, his blog. Even deleted his precious LinkedIn bio. He had swiftly bowed out not only of my sphere but the Sphere Entire. Our mutual acquaintances were polite enough never to mention his name. *Everyone* knew. But there was an undeniable sense that *everyone* had lost Connor. That some great force had surrounded him without contest—that he hadn't resisted as it built a wall, planted a flag, dug a moat, and scrubbed the maps clean.

Mindy had that effect on people. It only took seconds.

Early man didn't need to be told the value of gold. The glitter was enough.

It was a handshake in the dark, with deal terms forged in shadow. Her belongings had abruptly vanished from my apartment—and Connor McKittrick, social-network butterfly, had simply gone extinct. With no apologia to remember him by.

Eleven months. Six days. Two hours. And I was about to see him. The best friend who ruined everything.

And I hadn't brought a weapon. So much for those fantasies.

Mindy stopped halfway down the hall, far from the door of the place they'd been sharing. "It's gotten worse," she whispered. "The smell."

It took me a moment to pick up on it. But it was there, festering under the collection of odors wafting up from the dingy hallway carpet. A meaty stench, not of decay but rather of heightened *ripeness*. It was worse at the door itself—an apartment filled with a million flowers, blossoming all at once, spilling the sickly scent of their nectar into the air, to draw forth the pollinating insects. . . .

Every biologically innate alarm was blaring in my head but . . .

. . . *Anything anything but alive* . . .

But I'd come this far. I was at the door.

And Mindy needed me.

I showed Connor more courtesy than he'd ever shown me, in the act of stealing Mindy—I knocked on his door. "Connor. It's me."

Silence.

I didn't realize Mindy had shuffled forward until I heard her whisper close to my ear, "He can't answer you."

Those other alarms, the remaining few that hadn't triggered, that I guess I didn't even know I had up there?

Yeah. All at once.

"I'm coming in, Connor. I'm coming in. . . . I'm coming."

The stink rolled over me, filling every empty space, every available void, straight down to the gap between nucleus and electron. It was like I'd just belly flopped into a fetid, stygian pond straight out of Lovecraft's darkest nightmares.

But Mindy needed me.

The apartment lights were off, so I navigated my way using the feeble light from the hallway. I didn't want to risk touching anything, especially the walls. Not with that smell penetrating my soul. Not with the squelching sounds my feet were making on the floor.

My mind was conjuring some remarkable imagery, the things I might see if I dared find a light switch. And I had no interest in challenging their veracity. My eyes were adjusting well enough anyway— and it didn't take me long to zero in on what must have been Connor's makeshift office.

I could have found my way there with just my nose.

But instead it was the pulsing light seeping out from under the door, as clear as a homing beacon. It drew me into its gravity, the most careless of moths.

There were the screw holes, just as Mindy had described. If I hadn't checked for them, I might have missed the condensation that covered the entire length of the door. The paint was loosening, and peeling. It could have been made of . . .

. . . *Rotting decaying flesh* . . .

The knob was warm. Almost invitingly so.

"Connor." I tried to put some authority behind it. To establish a baseline. To ensure our positions in the world were understood. "Connor, can you hear me?"

There was a metallic creak from inside. His chair. A weight shifting.

"Mindy's here. She's worried." I wanted to spit, to clear my sinuses of the horrific stench, to clear my mouth of the shit-movie dialogue. I glanced back at Mindy, who had closed the apartment door. I didn't ask why.

I didn't think to.

"Do you want me to break the door down?" She didn't answer. Fuck it, *I* wanted to break the door down. And then I wanted to use my fists to beat Connor's face into . . .

. . . *Oh God why* why *couldn't you have just* . . .

Splinters of the door frame battered my face, the perspiration from inside the room must have been incessant, and finally weakened the wood. I brushed fragments from my eyes, staggering backward, momentarily blinded.

My vision finally cleared. And I saw the machine.

That's what it looked like, at first: a hulking metal morass in the center of the room, misshapen and angular, the creation of a tangled mind. The floor was nearly knee deep with snarled cables, some as thin as a straw, others as wide as a finger. Some fed into the desktops under the table—they'd punched through the outer casings, squirmed between the narrow cooling vents. Others wriggled into the walls and floor of the room itself, and a bundle of narrow ones even draped along the window ledge, ending in a fist-size hole they'd made in the glass. The shards around the edges sliced into their sinuous skins and a dark ichor flowed out, seeping down along the wall below.

It was a lair of sleeping serpents, undisturbed by the pulsing sapphire embers emitted by the computer monitors above them, swirling windows of fluid . . .

. . . *Saw me it saw me* . . .

That framed the oblong hulk of metal, giving it contour and—

The chair. The machine squatted right where a chair would have been.

I stepped tentatively over the coils, knowing before it became clear . . .

It wasn't a machine. It was Connor. He was the root from which all these branches emerged. His skin—what was left of it, anyway—bulged horribly under the tension of the cables . . .

. . . *The new wires* . . .

That had forced their way out from within. I found myself wondering if the thicker cables had hurt more than the slender ones, as they created a string of three-ring tents along his arms, his legs, his forehead. The wires that extended from his tear ducts were thin as gossamer, and connected to nothing but air. Tightly wound bundles that relaxed once they'd cleared his cheeks, and seemingly of their own power swirled independently, as if caught by some breeze I couldn't detect.

As if the current had abruptly ceased, the delicate eye wires slowed their movements, stiffening and coiling around one another, reforming into a tapered tip with a flattened face that *moved,* tasting the air, a scintillating gyre of an antenna.

The bundle slowly rotated toward me. Turning Connor's head along with it.

I could have sworn there was a hint of a smile on his lips, as he spoke.

"You came. You *came*."

When I emerged from the office, and couldn't see Mindy, I assumed she'd run. That the fear she'd been so futilely trying to bottle up had finally overwhelmed the container. But a whirring sound from the bedroom stopped me from leaving.

It was a nice bed, I'll give Connor that. For years I'd teased him about the crummy futon he insisted he'd never sell. I guess Mindy's moving in changed all that. It was double-thick, looked like a pillow-top mattress. He'd spent. And he wasn't a guy who liked to spend.

Mindy lay on her back atop the tousled sheets. The light from the screen of her laptop, perched on the nearby nightstand, gave away the movement of the gleaming strings that had begun to push through her skin.

. . . Small they start small . . .

I moved to the bedside, not interfering with the process. I wanted to. I imagined yanking the wires from Mindy, not caring about the damage I'd do inside her. Then I'd pull her onto my shoulder and burst into the hall, down the stairs, and into the night. The music would swell, and coalesce into a crescendo.

But her eyes denied me that fantasy. They were alert for the first time since I'd seen her . . .

. . . Eleven months six days but hey who's counting. . . .

She slipped her hand inside mine. Her lips moved, for the moment still under her control. "I'm—sor—so sorry—"

"Why did you do it? Why did you *play*, after you saw what—"

"He made me," she whispered. "He forced me."

Her hand tightened. She wasn't through.

"He forced me, like before. . . ."

I thought there were tears welling up in her eyes. But it was just the first glistening gossamer strands, curling and stretching in the air with what seemed almost to be *delight*. Soaking in their first sensations as newborns.

"He was drunk and I was drunk and he forced me and—oh God,

I couldn't kill it but I couldn't tell you and he—he said he'd change, he *promised.* . . ."

Somewhere, far above or maybe deep within, celestial bodies shifted. Moving away, on some new trajectory, once again letting in the scorching heat and the blazing light of—

. . . *Alive anything but alive* . . .

"It died, it died inside me, and we died, and I had killed you and—oh, oh God, Brendan, I can't feel you anymore—"

Her pupils dilated, wider than I would have thought possible.

Her lips parted. And then her perfectly crooked teeth.

Deep, deep inside her throat, I saw something stirring to life.

Two fifty-eight A.M. Almost out of time, now. So read carefully.

When it happens, it will happen like this: you will receive a phone call, or an e-mail, or a text. Or a pounding, pounding on your front door.

It could be a stranger. But most likely, it will be someone you know. Someone maybe you haven't seen in a while. Someone to whom you might owe a debt—or simply an unreturned phone call.

It might be someone you have hurt.

. . . *Ended her slaughtered her* . . .

You must fight every instinct you were born with. You must shove aside any feeling of guilt. You mustn't be moved by the clarity evoked by their return. . . .

. . . *Ended me slaughtered myself ripped out my own still-beating heart* . . .

You mustn't let it in. You cannot reconnect.

This is how it happens. This is how it *spreads.*

. . . *Coming I'm almost there* . . .

Searched the apartment, as much as I dared. Connor was a religious diary note keeper, but anything made of paper in his office had been rendered . . .

. . . *Almost home* . . .

Stopped typing a good ten minutes or so after I got the livestream feed up on her laptop just lying next to her now . . .

. . . *New wires new fingers* . . .

It says there's only fifty-two readers but I hope to God there's more.

. . . Let you down abandoned you won't leave you again ever . . .
Pulling words from my thoughts, a far better speller than I evAr
was ha ha . . .
. . . I loved you I'm sorry we'll be togeth . . .

ANTIPARALLELOGRAM

Amber Benson

TINTINNABULATION. Four silver bells on a loop of raw leather. Four silver nails pounded into the top of the metallic door frame, holding the bells in place. When the bells ring, sonorous and clear, you know that someone has come into the store.

Time to put down your book.

The store is cramped. Not overflowing with things, though, just small and cloying because of its shape: triangular, with two metal walls meeting in a sharp point, a large plate-glass front window making up the third wall. A shallow metal-and-glass counter full of tiny brown vials intersects the place where the side walls meet, but there's enough room behind it for only one employee, and a tiny stool for the employee to sit on—presuming the employee is thin and not too tall.

No bellies or giants need apply.

They won't fit.

Across the room, diagonally in line with the counter, is a perfectly rectangular doorway. Behind this metal door is another space, the mirror image of the first room—its equal and opposite—but chock-full of brown, square boxes labeled STANDARD TIME and TO SHIP. There is no counter, no employee, and no small metal stool to sit on.

Together, the store and its storeroom form an antiparallelogram, an incongruous shape that, along with the triangular aspect of the two rooms, makes the rent cheaper here than in any of the other storefronts on the block. No one wants to rent an oddly shaped space for his business: squares and rectangles and even ovals, yes.

But never triangles or antiparallelograms.

Nothing except bad will come from these angular shapes. Any

tenant of such a space will have no future . . . accidents will occur and death is a distinct possibility. There have been twenty-one employees since they opened the store—some quit early and were spared, but others were not so lucky. Triangular accident and death became their currency.

Now the store asks for only six months of time from prospective employees—this seems to be the upward limit before the bad things start to happen—and then the employees are free to go on their merry way, their wallets much, *much* fatter from the experience.

Hazard pay they call it.

Accidental-death pay.

The plate-glass front window is gritty, covered in three years' worth of debris, dirt, and grime. It's been that long since Demeter ran the store. Demeter, the only employee who ever washed the window. Inside and out, she made it shine, and sales were up for the six months she worked there. In the end, she left with the Schnaz, promises of marriage and a house in the suburbs hot on his lips.

I don't work in the store.

But I want to.

I've lived in the neighborhood my whole life. I've seen the comings and the goings. I've known all twenty-one employees. Some liked me, let me come and play in the store while they sat behind the counter, waiting and reading. Others shooed me away, forbade me from coming in. With the wrinkled purple jumpsuit I was forced to wear by circumstance, they knew I was the lowest of the low: an untouchable in a caste system that I hardly even understood.

I was found in a garbage bin behind a New Mexican burrito bar called Truth or Hotsauces.

No mother. No father. No name.

Just a scowling, yowling baby boy with dirty brown hair and a pinched, pink face nestled in a mound of flattened, yellow-corn tortillas. The MPs took me to a Pop-Up Green Crescent, where the nurse checked me out and implanted a Color ID under the skin of my left wrist.

Pink.

For Orphan and Ward of the Color Sector.

When I turned eighteen I was given a Purple Color ID, which signified me as part of the homeless population. Unless I managed to find a way to change my situation significantly before the day I turned thirty, the Purple would be swapped out for Orange. An Orange Color ID meant you were the walking dead. You had one year to enjoy life before you were collected by the MPs and euthanized to avoid overpopulation. Orange jumpsuits were to be pitied and given free alcohol and street drugs. But I'd spent my whole life feeling like the walking dead. When you're born with an expiration date, it's hard not to.

But we weren't given the *designer* drugs the triangular store sold. They weren't for the likes of the Purple, Pink, or Orange.

Of course, that didn't mean there weren't plenty of other-colored customers interested and affluent enough to afford them.

There were always plenty of other-colored customers who could buy what they wanted: special powers, included. Those customers came in sleek hover cars made of titanium and aluminum alloys, their fiberglass bodies spray-painted bright neon.

Colors, like shapes, had special meaning. Blue for the military. Red for business. Green for government. Yellow for the richest, regardless of what they did. There were other colors with their own designations— and then there were Purple, Pink, and Orange for people like me.

The poor.

Who did not have hover cars.

I liked to stand on the moving sidewalk across from the store and watch the rich come and go in hourly cycles. If you held the stationary metal handrail, you could walk in place for hours, as long as no MPs saw what you were doing and kicked you off.

I would count the hover cars as they floated in empty space, their passengers disembarking just long enough to secure their vials from the store and go. There were lots of Yellows. A few Reds and Greens. Very, very rarely was there a Blue.

Occasionally a Black hover car would appear in front of the store—the Black ones were "for hire," meaning anyone could rent them if he was willing to pay heavily for the pleasure. These hover cars I always watched intently because they were completely anonymous. They could be anyone.

Even a Purple like me.

One who had made enough money to escape the Color Sector.

This gave me hope.

And the vials that these anonymous people bought were a hope of another kind.

They could be my salvation, my ticket out of the Color Sector, if only I could talk my way into a job at the store. If only I could sell the vials for six months and collect the hazard pay. Then, and only then, would I be free, with no Orange jumpsuit in my future. With the money burning a hole in my pocket, I could go to the suburbs and look up Demeter. Maybe even get my own place there and live a fully homogenized, noncolor, shape-centric after-poverty life.

This was my dream.

It was a simple dream, but a hard one to attain.

First, I would have to catch the man who owned the store. He made oddly timed appearances, usually late at night when no one was at the shop. I'd seen him come in a Yellow hover car and I'd seen him come on the moving sidewalk. He always wore the same thing: a pale gold jumpsuit with a black zipper that split the suit in two.

He wasn't old—at least he didn't *look* old. He had a shock of black hair and pale blue eyes in a ratlike face. I didn't know if he partook of the vials he sold or even if he was the person who made the elixirs inside them, but I knew for certain that he was the man I would have to impress if I wanted the job.

Demeter had told me this, had confided the information to me because she liked me. She said I looked like her dead sister—though I was a boy—and that she wanted only good things for me. All this was before she met the Schnaz and went away, but I cherished her words just the same.

So I started coming out at night, later and later, watching and waiting. Trying to learn the pattern of the man's comings and goings. Half asleep, I stood on the moving sidewalk, yawning as the neon signs buzzed and flickered around me. But I could discern no pattern. The man was as random as the customers who frequented his store.

The other thing I would have to do, if I wanted the job, was to get a new jumpsuit. One in Black. Anyone could buy one of these nondescript jumpsuits, but the key word was *buy*. And I had no money. Only the Purple jumpsuit on my back and the scraps of rice and fish in my pockets—my favorite place to scavenge was from the garbage bin of Saw-She-Me, the floating sushi bar four stores down the opposite side of the moving sidewalk.

I didn't need anything else because the nicest part of living in the Color Sector was that it was enclosed and temperate. Here, I could scavenge food, use the public toilets to wash myself and eliminate the waste my body made, and get free medical care at any Pop-Up Green Crescent as long as I showed them my Color ID.

That was the beauty of living in the Chroma, the roughest neighborhood in the Color Sector, where I'd been born and existed for all my life. People minded their own business. Which left me free to sleep in whatever bolt-hole or empty doorway I could find without being harassed or kicked around. As long as I avoided the attention of the MPs, I was just another street urchin underfoot to the rest of the people I encountered: to be pitied by some and ignored by others.

Rarely did I find myself in any trouble.

There were the occasional scuffles here and there, but I was smart and stayed out of the way whenever possible. It was to my advantage that I looked unremarkable. I had dark brown hair, light brown eyes, and a forgettable face. I blended in with the crowd, with the garbage underfoot, with the grit and grime of the Chroma.

Only Demeter had ever looked at me twice—and only because I reminded her of her dead sister.

Mostly, I just kept my head down and my nose clean. Neither of which would help me get a Black jumpsuit or make the man—if I could catch him—give me the job I wanted so that I could move into the store and sell the vials that would collect me the hazard pay that would change my life.

It all seemed so simple.

It was the hardest thing I'd ever had to do.

And then there were the vials themselves, the elixirs that gave you special powers. Of course, the rub was that you had to keep buying if you wanted the gifts to last. One vial equaled one dose equaled one month. People quickly became addicted to the stuff. Spent vast fortunes so they could fly or walk on water or suck someone's blood.

The bloodsucking was on the weirder end of the spectrum.

The vials allowed you to become a vampire, a zombie, a werewolf— you name the monster and there was an elixir for it.

Call it the ultimate in role-playing.

To be fair, there weren't as many people interested in that kind of thing, but there were enough. Those people, the weird ones, came at dusk just as the store was about to close. They came in Black hover cars, wore Black jumpsuits, looked dodgy. Some had long, feminine hair. Some had faces pockmarked with acne. Some gave off a scent, a feeling, a *vibe* that made me uncomfortable as I walked in place on the moving sidewalk, watching them. There was something wrong about them, something *bad*.

Demeter said that those were the customers she liked least. The others she could tolerate—they wanted silly things—but the monster-lovers made her skin crawl.

I didn't care what the customers wanted. I would give them whatever vials they asked for. I just wanted the money.

The hazard pay.

So I spent my nights stalking the man who owned the store and my days standing in front of B-Suits-R-Us, staring at the Black jumpsuits gleaming in its front window.

The old Korean woman who ran B-Suits-R-Us didn't have to worry about the shape of her space—it was perfectly square, perfectly safe. There was no hazard pay, just the minimum seven chits an hour that was standard fare for people who wore Red jumpsuits and lived in the Chroma.

If the old woman noticed my presence, she didn't make a big deal out of it. I wasn't getting in the way of her customers or causing her to lose any sales, so it was no skin off her nose to let me stare at her window display. Besides, it would've taken more effort to run me off the moving sidewalk than she was willing to expend on ejecting some street kid.

There were only Black jumpsuits in the window, but I could see jumpsuits of other colors hanging on racks in the back. Unlike the Black jumpsuits, you had to have your Color ID with you to buy the other ones. Red IDs got Red jumpsuits, Blue IDs got Blue jumpsuits, and Yellow IDs got hybrid colors, like the Gold and Black jumpsuit the man who owned the triangular store usually wore.

Rich people could get whatever color they wanted, money being no object to them.

My Color ID was Purple. It was embedded in the skin of my left wrist, where it had been placed when I was an infant, and it would stay there, just like everyone else's, for as long as I lived in the Color Sector. It did not entitle me to buy anything. Purple, Pink, and Orange jumpsuits were given out for free at local shelters.

I went to the Order of the Cosmic Seed shelter once a year to get my new Purple jumpsuit, but I didn't take anything else they offered me. I didn't like the female monks who ran it, or the smarmy looks they gave you as you stood there, waiting to collect your jumpsuit. Their eyes gobbled you up like you were a piece of raw meat waiting to be spitted. We all knew the monks bought and ate the flesh of the Orange jumpsuits after they were euthanized—an electric poker up the ass kept the meat tender—but that didn't mean the ladies got a free preview.

I also didn't like the fact that the meals the shelter offered were laced with a sterilizing agent. I personally had no interest in adding to the population (who wanted to damn another child to the kind of existence I'd had), but I didn't want anyone forcing his will on me, either.

So I avoided the shelters and kept to the sidewalks, scavenging what I could from the garbage bins of the big chain restaurants that overpopulated the Color Sector. I knew they didn't dose their food with anything stronger than weapons-grade monosodium glutamate.

"Stop blocking the way, kid."

The sandpaper-rough voice was hardly in my ear before the man was gone, having elbowed past me without waiting for my response. I always had a hard time maintaining my watch at rush hour. That's when the sidewalks became extrajammed with multihued people trying to get through the Chroma as quickly as possible on their way out to the more staid neighborhoods of the Color Sector. The influx of people made it hard for me to remain motionless in front of B-Suits-R-Us and I let go of the metal bar the store provided in order to keep any window-shoppers from getting dragged away with the sidewalk.

Letting myself get sucked into the swirl of people, I relaxed my body and calmed my breathing.

Sometimes I got a little claustrophobic in the crush of colored jumpsuits and I'd found that concentrating on my breathing could get me through the worst of it. I would count to eight on the intake of one breath, then do the same thing on its exhale. It shut down the panic before it could build to a crescendo.

No one had taught me how to read or how to use basic mathematics, but that hadn't mattered because I'd picked it up myself. For as long as I could remember, I'd been able to read the flashing neon signs that hung on the buildings of the Chroma like infesting ticks, leaching energy as if it were blood.

Numbers had come as easily.

More than words, I liked numbers. Infinite and immutable, they were the building blocks of the universe. Everywhere I looked, numbers dominated, making me feel like there was some stability to my unstable world.

Having calmed myself down with the counting, I was able to open my eyes again and let the numbers go. The crush of sweating human bodies was still thick around me, but I ignored it now and went with the flow.

For the first time, I saw that I was wedged in among a group of Green jumpsuits. I counted seven of them, talking and joking among themselves. I figured they'd just come from the Municipal Building and were heading home for the night, but then they started moving to the right, grabbing on to the metal bar in front of the Strip and Dine, leaving me a little more space on the moving sidewalk.

I decided that the Green jumpsuits had the right idea.

Time to get off.

I reached out for the side of a passing building and swung myself off the moving sidewalk, my feet touching solid, stationary ground for the first time in hours. Mostly I stuck to the moving sidewalks and the first alleyways off the grid because they were safer. Going deeper into the grid brought you to the tenements that made up the majority of the Chroma. Anything could happen out there: too many poor Red jumpsuits, too many illicit Black jumpsuits running matter blasters, drugs, and other illegal substances.

For the most part, there were no MPs. Occasionally they would leave the safety of the moving sidewalks and venture out into the wilds of the tenements, but it was a rare sight.

Behind the buildings, in the first alleyway, was where the garbage bins were kept. This was my hunting ground, where I did my scavenging, and where I chose to sleep. There was a whole community of Purple and Pink jumpsuits back here, a few Orange jumpsuits, too, but I tried to keep to myself.

No one was your friend in the Chroma.

I'd gotten off the moving sidewalk just past the Strip and Dine, the steak-and-legal-prostitution joint the Green jumpsuits had gone into. Head down, I walked past the side of the building until I came to the first alleyway off the grid. Here, I made a left and entered a world full of garbage.

As far as the eye could see were giant, square metal bins overflowing with refuse that got collected only once a week by hover scow. In this part of the Chroma, the garbagemen came on Mondays, so by Friday the mass of crap was already piled into minimountains that threatened to topple at the slightest touch.

I passed two women in Purple jumpsuits inside one of the bins, collecting moldy chocolate muffins from the Pain-du-Pain chain bakery and stuffing them into a tattered mesh bag with a golden-eagle emblem on it. They ignored me, intent on scavenging muffins.

I did the same and kept walking, stuffing my hands into the pockets of my jumpsuit. I would hit the garbage bins later, but now I wanted to think. And walking was how I thought best.

Leaving the women behind me, I crossed over into the next alleyway. It was dimmer here, the garbage so high it blocked out the light, but I didn't mind. I liked the feeling of being hidden—that was until I felt a pair of strong arms wrap around my torso and drag me into the folds of waiting refuse.

The smell was tremendous. Like something had died, gotten back up, and then died all over again. I gagged as the stench coated my nostrils and the back of my tongue.

"Don't move."

The voice was guttural, the consonants hard and the vowels stringy.

The arms around my torso were muscular and very, very cold. I could feel the length of the man's body pressing against me—I assumed it was a man from the depth of the voice—and this made me feel even colder.

I started to shiver.

"I told you not to move."

"I can't help it," I said. "You're so cold."

The man growled, the sound scaring me until I realized it was a laugh.

"If I let you go," the man asked, "will you hold still?"

I thought about the request for a moment, then nodded.

The man released me and I remained where I was, not moving a muscle, the shivers slowing and then coming to a complete stop as the heat returned to my body.

Though the man was beside me, he stood in the shadow of the garbage bin so that I couldn't see his face. He was taller than me by a foot and bulkier in the middle, but his legs were thin. The light was too dim to make out the color of his jumpsuit, but I figured he was a Purple or an Orange from the size of him.

"I've been watching you," the man said.

I didn't answer.

He cleared his throat, the grotesque sound of sticky phlegm being sucked out of his nasal passage killing the silence.

"You're very obvious: the store, the jumpsuit, the store, the jumpsuit. Single-minded, I would call you."

Still I didn't respond.

"I need your help," the man said in his gravelly rasp. "And I'll make you a deal for it."

I was too stunned by the turn of events to answer him properly.

"Don't think about it. Just say yes."

The smell was getting worse, making my eyes water, making me want to throw up the mushy brown-rice roll I'd eaten that morning.

"What's the deal?" I heard myself asking.

The man growled—laughed—again.

"I knew you were a little weasel."

I didn't take offense.

The man sighed and I could feel the tension go out of his body, tension I hadn't even realized was there until it had gone.

"A Black jumpsuit for your help."

My heart stopped beating. I couldn't breathe. It was as if my greatest hope had been plucked straight from my chest and presented back to me on a titanium platter.

"What do I have to do?" I asked.

There was a moment of silent anticipation as the man reeled me in. "Steal something for me."

The man said it was called casing the joint, but it wasn't very different from what I'd already been doing with my time. Only now my goal had morphed. I wasn't chasing a Black jumpsuit anymore; a Black jumpsuit was chasing me.

I stood on the moving sidewalk, watching the triangular store.

Laguna, the girl who'd been there for five months and twenty-seven days of her six-month stint, was behind the counter, reading a book. Like many of the store's employees, she and I hadn't become very close, but she tolerated my presence, never yelling at me when I skulked into the store and looked at the glass case full of vials—all the ones on display were legal, the illicit stuff was kept in crates in the storage room—and generally made a nuisance of myself.

I knew from my hours of watching the store that Laguna was a user. She was addicted to one of the elixirs, a special potion that made you irresistible to the opposite sex. She was using it to trap one guy in particular, a handsome Yellow jumpsuit that came to the store every night at closing to pick her up. From what I could tell, she'd taken a loan out against her hazard pay so she could keep up with her habit. But I got the feeling that once her time at the store was up, life wasn't going to be so nice. A Red jumpsuit, she obviously wasn't rich, and after her money and stock of elixir ran out, she was going to be in serious, serious trouble.

Girls like Laguna, beautiful girls with expensive habits, usually ended up at high-class places like Strip and Dine. That lasted for a few years, and then after they'd gotten too old and saggy to tempt the men they serviced, it would be tenement city: low-rent brothels where the women were valued only by the number of holes a client could ram himself into.

I worried that Laguna was three days away from learning just how cruel the Chroma could be. Though I felt bad for her and her addiction, my chance to enter the store hinged on her need to get out of the store as quickly as possible so she could hook up with her Yellow jumpsuit. This was her weakness and I was going to exploit it to my full advantage.

Twenty minutes before the triangular store closed, it was time for the masses to go home. In the middle of rush-hour pedestrian traffic I took the Fourth Block Bridge over to the opposite moving sidewalk. Though I felt claustrophobic as I entered the transparent tube that led to the bridge and the cacophony of sweaty, rainbow-hued bodies that would press against me once I was inside it, I knew it was a necessary evil.

I did my counting trick, the numbers racing through my head. Once I was free of the bridge and the crush of bodies diminished, I was able to relax a little. Being out of the enclosed tube made me feel a lot better. I could breathe again.

I let the moving sidewalk ferry me along, reaching out to grab the metal bar in front of the store only so I could pause and look through the plate-glass window.

There were no customers inside.

I slid my fingers through the aluminum door handle and pulled it to me. Laguna was so engrossed in her book that she didn't even notice my entrance until the four silver bells above the door frame chimed, alerting her to my presence.

She looked up, startled out of her imagination.

"Yes?" she said, a smile enhancing the curve of her lips

Then she noticed it was me and not a paying customer. The smile vanished.

"We're closing soon, so . . ."

She let the sentence dangle, waiting for me to finish it.

"There's a man out there, looking at the store," I said, adding a touch of fear to my tone—just like I'd practiced.

Laguna set her book down, though her fingers still held on to its thick, white pages.

"Whaddya mean?"

I swallowed.

"He looks real bad. Like a . . ."

I paused here for dramatic effect.

"Like a *zombie*."

Laguna's face went white, her fingers starting to tremble so badly, the book shook.

It was a well-known fact that the elixirs used to create vampires, zombies, werewolves, and the like were highly unstable. Get in their way and things could turn ugly fast. There'd been a spate of serial killings a few years earlier—dismembered human body parts riddled with teeth marks and fingernail gouges, left to rot inside garbage bins all over the Chroma—that had finally been linked to a bad batch of zombie elixir. When the MPs finally caught up with the culprits, they had already returned to their human form, but the elixir had done something weird to their minds, had convinced them that they were already the walking dead and that the only way to survive was to keep themselves chock-full of fresh, human flesh. Their apartments were like charnel houses, full of their half-eaten kills. The whole episode had spooked the populace of the Chroma so badly that even the mention of zombies could still set people's teeth on edge.

Needless to say, the closer I got to thirty, the more I found myself empathizing with the poor creatures . . . we were all members of a unique tribe: the walking dead.

"Where is he?" she said, coming out from behind the counter and standing beside me at the front door.

I pointed out through the plate-glass front window, my finger spearing a tall man in a Black jumpsuit who was standing in front of the Strip and Dine. He had his back to us, but upon Laguna's arrival he turned around and it was immediately apparent that he wasn't a zombie. Seeing this, Laguna relaxed, reaching out and ruffling my hair.

"You're seeing things, kid."

Shaking her head, she turned away from me and went back across the room, sliding back into her spot behind the counter. Disarmed now, she picked her book back up and started to read again.

I continued to stand where I was, watching the man across the street—a total stranger I'd picked out of the crowd—as he finally went into the Strip and Dine and disappeared.

I didn't feel guilty about upsetting her. I'd scared her just enough that in her relief she'd relaxed any suspicions she'd held about me or what I was doing there.

I looked up at the clock on the wall above Laguna's head. Two minutes until time to close. Laguna was back inside her book, eyes glazed as she ate up the words in front of her.

It was now or never.

I pushed open the front door so that the bells began to tinkle, the noise from outside filling the room.

"Bye, Laguna!" I called out.

She didn't even look up from her book, just raised a hand in farewell.

But I didn't go through the front door. Instead, as it slowly began to crawl back to its frame, I tiptoed over to the other door—the one that led to the storage room—and gently eased it open, slipping inside just as the front door clicked into place.

From my time with Demeter, I knew the storage room was stacked with boxes, but without the light on, the darkness was absolute. I could see nothing.

Silence from the adjoining room. My heart raced inside my chest as I waited for Laguna to realize what I'd done and come kick me out.

Nothing happened. And then I heard it. The sound that assured me I was safe.

A soft rustling of paper as Laguna turned the page of her book.

I didn't have to wait much longer after that. As I'd hoped, Laguna didn't linger. Closing time came and I heard her turn off the lights and lock up, the front door closing softly on a heated embrace with her Yellow jumpsuit. I gave it ten minutes, a good margin of error, in case Laguna forgot something and came back unexpectedly. I did this by counting to six hundred, using that time to let my eyes adjust to the darkness. When I hit five hundred ninety-nine, I let out a long breath and started to move.

The man had told me the exact location of the vials he wanted me to steal, but getting to them proved harder than I'd expected. I wasn't worried about tripping any alarms—one afternoon Demeter had unwittingly told me that none of the motion sensors or cameras were hooked up to anything, just there for show—but maneuvering in the darkness was not easy.

Using my hands, I found the metal wall and began to follow it, letting it guide me to the other side of the room. I was nervous, worried about getting caught, but there was also something exhilarating about the whole endeavor. I had never done anything illegal before. Never so much as filched an apple, but here I was, burgling a store.

At the end of the wall, where I would've run into the counter if

I'd been in the main room, I squatted down and let my hands skim across the plush fiber of the carpet. The man had told me to look for a loose carpet tile, but no matter where I placed my fingers, I found nothing. After a few minutes of frustrated searching, I started to get scared. If I was caught stealing, my life would be worthless.

Worse than worthless.

Over. What time I had left would run out instantly.

My mind started to spin. If I wasn't going to find the hiding place, should I just steal some of the vials from the counter in the other room and then try to sell them?

I had no black-market connections, nor would I know how to go about getting any. I would probably get fleeced by any of the tenement lowlifes I went to for help, putting me back at square one. Besides, there was a part of me that was scared of the man who'd offered me a Black jumpsuit. I couldn't shake the feeling that he would come after me if I reneged on the deal we'd made.

The smell alone had been incentive enough for me to say yes. I couldn't imagine the man's stench covering me, overwhelming me as he wrapped his hands around my throat and squeezed the life out of me. I realized I would do almost anything not to incur his wrath, and that included finding the loose tile and getting what he wanted.

I felt the triangular walls closing in on me, the power of the antiparallelogram working to overwhelm me, screw up my mind, so that I didn't know what I wanted anymore. If I let it get inside me, it would be over. I would reveal myself and that would be the end. The police would come and take me away.

And that's when I discovered it. Right as I started hyperventilating and having heart palpitations. Right as my mind went numb with fear.

I dug my fingers between the carpet tile and the one next to it, prying the loose one up and flipping it over so it was out of my way. Instead of a stone floor, my hands grazed metal: a ring that I slid to attention and pulled upward, a square of the subfloor coming with it.

I desperately needed light. I thought about turning on the fluorescent overheads, but talked myself out of it.

I closed my eyes.

I dropped my hand into the hole in the floor, extending my fingers like tentacles. The metal box was exactly where the man had said it would be. I reached in with my other hand and brought the metal square out of its hiding place. It weighed very little and was the size and shape of a kid's jewelry box.

Relief flooded my veins and I grinned, pleased that I'd nearly completed my task. I replaced the subfloor and then the carpet tile, tamping it back into place before I ran my fingers over it to make sure it was even. With that done, I stood up and followed the metal wall back to the doorway.

I opened the door and quickly slid between it and the door frame, leaving the darkness of the storage room behind me. The main room was empty, the lights off. I could see the traffic on the moving sidewalk, the people still trying to get home after a long workday. I looked up at the clock that hung over the counter and I realized I'd been inside the storage room for only seven minutes.

It had seemed like hours.

I clutched the metal box to my chest, my heart thumping in my throat. My escape plan was simple. I would unlock the door and then just slip out onto the moving sidewalk. I would remain calm and I would not act as if I'd just done something highly illegal.

I walked over to the front door, turned the lock, and then I pushed it open, letting the sounds from outside wash over me. No one looked twice as I stepped through the doorway and grabbed hold of the metal bar in front of the store just long enough to pull the front door closed behind me. The metal box still under my arm, I moved into the throng, letting the moving sidewalk take me away.

I didn't turn around, didn't look to see if anyone had noticed anything unusual about my exit. Just kept my eyes trained forward and the box close to my heart. It wasn't until I'd reached the Second Block Bridge and crossed over to the other side that I let out a long, nervous breath.

I didn't know what was in the box. I hadn't asked, hadn't wanted to know, really. But now I was curious.

I was standing in front of the garbage bin where I'd originally encountered the man. We'd agreed to meet here exactly twenty-four hours from our first introduction, but he was late.

I'd taken the box back to a special hiding place I'd arranged before the burglary and then I'd spent the rest of the night scavenging food. After I'd eaten my fill, I'd crawled into the rear doorway of the Pain-du-Pain and promptly fallen asleep. I was stiff when I woke up the next morning, my joints sore from tension, but I was more excited than I'd ever been in my entire life. Today I was going to get a Black jumpsuit.

Tomorrow, I would be on the road to a job with hazard pay.

"You made it."

The voice was in my ear before I felt the hands slip around my shoulders and squeeze them. I turned around, the stench hitting me full in the face before I had time to draw a clean breath. Today the man was on full display, the rotting skin of his face and neck grotesque in the light.

I gagged, taking a step back and forcing him to let go of my upper arms.

"Not what you were expecting?" he wheezed, his bright blue eyes like rolling marbles.

From the man's rotten smell and chilled body temperature, I'd already deduced that he was a zombie—one of the role-playing weirdos that frequented the store and made employees like Demeter and Laguna uncomfortable. The zombie grinned at me, interpreting my silence as fear.

Yes, the guy standing in front of me scared me, but not because he was an elixir-made zombie. The real zombies were people like me, living a life without purpose, watching the minutes tick away until our lives expired. This guy scared me because there was just something plain wrong about him. Something crazy in his eyes.

I held the box close to my chest, my fingers anchoring it in place.

"Jumpsuit first."

The zombie shrugged, unzipping his own Black jumpsuit and stepping out of it. Unlike me, he wasn't naked underneath his but was wearing a moth-eaten Yellow polyester leisure suit that was probably standard wear in the suburbs, but unlike anything I'd ever seen on anyone in the Color Sector. He kicked the jumpsuit over to me and I released the metal box, letting it drop into his outstretched arms.

I hated to put on the Black jumpsuit he'd given me. I knew it would smell like rot and death, but I'd gone through too much to let the stench put me off. I unzipped my own Purple jumpsuit and shrugged it off, then I picked up the Black one and slipped it on.

The stench was overpowering, but I ignored it as I forced myself to enjoy the thrill of finally possessing a Black jumpsuit.

The zombie looked at me, cocking his head.

"Aren't you gonna ask what I wanted the box for?"

I had to admit that my curiosity was piqued. Of course I wanted to know what was inside the box, but I was smarter than that.

"Nah," I said, shaking my head and starting down the alleyway, proud in my new Black jumpsuit. "It's yours now."

I'd been around long enough to understand a few things about life on the street. And possessing too much information about something illicit was not a good thing.

But the hand on my shoulder—the one gripping my flesh so hard I knew it would leave a bruise—stopped me in my tracks. I stiffened, rigid with fear as the zombie's rancid breath, hot and foul, whistled against my neck.

"But I want you to understand what you've done."

I didn't want to know, but there was no polite way to extricate myself from the situation, so I shrugged.

"And what's that?" I asked.

The zombie released his grip and I stumbled away from him, the Black jumpsuit weighting me like a stone.

"You've opened up a new market, one that promises a different path to human existence . . . for those who can afford to pay," he said, a snaggletoothed grin splitting his face in two.

He lifted the lid of the metal box—and I don't know what I'd expected to see inside, but it certainly wasn't the six slim glass vials that were nestled against the blue-velvet inlay.

"These vials are very special, so special that they're not for sale just to anybody," the zombie continued. "The man who owns the store makes them only for the most elite buyers. Imagine how much money he makes from one, single vial, then imagine how much money someone else could make selling them at a lower cost to a much less 'select' clientele . . . that is, *if* one possessed the formula."

"Like you do now," I offered.

"Like I do now," he agreed, reaching inside the box and extracting one of the vials as though he were bestowing a gift upon himself.

"What's it do?" I asked.

It was the only question left to ask.

"It's a fixer," the zombie said. "Take the elixir of your choice once, followed by one of these vials, and your change will become permanent."

Uncorking the vial in his hand, he drew it back so that he could tip the contents into his open mouth.

I couldn't help wondering why someone would choose to remain a zombie permanently; what kind of a freak or fetishist would look forward to such a bizarre, rot-filled existence? And then I realized that the question was moot. No sane person would ever do what this man had just done.

"Zombiehood forever," he rasped, letting the empty vial drop to the ground, then crushing it underfoot.

Suddenly his body began to convulse as the fixer he'd ingested started to filter through his system—and in this moment of weakness, I acted.

I didn't think. Didn't let myself process what I was about to do. Just ripped the metal box away from the zombie, the lid slamming back into place as I turned and ran. I heard the zombie shriek in anger, felt the pounding of his feet as he lumbered after me, body still struggling to process the fixer.

When I looked back, I discovered that he was gaining on me, the change having made him even stronger and faster than he'd been before. Terrified, I did the only thing left to me: I turned around and slammed the metal box into the zombie's face, gristle and bone crumpling underneath its heavy weight. He gave a muffled cry and fell backward—and I was too worried about him getting up again even to think about what the impact might've done to the vials inside the box.

At that moment, it was either fight or be killed. And I was too close to freedom to stop now. Besides, I had the advantage. This was my home turf. I knew every hiding place in the Chroma. Once I'd lost him, I could disappear into the heart of the tenements, lose myself so completely that he'd never find me.

The Black jumpsuit might be enough to save me from my fate . . . but these vials . . . these vials were a sure thing. A one-way ticket to freedom *if* I was smart enough to use them.

I had already begun to formulate a plan: I would go to the sub-urbs and find Demeter, the only person I had ever trusted, then together we would discover a way to exploit the gift the zombie had unwittingly given me.

I was tired of being nothing, tired of waiting for my thirtieth birthday to come and go and for my life to end.

Tired of being the walking dead.

HOW WE ESCAPED OUR CERTAIN FATE

Dan Chaon

> I think of you when I am dead, the way rocks
> think of earthworms and oak roots . . .
> —Reginald Shepherd, "Also Love You"

THE ROBBERY WAS IN PROGRESS when my son, Peter, came out of the back storeroom. *Everything happened so quickly.* That's what we said to ourselves later.

I was on the floor by the cash register and the robber was pistol-whipping me, and without thinking Pete took our gun from its hiding place beneath the counter. At that moment the robber looked up and Peter shot him in the face.

This robber, this young guy that Peter shot, was a normal, living person, that was the weird part. He wasn't one of *them,* one of the infected—the zombies or whatever you want to call them.

In the last few years, we'd gotten used to having to kill a zombie or two every once in a while. If you weren't careful, they'd get in your backyard and attack your dog and trample your tomato plants; you'd come across them in parking garages late at night, or you'd accidentally hit one when it wandered onto the interstate as you were driving home after staying late at work.

But this robber that Peter killed was just a regular kid. Maybe eighteen, nineteen years old.

"Where's the money?" he was snarling. "Where's the money, where's the money, motherfucker?"—and then when he heard Peter behind him, he stopped hitting me with the butt of his revolver and started to turn, fumbling with his gun—

If he hadn't fumbled he would have killed Peter, so I don't know

107

why I should have to think about that expression on the robber's face when he realized that Peter was going to shoot him, the way he said, ". . . Hey, wait . . ." right before Peter pulled the trigger. Seeing the young robber's eyes widen, you might have thought, *why, he's no more than a child, he could be my own baby,* something like that, a foolish and sentimental thing to think because of course this thug would have murdered us without a second thought. People like that will only use mercy to their advantage and in the end it was probably better that he was no longer walking the earth, though I guess I'm sorry that I didn't do it myself.

The pistol that Peter had in his hands was a compact .380 semiautomatic, a Beretta Cheetah with a black matte finish, lightweight and easy to use.

We took the robber's head off, just like you do with the zombies, and we hauled him out back and put him in the Dumpster, just like you do with a zombie.

But this was the first living person we'd killed.

Afterward, I had some trouble sleeping. Insomnia. Nightmares.

Peter seemed to be getting by okay, despite everything. He continued to eat with good appetite. He was doing well in school, got good grades, was involved in activities, and came home and made supper for the two of us. He'd sit at the kitchen table finishing his homework while I did the dishes and I would try to engage him in conversation. How was school? What were his plans for the weekend? And he answered respectfully, looked me in the eye, seemed perfectly stable and reasonable. Despite everything.

Still, I worried.

More than a few nights I lay awake, listening to him moving from room to room in the house, checking all the locks, the creak of the boards as he went into the basement to check on the generator, the hum as he held open the refrigerator door and peered into it, wishing, I presume, that it was as full as it used to be. He turned on the television—even though, of course, they broadcast more and more rarely—and over the *shush* of the static I could hear him taking the guns apart and cleaning them.

His mom had died before any of this began to happen. How horrified she would have been to imagine him so devoted to weaponry, to see him go off to school in his youth militia uniform, ammo belt on his shoulder. She was in the hospital when the first reports of the infection had begun coming in, and I remember thinking that it was a hoax, some bizarre mass hysteria and media frenzy.

There was something on the news the day she died—some footage from Detroit that was playing over and over on CNN—and I remember pausing in one of the hospital waiting rooms to watch it, holding my bouquet of flowers, and then I turned and went down the hall to her room and she was no longer living; she had died in those moments that I was standing there mesmerized by the television. When I told Peter later that she was gone, I pretended that I'd been there with her. I pretended that I'd been holding her hand, and she'd let out a sigh, and closed her eyes very peacefully.

I've repeated this scene so often in my mind that most of the time it feels like a real memory.

For a time after the robbery, Peter was up at all hours, pacing and prowling, nearly every night. But then after a week or so, he began to calm down. Maybe he got worn out from so little sleep. In any case, when I woke in the night the house was quiet, and when I went into his bedroom I found him sound asleep in his bed, still in his clothes with his headphones on. The tinny specters of music wisped up as I detached the plastic branch of the earpiece from his head.

Sitting there on his bed—untangling the cord from his neck, hushing him as he stirred for a moment—I couldn't help but think back to when he was a baby. I could picture him in his infant carrier in the backseat of our car, the way I would play those children's lullabies on the tape deck, over and over, driving around the neighborhood until his bottle or teething ring grew slack in his mouth and his head lolled and his eyes lost focus and shut—at last, at last, I used to think, it was so hard to get him down for the night when he was little.

Of course he was not a baby any longer. Not at all.

At sixteen, he was already bigger than I. Six foot two, two hundred-odd pounds. A real bruiser, as they say, which was taking some getting used to. For years he was small for his age. It was embarrassing to recall some of the gushing, diminutive nicknames my wife and I had for him. Peter Rabbit, Mouse, Squeakie, Bunny. I loved to pick him up, to carry him in my arms or on my shoulders. I loved to rub his soft cheeks, tickle him, tousle his hair, and it may be that I kept him babified for too long after his mom died, because he was small for his age and I didn't recognize that he was growing up.

Now, of course, I was getting my comeuppance. His physical affection could be alarming. I'd often to speak to him sharply: I don't want to wrestle, I don't care to have my back slapped, I don't enjoy being lifted off the ground in a bear hug. His strength was unnerving. Was this the way he felt once? The looming larger adult, the implied threat of being overpowered, suffocated, crushed?

"Enough!" I told him that night, when he was pestering me and roughhousing after dinner. *Enough!* It never seemed to sink in with him until I raised my voice. *Quit it right now, Peter! I mean it! Get off me!*

His face fell, then, and he dropped his arms abruptly to his sides, backing away. "Fine," he said petulantly. "Jeez, I was just being affectionate . . ." and off he slumped to his room.

Then I felt bad, naturally. He had needed to be hugged, he had needed to be close to me, especially after all he had been through, after the robbery, etc. He had needed some comfort. How could I not realize that?

But there was no hugging him now. When I went to the doorway of his room, he barely looked at me. Headphones plugged into his ears, face hooded. Out came the solvents and lubricating oils, pipe cleaners and toothbrushes. Wordlessly, he began again to clean the guns.

So then, to make it up to him, I decided to take him out driving. He had been wanting to learn to drive—he couldn't wait to get behind the wheel, couldn't get enough of it—but there wasn't much opportunity for me to teach him, not much time in the day between work and chores, and of course it wasn't particularly wise to be out on the roads at night, especially with an inexperienced driver at the wheel.

But that night I saw that it was necessary. I had atoning to do, and when I went upstairs with the keys and held them out, he deigned to unplug a single ear from its headphone.

"Hey, buddy," I said. "Why don't we take the car out?" And it was better than an apology.

The power grid had become very spotty in recent years, and there were rolling blackouts all over the city. You'd see the lights shut down, streetlights fluttering dimmer, and then dead, block by block, vanishing, and some of the house alarms setting up a wail—

But at the same time, the city could be very beautiful in the darkness, very mysterious. The tree boughs hung over the road in layers and the sky intensified with starlight, constellations, the sheets of headlights emerging from the distance, the corona of a police cruiser's flashers, red-and-blue sheen circling over the surface of the bushes and houses and wet asphalt.

We drove for quite a while before we began to catch glimpses of zombies. By the park, we saw a naked female on the edge of a ravine, her skin almost fluorescently pale as she bent there, digging through the leaves, lifting her head as blankly and innocently as a deer, the headlights glinting in her eyes before she bolted. Behind the old Popeye's Chicken, we noted a bearded male emerging from an overturned Dumpster, scrambling on his hands and knees toward a hole in a fence, still dressed in a ragged lumberjack shirt and jeans, one foot missing, the other wearing a boot. Over on Derbyshire Lane, where most of the houses were abandoned, an elderly female froze in the road as we approached. It was carrying a dead shih tzu in one hand as daintily as a purse, and for a moment it appeared that it was trying to flag us down, that it was waving. Then, it tottered with surprising speed off the road and into a long-neglected yard overgrown with tall grass and butterfly weeds.

I watched as Peter straightened in the driver's seat, hands tightened on the wheel, face stern and alert, not reaching for the gun on the seat beside us, not overreacting. "Just go slow," I said. "Keep your eyes on the road," I said, and his expression was pinched but nevertheless I felt that this moment was better than any other kind of driving we'd done together. This kind of focus. Down the pitch-dark streets, our headlights pulled us across the surface of the road. We were as close to father and son as we'd ever be again, I thought. For a moment. For a second.

And then it was morning. I opened my eyes and my cheek was pressed against the passenger window and I could see, close-up, a smatter of rain droplets on the glass. We were pulling into the driveway and the garage door was folding open to receive us, and upon waking I didn't for a moment know where I was being taken or whom I was with. I blinked to see him behind the wheel, his big square head, his sideburns and chin hair, his stern eyes straight ahead as he settled the car gently into its place in the garage. Here was the gray dawn light, the sun spreading up into the sky and tracing along the branches of the trees.

"We drove all night," I said. "I can't believe I fell asleep."

"Yeah," he said, and smiled sheepishly. "I just didn't want to stop. I know it's a waste of gas, I hope . . ."

Then, abruptly, his eyes hardened. "Oh, crap," he said, and pointed to where our trash can lay overturned. Garbage was strewn about and clawed through. "Damn," Peter said. "Looks like they got into the backyard somehow last night!"

"I could have sworn I locked the gate," I said, and he frowned.

"Great," he said. "If they found any food in there, they're liable to come back, you know."

I slept for a little while and then got up around noon and went down to the store. Cleveland wasn't as bad as a lot of places—not like Atlanta or Chicago. The ratio of living to dead was still in our favor, and most of the basic services were still plugging along, police and firemen, water and electricity. I still had customers coming in—maybe more than usual. In such times, people needed a good liquor store.

The zombie problem had been spreading across the country for a while by that point—though not as exponentially as they'd first thought. It wasn't the end of the world, or at least that's what I kept telling myself. In most cases, a zombie was more like a pest than a threat. Of course, a bite would infect you, but they weren't terribly aggressive, in general. "They are more afraid of us than we are of them," people said; and they feared with good reason, since the militias and the national guard and police shot them on sight, and took their heads off and burned the corpses down at the old foundry by the river.

The truth was, the military was so efficient about it that it seemed like they should have just about finished them all off. But they clung on stubbornly. They were nocturnal, and seemed to have an instinctual sense of self-preservation, since it was oddly difficult to discover their daylight hiding places—the narrow little burrows they would find to curl up in, like culverts and the crawlspaces under abandoned houses and piles of junkyard debris. Some were even said to dig nests for themselves under overgrown bushes and shrubs, and then cover themselves up with leaves.

We had been assured that they had no thoughts or feelings, but sometimes I wondered if there wasn't some tiny little spark of memory or emotion left inside their skulls, still flickering from time to time.

That evening, I was locking up the store and pulling down the security gate when I saw one in the alleyway. A boy, maybe thirteen or fourteen years old, eating a pigeon. The zombie went stock-still when it saw me, its mouth full of feathers, its jaw working stupidly as it gazed at me. Its eyes were wide and alert, and when I looked into them I thought it seemed scared and sad. As if there were a shudder of remembering: a house, an old room with a bunk bed and football posters, a mother and father: all lost.

"Shoo!" I said. "Shoo! Get out of here!" and it took off with a hunched, ambling gait, pigeon still clutched in its mouth, vanishing into the alley, the tunnel of garbage bags and rubble and abandoned buildings.

Driving home, I couldn't help but wonder if my sentimentality would be repaid one day—that zombie kid popping back one evening to give me a quick, nasty death with its sharp teeth and ragged fingernails.

"Stupid," I whispered to myself. "Stupid, stupid," and I mentioned nothing about it to Peter when I got home.

He was in the backyard when I pulled into the driveway, pacing along the perimeter. We had lined the top of the fence with razor wire, and I watched as he tapped the wire with an old golf club, testing the tautness.

"What's up?" I said, and he turned to regard me with that soldierlike gaze he'd been developing.

"Just trying to figure out how they got in here last night," he said. "I think we need to get a chain and padlock for that gate."

"Okay," I said—though it seemed doubtful to me that a zombie would have been able to work the latch on our gate.

"Maybe it was something else," I said. "Like cats or raccoons or something . . ." Though this was equally unlikely, since most such animals had long ago been cleared out by roving, hungry zombies. You hardly saw squirrels anymore, let alone a skunk or an opossum.

"Anyway," I said, and showed him the bag I was carrying. "I got some ground beef! Pretty fresh, too! Some guy came in and traded it for a bottle of Absolut. You want to make some meatloaf?"

That was always his favorite when he was a kid, and his look brightened.

"Like Mom made it," I said. "With the carrots and onions chopped up in it."

"Yeah," he said softly.

Like a lot of things, meat had become a rarity, so dinner had a kind of celebratory quality. Our worries about the breach in the yard were forgotten momentarily, and we had the sort of cheerful, ordinary conversation I imagined fathers and sons used to have back in times past. Peter spoke enthusiastically about his day at school, where the kids were being taught to operate a flamethrower, and I listened and nodded, though of course a part of me was sad to think that this was the state of the world we lived in.

I didn't mention this, naturally. There were so many things we never talked about: that zombie kid with its puzzled, rueful expression; that dead robber, the way Peter had taken a hacksaw to his neck while I held the corpse steady on the plastic tarp in the back room; his mother in her hospital bed that last week of her life, the fitful way she drifted in and out of awareness, the way she tucked her face against her shoulder as she slept, frowning hard like an infant or an old, old woman.

For such things, what words could we find? A whole species of language seemed to have gone extinct. But maybe that had always been so between teenage boys and their fathers.

* * *

In general, I think, it was more difficult to find words for the things we did and saw.

Like the word *zombie;* for example. At first, people tried to believe the official pronouncements—that it was an "infection," akin to rabies, that a cure was being actively sought, etc., etc. They were sick people, not "zombies"—that was what the government and the news networks told us in the beginning.

But once you began to see them in real life, there was no way to deny that—whatever else they were—they were definitely dead. They came out of fatal car wrecks and morgues and graveyards and burbled up out of the bottoms of murky rivers. I had never seen an actual walking skeleton, but I'd come across plenty that were decayed or eviscerated or nearly limbless or essentially mummified, and it was clear that they hadn't been living creatures in a very long time.

Everyone had heard the stories. People swore that they had seen long-dead mothers, lost loved ones, people whose funerals were years and years past. One of my customers insisted that he had seen his son, Skittles, who was killed in a drunk driving accident a decade ago. That Skittles, still young, still with his long hair and bright blue eyes, had come to their front porch late one night and tapped gently against the door, and they'd been afraid, the old man said, blinking quickly, as if still astonished. "We were afraid, my wife and I," he said. "We didn't let him in, and he never came back again." He put his hand to his mouth.

I nodded thoughtfully, though I didn't put much stock in it. Skittles had been in the ground for ten years, I thought; Skittles was dust.

I thought of the story again that night, though. I had been asleep when I was awakened by a noise. I took out my little flashlight and looked at my watch. It was 2:30 A.M.

There was the sound of a rusty hinge—uncertain and irregular, an unlatched door opening and closing in the wind—and when I peered down from my second-floor window I could see her there in the backyard garden.

No, I'm not saying that it was my wife.

It was only that I was reminded of her in a powerful way. She was about the same height, and her hair was also blond, though matted and tangled. She wore a hospital gown, and she—it—was walking in our garden in the moonlight, stepping carefully, barefoot, through the rows of green-bean vines and carrots and cabbage, toward the corner where our corn was almost shoulder high, appearing to take care not to step on our plants. There was a kind of tenderness in its step, a sort of reverie or reverence in its movements.

Was this the way you would walk into a yard that had been lost to you long ago? A place from your past that was changed a little, but still mostly the same: that old apple tree, that little statue of Saint Francis with a bird alighting on his finger, that patch of garage wall where trumpeter's vine had rooted and spread?

I couldn't see her face, only the slow movement of her body and the white of the hospital gown, rustling in the wind of a summer night. Still, for at least a minute, every part of me believed. I stood there at the window, motionless, conscious even of the rising and falling of my chest as I breathed, fearing that any movement or sound would startle her and she would be gone. I just wanted her to linger a little while. Her face remained in shadows, turned away.

When people we love are dead, it's common, I guess, to keep looking for them, to be willing to give anything to see them again, even just for a moment.

I wanted to tell her about how the world had changed since she'd left it. To find a barometer in her eyes and voice: *Be honest, how bad are things, really? It will get better, won't it?*

I thought about how it would be to explain to her about Peter. *I know I haven't been the best father, I know I've screwed things up, but I've tried, really I have, and he's a good boy, despite everything. Didn't he turn out okay?*

She wandered around the backyard, aimlessly, as I watched. *They have no thoughts or feelings,* I told myself. *There is nothing human about them anymore,* I told myself as the zombie female crept along the edge of our fence. She scratched in the dirt under the apple tree, picking out morsels from the upturned soil—earthworms, maybe, or grubs—and putting them into her mouth. For a moment, she paused, as if struck by a thought; she passed her hand through her hair.

As morning was nearing, she left. I watched as she pushed open the gate and hobbled down the driveway, and when I went to a front-facing window to see which way she was headed, she was already gone.

I went to the front door and peered out. A breeze stirred the geraniums and the maple trees, and moths swam around the porch light. The squat fire hydrant stood at attention on the street corner, gazing back at me as blankly as a guard.

At the table, sipping my weak, contraband coffee, I felt embarrassed and ashamed. Such stupid, indulgent sentimentality! How angry Peter would have been if he'd known I'd willingly stood and watched a zombie traipse about our garden.

The first lesson everyone learned was not to anthropomorphize the dead. In the early days, the infection spread rapidly because we couldn't stop believing they were still human. Zombie mothers preyed on their children, biting them, often eating them. Zombie husbands sought out their wives, zombie neighbors would seem to be merely confused and then would rush at you, teeth bared. An infected person would go to work in the morning and by midafternoon would have transformed, often managing to drag down and contaminate a good number of their coworkers in their wake.

After that first wave, we learned quickly that the infected would always first seek out those they knew, those they had once loved. With strangers, they were far less aggressive. Almost shy, you might say.

After that first wave, most people learned quickly how to harden their hearts. It reminded me a little of the way, when I first moved to a city in my youth, I had to teach myself to ignore the homeless. No eye contact. No acknowledgment when they called out after you as you passed. Only fools would interact with them or give them money or linger on their condition, no matter how wretched or pathetic they might seem.

But I never perfected that thousand-yard stare of the true urbanite, never quite figured out how not to look, how to make my face and mind as blank as outer space, and it was in this way that even now I created problems for myself. Thus, watching silently as a zombie invaded my yard or crept around my place of business.

Thus, the last words of the young robber still vividly imprinted, right on the surface of my consciousness when I closed my eyes: "... Hey, wait ..."

* * *

When I got home from work that day, Peter was back out in the yard. He had a colander and was working his way along a row of our green beans, but when he saw me drive up he stood and came to meet me.

"There was something in the yard again last night," he said, and he pointed over to a spot beneath the apple tree where it was clear that digging had occurred.

I recognized the spot, then. It was the place where, many years ago, we had buried Peter's pet turtle, Louisa. She had lived her life in a terrarium in Peter's room, swimming in circles around the edges of a plastic tub or sunning herself on a rock in the middle of her enclosure. She had been unusually responsive for a turtle, we believed— she seemed to become eager and even playful when it was her time to be fed, and she would often stretch her neck out to its full length and regard us flirtatiously with her yellow reptile eyes. When she died, it was the first real death that Peter had experienced, and my wife created a fairly elaborate ceremony for her funeral, with songs and flowers and a little cardboard coffin that she and Peter decorated with crayons and ribbons and glued-on sequins.

The coffin, of course, had rotted long ago, but the turtle's shell and skeleton remained. This is what had been unearthed. We saw that Louisa's carapace had been dug up and broken open, and whatever had still been contained in it had been picked over.

I watched as Peter bent down and fit the pieces of the broken carapace together, as if they were shards of a smashed vase. He looked up at me grimly.

"I think we better start keeping a watch," he said. "We can just do it in shifts." He looked back down at the turtle shell and shook his head. "If one of them is getting in here, before long it's going to bring others. And then we could end up having some serious problems."

"Right," I said. "You're absolutely right."

There was a dinner of rice with a few frozen peas and carrots thrown into it, and some of the green beans, which we stir-fried with some hot pepper flakes and oil, and I sat there touching my plate with my fork, thinking for some reason about the boy we had killed, the robber. He might have been very hungry, I thought.

And I thought, *Should a hungry man be punished for stealing bread?* It was one of those old ethical riddles. Probably not applicable in this case, since it was a liquor store and the corpse of the perpetrator, when we dismembered him, was not the body of someone who was starving. And he probably would have killed us if we hadn't killed him, I reminded myself.

"This is really good," I said, and put a green bean to my mouth. "I like the spices."

"Mm-hm," Peter said.

He was already deep in thought—thinking about killing, I assumed, thinking about his gun and the bead he would draw on the garden from the upstairs back landing, and the things they had taught him in school about crosshairs and accuracy.

When she arrived at our back gate, it was almost midnight. It was my shift—Peter was asleep, and I was sitting on our second-floor porch, staring down. Not really "keeping watch," I have to admit.

I was thinking about Peter. Peter, that little rabbit we had loved so much, the way he fit in my arms and nuzzled against my chest; the way he had walked between us, my wife and me, as we waded in the lake, the way we lifted him as the water got deeper, his little legs paddling along without touching bottom. The way we would sit on his bed, the two of us, singing softly together, taking turns stroking his hair until he fell asleep. It is not until much later that you realize that the child you once had is lost to you; you cannot even pinpoint the moment when it happens, when you understand that you will never see that little boy again, you will never again hold him in your arms. There is the other person that he has become, of course. But that baby, that child—that is something you will never get back.

It sent a kind of keen shudder through me, this thought. And then I looked down and the gate was opening. There was the familiar creak. She knew how to work the latch, I thought. How was that possible?

In any case, here she was again. White cotton hospital gown with periwinkle pattern. Long, matted blond hair. The old rifle was beside me, which my father had given me when we used to hunt deer, but I didn't pick it up.

As I watched her, I thought of my wife when she had been in the hospital right after Peter was born. The zombie walked like a woman who had just given birth, that kind of dreamy, exhausted intensity. I watched her pale bare feet move through the grass toward our garden. I watched as she knelt down and began to dig in the soil.

If Peter had been there, he would have aimed and taken the head shot without a second thought; after the zombie fell, he would have gone down and removed the head with an ax or a saw, and it wouldn't have perturbed him. It would have seemed like the right thing to do.

And it was. It *was* the right thing to do.

When I went to the back door, she didn't notice me at first, she was so involved. She ran her fingers along the garden soil as tenderly as a fortune-teller reading a palm. As if she was searching for something fragile and precious. Or so it seemed.

"Hello?" I said. I took a cautious step forward. I couldn't say what I was thinking, really. I spoke more clearly. "Hello?"

And then she turned. Her pale, unnaturally cloudy eyes lit upon me, and it was not clear if she saw me, or smelled me, or sensed me in some other way, and she gave a low, trickling growl.

I put one foot, then another, down the back steps. "It's okay," I said softly. "Hi there." My flashlight ran across her face—which was so torn and ragged that little remained of the cheeks or nose. Perhaps the word *face* isn't the right word, though she lifted her head and glared into the light. Looking at those eyes, those bared, lipless teeth, I wouldn't have said that there was anything human about her. But she didn't rush to attack. She cocked her shoulder with a kind of dainty puzzlement. Then she stood.

"Come on," I said softly. "It's time to go. Let's go now."

And I began to step slowly toward the gate. "Come on," I said, and I made a little whistling, kissing sound, like you would do with a dog you were trying to lure.

I opened the gate wide, like a gentleman, and moved gently into the driveway, walking slowly backward. "C'mon, baby," I whispered. "C'mon, sweetheart. Let's go. It's time to leave now."

And after a moment she began to follow me. She held her arms out, and tottered forward, the way that zombies do, a wet, thick sound whispering from her lungs, and I waited until she'd gotten close before I took another step back down the driveway.

"That's right," I whispered. "Here we go. Come on." And she followed.

There was something so gentle and hopeful about the way her hands groped forward. I thought of the way that we reach out to try to touch something insubstantial in the darkness. I thought of the way Peter had toddled forward to me when he was first learning to walk, the way his arms stretched out for me to catch him. I thought of my wife the day she had gone into the hospital, the way her hands had risen, pleading and comforting, to touch my face. "I'll be all right," she'd said. "Don't worry."

By this time we had reached the street, she and I; I was backing up and she was following, and she was coming on faster, more determined and hungry. I could see Peter's darkened window above me.

"Come on," I whispered. "Come on."

What would it feel like to let her embrace me? I wondered. *Would it be so bad?*

A MOTHER'S LOVE

John McIlveen

COLICKY, FINICKY, and just plain cantankerous, six-month-old Cedric had been trouble right from the moment Dr. Gregiore slapped his too skinny bottom. Marissa prided herself on the patience she had displayed since the birth of her irritable infant, but Cedric had become ravenous four months ago and it just kept getting worse.

It would have been so much easier if she hadn't loved her insatiable child. She could have tossed him to the wind like they did in population-controlled nations, or taped him up and popped him in the freezer for safekeeping, or maybe buried him in the backyard . . . if she'd had one. There had been a time in America when these things weren't allowed, and the idea of disposable children was unthinkable.

Just a few months earlier, Uncle Sam had monitored everything: how much you earned, what brands you used, and where you bought them, if your taxes were short, and if your kids were in school and up-to-date with their shots. But things had changed. Now they monitored nothing and *all* life was disposable . . . at least all human life. Now you could bury your kid in the backyard. Hell, now you could tie your kid to your car bumper and take him for a spin, because there were painfully few people—if any—who had the wherewithal to monitor you. There were even fewer who gave a shit.

Marissa moved a little morsel of food around on the plate, sliced off a small section, and dropped it into Cedric's mouth. It was so much nicer now that he could take small bits of solid food, instead of her having to prechew it, dice it, or somehow break it down. Cedric gnawed on the offered tidbit with great passion, accenting his toothless chewing with the guttural sounds of gnarling hunger. He swallowed and shrieked angrily for more.

Keeping Cedric fed and happy was a grueling, thankless, and endless task that only got harder as the baby grew older. The fact that food became scarcer by the day only exacerbated matters. In retrospect, it had been easy enough at first. Living flesh had been plentiful. This was Boston, for Christ's sake. The streets had always been teeming with people of all shapes, sizes, genders, and flavors, so finding a little food for Cedric had been, if not easy, at least easier.

The pandemic had spread through Boston like hot molasses and then through New England even faster. The CDC, with the full backing of the United States armed forces, the CIA, FBI, and possibly the NFL and AARP, tried to contain it. The last Marissa knew, all flights nationwide had been canceled and a desperate stand had been set up all along the Mississippi River and along the Canadian border in an improbable attempt to control the spread of the plague. Now, three months later, there were no flights at all.

It had begun with a new species of spider discovered in the rain forests of South America. Apparently, some ambitious young biologist, botanist, or whatever the hell he was, took it upon himself to pack up one of these exotic little arachnids and bring it back to MIT for research. Unfortunately, the scientist didn't stop to think that his little spider didn't want to be dissected, was faster than shit, could jump like it had a rocket up its ass, and could make small work of whatever protective materials were covering his hands. He slapped and killed the spider immediately, but that was too little, too late. The deadliest and most contagious toxin ever encountered was on the loose, and the Araneae Plague, or Plague of the Spider, was born.

After his litter spider kiss, our scientist went home and kissed the wife and his two kids, the wife kissed her mother, and then she made love to her best friend's hubby while the kids shared their Kool-Aid–filled sippy cups with their cousins. Next thing you know, our scientist is eating the cheerleader next door, and not in the way you brag about. By noon the next day, half of Arlington is sharing their newfound strain.

Twelve hours from point of infection to living-dead condition.

Catch the toxin, spread it everywhere, puke and shit your guts out, and then keel over dead. Five minutes later, up and at 'em and voilà . . . you've got yourself a zombie!

They tried to be politically correct by calling it "suspended life." *What the hell was that all about?* Marissa had wondered. The shit was hitting the fan in copious amounts from every feasible direction, and they were worried that people would be offended by calling a spade a spade. If you're dead but you're still walking around all growly and shit and eating everyone from your barista to your pastor, sorry, honey, you're a zombie.

At the onset, all Marissa had to do was move fast. Food was plentiful for the living dead, and they moved slowly, but not as slowly as some would think. Regardless, if you were sluggish and had a propensity to dining daily on fast food, chances were you'd become a first course.

She had found a Smart car that worked pretty well for weaving around, through, and under hard-to-fit spaces, and was near enough to the ground to push the ravaged bodies of the unfortunate aside. Marissa could jump out of the Smart car, hack a foot or hand off, and be back in the car within ten seconds without a feasting zombie even noticing her, or if they did they didn't give much of a shit as long as they were eating well. Soon, however, there was far too much congestion from crashed or abandoned vehicles, other debris, and, of course . . . bodies, for the Smart car to be a long-term solution.

The second month was more difficult. Cedric was four months old, two months living dead. The survivors had all but disappeared. Whether they escaped out of Boston to safer grounds or had all perished Marissa wasn't sure, but she would occasionally hear the tortured shrieks of some poor bastard who'd been caught napping. From her eighth-floor condo she could see the rush of the dead as they responded to those screams.

Now she had to use her wiles when it came to feeding Cedric. She had tried freezing a hefty collection of body parts she had gathered, but Cedric wanted nothing to do with them. Fried, microwaved, blended, souffléd, it didn't matter. Unlike with the living, frozen meats didn't quite cut it with the living dead.

The power had failed shortly after that second month. Despite its being one of the old-fashioned horizontal types with a latching lid, some of the smell did manage to squeeze between the seal and the frame, and there was no way she'd open that freezer now.

Another reason for not opening the freezer was that Cedric's daddy was in there. Marissa knew next to nothing about zombies. She had been so focused on Cedric that she hadn't spent much time studying them, which meant she had no idea if they could starve to death or if their eating was just fueled by memory or a motor function. Nor did she know if they reanimated after being frozen and then thawed. She hadn't heard any noises from within the freezer, but finding out was not on her list of options or desires. Besides, he was the dumbass who had infected Cedric; he didn't deserve to get out. Where he got it—the plague—she had no idea, but if it had come from that ho Keisha Jordan it wouldn't surprise her, the way she kept giving her stuff away to anyone who cared for a sample, rubbing that big old ass all over anyone who looked twice at it. Didn't matter none, now. Keisha Jordan had been Cedric's dinner about a month ago. The leftovers had gone out the window and down eight stories.

"Ain't you ever full?" she asked her son. Cedric twisted and heaved in response, little impish clicks and snarls spilling from his mouth. His eyes bored straight into her, burning with hunger and an intensity far too direct for his age.

He was now six months old. Before he'd been infected, his skin had been healthy and unblemished, the powdery hue of cocoa. Now it was as ashen as storm clouds, with splits beginning in the webbing of his fingers and toes and blood seepage from around his eyes and the corners of his lips.

Marissa lifted him and raised him to her shoulder. The intimacy of motherhood had disappeared upon the acknowledgment of what her sweet baby had become, yet her heart was still tied to him. She patted his back until he released a fetid belch, all the while trying to sink his nonexistent teeth into her shoulder and drooling all over her. She wore a fisherman's raincoat while dealing with Cedric, though it made her feel and look more like Paddington Bear. Cedric protested loudly, screeching his wrath as she laid him back in the crib, his eyes never swaying from hers.

"There you go, you little demon," she said sweetly. She carefully removed her coat, carried it to the bathroom between thumb and forefinger, and dropped it into the tub on top of two others. It was so much easier when there was hot water: she would just turn the shower on full heat and dump in a bottle of chlorine. She gingerly peeled the Playtex gloves from her hands, rolling them inside out, and dropped them into a lined barrel.

She'd known that Robert, Cedric's daddy, had the plague before he even knew it; she'd seen it in is his eyes, how they darted back and forth, always wary and shying from the light. When Robert started puking and messing damn near everywhere, even he couldn't deny it. After Robert had passed out, she'd brained him with his own softball bat, as he had instructed her. It was the same one she had later used on Keisha . . . a little poetic justice, she figured.

Needing out of that vile apartment, Marissa had moved the bare necessities up to the eighth floor of the ten-story building and begun stocking it with water, nonperishable foods, medical supplies, and propane to fuel the Coleman camping stove she had set up. She had observed that the zombies had no particular desire to ascend steps unless enticed, so the higher the better. She had also developed a pretty clever route from her apartment to target sites like stores, pharmacies, and even a hospital, snaking through the upper floors of buildings and employing ladders, bedrails, planking, and anything else useful for traveling between buildings and over rooftops, keeping any proximity to the zombies to a minimum.

By the third month, the living dead had far outnumbered the living alive. The only advantage to this was that the living population that had perished had done it so quickly that it had left plenty of food and fuel for the survivors, as long as they didn't mind eating canned and dry foods and siphoning gas . . . and could outmaneuver the zombies. The biggest disadvantages were that there were so many dead the streets resembled Times Square on New Year's Eve, only without the lights and fanfare, and that living flesh was now so rare that Cedric was eating less and less, though his ferocity remained at the same searing level.

Marissa's maternal instincts had kicked in. She needed to feed her baby. Marissa knew that if *she* was alive, there had to be smarter and more-adept people who had survived as well, especially in a city the size of Boston. Cedric had needed food, which meant that she, just like the living dead, would have to hunt for living flesh. Her advantage was that the survivors knew the mindless dead were after them, but they never expected a gritty, strong-willed mother. The realization that she didn't have to carry Cedric everywhere with her made things a bit easier, and travels much lighter. He was safe when left behind at the apartment. The dead didn't want him: he was one of them.

By the time Cedric reached five months old his appetite was voracious, yet he was an infant, so he still ate relatively small amounts. With no way to preserve the dead bodies and the number of survivors nearing nil, Marissa had been forced to take prisoners, luring them to her apartment and then handcuffing them to the cast-iron steam radiator. She kept them alive and fresh, making sure they survived as long as possible. She'd start small, with the toes and fingers, then the feet and the legs. She didn't like putting them through all the pain and terror, so she'd shoot them up pretty well, at first with morphine, and then Darvon, Fentanyl, or Sufenta, all of which she had in ample supply thanks to the empty hospitals and pharmacies. You never knew when you might need serious narcotics.

She found the woman first, practically slammed into her as they both ran across an anonymous rooftop that connected apartment complexes, turning the same corner at the same time in different directions. Sue wasn't an easy catch. Marissa had to work on her sympathy by telling her that her baby's head was trapped in the stair railings and she needed help. Damn fine bit of acting, too. Tears, sobs, and all.

But Sue had tricked her. After drugging her, Marissa had searched her for weapons, but hadn't thought twice about the Tylenol bottle in her sweatshirt pocket, where the clever young lady had stashed a razor blade. The evening after Marissa had cut Sue's foot off and fed it to Cedric in small, nibble-size pieces, Sue had slashed her own wrists while Marissa slept and the zombie child watched her hungrily through the prisonlike bars of his crib.

Marissa didn't make the same mistake twice.

She could see the flicker of candlelight around the edges of a window about an eighth of a mile away. It was astounding how dark Boston could become on an overcast night now that there was no electricity. The flickering was like a beacon.

She waited patiently until morning, sitting on the balcony two stories above her apartment, where Cedric's shrieks and guttural noises couldn't reach her. It was a man, evident by his size and the Celtics tank top, even at that distance. He climbed out onto the ledge, stretched, and stumbled, nearly plummeting six stories down. Marissa jumped around, waving her arms boldly until he noticed her.

The guy was easy to bait, as most were . . . or had been. He was a sucker for the lonely woman with her pouting lips and amazingly tight jeans. Promise a man the best blow job of his life and he'd follow you damn near anywhere. Kneeling in front of him also offered the best possible position for jamming the needle into his ass before he could even free his redheaded friend from his Levi's. She searched him as soon as she had him restrained, feeling a tinge of regret. He wasn't terrible, a little daft-looking maybe, but he had a fine body.

But baby came first.

Troy fed Cedric for nearly two weeks, until fever from all the cutting and amputations overtook him. Only an hour after Troy died, Cedric refused the meat. Dead was dead, and who would know this better than the dead? As she had done with Keisha and Sue, Marissa unlocked the handcuffs and wrestled the body out the window, letting if fall eight stories to the pavement below, hopefully taking out a few of those deteriorating bastards in the process.

Eight days later, Marissa's search for food for Cedric kept coming up short. She traveled the rooftops at night, looking for any signs of life. Many of the zombies seemed to have redirected their searches to greener pastures and the reek of death and decay seemed to be lightening, though many bodies were still visible in the streets. Cats and dogs weaved among the ownerless vehicles, every so often yanking a bit of flesh from a corpse, sometimes fighting over some delectable treasure. She herself had plenty of food. The apartment was stocked with Spam, Bush's Beans, ravioli, rice pilaf, and a cornucopia of other foods, none of which was beneficial to Cedric, who was at that moment shrieking like a siren inside the apartment. It was time for his second feeding of the day.

"I'm coming, I'm coming," she said wearily as she hoisted herself through the window and sat on the ottoman near the crib.

The first Novocain stab was always the worst, even all hopped up on Sufenta. She inserted the needle between the big toe and second toe and pressed the plunger. After waiting five minutes she gave the toe a good snap. There was a bite of pain, but she'd deal with it.

She took the cable cutter and placed the open jaws around her second toe.

Two feedings a day seemed to get Cedric through. The first day it had been her ears.

Eight days.

All that remained of her digits was the big toe on each foot, and her index fingers and thumbs. She wondered where his next feeding would come from. A big toe would really mess up her balance, but any of her remaining fingers would leave her helpless.

She figured she'd cross that bridge when she got to it.

On the count of three, she slapped her hands together over the handles of the cable cutter. With a loud snap that sent tremors through her body, her toe fell to the plate below. The pain was immense, but she clenched her teeth and inhaled slowly, counting each breath. For Cedric she could handle it. For her baby.

DOWN AND OUT IN DEAD TOWN

Simon R. Green

WHY DON'T the dead lie still?

I suppose everyone remembers where they were, and what they were doing, the day the dead came back. Mostly, I still remember it as the day I got laid off. It came out of nowhere, just like the newly risen dead. The boss called me into his office and told me I didn't have a job anymore. The company was sending all our jobs abroad, where they wouldn't cost as much. And that was that. One minute I had a job and a regular wage, a future and prospects, and the next my whole life was over. I went home early, because nobody cared anymore, and watched the dead walk on television. Just like everyone else.

It was pretty scary at first. We all gathered together in front of the set, the whole family, to watch blurred pictures of dead people stumbling around, with blank faces and outstretched arms, trying to eat people. Luckily, that didn't last long. Just a few last hungers and instincts firing in damaged brains, the experts said. The dead calmed down soon enough, as they forgot the last vestiges of who and what they had been. They stopped being scary and just stood around looking sad and pitiful, hanging around on street corners with no-where to go.

At first, their families were only too happy to reclaim them, to have their lost parents and children and husbands and wives back again, and take them home. But that didn't last long. They soon found out you couldn't talk to the dead. Or you could, but they would never answer. They were just bodies; nobody home. They didn't know anyone or remember anything. Didn't want to say anything or do anything. And they smelled bad, so bad. . . .

Soon enough the dead started turning up on the streets again, put out by their horrified and terribly disappointed families, and the government had to do something. They couldn't just leave the dead standing around, stinking up the place, getting in everyone's way. And so they built the dead towns, thrown up quickly, as far away from the rest of us as they could get, and put the dead there. And the world . . . just went on with business as normal.

I didn't. I had experience and qualifications and a good attitude; it never even occurred to me I wouldn't walk right into another job. But it turned out we were in a recession, or a depression, or whatever it is when there just aren't enough jobs to go around. There was a glut on the market for people with my experience and qualifications, and apparently I was too old and overqualified for what entrance-level jobs there were. And every time I turned up for an interview my clothes were just that little bit shabbier, and my manner was just that little bit too desperate, and after a while no one would see me anymore.

My savings ran out, I lost my house, my wife went back to live with her parents and took the kids with her, and almost before I knew it, I was living on the streets. With all the other people who'd lost everything. It's a lesson you should never forget. It doesn't matter how hard you work or how much you have, there's nothing you've got that the world can't take away. The only thing standing between people like you and people like me is one really bad day.

It's not so bad, really, living on the streets. It comes as something of a relief, finally, when you realize you can stop struggling, stop fighting. That it's all over. You don't have to worry about your job or paying the bills. No need to look after your family or make decisions. No more responsibilities, no more lying awake in the early hours of the morning, worrying about the future. On the streets, everything comes down to what's right in front of you: finding something to eat and drink, something to keep the warmth in and the rain out, and locating somewhere reasonably safe to sleep. You don't have to worry about yesterday or tomorrow, because you know they're going to be exactly like today.

It's interesting that you don't call us "homeless" anymore. Just "street people." Like the street is where we chose to be; that the street is where we belong. You don't call us homeless because that might imply that someone should give us a home. If you came across a stray dog in the street, wet and shivering and hungry, you'd take it home with you, wouldn't you? Give it food and drink and a blanket in front of the fire. Been many a cold night I'd settle for that. But no, you just walk straight past, ignoring our outstretched hands and handwritten signs, careful not to make eye contact because then you'd have to admit that we are real, and our suffering is real.

We're dead to you.

I don't know why I left the city. No particular reason. Just started walking one morning and didn't stop. Walked till I ran out of streets and just kept going. Are you still a street person if there aren't any streets? The countryside was pretty, and entirely unforgiving. The elements are just that much closer and more pressing; you miss the company of people. Eventually, I came to a dead town. I stopped to look it over. There aren't any fences around a dead town, no gates or barbed wire. Nothing to keep the dead in, because they don't want to go anywhere. They have no purpose, no ambition, no curiosity. They're dead. They don't want or care about anything anymore. Just bodies, called up out of their graves and given a bit of a push to set them going. We put them in dead towns because they had to be somewhere, and that's where they stay.

I'd never been inside a dead town, so I went in. Just to see what there was to see.

The dead took no notice of me, looked right through me as though I weren't even there. But I was used to that. Wasn't much of a town, just blocky houses in straight rows on either side of a dirt street. No lights, no amenities, no comforts. Because the dead don't need them. They didn't even walk, just stood around, looking at nothing. A few still stumbled or staggered from one place to another, driven by some vague impulse, some last dying memory of something left undone. Their clothes were rotten and ragged, but most of the bodies persevered. They didn't acknowledge one another or the world around them. Their brains were dead in their heads, bereft of reason or meaning.

Their town was a mess and so were they. The dead don't care about appearances. They didn't smell that bad, so far from their graves, just a dry dusty presence, like autumn leaves in the wind. I was used to the stench of people who live on the streets. Life smells worse than death ever will. I walked down the dirt street, picking my way carefully among the dead. Not because I was afraid of them but because I didn't want to be noticed. I still half expected someone to come up and tell me to leave, that I didn't belong there, that I had no place in a dead town. But no one looked at me as I passed, or reacted to the sound of my footsteps in the quiet street. The dead had this much in common with the living: they didn't give a damn that I was there.

I never saw the dead make much use of the houses they'd been given. Sometimes they might lie down on a bed for a while—though of course they didn't sleep—as though that was something they remembered doing, even if they no longer knew why. And sometimes they would walk in and out of a door, over and over. Presumably for the same reason. I never really saw them do much of anything. Mostly they just stood around waiting for something. As though they felt there was somewhere they should be, something they should be doing, but no longer knew what, or why.

I found a bed, in a room in a house that was still reasonably intact. I barricaded the door so I wouldn't be disturbed and got some sleep. Even a damp and dusty bed can be the height of comfort when you're used to shop doorways and cardboard boxes. The dark didn't bother me, or the dead outside. In the morning I went looking for food and drink, but of course there wasn't any. I walked up and down and back and forth, but there were only the dead and the houses they didn't need.

I watched one dead man just fall over for no obvious reason. None of the other dead noticed. I went over to him, and crouched down a cautious distance away. His face was empty and his eyes saw nothing. He was gone, now. Nobody home. I could tell. His boots looked to be much the same size as mine, and in much better condition, so I took them. Good footwear is important when you do a lot of walking.

I knew why he'd fallen over, why he'd stopped moving. It meant the last living person who knew or cared about him was gone. Nobody remembered him, so there was no one to hold him here anymore. That is why the dead came back, after all. Because we just couldn't let them go. Because we all had this selfish need to hang on to our loved ones, even after their time was up. We thought of our friends and families and loved ones as ours, our possessions, and we wanted them back so much that we called them back up out of their graves. Unfortunately, the part we cared about, the personalities, or souls, had passed on to wherever personalities or souls go. Beyond our reach. All we could bring back were their bodies.

I'd seen people try to talk to the dead, speaking earnestly and emotionally to blank faces, trying to reach someone who wasn't there anymore. Heard people raise their voices, in anger and anguish, trying to force or cajole a reaction of some kind from their returned loved ones. Sometimes the living even hit the dead, and screamed abuse at them. For not being what the living wanted them to be. The dead didn't react. The dead didn't care.

I didn't stay long in dead town. I had some thought of bringing other street people here, to make use of the empty homes. It was a lot safer in the dead town than it was in the city. The dead had no reason to attack us or insult us or steal from us. But I left, because even as far down as I had fallen, I was still better than the dead. I still had hope, and dreams, and somewhere to go. My life wasn't over till I said it was.

I went back to the city and the people I knew. Because even if people like you won't admit we exist, street people still have one another.

DEVIL DUST

Caitlin Kittredge

THE LIGHT ON THE HOSPITAL CEILING buzzed like a humming-bird's heartbeat, like it was alive. Lizzie asked, "Am I dead?"

"Not hardly," the doctor assured her, and Lizzie's eyes roamed to the machine wires and tubes running to and from her body.

She didn't believe him.

"Where's Stephen?" she said, and the doctor's face told her everything she needed to know.

There was a funeral, which Lizzie was too weak to attend. A parade of well-meaning deputies and their wives. Even Dickie Bonner, the sheriff himself, came in and sat with her and quoted passages from the Bible, as if that'd somehow make her feel all right, more than the morphine.

An investigator from the Louisiana State Police, Detective La-Rochelle, came by after a few weeks, or months. Time bled together when you were dead, Lizzie was learning.

The detective was unsmiling and smelled like cigarettes and rose-scented body spray. "I hear you don't remember anything," she said.

Lizzie nodded. Sometimes she swore the steel plate in her head picked up the buzzing light fixtures, until her skull was full of nothing but the hum.

"I hate to be the bearer of bad news," Detective LaRochelle said, "but without your testimony it's a pretty shaky case. Mostly circumstantial. Y'all live so far off the beaten track we don't have any witnesses, and Dewey Proctor and his buddies have the best beer-soaked alibis a twenty-four-pack can buy."

"Sorry," Lizzie said, and turned over to face the wall.

* * *

Dewey Proctor had the eyes of a bird, something that eats dead flesh on the side of the road. Lizzie saw him only once, coming out of the Winn-Dixie on 119, and she sat patiently until he'd loaded his beer and groceries into his lifted truck and driven away.

She rented a trailer on the opposite side of the bayou from the house. It was on the market, and Stephen's life insurance was paying the mortgage, but Lizzie let the lawyer handle most of it.

After a month, the grief counselor who'd dogged her endlessly in the hospital came by. Lizzie had no idea how the woman had even found out where she was living, but she sat down like she belonged there.

"Lonnie Thibodeaux is going to be released from prison," said the woman. "He's asked to meet with you, to make amends."

Lizzie stayed quiet. She'd found that people tended to assume you were either prostrate with grief or taking them seriously if you just shut your mouth.

"I know what he did to you was unforgivable," said the woman. "But he's sober and I think it would be a good idea for both of you. For closure."

"If you think so," Lizzie said, and the woman blinked at her, eyelids heavy with purple shadow. She looked a lot like Lizzie had just after she'd woken up, black-and-blue from head to toe.

"Well, great, honey," she said. "We'll set up a time at the halfway house."

Lizzie drove to the hunting camp Stephen and his father had used, before Doug's heart attack and Stephen's promotion to sergeant. The smell tickled her nose as soon as she got out, but there was nobody else for miles. You could go for hours through the delta and not find anything besides gators and meth labs. Dewey Proctor had counted on it, and now so did she.

She put on her mask and coveralls and went in, checking on the levels before she scraped some of the long, pinkish crystals into a baggie and crushed it up under the heel of her hand.

You could learn how to make street meth on the Internet. Any moron could do it. Dewey Proctor was living proof of that.

But this required some finesse, something extra. When she could sit up in the hospital, she spent the time figuring out how to get the plants into the country and where she'd put the batch togther. When she was out, in physical therapy six days a week, she worked on setting up accounts to order the supplies she needed. The St. Bernard Parish Alternative Day School had a fully stocked chemistry lab, courtesy of Lizzie's teacher's license. Pretty good for a one-room schoolhouse.

She looked at the dilapidated little shack that smelled of cat piss and laughed before she shut the door.

Lonnie Thibodeaux had put on weight, and his eyes bugged when she walked into the dayroom. Lizzie sat across from him and didn't speak. Lonnie pushed the cap back on his head, Confederate flag and NASCAR flag crossed, embroidered on the bill.

"Well, reckon I should just get this out. I'm sorry as hell for what happened, Miss Dodge. I weren't in my right mind, and, well. When Dewey Proctor tells you to do somethin', there's no good way to say no. Scary son of a bitch."

Lizzie didn't speak. Lonnie swallowed, and his brown teeth clicked. "They showed me the photos of you and Sergeant Dodge, when they arrested me. That was what snapped me out of it. I knew I could never go back from that. Dewey . . . he told me to do it and I was so out of my mind I just . . ." He sniffed, wetly. It ate your sinuses away and went into your brain if you smoked enough of it. "Just tell me what I gotta do so I can close my eyes at night, Miss Dodge," Lonnie said. "All I see is you and your husband. Lyin' on that kitchen floor . . ."

Lizzie took the baggie from her purse and slid it across the table. She moved her hand like a magic trick. "Take it."

Lonnie stared at the baggie, then at her. "Miss Dodge, I don't . . ."

"You want to ease your pain? You want to stop thinking about the man you killed? Then you smoke that shit down to the burn marks, Lonnie. That's what you do." Lizzie stood up. "And it's Mrs. Dodge, no thanks to you."

She left Lonnie crying in the dayroom, sobbing even as he tucked the baggie into his shirt quicker than you could blink, and went to her car, and waited.

* * *

Lonnie waited until dark. He went to a 7-Eleven and bought a pack of disposable lighters, and used an empty soda can in the alley behind it to smoke up.

Lizzie waited until he was sprawled on the ground, until he might as well have been dead, and then went to him and kicked him in the stomach. "Wake up, asshole."

Lonnie's eyes flew open. He tried to breathe, but nothing happened.

"Here's how it works," Lizzie said. "You might think this is a bad dream, but it's not. You're under my control, and you're going to tell me what I want." She crouched, using her small flashlight to light up Lonnie's pale, deceased face. "You can't refuse me. What's in you now will burn out in a few hours, and then you'll die for good. But before you do, answer me."

Lonnie nodded, and the panic in his eyes was absolute. The panic of a man looking into the light and not liking what he saw.

"Where does Dewey Proctor run his labs?"

He tried not to talk. She saw his throat working. "I . . . don't . . . know. . . ."

"No," Lizzie said. "A junkie like you who runs his errands in exchange for dope knows. If only to have something to give to the cops when they get caught." She grabbed his chin. "Answer me, Lonnie. Where's the lab?"

"House . . . house . . . in his Mom's . . . name," Lonnie gasped. "Back on . . . Route 17."

Lizzie stood up and brushed off her pants. "Go walk into traffic, Lonnie. I don't want that bitch wife of yours having an open casket."

Lonnie did as she'd said. Lizzie listened to the semi's air brakes scream, then took the opposite way through the alley. The formula was almost perfect. She was almost ready.

Dakota Bonner spent most of her time on the elementary-school playground, drinking out of paper bags and texting her friends, who came and went. Only Dakota was always there. Lizzie didn't blame her. With a father like Dickie Bonner, a red-faced, thick-fisted drunk, she'd stay away, too.

Dakota stared at her, face crinkled and suspicious, as she approached. A white kid with a backward hat and baggy jacket grinned at her, started to say something, but Lizzie lifted the hem of her shirt.

"Fuck off."

He saw the gun and took her advice. Dakota watched him go, and turned back languidly. "What's your problem, bitch?"

"You're really such a burnout you don't recognize me?" Lizzie asked her.

Dakota thought for what seemed to Lizzie an excessively long time. "Oh yeah. You're that lady whose husband got killed by that tweaker."

"Something like that," Lizzie agreed. "My husband worked with your father—as much as he could, with your father being a corrupt son of a bitch."

Dakota's gears ground again. Lizzie could practically see the smoke. "Fuck you," she said finally. "My dad didn't do shit to you."

"That's funny," Lizzie said. "Is that why all those guys hang around you, Dakota? Your sense of humor?"

She started to rise, and Lizzie jammed the needle into her neck. The pink liquid looked like some kind of sci-fi chemical, a formula to bring out Mr. Hyde, but Dakota just slumped at the picnic table.

Lizzie lit a cigarette and waited for her to come around. She snapped back faster than Lonnie. Younger, brain less fried, Lizzie guessed.

"Wha . . ." Dakota said. This time, Lizzie was ready. She knew it would work.

"Be quiet," she said, and Dakota's pink-painted mouth snapped shut.

The panic was the same—waking up and knowing your body is no longer yours, that your veins are full of fire, and the devil is turning the spit. When she'd woken up, unable to move from the drugs and the casts on her arms and legs, she'd felt the same panic. Knew it as intimately as she'd once known Stephen's hands.

"Funny," Lizzie said, "how Stephen managed to fight off Lonnie *and* Dewey, but there's not a shred of physical evidence. Funny how nobody saw them going off in Dewey's truck to do the deed. Somebody in the department must have an interest in keeping Dewey Proctor in business."

She made Dakota stand up and told her where to go. She put the scalpel she'd lifted from the hospital in the girl's hand.

"Your father," she said. "Then yourself. In the bathtub. Hurry, so your mother can come home and find you."

Dakota walked, pale and shuffling, in the fading daylight, and Lizzie didn't bother to watch her go.

The headlines shouted at her when she walked into the Winn-Dixie: murder-suicide, molestation, child abuse, revenge. Lonnie had never even made the paper.

Lizzie found Dewey Proctor in front of the beer cooler, sucking on his teeth while he examined a coupon for a case of Miller Lite.

Lizzie waited until he noticed her, and he smiled when he did. "You got something to say to me, gorgeous?"

She folded her arms. She'd worn a black shirt Stephen had always liked, with a bow in the V of her breasts. "I need money," she said.

Dewey snorted. "I don't think that's my problem."

"Stephen's pension isn't coming through for another six months," Lizzie said. "And my mortgage is upside down. I've seen what the shit you cook out there on 17 does to people, and I can do better. I can deliver you pure product and all I want is ten percent. I know that's what you gave Bonner to stay out of your hair, and considering you murdered my husband, I think it's the least you could do."

Dewey recovered instantly, that mask of hillbilly good looks sliding back into place almost before the shock could show on his face.

"I don't know what you're talking about," he said. "And you can tell your state-police buddies on the wire the same thing."

Lizzie pulled up her shirt. The scars branched out from her belly button. One for internal bleeding. One for the collapsed lung. "No wire, Dewey. Just business."

He snatched at her hand. "Pull your shirt down, for fuck's sake. You want us both tossed in jail?"

"I want us to do business," Lizzie said. "This was the only spot I knew I'd get you alone." She gestured at the shopping cart, full of shampoo and potted meat and the fixings for a roast chicken. "How is your momma, anyway?"

"So senile she thinks the mailman is my daddy most of the time,"

Dewey said. "And how the hell do I know you can deliver a product? You're a cop's wife. Jesus, woman."

"I'm a chemistry teacher," Lizzie said. "And let's face it, Dewey. If an inbred jizz stain like you can cook meth, then I can do it ten times better."

He grabbed her, slammed her against the beer case. Cold went up her back, tickled her spine. "I ain't no retard," he said with a snarl. "And if you wanna cook with me for real, you better watch your whore mouth."

"Sorry," Lizzie said, and let herself go limp.

"Is there a problem?" said a stockboy, staring at them like they might bite him.

Dewey released her.

"No problem, son," he said. "Just working a little something out."

Lizzie suited up and made Dewey wear a respirator, too. "You pass out and you're useless to me," she said. Dewey thumped her on the side of her skull. Her brain buzzed, making contact with the plate.

"What'd I tell you about that mouth?" His voice came out muffled and high behind the air filters.

Lizzie took the plants from her duffel bag. She'd kept them in the plain boxes, the crooked stamp PRODUCT OF HAITI faded and curdled from the exposure to the fumes.

Dewey prodded the plants. "The fuck's this shit?"

"Additives," said Lizzie. "It makes the smoke smoother, lets your customers smoke longer. Means they buy more product."

Dewey looked blank, and she sighed. "You ever smoke a clove cigarette?"

"Ah, yeah," he said. "Get on with it then."

Lizzie cooked a batch, and Dewey let one of his boys test it. The guy blissed out, then fell asleep on the sofa outside the bedroom Dewey had made into a lab.

Before she left, Lizzie leaned over and breathed, "Wake up. Go home. Die there," into his ear.

Dewey didn't say anything, but she could tell from the glint in his eye he was already seeing more piles of cash than he could spend in a lifetime, more even than Stephen had found in his trailer, when he'd broken the door down on that domestic call. Months ago now. Another lifetime.

The batch went out, and two days later Dewey called her to the house on Route 17. Grinning from ear to ear, he handed her a stack of wrinkled, crystal-crusted hundreds. "I don't know what you did," he said, "but damn, bitch, you sure showed me." He patted Lizzie on the shoulder. Fortunately, not the one Lonnie had smashed with the bat, the spot that could still make her cry out in pain. "Who knew the cop's wife had it in her?"

"Desperate times," Lizzie said. She eyed his hand like a snake. She thought about what it would be like to burn it with the chemicals in the lab next door. How Dewey would carry his melted skin and scars for what remained of his shortened life, as the chemicals worked their way through his bloodstream.

"I don't know and don't care to know how you cooked it," Dewey said. "But more. More and we'll run the Arkansas oxy boys out of here—shit, we'll run the *cartels* out. Nothing can touch us. Just keep making cookies for the bake sale, momma, and life is good."

Lizzie covered Dewey's hand with her own. "Sure thing, Dewey."

Detective LaRochelle almost caught her the next week, pulled into the drive as she was leaving for the hunting camp. Lizzie threw Stephen's old jacket over the vials and respirators in the backseat.

"Your psychiatrist—or the fella supposed to be your psychiatrist, if you ever made an appointment—told me where to find you," she said.

"I'm pretty sure that's against the law," Lizzie told her.

LaRochelle drew her eyebrows together.

"You know, I see a lotta victims. Lot of people who get the shit end of the stick. What happened to you wasn't right, but running off, living in this dump?"

The trailer was rusted along the roof and sagged at one end. Water had seeped into the paneled walls, painting flowers and feathers of mildew.

"You need to learn how to live again," LaRochelle said. "Take it from me. Otherwise, you let Dewey Proctor win."

"He did win," Lizzie told her, looking at her feet, praying LaRochelle would just turn around and leave. "I'm already dead."

"Will you at least talk to someone about what happened?" La-Rochelle said. "I know it must have felt good that Lonnie Thibodeaux walked in front of that truck, but you need more. Take it from me."

"Oh, I know I do," Lizzie said.

LaRochelle drove away, and Lizzie went back to the camp, where she practically lived now. Dewey had gotten her a bed and a composting toilet so she could run both labs at once, batches going out all across southern Louisiana. She hauled the bed outside and lay on it, looking up at the lattice of trees. This was the last batch. The last time.

She packaged up the pink stuff and then set the road flare next to the plastic drum. She'd be far enough away to avoid blowback by the time it melted the vessel and ignited the chemicals inside, and then nothing but ashes would remain of the place she'd gone with Stephen so often.

It was better that way.

Dewey was ecstatic. "If you were more my type, I'd marry your ass," he proclaimed, hefting a bag of pink.

Lizzie looked out the window. Almost sundown. Almost time.

Dewey was making up shots. He doled them out to his buddies, but she'd never seen him partake. That was all right, though. She wanted him aware.

The knock had come around this time, just as the horizon was gold and the sky was black. Lonnie, cap over his eyes, mumbling some bullshit about a car breaking down. The door slapping her backward, the bat landing once, twice across her back as she tried to crawl away.

She screamed for Stephen, and then Dewey was over her, holding a pistol to her forehead. Lonnie did as Dewey said, and she heard the crack, over and over. The sound of meat tenderizing.

Nobody steals from me. Not even some tight-assed sheriff who thinks he's Captain America.

"You know, it's probably for the best," Dewey said, sweeping the disposable syringes of pink into a paper bag. "You're destined for better things, Elizabeth. You didn't need that piece of dead wood weighing you down."

He grinned at her. Straight, perfect teeth. "You're a wild one, sweetheart. I knew it from the moment I saw you. A fighter."

Lizzie pulled out the stun gun she'd bought off the Internet through the same fake account she'd used to order the plants. She took a few seconds to aim—aim right the first time, Stephen had said, and the rest is easy.

Dewey gave half a yell, then he went down. Lizzie left him on the floor, his pants piss stained, and peered through the curtains. In the woods, things moved. It was full dark. It was time.

She unlocked the three dead bolts and threw the steel door wide open. Stupid, anyway—if the DEA wanted to break in, they'd just go through the flimsy, half-rotted wall around it.

Dewey moaned, then sat up. "Fuck! What the *fuck*?" he shouted.

Lizzie tossed the stun gun aside and stepped on Dewey's chest, holding him down. "Feel that?" she said. "It doesn't take much to crush a lung. Far fewer pounds per square inch than you'd think. My doctor told me that."

"You fucking bitch whore!" he screamed. "The hell you think you're doing? You going to steal from me?"

"No, Dewey," Lizzie said. "I know what happens to people who take what's yours." She watched the first white shape lurch up the weed-studded walkway and through the door. One of Dewey's pals, the one she'd told to go home and die. His arm hung flimsy and mangled, like he'd been sideswiped by a car, and he limped. His eyes were white with cataracts.

Dewey started up again, and Lizzie kicked him down. "I don't want your meth, Dewey. I don't want your money. I didn't want Lonnie's apology and I didn't want to pretend that I don't know you and Dickie Bonner were thick as thieves."

She grabbed a bag of the pink stuff, ripped it open, and threw it over Dewey. He thrashed, noticing the lurching figure for the first time.

"What is going on?" he screamed.

"Best question you've ever asked," Lizzie said. "See, you didn't know me, Dewey. You *don't* know me. Stephen was just doing his job when he seized that cash. I figure it was probably to pay off the cartel or somebody else, and you were in deep shit. You got one of your pet tweakers to beat him to death as payback, and I was collateral damage. That about right?"

The figure clawed at Dewey's pant leg, and he kicked and screamed.

"I had a lot of time after I woke up," Lizzie said. "A lot of time to research. Any moron can learn how to make meth, but it takes a little more doing to come up with a way to cook in *Datura stramonium*." She took another step toward the door. More figures were crossing the highway now, coming from the woods. "That's jimson weed to you, Dewey. The devil's trumpet. A few other toxins, a few additives, and you know what you've got?"

Dewey was screaming, and two of the things held him down, clawing deep furrows into his flesh as they tried to scoop up the crystals.

"A dead man," Lizzie said. "A dead man who can't be bargained with, can't be intimidated. A dead man who will listen to whoever puts an order in his ear. A dead man who, once he dies and wakes up again, has a jones like the devil sunk his teeth into your soul. A junkie who'll do anything to chase that high."

She glanced out. She needed to go if she was going to avoid the majority of the crowd converging on Dewey's momma's place, hunting their next fix of the pink stuff.

"Half the tweakers in this parish are in NA, which meets in the hospital, which is where I go twice a week for physical therapy," she said. "Pretty easy to plant a suggestion. To tell everyone that their favorite pusher is holding out on them."

She ripped two more bags for good measure, as Dewey screamed. The figures had given up on the crystals now and were licking and biting at his clothes, his skin and hair.

Lizzie raised her voice to be heard. "I could have lost Stephen," she said. "I could have lived with pain every moment for the rest of my life and a brain so scrambled I can't think half the time."

She lifted her shirt, exposing the scars. "But you took this from me, too, Dewey. Stephen was so excited to be a father. You stole that."

He met her eyes, blood running down from his scalp, mouth open so far that she couldn't believe he hadn't unhinged his jaw.

"Nobody steals from me, Dewey," she said, and slipped out.

She could still hear his screams from the highway.

* * *

Stephen's grave was covered with rotting flowers and tilted wreaths, personal messages from deputies and people he'd helped during his time with the department.

Lizzie moved them aside, the sweet scent of death rising, and sat cross-legged, leaning against the stone. The night was close and heavy, but the stone was cool.

She took out the disposable syringe, the shot she'd kept hidden in the back of the trailer's refrigerator until tonight.

Lizzie slipped off her belt and tied off her arm. She'd watched the nurses do it so much that she found a vein the very first time.

She watched a little blood swirl as she drew on the syringe. Nobody would question it. She was grief-stricken, she wasn't thinking clearly. She'd never visited her psychiatrist. Nobody knew about Dewey. Who'd believe it if they did?

Lizzie paused to see if she was afraid, if she had the flutter in her stomach she used to get as Stephen would leave for his shift, the flutter that wouldn't entirely subside until she saw him again.

Nothing. That wasn't too surprising, Lizzie thought as she depressed the plunger.

She was already dead, after all.

THE DEAD OF DROMORE

Ken Bruen

THE DEAD ARE DIFFERENT from you and me.

Well, duh!

Hello, like we didn't know.

Major Sean Fitzroy, in charge of Special Operations, told me this. He was in the process of warning me that no protection could be guaranteed if I persisted in entering Dromore.

We were standing in his distinctive black tent, Command Center.

Fitzroy was one of those Irish who believed utterly in the magic of his own words. If he said it, then you better heed it. He had a point. The village had been sealed off since the outbreak, nothing in or out. But a distress signal had been issuing on the hour from the tiny church in the center of Dromore. In Morse, it spelled simply

"Help."

I said

"Someone is holding out there."

He shook his military head.

"They're all dead."

Paused

Added

". . . Ish."

I said

"Someone is sending the signal. I don't think it's one of the infects, unless they're a whole lot smarter than you think."

Infects. The term for the victims of the infection. If infection it was. The military felt better about destroying something they had labeled. Made it, to use another of their buzz terms, an operation.

"Operation decimation."

Due in twenty-four hours.

I said

"I'm not Jack Bauer. You need to give us more time."

Us being my team.

He stared at me.

"Jack who?"

Not a TV aficionado, then.

Zombies already ruled the virtual world. From HBO, *The Walking Dead,* to movies, comics, DVDs, zombies were more popular than vampires. Could only be a matter of time until *American Zombie.* The judges' panel there already seemed half dead. George A. Romero was enjoying a huge revival and so was his catch phrase,

When hell is full, the dead will walk the earth.

As if even hell were running a strict immigration bureau. Real life came late to the show. The devastating earthquake in Japan had unleashed a cloud, not unlike the Icelandic ash, but smaller and faster. It moved from place to place for no apparent reason, hovered over certain regions, then disappeared. The affected region was soon overrun by the reanimated dead.

It was beginning to be believed that all the data on Hollywood zombies must have been based on facts the human race learned eons ago, as much of it proved to be true. The principle being, you could put the infects down permanently only by destroying their brains, what was left of them. The movie *Zombieland* made the double tap derigeur.

The World Health Organization got militant. No crap about finding a cure, seeking to help the afflicted, it was a straightforward directive.

"Turkey shoot."

The anticipated protest from liberals and prolife were quashed and it was rumored that Amnesty International was under a cloud. The small, deadly one. Helped there by a combination of

The CIA

Mossad

And the Chinese.

The military moved in jig time as soon as the cloud hovered. Immediate cutoff, fences erected to keep the inhabitants in

then nuke time.

No debate, exceptions, help, or quarter.

The cloud appeared, the area was gone. And now it had shown up in Ireland, over the tiny tourist village of Dromore. Not even a claim to be the ancestral home of the secretary of defense was going to save it. The cloud appeared on a Tuesday, by Thursday the fences were up, and on Saturday the bombers would fly. Where I came in.

I'd been trained as a marine, my family having emigrated to the United States when I was a child. Was spotted at being adept in black ops, saw service in all the hot spots, then invalidated out when my state of mind raised alarm bells. I liked my duties too much and wasn't too pushed about covering up. Civilian life was never going to work for me. I had a taste for killing. Went freelance. And oh Lordy, the pay was awesome. I formed my own crew, four apprentice psychos, and we rocked.

Slade, my second in command, a black guy from Jersey.

Turner, from, he said, "everywhere *and nowhere, baby.*"

Kelly, from San Francisco. The sole woman.

Reilly, from Belfast, veteran of the street in The Troubles. Word was, he *was* The Troubles. We were the call of last resort and we delivered.

Fast

Furious

Fatally.

Our crew gradually evolved from random acts of retaliation, revenge, and retribution to a specialized snatch team. Business was brisk. Samuel T. Rubin was one of the richest men on the planet. His daughter, Debbie, the only love in his life, power of course not included. Debbie was on a sabbatical and had traveled to Ireland.

To Dromore

Dumb broad.

Didn't kids rock in Ibiza anymore?

Rubin flew me and my team to Ireland, the biggest check of our career in my pocket. With the admonishment

"You can't get her out? Don't come out."

I'd been threatened by the best, relayed his sentiment to the crew. Kelly, God love her, said

"Him and what fucking army."

Why I loved her.

Fitzroy was aware of my rep, and despite his objections to my plan, he was powerless against a man of Rubin's stature. Now he said

"You haven't a freaking prayer."

I was cleaning my weapons, racked an Uzi, said

"Ain't about prayer."

Nothing wrong with arrogance if you can back it up.

We had always had the most phenomenal luck, as if the devil paved our way. Reilly, with his Irish fatalism, believed we were due a fall and that it would be the "bollix of 'em all."

I had a map of the village spread on the hood of the Bruiser. Our custom-adapted armored car. Bulletproof, reinforced with the lightest metal and alloy available. It was awash in hardware and never yet failed us. I drew my finger along a line from a breach in the fence right to the church, said

"We're playing it real simple."

Behind the church was a small hill. An Irish one, meaning it had aspirations to be a mountain.

The one road led to the church, that was all she wrote.

Slade removed his earphones, from which heavy metal dribbled, said

"Kill 'em all."

Well, yes.

I looked to Turner, who said

"We'll lay down withering fire from the moment we hit the village, right up to the church. Anyone not in the church goes down."

The crew agreed.

Kelly and I would enter the church, grab Debbie if she was still there, move out.

Reilly was smoking, the only one of the crew with the addiction, took a deep drag, asked

"What if there are other survivors in there and they want, you know, to get the fuck out of Dodge?"

I let that simmer, hover for a bit, then he answered his own question:

"Fuck 'em if they can't take a joke."

We prepared to lock and load. I reminded them

"Head shots."

Kelly, in almost-designer fatigues, shifted her shades to rest on her blond locks, said

"I give good head."

As we battened down the hatches, Fitzroy watched with bemusement. I was adjusting my battered leather jacket, pockets full of death, and I asked Fitzroy

"Any last words of wisdom?"

"Oh yeah, don't go."

When we reached the fence, we paused. Turner moved topside, manning the machine gun, tailored to pump nearly five hundred rounds without jamming.

I asked

"See anything?"

"Nope."

We moved, gathering speed as we approached the village.

Turner shouted

"Bogeys at twelve o' clock."

I didn't get much of a chance to observe as Turner opened up. The main and only street in the village was literally a sea of walkers.

Reilly went

"Holy fuck."

Turner had the gun trained on them, asked

"Yeah?"

As I watched the seething, teeming mess of infects, something stirred in my heart, something I couldn't name. I was momentarily lost, and Kelly, catching on, snapped

"Skip, what's the haps?"

"Clear a path through the bastards."

Kelly and Reilly were out of the truck, the mortar primed

. . . to watch them tag-team that baby was beauty in motion.

One

Two

Boom.

Again, again.

I shouted

"Let's rock now."

Back onboard, we moved through the path of destroyed, still-moving bodies, or rather parts, a loud growling, moaning growing in intensity.

Kelly said

"Jesus, it's freaky."

Slade, who'd been ominously quiet, shouted

"Shut the fuck up."

We'd got halfway up the street when we stalled.

Slade was up beside Reilly, and the Bruiser lurched downward, a jolt threw us roughly around inside.

Slade shouted

"Ah fuck, the mortar tore a crater in the road."

And our front end was stuck in it.

Not good. I untangled myself from the twist of limbs, pulled my body up.

Slade said

"Look."

Both sides of the street, the infects were still.

WTF.

Not moving. Just staring blankly at us.

Kelly, moving to the rear, asked

"I thought they never stopped moving."

Moments like this, your whole team could fall apart, you had to act, even if rashly. I said

"Get your shit together, Slade; you stay with the truck; and, Turner, see what you can do to get the truck moving."

We were on the street, knee deep in limbs and gore, the silent infects not five feet away.

I said

"Anything moves, nail it."

Reilly, Kelly, and I began to move, laden with hardware, our fingers on triggers, the silence spooking us.

Turner said

"This truck ain't going nowhere, skip."

I didn't look back, said

"Stay on the radios. If the infects remain like this, maybe we can walk out."

Like it would go down that easy.

I took the lead, Reilly at my shoulder and Kelly on point. We got to the door of the church, and I was about to hammer on it when Kelly screamed.

The remains of what had been a cop, half his head gone, sunk his teeth into her shoulder. Reilly turned as a group of infects moved behind the cop. Slade opened up, mowing them down. Turned the barrel on Kelly, literally blew the cop's head off her shoulder. I was banging on the door,

"Let us the fuck in, we're here to help."

Turned to grab the fallen Kelly, got my arm under her shoulder, and Reilly gasped.

"Oh, sweet Jesus."

Crowds of infects were moving toward us. I heard rapid fire from the Bruiser and a babble from the radio.

The door opened and we piled in. Fell on the stone floor as the door was slammed, heavy boards rebarricading it. A priest offered his hand and helped me to my feet. He was in his thirties, dressed in a brown cassock, Franciscan? The cassock was covered in dust and grime and he looked exhausted. He said

"I'm Seamus and these are . . ."

Swept his arm to the interior of the church,

"My flock."

Bitterness spilling over the words. A bunch of about ten, armed with clubs, Hurleys, legs of chairs, even a pitchfork. Kelly groaned, got to her feet.

Seamus asked

"Is she bit?"

Then I saw the rusty machete in his right hand, down alongside the cassock. No hesitation, I said

"Not her blood, from one of them."

Reilly moved in front of her, blocking the priest's view of her wound. I could see the shock on her face, her eyes going out of focus.

I asked

"Is this all of you?"

A burly man came forward, said

"Meet the population of Dromore."

Behind him, a young man, maybe twenty, carrying a shotgun leveled at us, said

"And not due for a growth spike anytime soon."

Reilly, his AK resting on his folded arms, said quietly

"Son, you want to point that somewhere else."

We were off to a dandy start.

The shotgun was lowered.

I asked

"Is there a Debbie Rubin here?"

A girl came forward, the all-American teen, her face wearing a look of trepidation and disbelief.

The shotgun guy moved in front of her, demanded

"What do you want with her?"

A blur, as Reilly moved, kicked the guy's feet from under him, wrenching the shotgun from him as he fell.

He said

"I'm really sick of your attitude, fella."

The priest looked like he might intervene and Reilly laughed, sneered

"Don't even think about it, Padre."

I said to the girl

"Your dad sent us."

She seemed as if she might burst into tears but held it.

The guy on the ground asked

"You're saving her? And what, leaving us?"

I kept my attention on the priest and his machete, said

"Her father didn't mention you."

A man with gray hair, in his fifties, broke in

"Might we all take a moment, we're in this together."

Reilly never even glanced at him, muttered

"Dream on, sucker."

The man said

"I'm a doctor, Dr. Driscoll. The *creatures* out there—at first they seemed to go still every hour but then the intervals became longer, and it appears the episodes of this are gradually fading."

I asked

"Your point?"

He was furtively polishing a pair of horn-rimmed glasses, as if they'd provide comfort, said

"This is only my theory but it seems the human side—the very life, as it were—was fighting to stay, but the infection is gradually completely taking over. From the time of infection, a person becomes one of them in about four hours."

Neither Reilly nor I looked at Kelly, who had moved to a far wall and sat slumped, her head down.

The doctor continued

"I'd hazard there may be one more episode of stillness, then transformation is complete."

I pushed

"Meaning?"

"The next stillness could be our last opportunity. We have to try to break out then."

I took Debbie's arm, moved her behind me. This caused a ripple in the crowd. What they might have done was averted by a rapid static of gunfire, then silence. The church windows were high on the walls so we were effectively blind to the outside.

The guy on the floor spat

"If you had men out there, they're chum."

I kicked him in the head, brought my Bren up, leveled it, said

"Any more smart asses?"

No.

Reilly was on the radio, calling Slade, tried over and over, then shook his head.

I said to Seamus

"Get someone up to the window, let's see if the doc's theory holds."

I couldn't even think of Slade and Turner, an image of them overrun by those . . *creatures* . . . freaked me. And worse, that they'd become the infected. I swallowed hard, moved over to Kelly, bringing Debbie with me. The priest watched me with those dark eyes. He had some moves yet and I'd better be ready.

Reilly whispered to me

"Skip, you want me to waste the padre?"

Tempting as it was, it would only up the already knife edge we were on.

I said

"Not yet."

Debbie asked me

"Are we going to survive?"

I said

"Absolutely. Never failed a mission yet."

Never lost a crew member, either.

I bent down. Kelly seemed to be in a fever, her eyes closed but a steady murmur/groan coming from her chest.

Reilly hunkered down beside me, said

"Not good, skip."

I knew what I should do. Reilly would even do it for me. But I waited. For what, a miracle? Dromore was the end of life, the living, hope. Kelly had been on my squad for five years, we'd even had a brief fling. I couldn't imagine the crew without her.

The voice in my head

"Wake the fuck up, what crew? There's you and Reilly."

I stood up, took her beloved Walther PPK, handed it to Debbie, asked

"You ever use a gun?"

She'd grown up with hunting in her family.

Reilly said,

"Alana, we are the hunted."

The priest came over, asked

"How is your friend?"

"Good."

I thought, *Fuck with me and I'll gut you.*

He said

"Her life is flowing fast, and soon she'll have the thing that passed for new life, an abomination."

Reilly stood right up to the priest, asked

"Isn't all life sacred to you crowd?"

The doctor said

"Would you like to see the view from the roof?"

Reilly nodded, indicating he'd manage.

I said to Debbie

"Hang in there, we'll get you home."

She didn't seem convinced.

The view from the roof was bleak, the hill behind the church, the only area free of the infects. I noticed a flatbed truck a few yards from the church rear, and the doc, reading my mind, said

"Might work."

I asked

"Is there a path along the hill?"

And the doc suddenly pointed, went

"It's happening."

The stillness.

We came down those stairs like banshees. Shouting

"Everybody to the back, there's a truck, we're running."

I said

"Reilly drives the truck, injured in the back, the rest of us on foot, and hope to fuck we get to the hill before they come back to . . . whatever."

The priest blocked my path, the machete half raised, the belligerent young guy beside him, ordered

"The infected stay here."

Reilly shot him.

Stunned us all.

He said

"No time for bullshit, we've got to boogie."

We laid Kelly in the back, the doc with her, the young man still with the priest.

I said to Reilly

"Take off, I'll catch up."

Watched the pathetic convoy of souls start toward the hill, went back to the church. The young guy was kneeling by the priest. I hit him hard with the butt of my gun.

As I caught up with the convoy, the doc shouted

"Where's Flaherty?"

There was no answer that contained sanity so I gave none. We were moving well when I sensed the change, looked back to see the swarm of infects begin to move. I could see the protective fence and shouted

"Book it."

Debbie, who had been in the front, got out and said

"I'm staying with you."

The truck stalled.

I said

"Lighten the load, get more people on the ground."

Got as many as possible off the truck and it began to move. We could see it approach the fence as we hurried to catch up. I also saw Kelly rise, fall on the doc. The truck began to veer, lurch, and then it slewed into the fence.

I muttered

"Jesus."

People were spacing out, trying to get away from the infects, from . . . Kelly. Reilly was out of the truck, seemed dazed from where we were.

I screamed

"Shoot her, for Christ's sake!"

My own words nigh to death in my throat.

I froze. First time in my career, I lost the plot.

Debbie grabbed my arm, urged

"The fence, over there, it's cut, come on."

And led me to it. I could hear screams, cries from the truck, but couldn't look back. Through the fence and flat out running, until I saw the camps of the military. Muttered

"Thank Christ."

The distinctive black tent, Fitzroy's, came into view. I said to Debbie

"The Command Center."

As I rushed up to it, I could see a figure moving inside. My relief was palpable. Debbie behind me as I tore open the flap.

Fitzroy lunging, sinking his teeth into my outstretched arm.

A thought burning in my head

Debbie. Run.

ALL *THE* COMFORTS OF HOME

A BEACON STORY

John Skipp and Cody Goodfellow

I.

LIFE WAS NOT TOO SHABBY in room 4037 of the former Le Meridien Hotel. Luxury accommodations had been the name of the game long before Bryce Hatfield took over the City, and in that respect very little had changed, even after the building had been entirely repurposed.

Same king-size bed, soft sheets, and warm blankets on a pillow-top mattress sweet enough to kiss. Same thirty-two-inch LCD HD flat screen and fully stocked minibar. Same pervasive AC, only slightly more filtered, comfort-adjustable within three degrees of Fahrenheit seventy-five.

Tom had built bookshelves to make 4037 feel more like home, adorned them with Godfrey-Huft family photos: his wife and kids, his mom and dad, his brother, his niece, his wife's parents, and so on. He'd designed them to match the decor, secured management approval. It was, after all, his home now. The result, as intended, was cozy as all get-out.

He'd definitely gotten a lot of wear out of the complimentary robe. Was wearing it now, over crisp navy drawers and freshly scrubbed skin. After a day like today, the hot shower alone was worth the price of admission.

If only he could get the lingering stink out of the air.

The million-dollar view wasn't quite what it used to be, either. He kept his thick curtains closed almost all the time. And had specifically requested a room with no view of the bridge.

But tonight, if he could have opened the windows, he would have. The panoramic expanse of city ending in the new workers' housing compounds at Pier 9 was ugly, but they made him think.

Not everybody in the new San Francisco was nearly as lucky. Hard work paid off in the new regime as it never had before, but the winners in the New Deal had come by their cozy creature comforts the old-fashioned way—by dumb, cussed luck.

Le Meridien San Francisco had become the de facto family building at Embarcadero Center. Very smart move on Emperor Hatfield's part. The school for kids grades K through twelve, the library and rec center, the gym and basketball court had all been reconstituted from stately ballrooms and vast high-tech conference halls down on the lower levels.

Just part of the incentive program.

The restaurants in the lobby, as well, had been converted into family-style feeding grounds: an immense salad bar stocked with fresh produce from Embarcadero Three; an all-day breakfast-cereal bar, long on granolas, woefully short on Cap'n Crunch; co-op kitchens where hot meals were served from 6:00 A.M. to midnight.

Round-the-clock room service was a thing of the past. But you could go down and whip up some leftovers 24/7, if you had the proper clearance, kept a record, and cleaned up after yourself.

From the mezzanine up, Le Meridien was all family dwellings. So far, only the first six floors were in use, with room to grow as more families arrived, or more singles decided that breeding wasn't such a bad idea after all.

Not that the Hyatt was a dump. Far from it. There were times he wished he lived there instead. The noise of endless parties and kids jamming on guitars at all hours was less a nuisance than a loud reminder that life went on, with or without you.

But there were definite perks to family life. In the thick of the parental herd, he could finally afford to let his guard down. To believe they could be safe.

And that their lives might be worth living.

On weeknights, the father-daughter deal was that nine forty-five was lights-out time for Molly, next door in room 4039 (*her own room*, as the crotchety nine-year-old never failed to remind him). She'd wanted to finish her chapter—she was reading Heinlein's *The Door into Summer* again, and he couldn't fault her taste—he'd loved that book as a kid—but a deal was a deal.

Tonight's round had ended, with a hug and a kiss, in just under fifteen minutes; and now it was Off-duty Daddy Time. An hour at most, before his own lights-out.

One beer. One smoke. And a little TV.

Before having to face his dreams.

II.

IN THE WORST ONE, he's walking through a field of deep mud in an endless green-black night. He doesn't know how long he's been walking or why, but he knows he's in trouble. Kristin will be angry when she comes home, will be devastated because of something he's done or hasn't done, something so enormously, unacceptably wrong that it won't fit into his head.

The gelid air crushes him down and the mud holds him back. But he struggles forward, thrashing and gasping, until he sees someone standing alone out on the plain.

The resistance grows worse, but he fights it now with new strength, because he's saved, the bad thing he did is undone. Hot tears of relief streak his face as he comes closer and sees that yes, it's Geoff, looking up at him with his backpack in his little shaking hands.

His son's eyes go wide and white when he sees his father coming. He raises his arms, holding out the backpack. It tilts in the frigid wind so that Tom sees Geoff's face through a hole in the bottom. All his art stuff is gone, but that's not why Geoff looks so frightened, so utterly unhinged and, yes, even a little angry with his father.

"Geoff, where did you go?" he asks, but the words won't come. His mouth won't make sounds.

Geoff drops the gutted backpack and reaches out for his daddy. When he opens his mouth, his blue lips frame a stream of silver bubbles that shoot upward like a swarm of ghost jellyfish.

And even though he's had the dream more times than he wants to count, Tom is shocked once again to find his son at the bottom of San Francisco Bay.

III.

TOM GODFREY HAD BEEN IN THE NAVY for seven years— Amphibious Construction Battalion 1, stationed in Coronado—

when he met Kristin Huft. He was an earnest young career man with a minor in bourbon and a yearning for stability, meaning, and purpose. She was one of the first enlisted women to serve on a submarine, a straight arrow with her eye on the prize, secretly battoning down the hatches on her fierce mommy-urge.

They were both short and burly—neither of them beauties—but they looked good together. And felt that way, too. He hailed from Missouri. She was born and raised in Kansas. They had a lot in common.

Both of them had dreamed of oceans from the time they were born.

She got pregnant with Geoff on their honeymoon. They told their friends they had a rock-paper-scissors tournament to decide who'd stay home with the baby, but it was no contest. His enlistment was up, and all the fun jobs were being subbed out to private contractors, anyway. There were plenty of companies in the market for a former Seabee but not many jobs out there for a former submariner.

His real friends kidded him about it and a lot of others simply dropped him, but Tom didn't lose anything staying home with his son. They set up housekeeping in Richmond, and Tom carried Geoff in a sling when he went out to oversee the new fuel-storage facility at Alameda, or to the new sewage-treatment plant the city almost ended up naming for Bush the Younger.

Kristin was out with her crew in three-month rotations, playing hide-and-seek with the Chinese just as they'd been trained to play with the Russians. He missed her, and he worried that Geoff did not miss her enough.

She took leave when she had Molly, but she came back to find herself promoted to fire control officer and even longer duties away.

But somehow, it worked. He fretted that maybe it was *he* who didn't miss her enough; that maybe he'd needed the idea of Kristin more than the reality. As their children grew up, they called him Mommy and Daddy interchangeably. When Kristin came home, they treated her like a goddess.

Time flew. Geoff started school. Tom went independent, opening his own engineering-consulting firm. Kristin applied for an instructor's position at the Naval Undersea Warfare Center. When her next tour was over, they planned to move to Newport, Rhode Island.

Tom was looking at houses on a Realtor's Web site when the news about the outbreak reaching America first broke through Game 6 of the World Series.

IV.

THERE WAS NO MORE WORLD SERIES, of course. No more world. No more series.

But looking at the screen always threw him back. Sometimes, it even let him forget.

Tom scrolled down the menu of stations and shows. It was amazing, how much of the old world was still available in digitized form.

There was, in fact, a World Series Channel, with every championship and playoff game ever broadcast on file. It was right next to the Super Bowl Channel (itself bracketed by all Olympics, all the time). A couple of dozen other slots were devoted entirely to basketball, tennis, poker, pool, horse racing, car racing, boxing, and wrestling, and a raft of channels dedicated to all things Xtreme.

Tom had a few minutes to kill before *Beacon News* came on. He slipped past sports to the multiple science and technology streams. Again, Hatfield had smartly had his teams sift through gajillions of Discovery, National Geographic, and History Channel programs for useful data, as well as produce original shows. As such, there was very little bad science left in the programs they aired, except in context, and only to show how far we'd come.

This was genuine public education, the kind of programming he generally preferred. The world was full of stupid stories. Tom just wanted the facts, wherever they might be.

There were dozens of stations devoted to movies and sitcoms and other fanciful relics from the bygone days, subcategorized by geeks who knew and cared way too much about it, and were determined that not a speck—from *Citizen Kane* to *Three's Company*—was lost.

Because this was San Francisco, there was a lot of weirdo stuff that Tom did not approve of, although the hyper-V-chip security-clearance systems did a great job of screening it from the kids. There'd been only one recorded case of porn getting leaked into scholastic feeds; quickly corrected, the clown responsible got reassigned to the sewage-reclamation plant.

He couldn't get over the prevailing tone of hedonism and licentiousness, any more than he could blame them, after all they'd been through. Ads for weed and worse on most adult stations, not to mention the Cannabis Channel. Personals and pros put their assets on the glass on the Hook-up Channel. Way more hippie nonsense on the San Francisco History channels than he cared to have shown to his nine-year-old. Gladiator stuff on other channels—where contestants dispatched defanged dead folks with flamethrowers and monster trucks—that he blocked so he didn't have to see it himself.

Which led him to the religious and spiritual section. This was where the whole thing got murky for Tom, and also simultaneously fascinating.

He'd been relieved to find that they did *not* have a thousand Christian stations endlessly rerunning the *700 Club,* the long litany of televangelism from Billy Graham to the end. He was a Methodist himself, and that was not how he wanted to remember Jesus. Or have Jesus remembered.

In the same way as Bryce Hatfield—CEO of the City and lord of all that he surveyed—had urged his media staff to weed out the bad science, he had also insisted they weed out the bad religion. No hateful, money-grubbing ministers made the cut, no fire-breathing talk of the Rapture or the Last Trump summoning the dead to judgment.

Instead, the God and Oneness streams were widely representative. There were Christian streams, Islamic streams, Jewish streams, Confucian streams, Buddhist and Hindu and Taoist streams, and so on, down the road.

But they were all presented as relative options of faith—different ways of approaching the ineffable—flensed of primacy, with an emphasis on the cuddly love-and-cooperation bits.

That was kind of okay with Tom.

Much like the political parties had been dissolved—and good riddance to that two-headed nonsense machine—the churches had also been taken down a peg. There was only one line left that truly needed to be toed.

The City was not a democracy. It was a corporation.

You learned to work together.

Or you were on your own.

In the eighteen months since Hatfield's people had gassed the dead-infested City and begun reclaiming it block by block, Tom had seen it mushroom from a few hundred sailors and tech geeks to a stable and diverse city of nearly ten thousand. They grew their own food, used the ocean's currents to generate their own power, and they even had a decent chunk of the old Pacific Fleet. None of that would've gotten done, Tom believed, if someone had stopped to take a vote.

He rubbed his eyes, overwhelmed by the bottomless pit of programming—a trillion trails to distraction—but it was less than a minute to ten, and there was something he wanted to see.

He punched 001 into the remote and was rewarded by Bryce Hatfield's ubiquitous face. Fearless Leader was not a handsome man, but he was impressive in close-up: the once-doughy features chiseled by crisis and gravity, his eyes far too blue, windows into his exorbitant IQ.

"We are all," Hatfield was saying for the umpteen millionth time, "in this together. That's why we count on *Beacon News*. The live local news network that connects San Francisco, 24/7. Letting us all know where we stand. Shining a light on a world gone dark.

"A light you can trust."

The staring contest dissolved to a fancy CGI lighthouse, blazing lamplight endlessly rotating behind the words:

BEACON NEWS.
SHINE THE LIGHT.

Only then could the news begin.

Tom popped his beer with his lighter, watched the bottle cap flip and land in his lap. One of the last Sam Adams in captivity, and cherished as such.

He had a salvaged pack of Lucky Strikes in the left pocket of his robe: twelve left, as of this moment. The second the City ran out of Luckies would be the day he quit.

One cigarette a day was not a big deal. Based on his current stash, he had at least 312 days to go.

Then "*Hello!* And pee-yew!" said the beautiful woman on the screen. "It's ten o'clock, and this is *Beacon News*. I'm Trini Dee. And these are today's headlines."

Tom took a swig of Sam, lit his smoke, and settled back to watch the City's last remaining golden goddess deliver the spin.

Trini had the six-to-eleven slot Monday through Friday. She was stupidly gorgeous and alarmingly smart, with wheat-blond dreadlocks and cocoa skin, almond eyes, and lips that knew just how to grin and win you over, whether you believed what she was saying or not.

Yet another brilliant choice by Hatfield.

That lucky son of a gun.

"The big local story today," said Trini Dee, "will hardly be news to anyone with a nose." A snarky Photoshop graphic flashed a headline over her shoulder: THE REVENGE OF THE TURDS. "It was black and came gushing out of the ground, but it sure wasn't oil. A critical drain blockage sent tons of raw sewage up through toilets and sinks in the Hyatt food court, ruining lunch for hundreds of second-shifters and leaving a stink that Central Air is still trying to disperse.

"Here with a report is Zach Chassler, our man in the underground. Zach, how are you doing?"

The image split-screened to Trini on the right, gas-masked Zach on the left. In the background, someone was laughing.

Tom sucked hard on his smoke, took half the bottle in a swig, closely watching the infotainment.

"Well, Trini," Zach said, "as you can see, things are almost back to normal down here. The block is cleared and City engineers have already restored water and sewage service. Now it's just a matter of venting the lingering, unbearable stench."

"Tell me about it!" Trini pursed her lovely lips. "Any word on how it happened?"

"Trini, no official statement has been released, but rumor has it that a combination of old-city pollution build-up and last night's burrito buffet were to blame."

"And there you have it," said Tom, weary of the fun already.

He didn't blame them for skirting the real cause of the backup. The truth was often too horrible for TV.

What they couldn't say was what hurt him most.

Stuck, as he was, with the facts . . .

V.

TOM HAD BEEN HALFWAY into his eggplant parmesan when the kitchen staff came hopping over the counter, screaming and cursing in four languages.

At first, he thought it was a bomb.

Hot on their heels came the ripe brown stench he'd come to know so well of late: rich as a symphony in its ugly aromas, like a padded brown fist between the eyes.

A moment later, people came sloshing out of the restrooms, shrieking and tracking the awfulness behind them.

Tom swallowed fast, threw down his fork, and began to push upstream against the panicked crowd.

This looked like a job for Sewerman.

Ten minutes later . . .

"Yeah, it's blocked," said the Jeep.

In his rubber hip-waders and matching slicker, the Jeep looked more like the Gorton's Fisherman than a master civil engineer. But he knew the City's tangled underworld of tunnels, sewers, and shafts better than anyone alive before Z-Day.

Tom looked up at the stout outflow pipe that clung to the ceiling of the service tunnel beneath the mall. "But this is just toilet drainage, right? We switched all these things over to the new network last month."

"Yep. And she's already clogged. I told them, but nobody listens." The Jeep cracked three nuggets of Nicorette gum into his mouth, hidden under his full, white beard and curly handlebar mustache. The Jeep normally smoked his pipe like a locomotive, but methane hung thick in the air. "You got rubber boots?"

They called Eugene Prosky the Jeep because he always had all the answers, like the magic little critter from the old Popeye cartoons. After he retired, the Water Department had kept his home number on speed dial. When the City fell apart, the Jeep and six other people, including his grandkids, had holed up in a Civil Defense shelter under the old U.S. Mint. Six months later, the Jeep and the kids were still there. The others tried to escape through the BART tunnels and never came back. Should've listened to the Jeep—

"No, I'll just stand back and let you do the honors. But unless they're dumping trash down the toilets—"

"All kinds of trash ends up down here."

At the end of the tunnel, the Jeep unlocked a gate with his massive ring of skeleton keys and entered the pump house. The toilets and sinks for the entire mall converged on the big pipe that filled the small room. In the past, it had fed into the main sewer line and gone to the southeast waste-treatment center. But in the last few months, Tom had drafted a plan to redirect the sewage lines to the old storm-runoff-control center near the ferry terminal. The plan was to close the loop and recycle the City's waste for the gardens.

It was an elegant solution. Bypassing all the old infrastructure cut through a gordian knot of two centuries of stopgap solutions. It would be simplicity itself, if the fucking thing would just work.

"Stand back," said the Jeep as he gripped the first bolt on the pipe's filter housing with his wrench. "A little more. It's gonna come right at you."

Tom backed up into the doorway. "It's not under pressure. Why don't you just drain it first?"

"I did." The Jeep worked around the housing's hex bolts with the wrench like he was tying his shoes. "Not worried about shit on your shoes . . ."

The Jeep had to stop to cough up a dollop of black snot. Worried, Tom went over and reached for the wrench.

"It's all right, dammit," the Jeep grumbled. "I can do it."

The filter housing tore off the pipe junction all by itself. Tom jumped back, slipped in the gusher of black sludge coating the floor.

"We turned off the intakes at Two and Four, but the pipe kept making noise. Tapping."

The tarry black stew of human waste bubbled and parted. And a hand shot out of it to fumble at the lip of the pipe.

A head rose out of the ooze, bobbing with an infant's wobbly motor control. Bloated and burst and shriveled to the color and texture of a prune, the dead thing looked like a fat old man. But when it lurched halfway out of the pipe and stretched out fractured arms for the Jeep, Tom threw up in his mask.

It was a little kid, maybe seven or eight.

It looked, for just a moment, like Geoff.

Its flesh sagged off the bone like a full wineskin. It had been trapped in the filter screen with hundreds of gallons of sewage blasting over it for God only knew how long. Pinned against the screen, it had swelled up like a water balloon, and now its ruptured innards and stretched-out skin draped from its ribs like a repulsive tutu.

"Jesus, he's a ripe one," said the Jeep. The claw hammer slid out of his belt and neatly crunched up to the hilt in the crown of the mud puppy's skull. It wriggled and tried to twist around on the hammer for far too long, but the Jeep held it with a snake wrangler's ease. "Doesn't look like one of our workers, does he, Tommy?"

Tom had to peel his mask off to wipe his eyes and shake out his lunch. The smell steamrolled his nose plugs and flatlined his sense of smell, leaving it in shock.

"I thought there were no more free-range dead in the Green Zone, Jeep. You said that, and you're always right."

The Jeep shrugged, taking it in stride. "I could think of a lot of things I've been wrong about." He lifted the dead boy's corpse out of the filter by the hammer and dragged it onto a plastic tarp.

"It's a brave new world, all right. And I wouldn't want to meet the fella who's got all the answers now. . . ."

VI.

THERE WAS A KNOCK on the door, but Tom was more surprised by how long and how far he'd gone away. He jerked, and half an inch of Lucky ash collapsed on the sheet beside him, no longer hot.

"Molly?" he called. If it was her, she'd use the key.

The knock sounded again, both reluctant and insistent. Not Molly. Some neighborly thing. But halfway to the door, he noticed the smell.

Despite the AC, it was thick enough to taste.

Dead things.

Tom got his handgun out of its holster on the hat rack by the door. His head went cold and his heart leaped into his throat, but he clenched his hand into a fist until it stopped shaking before he cracked the door to the length of its security latch.

"She's crying again," said Lucius from 4043. Lucius had been a mailman before, but now he supervised a border-patrol squad in the Red Zone. He looked as tired as Tom felt.

"I'm sorry," Tom said. "Is she keeping Terry up?"

"I don't think so. I just heard it from the hall. And, you know . . ." Lucius threw his hands up.

"I appreciate it. Thanks."

"It's cool," Lucius said, pinching his temples. "My boy cries, too."

"If she's still going in another ten minutes," Tom said, "I'll step in."

"Sometimes you got to just let 'em go."

"I know." He looked away from the other man's concerned expression. "You know anything about the smell?"

"New family moving in, down the hall. Think one of the workers sprung a leak. You know, some people actually sabotage them, so they bust open in public. . . ."

They came down the hall toward him on padded sneaker feet. Each carried a stack of cardboard cartons or a bulky piece of Danish modern furniture from the local Ikea warehouse. Tom flipped the safety on the gun and stepped back into his doorway to let them pass.

Their dark green neoprene uniforms were supposed to keep in the stench, but under all the surgical and cybernetic modifications, under all the Z-chips and antibacterial shrink-wrap, they were still dead people.

Eighteen months ago, they ate the world alive, Tom thought. *Now they're helping move the furniture. Tell me that's not progress.*

Tom noted a few pieces of pink kids' gear in the queue and said, "Look out, man. Another family with girls. Your son's gonna be outnumbered."

"Don't worry about him. It's the girls' dads who gotta worry. No new names on the duty rosters, but I heard they came in from outside. Probably pretty shaken up. It must be hell out there."

"Yeah, it must be." The family wouldn't be moved in until after the workers were gone. It would take some getting used to, being waited on by the dead. And it would probably take almost as long to get used to their neighbors. Well-fed, healthy, happy people would be a far stranger sight than walking dead folks.

At the end of the long line of slave units, an operator came shuffling up, whispering and typing commands to his crew on a souped-up BlackBerry. He looked little better than a zombie himself, with dark circles under his beady eyes and a straggly beard. "Sorry about the smell," the operator mumbled. "You got an extra smoke, man?"

Tom almost told him there was no such thing, but then shook one out. Only a shitheel begrudged a working man a smoke. "Take them back down on the service elevator, would you? Our kids don't need to smell that shit in their sleep."

"You got it, dude," the operator said with a flick of his lighter, and skipped off to catch up with his mule train.

Lucius looked after them and then turned back to Tom. "You know what bugs me, man? Our kids are growing up with this. To them, it's going to seem normal."

Tom nodded and sighed. "G'night, Lucius."

Click. And the door was shut, Tom leaning against it, while the dead weight fell inside him.

Listening for Lucius's retreating carpet footfalls.

Listening for Molly, through the wall.

VII.

WHEN SAN FRANCISCO FELL APART, Tom already had a plan. He kept Molly home from school and picked Geoff up from kindergarten. The SUV was loaded with supplies. They were going to the cabin up at Clear Lake.

Between the announcement that there was no reason to panic and the order to evacuate, the freeways out of the Bay Area were hopelessly gridlocked. The army was trying to run checkpoints on the 80, the 580, and the 880, and tempers were wearing thin.

Images of soldiers shooting at cars as they bulldozed through the sawhorse barricades were scary enough, and nobody even knew yet what they were really running from. The blow-dried idiot on the local Fox affiliate called it an outbreak of political street violence and even speculated that immigration protesters were to blame.

Tom's digital scanners were not much help. The police called it a rabies outbreak, then a terrorist attack.

SFO was shut down that morning after an American flight from China disgorged a hundred rabid passengers into the international terminal. Oakland and San Jose kept pushing out flights until the military shut them down.

Watching the chaos on the freeway from his backyard in Richmond, Tom started making calls. The lines were overloaded, but he had a satellite phone, and was able to get through to his friend Russ Blevins, who ran daily operations on Treasure Island.

"Get over here, Tom," Blevins told him. "Get your kids and get out of the house. Don't take the bridge. I don't know who they're trying to fool on the TV, but it's way worse than anybody's saying."

Tom's questions about the attack went unanswered. Russ was shouting at ten other people while Tom bugged him. It wasn't until he insulted the navy that he got any answer at all. "Russ, is the fucking navy retreating?"

"Retreat, shit. We're in free-fall. I have—"

The line went dead.

Tom went out on their balcony and looked at the Bay. A few pillars of smoke rose out of San Francisco—in the Castro, the waterfront, and Japantown, the smoke looked like new instant skyscrapers. Oakland was a funeral pyre.

"Molly? Get your brother and get in the SUV!"

Geoff was on the couch, eating Oreos and drinking milk out of the carton while watching a Batman cartoon, enjoying the holiday to its fullest, even if he had to share it with his sister. But he dropped everything at the commanding tone in his dad's voice, let his sister lead him by the hand into the garage.

They took side streets down to a swaybacked boat dock with a couple of old houseboats tied off on it. Molly helped Tom drag the Zodiac raft off the roof and down to the landing. He strapped the kids into their life jackets. Geoff tried to carry his big sister to the raft, so her feet wouldn't get wet. He'd forgotten his backpack of drawing stuff in the RAV 4, and Tom had shouted at him when he went to get it.

There was a woman standing by the open doors of the SUV. She wore a frilly pink negligee with marabou stork feathers at the cuffs and collar. Her lower jaw hung from the ruin of her face by a few thongs of gristle. Her eyes reflected the reddening sunset, but nothing else.

Molly screamed and hid her face. Tom grabbed Geoff by his windbreaker and threw him into the raft.

The woman came running down the boat landing after them. Her shambling, drunken gait spilled her down the concrete slope. The wind tore open her flimsy wrap. Everything underneath had been bitten off.

Tom had a gun in his breast pocket, but he had no time to draw it. He shoved the raft off and dived into it, yanked the starter, and gunned the throttle.

The poor, ravaged woman wallowed in the shallows, waving her arms like she expected to be rescued.

The water was all choppy whitecaps, and a jolly impromptu regatta was strewn across the Bay, headed against the tide for the Golden Gate. Tom cut among them in the little raft, wondering that more of them weren't seeking shelter at the naval station.

Molly hugged him for dear life. Geoff rode the nose until he was soaked, happy as a dog. The wind coming off the City reeked of charred buildings. His mind raced with all the methodical things he was trained to think in a crisis, but he couldn't imagine how anything could turn so bad so quickly.

He almost got shot landing at Treasure Island. He was warned off by screaming buoy-beacons, and a cruiser anchored off the northern end of the tiny island tracked him with its guns. He wondered if they were shooting civilians yet.

The island was overrun with vets and families and a few hundred lucky refugees. Russ couldn't see him, but passed down orders. He was needed to reinforce the barricades for the offramps on the Bay Bridge on adjoining Yerba Buena Island, and by the way, could he see about helping to arm charges that were set in the spans east and west of the island?

Tens of thousands of angry commuters had faced down the army and were flowing out of the City on both decks of the Bay Bridge and all seven lanes of the Golden Gate. But now the orders had come down from a different authority to "hold and contain" the cities. The infected had breached the Civil Defense perimeter, and the National Guard was swept away by what one short-lived TV reporter described as "really sick people." Oakland and Berkeley were on fire, and mobs of the infected roaming en masse onto Interstate 580 caused traffic to grind to a halt.

Traffic was stopped dead on both bridges, and some idiot had set tanks and bulldozers to work pushing the stalled traffic across the bridges. Trapped in their cars with roving, drooling dead people climbing on the hoods, they were shoved out of the City, into darkness and fire.

Tom saw all this on the news while he and his kids ate hamburgers and chocolate pudding in the officers' mess. He started to ask his kids to leave the room, but they tuned the TV out anyway. Kristin craved Indian food throughout her pregnancy with Molly, and their daughter called anything without hot sauce on it "boring." Geoff played his PSP.

In between jobs, he'd tried to get a message out to Kristin, but the whole Pacific Fleet had gone dark. Nobody knew what they were dealing with, or if they were at war.

Three hours later, they got the order to blow the upper span, dropping it onto the eastbound lower deck to stop any more cars from leaving.

Tom wasn't in the navy anymore. They couldn't order him to do it. They didn't want to do it themselves. If it was him on that bridge, with his kids, struggling to get out of a city gone mad, he'd damn the cowards who shut the door on them with his last breath. But his kids were right here, safe for now, because of his good planning and great luck. The people on the bridge weren't so much like him. They were out there, with the infected. When they couldn't get across the bridge, they would come in here, and there'd be no sorting them out.

He could go on for the rest of his life rationalizing the decision, but it was made for him with one look at his kids as they did look up at the TV screen, and Molly asked, "When is Mommy coming home?"

He left the kids in an impromptu day-care center and joined Russ on the roof of the command center with an older man whom Russ introduced as Rear Admiral Thatcher.

Tom shook the officer's hand and asked, "Admiral, how are the people supposed to evacuate San Francisco if we blow the bridge?"

"We're trying to steer them south down the 280. There's no way out, to the east. Most of the people on that bridge are already dead. And there are several thousand infected crossing the bridge from Oakland. We're not going to contain this situation any other way."

The evening fog had wrapped the whole island in cotton, but it seemed to amplify, rather than muffle, the sounds from the bridge—

wailing sirens, gunshots, and screams like a whole stadium in a meat grinder. The news told them to evacuate to the south. Couldn't be more clear.

"Sir, I've got kids of my own. You can't seriously ask—"

"I'm not asking," Thatcher snapped back. "We already tried it, but some candy-ass civil engineers sabotaged the charges. Give me the goddamn thing."

Russ handed him a cell phone. "This is Thatcher. Tango-72 authorized. Cut the cord, son."

He pocketed the phone and turned away, bowed his head. Something high above the fog roared. By the time he heard the sound, they were way out over the ocean. Fighter jets—F-18s out of Alameda—passing low overhead, just once.

The Bay Bridge was a spectral, impossible landscape unto itself, a miracle too big to have been made by men. But it took them only seconds to take it down.

The concussion was a flat, unpowerful sound, but the fog jumped with the incredible displacement of force. Bulbous fireballs erupted in midspan, halfway to Oakland and halfway to San Francisco.

The building shivered beneath Tom's feet. The night screamed with steel teeth and concrete tongues and bloody human lungs, and then a huge wing of the bridge, so fundamental to the landscape that it seemed like a chunk of the sky itself, subsided and fell thirty feet onto the lower deck, crushing dozens of cars in a concrete sandwich that slowly sagged and tumbled into the Bay.

The steel suspension cables twanged like a gigantic harp, a horribly musical sound louder than the explosions themselves.

And it started to rain.

It rained cars and people. Horns honked and bleated as they fell two hundred feet to smash into the stone-hard face of the water. Headlights made firefly flickers in the mist, picking out awful glimpses of people twisting in the air, clawing at falling cars and at one another, eating and being eaten all the way to the bottom.

"God knows," Russ kept hissing. "God knows why . . ."

If God knew anything, it was that they deserved his worst, and He had clearly sent it.

There was more work to do, and Tom pitched in until he was no good to anyone, and they sent him to his room. Refugees had continued landing on the island throughout the night, and a flotilla of yachts and dinghies filled the harbor. Angry civilians filled the halls. Tom had never been happier to be out of uniform.

A burly older guy grabbed him by the lapels anyway and demanded to know what the navy was doing. Tom hadn't been in a fight since grade school, but he almost decked the guy. "You're scaring people with your noise," he said, as reasonably as he could.

"Scared? Hell, we're furious! I pay taxes, asshole, and I deserve to know what you're going to do!"

"We're trying to keep you people alive. But if you wake up my kids, the navy's gonna have to keep me from kicking your ass off this island."

The guy's wife pulled him away, and Tom shuffled into his room. The guy was just afraid, like anyone, but he was asking the wrong guy for answers.

He eased the heavy, unfamiliar door open slowly, fearful of making a sound. Molly was sound asleep, but Geoff sat bolt upright on his cot. His hands lay in his lap like he was still holding his PSP, but they were empty. He just sat there breathing heavily with his eyes open and unseeing. Tom remembered shamefully those moments when Geoff was throwing a tantrum or something, and Tom had reacted by losing his temper. When Geoff was suddenly shocked out of his whining by the unwarranted volume of Tom's response, he looked just like that. He looked like he was falling inside his own head. He looked like he'd been like that for hours.

"Geoff?"

The boy didn't respond. Tom went over and touched his son's clammy forehead. Geoff jolted in his arms. He'd been asleep with his eyes open.

"Daddy, what happened to my backpack? I need my art stuff—"

"It's in the car. We'll go back for it. . . ." When? Tomorrow? Would all this go back to normal before the weekend? "Or we'll find you something here you can draw on, tomorrow. Right now, you should go to sleep."

"I was asleep, Dad." Putting a healthy dose of offended dignity into his bleary voice, Geoff turned over and slapped an extra pillow on top of his head, just like his dad on a Sunday morning.

Tom lay down and, after washing down two of Kristin's sleeping pills, he did the same.

Even at home, without a pillow over his head, he couldn't get to sleep. The slightest sound would jerk him alert and he'd start thinking, and then he might as well get up. Geoff had inherited his father's nerves.

But they were safe, here. Safe with the navy. He could sleep.

So Tom didn't hear the door open and shut, or anything else, until he woke up six hours later.

And he never saw his son again.

VIII.

SOFTHEARTED MODERN FAMILY MAN that he was, Tom was strictly old school when it came to tears. He wasn't raised to respect or excuse them. Where he came from, they were still a mark of weakness.

He wiped them off before he got out of his chair, and noticed the smell, so thick he was swimming in it. Death.

And burning.

Flipping the safety off his pistol, he grabbed his doorknob. It wasn't hot, but his hand slipped on it, slick with tears and sweat. Cursing, he threw it open and followed his gun into the hall.

The corridor was dark for a split second before the motion detectors activated the lights, but it was long enough for him to sense that he wasn't alone. There was no smoke in the air, no fire, but the stench of scorched flesh—sickeningly, repulsively sweet on the disinfected breeze—made him gag.

When the lights came on, he jumped backward into the wall.

Someone had tagged the wall. In red letters six feet high that marched down the hall—from the elevators to cover the door opposite his room—a huge dialogue balloon said: YOU NEED ME MORE THAN I NEED YOU.

The dialogue balloon's long, slender tail pointed to a service worker standing against the wall opposite Molly's room. A spent spray-paint can was clutched in one gloved claw.

It didn't move as Tom cautiously circled behind it to put his gun to its skull. Stray wisps of noxious smoke leaked out of seams in the service worker's green neoprene cowl.

Pulling the trigger would wake up everyone on the floor, and there was no point in executing it now. Whoever had hacked the worker's Z-chip must've programmed it to fry the worker's brain when it was done with its little act of viral vandalism.

Tom shook himself to get hold of his rage and the fear that pulsed underneath it. Not everyone in the City was as grateful for the safety and luxury they'd carved out of the chaos. Not everybody wanted to go along to get along.

And if they could take control of workers, they weren't just vandals. They were terrorists.

He called downstairs and chewed out the manager, who promised to send a maintenance crew up ASAP. "You're not the only ones who got hit, sir," he said with a groan as Tom hung up.

Tom tucked his gun into his bathrobe pocket and went to his daughter's door.

All was quiet in 4039. He peeked under the door and saw no light. She was now either thinking or dreaming. Either way, the crying had stopped.

But there were whimpers up and down the corridor. Little audible ghosts of orphaned sorrow. Not all of them children.

He sat by her door, staring down the broken worker until he heard her snoring, a half hour later. The big red slogan on the wall ran through his mind, chasing its tail.

And all the while, he listened for the ding of the elevator.

Imagining the dead, pouring in.

He imagined his son clumsily rounding the bend in a natty rubber jumpsuit, now marinated and gravid with shit like the boy the Jeep had plucked from the sewer. Forehead ripe for crushing.

And he asked himself, *If Geoff did come back . . . could I do that thing?*

And the answer was, horribly, yes.

Because something had emptied them. Emptied them all. All the lights and noise and creature comforts couldn't drown out the hollowness at the heart of everything and everyone in the City.

Making the dead much more like the living, and the living much more like the dead.

Violating all our barricades, no matter how well crafted.

Overwhelming all the comforts of home, no matter how painstakingly reconstructed, maintained, and controlled.

"I love you," Tom said to the door of 4039, and the daughter he hoped he'd never have to kill, or live to see repurposed, a year or twenty down the road.

Waiting for the uncontrolled billions that still hungered outside their tiny, frail, brave oasis. Their light in the darkness. Their lone beacon. Their home.

Listening for the ding that—this night—never came.

"I love you," he said.

GHOST DOG & PUP

STAY

Thomas E. Sniegoski

Murphy missed the smell of the air after rain, the multiple scents carried on a cool breeze as he closed his eyes and turned his snout to the wind. He missed the feeling of the moist ground cool against his belly after a hot summer's day, and the refreshing taste of rainwater as it overflowed his water dish.

But more than anything, Murphy missed his boy, the musky smell of him, damp with sweat after a long walk in the woods, the feel of his young but strong hands as they stroked his fur, the salty taste of his boy's skin as Murphy licked his face.

The dog was lying in the grass at the back of the wooded yard that had been part of his home for nearly eleven seasons, watching his boy as he knelt before a mound of earth that had just begun to sprout new grass. The boy was crying as he placed a worn tennis ball in the center of the patch of recently disturbed soil.

So many tears, Murphy thought. *So much sadness.*

He wanted to go to his boy and press himself close, nuzzling his hand to tell him that everything would be all right, but the boy would not have felt him. The boy would not even have known that Murphy was there.

"Mitchell," the mother's voice called out, and the boy lifted his damp face toward the sound, wiping away the tears.

"Yeah, Ma?"

"Supper's just about ready. Why don't you come in and wash up."

The boy turned his reddened eyes back to the small grave. "I've got to go," he said in a voice filled with emotion. "I'll try to come back after I eat." He placed his hand on the disturbed ground beside the ball, as if waiting for some sort of reply.

Murphy stood and barked, as he had every time since . . . but in his current state, he could not make himself heard, no matter how loud his voice. The boy could not hear him.

The boy rose from his knees, brushing away the dirt that clung there, and reluctantly headed for the house as his mother called again.

"Mitchell!"

"Coming!" he replied, chancing a quick look back over his shoulder.

Murphy's thick yellow tail wagged reflexively as the boy turned. He was going to follow Mitchell, running beside him as they had done countless times before, but something distracted him.

Something in the deep woods beyond the yard, stronger now than it had been on that fateful day when the great storm had come.

The day Murphy had lost his life.

Two Weeks Ago

Irene was coming, and everyone was talking about her.

At first Murphy had been excited by the idea of a visitor, but he had soon come to understand that Irene was a storm, growing stronger by the minute as it headed for his home. That morning, as he went out to do his business, he could smell it in the air. It wasn't like any other storm he had experienced: this one smelled different. This one smelled of danger.

The parents had not wanted to go to work that day, but they had to—the mother was a nurse and the father worked for the electric company. Murphy had listened from his place on the kitchen floor, beside his boy's chair, while the mother and father repeatedly told their boy to stay inside, and ensured that the neighbors would check in on him. "I am ten years old, y'know," Mitchell had grumbled as he shoveled another spoonful of cereal into his mouth, milk spilling down the front of his pajama top.

Murphy could understand the parents' concern, but the boy wasn't to be alone. Murphy was there. He would watch over his boy and protect him, even from a storm named Irene.

The morning went along as summer mornings did, Murphy by

his boy's side as Mitchell played video games and watched TV. But the dog could feel Irene approaching, and it made him anxious. He could see it from the windows as the sky grew dark and the trees bent with the gusting winds. Sometimes the rain fell in what seemed like sheets of water, but he had to be brave for his boy.

Murphy had been dozing, flat on his side in the middle of the living-room floor, when he was awakened by the sudden realization that Mitchell was no longer in the room. The dog lifted his head, sniffing the air for anything out of the ordinary, but could find nothing. He had risen to go in search of his boy, when Mitchell came bounding down the stairs, fully clothed, and headed straight for the kitchen.

Curious, Murphy trotted along beside his charge, then sat and eyed his boy warily as he took his hooded, yellow rain jacket from a hook inside the cellar door.

"What are you looking at?" Mitchell asked, pulling on the slicker and snapping it up. "I'm going outside."

Murphy continued to fix the boy in his unblinking stare, trying to convey his displeasure.

"You comin', or are you stayin' inside?" the boy asked, pulling open the back door to a tremendous gust of warm, moist air.

The dog recoiled from the rush of wind, and the boy laughed.

"It's really blowing," he said as he stepped outside and turned to pull the door closed. "Comin'?" he asked, looking at Murphy.

The dog had no choice: he had to protect his boy. He bolted across the kitchen floor and out the door and Mitchell shut it tightly behind them.

It was late morning, but the sky was as black as night, as if the sun, fearing for its safety, had gone into hiding. Murphy didn't care for the way it felt outside, the hackles of yellow fur around his thick neck rising to show his disapproval. The rain was falling even heavier than before, and the dog was tempted to run back up onto the porch, but then he saw the boy, his arms spread to catch the gusts of wind that propelled him farther and farther back through the yard.

Murphy let out a bark and ran across the saturated grass to join him.

"Isn't this great?" Mitchell yelled over the yowling wind and the hiss of torrential rain. Powerful gusts caused the trees to bend precariously, while pushing the boy toward the wooded area at the back of the yard.

Murphy's barks fell upon ears deafened by the storm as he tried to call his boy back. Squinting against the whipping wind and water, Murphy watched as the boy leaped into the air and was carried a great distance closer to the woods by another powerful rush of air. Mitchell laughed uproariously as Murphy crouched low to the ground while the surge of wind tried to toss him away as well. The boy could be a stubborn one, sometimes unaware that he had gone too far, until it was too late.

And suddenly it was.

Murphy watched as the boy leaped again and landed on his hands and knees, the winds immediately trying to haul him up from the forest floor to throw him even deeper into the woods.

There was that feeling again, that one of danger, and it seemed as though Mitchell was finally aware of it, too.

"Think we might need to go back," he yelled, fighting to stand.

The dog couldn't have agreed more, already turning toward the house.

Mitchell took a step in the same direction, but was blown violently backward by a blast of wind even more powerful than the ones before. The sound of the boy's cries as he tumbled along the ground drove the dog to action.

Murphy dived forward, capturing the boy's pant leg in his mouth, and planted his feet firmly, fighting to stop Mitchell's progress. It was enough for the boy to turn onto his belly and grab a protruding root to keep from being carried farther from the house.

Releasing Mitchell's pants, Murphy began to bark furiously, urging the boy to follow him. He could see the fear in his eyes as the boy struggled to his feet.

And then it all came to a sudden, frightening stop, as if it were somehow another day, and there was no such thing as a storm called Irene. There were no howling winds, or driving rain. It was as quiet and still as the early morning.

Mitchell stood, frozen in place, eyes wide with wonder as he looked about. Murphy began to growl, then lunged at the boy, barking wildly. *Can't you feel it? Don't you know this isn't right?* He grabbed the rubbery sleeve of his boy's raincoat and tugged. It was almost as if the boy had been held in some sort of trance, and snapped out of it only as the dog pulled at him.

"Hey," Mitchell said as he yanked his coat from the dog's mouth and rubbed at the sleeve. "Knock it off."

The quiet in the woods was deafening, but as the boy took his first step toward the house, Irene descended upon them again. It was as if she had been waiting, like a cat in a tree ready to pounce upon its unsuspecting prey. She dropped on them, twice as furious as she was before.

The rain fell so hard that it obscured Murphy's sight, and he lost track of Mitchell. Panicked, he ran through the growing puddles, so much water falling from the sky that there was no place for it to go. The wind was like a living thing, screaming and thrashing as it showed how angry it could be. Murphy finally found his boy moving in the wrong direction. He raced to his side, herding him back toward the house.

This time the boy paid attention, grabbing hold of the dog's collar as Murphy began to lead him. But the storm had other ideas. It had more to show them.

The trees started to fall, as if some great beast, invisible in the storm, were snapping them in half and tossing them down, the ground trembling as their weight landed upon it.

His boy was crying out in fear now, but Murphy continued to lead them out, hearing attuned to the sounds of falling trees, trying to steer them clear of every crack, snap, and eventual thud. Mitchell's grip remained tight upon his collar, and Murphy prayed to the Great Old Dog, hoping He would help get them both to safety.

But Irene did not yet care to dismiss them.

There came the most horrible of sounds, a deafening groan like no other, and as they spun around, disoriented by the elemental and sensory onslaught, the ground beneath their feet seemed to open up.

Murphy reared away from the disturbance, and although Mitchell cried out, his grip upon the dog's collar remained firm. The two stood frozen in the storm, trying to get their bearings, and that was when Murphy saw a large, old tree toppled directly in front of them, the muddy earth no longer able to hold its tremendous weight.

Murphy backed away, and felt his boy's hand suddenly absent from his collar. He glanced at the great hole near the base of the ancient tree, and saw Mitchell squatting at the edge, looking down into the crater created by the mighty tree's fall.

"What is it?" the boy hollered over the raging storm, as Murphy came to stand beside him.

But the dog had no answer as he peered down at the strange, flat blue stone at the bottom of the hole.

Now

The sound of his boy yelling inside the house drew Murphy from the painful memories. He trotted across the yard, and passed through the heavy wooden back door into the kitchen. His concern was always for the boy, and he at once located him, standing rigidly in the center of the room, his face splotchy with rage. Murphy was moving toward him when he heard the whimper.

The dog stopped, his blocky, yellow head whipping around toward the frightened sound. The father was standing in front of the stove, the mother by his side, and in his arms he was holding a tiny puppy.

"Mitchell, please," the father began, but the boy would not hear it.

"No, I don't want him; I don't want another dog—ever!"

"Honey, we thought with you being so sad since Murphy . . ."

"You're trying to make me forget him, and I won't," Mitchell screamed, stomping his foot on the floor. "I won't ever forget him and I don't want some other stupid dog to try and make me."

The boy was crying, his entire body quivering with rage and sadness. Murphy was compelled to go to him, to reassure him as he had countless times before, but it was all for naught, for he could do nothing now.

"Couldn't you give him a chance?" the father asked, holding the trembling puppy out to the child.

"No!" Mitchell screamed all the louder, his hands clenched in fists at his sides as he unleashed his anger. The stained-glass panels in the kitchen cabinets suddenly cracked, followed by the shattering of a vase of freshly cut roses that had been placed in the center of the table.

The room was eerily silent, the only sound being the pathetic whimpering of a frightened little dog.

The parents looked at each other, then turned their eyes to the boy.

"I'm sorry . . . I just don't want him," Mitchell cried, then turned and ran up the stairs to his bedroom.

The mother and father looked at each other with concern in their eyes, while the young pup, still cradled in the man's arms, cried out in fear. Murphy stood for a moment, head hung low. He had been afraid of something like this and knew it was only going to get worse. The ghost dog left the kitchen, climbing up the stairs to make sure that his boy was all right. The door to his room was closed, and in the past that would have stopped him, but now . . .

Murphy passed through into the room to find the boy standing perfectly still, staring out the window at the falling night. He padded silently across the room and, standing on his haunches, looked out as his boy did. The sun was failing, and the shadows were growing, and in the darkness beyond the yard, something was stirring.

The same something that had been awakened on the day Murphy died.

Two Weeks Ago
Murphy had never seen its like.

The stone lay at the bottom of the muddy hole, entwined in thick, twisting vines, as if their job was to hold it firm.

Even above the noise of the storm, the dog could hear the sound it made, tickling the sensitive hairs inside his ears. He could see that Mitchell heard it as well, the boy smiling as the song—*that's what it sounded like*—slithered its way inside their heads. And then images began to appear.

They saw the Earth when it was young, a world filled with much beauty—so much green, so much life.

Murphy wanted to run through these primeval fields with his boy, run and run and run, until they were so tired and thirsty. Just beyond the green was a stream with water so cold and fresh that it made them want to run and play some more.

Until a shadow fell over the land of green, blotting out the warmth of the sun, causing the grass to wither and brown and the stream to become stagnant, a breeding place for bugs that would carry disease.

In this new but ancient darkness they saw shadows coalescing into a new form, a skeletal thing that fed on the life of the young world, an evil spirit that grew stronger with the stolen essences of the living, plaguing the earliest tribes of man, drinking in the anguish of each human death and turning loss and rot and decay into its own weapons.

But the world did not care to be fed upon. As Murphy and his boy watched, it gave birth to something new, a comparable force to fight against the evil blight of the shadow thing. A great wolf, full of vibrant life, a beast totem and champion for nature. The world trembled as the opposing entities battled, light against dark, life versus death. The powers were evenly matched, their conflict ravaging the land, until a boy was born from the ranks of one ancient tribe . . . a boy who could stand with the great wolf and add his strength to that of the beast. Murphy and Mitchell were in awe as the primal battle played out before them—the boy and the great wolf dog standing side by side as the battle that would decide the fate of the world raged around them.

Driven to submission by that special boy and his wolfen companion, the evil spirit was bound in the vines of life, and dragged down into the earth, surrounded by the perpetual presence of the world's consciousness, imprisoned by the force that it had sought to feed upon.

Murphy suddenly saw the evil spirit, its body like thick, black smoke, flowing around his boy, and the world going gradually dark as Mitchell began to scream.

Murphy emerged from the dream with a start, jumping back from the edge of the gaping hole. The wind wailed, beating at the woods, as the rain fell again in driving sheets. Mitchell still knelt at the lip of the hole. Fearing for the boy's safety, he approached with caution, hoping to pull him back and away from the hole, and the strange blue stone that filled their heads with images of the past.

Murphy realized in horror that the boy was still in the grip of the stone, staring with unblinking eyes at the unearthed artifact. The stone continued to hum like a hive of angry bees, the sound gradually intensifying, and Murphy sensed that nothing good would be coming from this. Carefully he extended his snout, grabbing at the pocket of Mitchell's raincoat and pulling.

Then he saw it, tendrils of oily black, snaking out from tiny cracks that had formed upon the surface of the wet, blue stone.

Snaking tendrils that were slithering up toward his boy's outstretched hand.

Murphy reacted in the only way he knew how. Throwing the weight of his body against the boy, he knocked him down and away as he placed himself in the path of the striking feelers.

The dog felt a moment's relief as the boy thrashed upon the ground, cursing as he struggled to get to his feet.

But that relief was quickly replaced with incomparable pain as Murphy felt the spirit's bite.

The tendrils of black struck like snakes, darting forward to stab beneath his thick yellow fur, entering the flesh beneath and filling his body with a cold unlike any winter he had experienced in his eleven years upon the world.

Murphy yelped, falling on his side as his boy's cries rose above the storm. The dog felt the dark spirit flowing inside him. He felt its anger at him for thwarting its attempt upon the boy, and even though his pain was great, Murphy took pleasure in the black spirit's frustration, and failure.

Mitchell was at his side, shouting his name over and over again, and it was his boy's plaintive voice that brought Murphy back from the brink. He had to get his boy to safety, he had to get him away from the woods and back to their home.

Murphy managed to crawl to his feet. Mitchell threw his arms about his thick neck, hugging him and asking if he was all right.

Murphy knew the answer, but would not have shared it with the boy even if he could have spoken. They had to get away from this place as quickly as they could.

Looking into his boy's eyes, he barked once, weakly, and turned his head to run. He stumbled slightly, as a numbness began to spread through his legs, but he quickly regained his footing. He barked again, urging the boy to follow.

Mitchell did, following him closely, away from the toppled tree and the gaping hole that held an evil as old as the beginning. Murphy knew that the spirit would not pursue them, its unsuccessful strike on his boy having weakened it, but they still had the storm Irene to deal with.

The wind fought to push them back, and Murphy struggled against it with dwindling strength, hopeful that he would be able to get his boy out of the woods before he was too weak to continue.

His back legs were the first to fail him, and the dog felt himself dropping to the ground, front paws desperately attempting to drag himself farther.

Mitchell cried out, falling by his side, trying to help him rise, but it was too late. The numbness was spreading quickly, and Murphy could not remember ever feeling so cold.

"C'mon, boy," Mitchell said frantically. "We'll get you home and you'll be fine."

For his boy, Murphy struggled to rise, but it was to no avail. Mitchell tried to pick him up, but he was too heavy and they both fell upon the muddy ground as the storm continued to pound them.

"Help!" Mitchell cried above the yowling winds. "Help us . . . please!"

Murphy wished that he could have helped his boy, adding his own barks and howls, but all he could do was lie there, feeling the touch of evil spread through him, stealing away his life.

He felt the boy's tender hand upon his head, and heard his voice in his ear. "I'm gonna go for help. You stay here and don't move. I'll be back as soon as I can."

And then he felt Mitchell's lips upon his brow, a gentle kiss that made him hope he was strong enough to survive until his boy's return.

Murphy angled his head upon the leaf-covered ground to see the boy running away from him, only to be stopped by a much larger shape that emerged from the shadows to block his path. Finding some last reserve of strength, Murphy managed to leap to his feet with a ferocious snarl, ready to defend his boy with every last ounce of his dwindling life, but he quickly saw that there was no need, for it was the father who appeared.

The father had come searching for them in the storm.

"Something's wrong with Murphy, Dad," he heard the boy say, just before all was given up to darkness.

* * *

Now

The thing in the woods—in the hole beneath the tree—had retreated, but Murphy knew that its withdrawal was only temporary, for it badly wanted his special boy.

Murphy turned from the window to Mitchell, who had climbed into bed and was already fast asleep, safe.

For now.

The dog left the room with a new purpose, descending the steps to the first floor in search of the thing that might have been the best hope for his boy's continued safety.

What are the odds that a dog pup would be brought into the house at this very time, when the evil spirit is stirring? he wondered as he padded through the kitchen.

The pantry door had been left open, and newspaper spread out on the floor. He stood in the doorway and stared at the puppy, asleep atop a blue blanket inside a small crate. He had to admit, this pup was one of the odder-looking young dogs that he had ever seen, with his squat muscular body, round head, and pointy ears, just like a bat.

The pup's large, round eyes suddenly opened.

"What are you looking at?" he asked.

Murphy was startled, looking around to make sure that he was alone.

"You can see me?"

"Of course I can see you," the pup answered.

Again Murphy experienced the slightest hint of hope.

The pup lifted his round head, the black nose on his flat face sniffing the air.

"How come you don't have a smell?" the pup asked curiously. "Did you just have a bath?"

"It's a side effect of my current condition, I'm afraid."

"Your current condition?" the pup asked him. "What's that?"

"I'm dead," Murphy said flatly.

"Dead?" the pup squeaked. "As in dead-dead? As in not alive anymore?"

Murphy remained silent, letting the pup work through his reaction.

"You . . . you're a ghost dog?"

"I am at that," Murphy said.

"How did you . . ." The pup gulped, retreating to the back of his crate.

"Die? I died while protecting my boy," Murphy began to explain. "A duty that has now been passed to you."

Then

The pull of the end was getting stronger.

Murphy did not remember much after the father had lifted him up from the forest floor and carried him back to the house.

What he did remember was the sense of relief as he and his boy were taken farther from the woods, the toppled tree, and what was stirring at the bottom of the hole.

Murphy could hear his boy's plaintive cries, commanding him to get up, telling him that he was all right, and if Murphy had been able, he would have happily complied, but the spirit's touch had made that impossible.

The darkness had taken him for a time, and when he managed to stir again, he was no longer at the house. The scent told him he was at the doctor's place—the veterinarian's office—where his boy and the father took him when he was sick or needed his shots.

It was not one of his favorite places, but he knew it was probably the best place for him to be at that particular moment. He could hear the doctor's voice and smell the nice people who usually gave him treats as he left the office. He understood that they were all trying to help him, but Murphy feared that there was very little they could do.

The sudden cold of the examination table through his fur made him realize that the darkness had taken him again. This time he could hear the father's voice as he spoke with the doctor, and felt the touch of his boy as Mitchell gently stroked the fur about his neck.

"I'm sorry," the doctor was saying. "Whatever is causing Murphy's condition is moving too fast for us to stop it."

"Isn't there anything . . ." the father began.

"I'm afraid we've done everything we can," the doctor replied.

His boy was crying now, burying his face in the fur at his throat. Murphy wanted so much to lick his tears away, to press himself against him, to show him that it would be all right, but what the spirit in the woods had done to him . . .

"Please don't leave . . . stay with me," Mitchell whispered, rubbing one of Murphy's velvety ears between his thumb and finger. "Please stay. If only I'd stayed inside like I was supposed to . . ." The boy was crying all the harder now, and Murphy could feel the dampness of Mitchell's tears upon his fur, though he could feel little else.

"I'm so sorry," the boy cried. "I'm so, so sorry."

Murphy hated to leave his boy this way, but he had no choice. He tried to remain longer, to hold on to a body now numbed with sickness, but there was a stronger power at work, and Murphy found himself drawn from his form. Like a bird, he was hovering above the scene in the office. He saw his boy overcome with emotion, holding on to the body of a dying dog.

And suddenly Murphy knew that he was no longer part of the living world. He hesitated for a moment, already missing the touch of his boy, watching as the father tried to comfort him. But Murphy knew it was time to move on.

He traveled up through the ceiling of the veterinarian's office and beyond, higher than any bird had ever flown.

Any living bird.

And he found himself in the most incredible place. It was greener than any other place he had ever seen, and the air was filled with a multitude of incredible smells for him to investigate.

Murphy moved through the tall grass, the urge to run energizing his every limb, when the rabbits appeared. The two emerged from the grass before him, noses twitching, and he let out a bark to scare them away so he could give chase, but they just sat, staring at him with their small, black eyes.

"Why aren't you running?" Murphy asked, bending low and sticking his rump into the air. "I want to chase you."

"Not yet," one of the rabbits said with a shake of its head.

"You can chase us another time," said the other. "When the boy is safe."

Murphy tilted his head to the side, suddenly remembering his boy.

"I'm afraid they're right, Murphy," said an unfamiliar voice, and Murphy turned to see an old man and an equally old dog moving toward him through the grass.

It was the dog that was speaking.

"You look troubled," he said. "What's wrong?"

"I had forgotten my boy, until the rabbits spoke of him," Murphy replied sadly.

"That's to be expected when one travels from there to here," the old dog explained. "Usually one doesn't have to even think of the old life, but I'm afraid that you don't have that choice."

Murphy studied the old man and dog, feeling a strange familiarity about them. "Who are you?" he asked as the sweet-smelling wind rustled the tall grass and made it sing.

"You and your boy saw the message we left," the old dog said. "The one beneath the tree."

And then Murphy knew who they were, only now they were far, far older.

"The boy and wolf dog, the ones that helped the earth capture the evil spirit."

"Yes. We were the first," the old dog said as the man reached out to scratch behind his ears. "As you and your boy are the last."

Murphy didn't understand. "The last? The last of what?"

"The last in a line of protectors," the old dog explained, the breeze ruffling his fur as he turned his dark snout to the wind. "You were supposed to protect and guide him."

"Who?" Murphy asked. "My boy?"

"Your boy is special." The old dog turned his large head toward the old man beside him. "As was mine."

The old dog returned his deep gaze to Murphy.

"These special boys have the ability to shape the world and protect it from darkness. Equally special dogs are born to watch over them and guide them down the correct path."

"Am I one of those dogs?" Murphy asked.

"You were," the old dog said. "But the spirit has grown stronger over the millennia. It sensed a power in your boy that could free it from its prison, and so it struck."

"But I stopped the spirit," Murphy said. "My boy is safe."

"For now," the old dog agreed. "But there is no dog to guide him."

Murphy felt a shudder of fear pass through him.

"The spirit is awake," continued the old dog, "and will try for your boy again."

"We have to do something," Murphy said anxiously. "We have to protect my boy."

"And that is why you will not be chasing rabbits," the old dog said, and the old man nodded sadly in agreement.

"Are we going to return to the living world?" Murphy asked.

"In a sense. But you will be returning alone, and you will not be alive."

Murphy's head tilted quizzically.

"You will be a ghost dog, invisible to most—"

"A ghost dog?" Murphy interrupted. "How can I protect my boy if he can't even see me?"

"The boy must have a guide," the old dog said.

"Yes, but what kind of guide can I be as a ghost?"

"A special boy without a guide can be a terrible thing for the world," the old dog continued as if he hadn't heard.

"Yes, I know, but how can I guide him if . . ."

"A boy must have a guide," the old dog repeated one last time as he and the old man slowly turned, walking away through the tall grass.

"Wait!" Murphy barked. "I don't understand!"

But the ancient pair did not stop. Murphy was considering giving chase when he felt tiny eyes upon him. He turned and saw that the rabbits were still there, watching him.

"I don't understand," he told them. "I was the special dog . . . the guardian . . . but I'm no longer alive."

"You're a ghost dog," one of the rabbits said, pointing at Murphy with a puffy brown foot.

"I am," Murphy agreed. "But if I'm a ghost dog, how can I be a guardian?"

"You need to find a new one," the other rabbit said matter-of-factly.

"A new one?" Murphy asked.

"A new one," the rabbit repeated. "A new guardian."

"A new guardian," Murphy echoed, knowing the rabbits were right. "But how do I . . . ?"

"You're the special dog," the rabbits said in unison, and then they, too, turned and scampered off into the grass.

"You figure it out" were the last words Murphy heard before they were gone.

And in turn, so was he.

Now

The little dog stepped cautiously out of the pet carrier to address Murphy.

"So now you think I'm the special dog?" he asked incredulously after listening to Murphy's tale. "That boy doesn't want anything to do with me, and his parents seem to agree."

"What do you mean?" Murphy asked.

"They think I don't understand, but when they put me in the crate, they were talking about taking me back where I came from."

"But they can't," the ghost dog said, trying to control his brewing panic. "The boy must have a guardian. . . ."

"Yeah, well, I don't think I'm it." With that, the little dog turned away and curled up on his blanket. "Besides, I'm the runt of the litter . . . nobody wants the runt."

Murphy was about to argue that Mitchell was still dealing with the grief of Murphy's own death, but the puppy was snoring, already fast asleep.

The disappointment was nearly overwhelming.

For the briefest of moments, Murphy had believed that he had found his boy's new guardian.

But now he realized it had been just too good to be true.

The ghost dog lay in the grass beside the mound that was his grave. There was still an air of sadness about it, a heaviness in the atmosphere that forced him to remember the day his body had been laid to rest.

He saw it as he'd seen it then, the boy and the father and mother digging the hole that would hold his material shell. They had wrapped his body in his favorite blanket and gently laid him at the bottom of the hole.

Murphy had watched them standing at the edge of the hole, staring down at his body. They were all crying as the boy slowly dropped a shovel full of dirt atop the wrapped and lifeless body. Then they took turns, covering up his earthly remains. And when they'd finished, they laid flowers upon the overturned ground, as the ghost Murphy turned his face to the setting sun and silently howled for the life that had been lost to him.

The ghost dog blinked away the memories, noticing that his boy had come out of the house again. It was late, now, past Mitchell's bedtime. In the days since Murphy's death, the boy had had difficulty sleeping and had often come out to stand, exhausted, keeping sorrowful vigil by the grave in the backyard. And always, the ghost dog kept a close eye on his boy, even though there was very little he could do if the evil forest spirit had chosen to . . .

"You miss him very much, don't you?" asked a voice, carried upon the wind.

Murphy lifted his head in alarm, watching as his boy started and looked about the yard for the source of the voice.

"Hello?" Mitchell called out.

"He was a very good friend, by your side until his end."

Murphy rose to his feet, growling, his eyes scanning the yard for the intruder but finding nothing. And suddenly he knew who— *what*—was speaking to his boy.

Mitchell turned slowly toward the back of the yard, to where the tree had fallen that fateful day.

"It's a shame he had to die for such a foolish reason."

"He was protecting me," Mitchell argued.

"Protecting you? Pray tell, what did you need protecting from out there in the woods?"

Murphy took a stance by his boy's side, barking furiously into the woods, hoping his voice would dissuade the spirit, but it kept right on talking.

"I only wanted to help you . . . to make you stronger."

"Make me stronger?"

"Oh, Mitchell, you are quite the powerful little boy."

"I am?"

"Oh, yes, but you're still very young, and you've not yet learned how to tap in to the special power that lives inside of you."

Murphy could see the spirit's words having their effect upon his boy, wheedling into his mind, making themselves right at home.

"I just wanted to show you how strong you are . . . I just wanted to teach you."

"You killed my dog," Mitchell cried to the woods, his fists clenched in anger. "You killed Murphy."

"A tragic mistake," the spirit whispered. *"One that I wish never had happened . . . but one that I can fix."*

Fingers of dread clutched at the ghost dog's heart.

"Fix? What are you talking about?"

"Your dog's death . . . you . . . we . . . could fix that terrible, terrible mistake."

The boy looked confused. "How? How can we fix something like that?"

"Together, we can bring him back," the spirit whispered seductively.

"That's impossible," the child proclaimed. "People can't bring the dead back."

"People can't . . . but you and I can."

"You're lying," Mitchell said, but it came out more as a question, a question that begged to know if the spirit's words could be true.

Murphy continued to bark, charging into the woods, but it had no effect, the spirit kept talking, slowly drawing the grief-stricken child closer.

"You can't do it alone," the spirit said. *"You need me to help you . . . but in order for that to happen, you must accept my offer."*

The child stood there, fists still clenched, eyes filled with tears of hope.

"Will you do that?" it asked.

Murphy watched the child, hoping against hope that his boy would realize that nothing good could come from accepting the offer from the mysterious voice from the woods.

"Will you accept my offer?" the voice asked again.

"No!" Murphy barked. "He doesn't accept . . . he doesn't want anything to do with you!"

"Yes," Mitchell said at last, and the world suddenly turned to darkness, and the voice from the woods was louder.

"Excellent."

"Who are you talking to?"

The childish voice startled Murphy, and he realized that he was still in the backyard, staring at his grave. It had all been some strange kind of dream.

Or had it?

The ghost dog whipped his head around to see the odd-looking puppy sitting beside him, head cocked to one side.

"Is something wrong?" the pup asked.

Murphy was just about to answer the young dog, when he saw it—a thick mist moving across the ground, an undulating, gray blanket over the forest. It moved as if it was alive—moved as if it had a purpose.

"It's happening," Murphy said as the fog crept toward them.

The pup jumped to his feet, watching the mist advance. "Is that normal?"

"Far from it, I'm afraid," Murphy told him. "What I've feared is happening . . . it's happening too soon . . . it's happening now."

"What is?" the pup yelped. "What's happening?"

"The spirit in the woods, it's coming for my boy."

And with those words, Murphy spun around and bounded toward the house. He had to do something—anything—he had to try.

The puppy didn't know what to do.

He felt the cold touch of the flowing mist before he'd even realized that it had arrived. It touched his paws, moving between his toes, up his legs, filling him with a cold that made his body ache.

He crouched low, barking as ferociously as a puppy could. He might have been young, and little, but he could still do some damage with his needle-sharp teeth.

"*Well, aren't you a ferocious thing,*" said a voice that seemed to be coming from within the mist.

The pup growled menacingly as the mist flowed around him, moving with great speed across the yard toward the house.

"*I could use someone like you,*" said the voice. "*A guardian to watch over and protect me.*"

"Where are you?" the pup asked the fog. "I can't see you."

"*I'm here . . . in the woods . . . I want you to be mine . . . isn't that what you want, too?*"

Images flashed before the pup's eyes, from a time not long ago when he was with his brothers and sisters, so happy with his family. And then his mother had told them how it would be. That her puppies would soon be leaving to be made part of other packs, and that it was likely that they would never see one another again; and if that wasn't bad enough, she had then fixed her eyes upon him to explain that he was the runt—the smallest and weakest of the litter—and that there was a chance no pack would want him. The puppy had howled in sadness, hoping that if he carried on enough, perhaps it would never happen, and his brothers and sisters would remain with him, but one by one, as his mother had foretold, they were taken, until he was the only one left.

And he'd remained that way for quite some time until the man came, and told him that he was needed to make a little boy happy.

Desperate to know the feeling of family again, the pup was excited to belong, even if he was a runt, but the boy who was to be his new littermate had rejected him.

"You can be mine," said the voice. *"You will be my guardian, and I will give you a pack the likes of which you could never imagine."*

The pup waded through the cold mist, moving closer to the forest beyond the yard.

"Will you help me?" the voice asked. *"Will you be mine?"*

"Yes," the pup said cautiously, so desperate to belong.

"Come to me then," the voice cajoled. *"Come and aid me in my efforts to be free, and we shall form a pack that will make the world tremble."*

The pup moved deeper into the shifting fog, and deeper into the woods.

"Come."

Murphy's ghostly form bounded silently up the staircase, determined to get help. The mist was already there, covering the floors in a carpet of gray, like thick spider's silk. The strange thing was that he could feel the cold of it. If he hadn't been so fearful, he would have reveled in the sensation.

The door to the parents' bedroom at the top of the stairs was partially open, and he was disturbed to see that the mist had already found its way inside, making itself at home, lying atop the sheets and blankets, inching its way upward to cover their faces.

Standing in the doorway, Murphy realized that there was nothing they could do to help, and nothing he could do for them. He listened as the parents moaned in the grip of sleep.

In the grip of nightmare.

Murphy retraced his steps, racing down the stairs and back out into the yard, knowing that if his boy was to be saved, he could not rely on anyone but himself. The boy stood by the mound of dirt where Murphy's body lay buried. The cool, gray mist swirled at the bottoms of Mitchell's pajama legs. The dog could see—could sense—that the boy was no longer truly awake, but was being influenced by something else.

Something that had found its way out of the woods.

Murphy hung his head in sorrow as the boy spoke the most disturbing of words.

"I'm gonna bring you back."

And the world moved that much closer to being a far darker place.

The voice had led the puppy to the hole.

The little dog cautiously approached the edge, eyeing the toppled tree and its broken roots that radiated outward in a circle around the base like the dirty rays emanating from a filthy sun.

"Hello?" the pup called out, and the blue stone that covered the floor of the hole began to glow in the softest of lights.

"Hello, pup," said the voice. "Why don't you come closer?"

The pup hesitated and began to back slowly from the edge, but the dirt beneath his feet started to crumble, and he found himself sliding into the hole.

He began to panic, the hard dirt-covered surface beneath his feet making him feel strange.

Making him feel wrong.

"Here you are," the voice whispered from someplace beneath the stone. "Just where I need you to be . . . just where I need you to be so that I might be free."

There were some small cracks in the blue stone, and a cold white light began to seep from them.

"Where are you?" asked the pup.

"Beneath the stone," the voice told him. "Can you see me?"

The white grew brighter—colder—and the pup leaned in for a closer look and a sniff.

"What are you doing under there?"

"A very long time ago, when the world was young, I was put here by someone who felt that he knew better than I," the voice explained. *"I had a vision for the world that he disagreed with, and for that I was placed here, with the enchanted stone above my head to forever remind me of who placed me here."*

"And now you want me to . . ."

"Help me to be free. The stone is already fractured . . . the magic weakening . . . all I need is for you to pull up the pieces."

Something at the far back of the pup's mind told him that it probably wasn't a good idea, but he hadn't been alive long enough to realize the importance of that inner voice, and so he decided to ignore it. He pawed at the larger of the cracks, his black claws clicking upon the hard surface of the blue stone.

"That's it," cajoled the voice. *"Pick at it . . . break it away. Good dog."*

The praise crept into his mind, and the puppy dug all the faster, eager to please.

The crack grew larger, and as the pieces of blue rock broke away, the cold light escaping from the fissure grew all the brighter.

"Yes!"

The pup felt his claws slip into the fissure, hooking the bottom of a fragment of the stone. He pulled it up a bit, before it thudded back down into place.

"Yes!"

The young dog tried again, and again the fragment fell back down. He growled as he continued to dig, becoming more and more frustrated. Finally, he felt his claws take hold, and he managed to pull the large fragment of the enchanted stone upward, so that the cold, white light filled the hole.

And the spirit was free.

The thick gray fog swirled around the boy as if he were wearing a cape.

"Please, Mitchell," the ghost dog begged. "Don't say such things . . . go back to bed."

But of course the boy could not hear him as he stared fiercely into the dirt, his focus so intense that Murphy was certain he could see straight through the earthen layers.

Something moved in the mist behind the boy, and the dog immediately went on the offensive, taking a crouched stance and baring his ghostly fangs as he growled.

The figure in the fog came to stand behind the boy, its features indistinct other than its eyes, which glowed a fiery red among the sooty gray. Though he had never seen it outside the dream, Murphy knew exactly what it was that now stood behind his boy, free from its prison in the deep, dark hole beneath the tree.

"Get away from him," the dog warned with a ferocious snarl, but the spirit moved closer to Mitchell, flowing around the boy in an embrace of greeting.

It was torture to behold, the smoky form of the evil spirit touching the boy, flowing up into his nose, his mouth, and in through the corners of his eyes.

"Stop it!" the dog barked. He lunged at the fog, trying to sink his ghostly fangs into the equally insubstantial mist.

But there was nothing he could do except watch, sickened by what he saw.

Mitchell was smiling now, filled with the dark spirit of the woods, and he dropped to his knees upon the funeral mound, plunging his fingers into the soft ground. His eyes were closed, beads of sweat forming upon his brow despite the cool evening temperatures. The smile that had previously adorned his face contracted into a grimace, his head began to thrash from side to side, and the boy that Murphy loved so very much, and whose safety he now feared for, began to scream.

The dog twitched at a sudden sensation coursing through his ghostly form. Murphy looked around, realizing that something was different—that something had changed—but all he saw was the shifting mist moving across the grass.

His gaze turned back to the boy, who still knelt upon the grave, hunched over, hands buried in the dirt, and then he noticed the strangest of things. The ground was moving, pulsing ever so slightly, and more movement—caught from the corners of his eyes—showed him that this wasn't an isolated event: the dirt all around the yard had started to churn and bubble as if suddenly liquid, as if something was pushing up—rising from beneath.

He heard his boy gasp aloud, and was captured by the look of absolute euphoria upon his young face. The tears were flowing now, streaming from his eyes to dapple the front of his pajamas.

Murphy did not want to look at what it was that filled the boy with such emotion.

All around him things had started to emerge from the dirt—things no more than bones, but now filled with the essence of life.

"I told you I'd bring you back," he heard Mitchell say.

Murphy looked toward the churning mound before the boy, watching as something covered in a filthy blanket pushed itself up from below.

What had once been dead, now alive.

The pup opened his eyes to a brand-new world.

Somehow, he was no longer at the bottom of a muddy hole, but was instead lying upon a freshly mowed lawn, the smell of cut grass and springtime heavy in the air.

The pup raised his flattened snout to the air, breathing in the freshness of the air. It was taking a little while for his young brain to process, but somehow he must have found his way out of the hole and back to the house that was supposed to be his new home.

But something didn't feel quite right. Something was . . . off.

The young dog got to his feet and was slowly making his way toward the house when the porch door opened and the boy stepped out, talking. There was something different about him, he seemed older, his voice lower, more mature, and he was holding the door open as he continued to speak to somebody still inside.

"C'mon, Jack," the boy urged.

The pup watched as a dog trotted out, and was shocked by what he saw. It was a dog, just like him—same color, same everything—only older.

"That's a good boy," the older Mitchell said as the dog happily ran down the steps to the yard below. "I even cut the grass for you."

The pup walked closer so that they might see him, even letting out a yelp that they might notice all the sooner.

But the boy and dog did not react. It was as if he wasn't there.

"They seem pretty happy, don't they?" said a voice from somewhere behind him, and the pup turned to see who it was.

He didn't know the older man or the big black dog with the graying snout. They, too, were watching the boy and his dog as they walked about the yard.

"I don't think they can see me," the pup said.

"You're right," the old dog answered. "It's because you're not really here."

"I'm not?" the pup asked.

"You're here, but you're not."

"I'm confused."

"You're here," the dog said again, looking at the dog named Jack that was now playing fetch with the older Mitchell. "But you're not."

"I'm here," the pup repeated, watching as the ball rolled across the lawn toward them and Jack barreled across the lawn to retrieve his prize.

"That dog is me," he suddenly realized. "That dog Jack is me." He looked to the older dog for further clarification.

"You got it," the dog said. The old man accompanying the dog just smiled and slowly nodded.

"But how can that be me when I'm right here?" the pup asked frantically.

"It's because you're getting a glimpse of something that hasn't happened yet," the old dog began. "You're getting a chance to see a possible future for you and your boy."

"My boy?"

"If you accept your potential as guardian, and Mitchell accepts you."

"He's calling me Jack," the pup said.

"Yes, he is. That's the name he's given you."

"Jack," the pup repeated. "I like it."

"It suits you," the old dog told him.

"So this is what it will be like if . . ." The pup turned his large, brown eyes to the old dog.

"One of the possible views," he said. "With a proper guardian, the boy will grow up a warm, loving person, using his special gifts for the benefit of the world."

The pup, the old dog, and his man watched as Mitchell grabbed hold of Jack, taking him into his arms, hugging and kissing him, as the dog playfully struggled.

"He seems to love me," the pup said.

"Very much," the old dog agreed. "And it's that love that helps to make the boy into what he will be for the world."

"But he doesn't want me," the pup said, tearing his gaze from the affectionate display before him. "They're going to take me back."

The old dog suddenly looked very worried.

"Yeah," he said. "That's a possibility also."

It suddenly became very dark around them, and the pup felt dizzy, stumbling in the darkness.

"What's happening?" the young dog asked.

The old dog and the old man were still with him, but they were no longer in the yard, the wonderful smell of freshly cut grass having been replaced by something foul.

Something that stank of death.

The pup looked around him and was at once afraid. He had been someplace like this before, remembering that he had been taken to another family that had not wanted him, choosing one of his sisters instead. The pup recalled how afraid he'd been of the smells, sights, and sounds of the place: the cars and trucks, the structures that climbed so high up into the sky, and the people.

So many people.

"This is a city," the pup said, looking over to the old dog and man standing beside him. "They scare me."

They were standing just inside an alley between two towering buildings, looking out onto the city street. There was something different about this city, something terribly wrong.

He could feel it all around him, smell it, taste it in the air.

"Something really bad has happened," the pup said, the flames from the burning buildings and vehicles across the street from them reflected in his round eyes.

"You're right," the old dog said, as his man nodded yet again, the look upon his withered face exceedingly grim. "This is one of the other possibilities . . . if you don't accept your role as guardian."

The puppy was scared, but he found himself stepping farther out into the street, taking in the horrific sights around him. The air was filled with thick, black smoke that blotted out the sun, making it appear as night, and there were people running away from something, the look and stink of fear about them.

In the center of a street clogged with burning cars, the pup gazed down its length to see a group slowly approaching.

Is this who those people are running from? he wondered, watching the figures as they grew closer. He noticed that they moved oddly, stiffly, lurching with every step.

All except for the one who led them.

The boy and his dog were in the lead, an army of strangely moving people following behind them.

"That's not me with Mitchell," the pup said, looking toward the old dog for clarification.

"No, it's not," the old dog agreed as he and the man joined the pup in the middle of the street.

"It looks like Murphy," the pup observed. "Did Murphy not die in this view of the world?"

"No, he died," the old dog said.

"But how is he dead if I'm looking—"

"The boy . . . Mitchell . . . brought him back."

And that was when the pup got a good look at the dog walking slowly at the boy's side: the missing patches of fur, the rotting skin covered in feasting insects, the milky white eyes.

"And in bringing Murphy back, he brought them all back," the old dog continued.

The figures behind the boy and his dog were equally disturbing to behold: bodies pale and rotting, covered in dirt, some displaying gaping wounds—bite marks—that had taken their lives.

But had filled them with something dark that had allowed them to come back.

"How could he do this?" the pup asked, watching as Mitchell strode down the street, his dead dog by his side, leading a legion of living-dead monsters in an attack upon the city. "Where am I?" the pup asked. "What's happened to me?"

The old dog and the old man glanced off in another direction, toward a building engulfed in fire. Out in front, a dead man had pounced upon a living one, had driven him to the sidewalk, and was now biting him . . . eating him.

"You were taken back to where you came from," the old dog

said. "A bond was never forged, and the boy was left to the mercies of the spirit from the woods."

The pup stared in a mixture of awe and horror at the sight of Mitchell as he and the living-dead version of Murphy advanced, leading their growing army of the dead.

The boy's eyes were dark and cold, absent of life even though he still had a pulse, unlike the dog and the shambling legions behind him.

"Now do you see how important it is?" the old dog said.

"Yes," the pup answered, but he was suddenly very afraid. There was so much riding upon him, and he was such a little dog.

"There comes a time when one has to open his eyes and become more than how he sees himself," the old dog told him. "To become more than just the runt of the litter."

The pup turned back to the advancing horrors to see that Murphy now stood directly before him, dead white eyes staring him down, the stink of rotting meat and dirt forcing its way up into his nose.

"*You're too late,*" the dead dog said, yet it wasn't Murphy's deep, soulful voice but the one that the pup had heard from the fog, that had lured him into the woods.

And before the pup could react, to tell the dead dog that they'd just have to see about that, Murphy's mouth opened up incredibly wide, so wide that his jaw unhinged with a disturbing pop, and dirt started to pour from his open mouth.

So much dirt that it started to cover the puppy, no matter how hard he struggled to stay above the flowing soil.

"*Too late,*" taunted the voice again as the dirt washed over his head like an ocean wave.

The filth filled his mouth and nose, and the pup struggled beneath its oppressive weight. For a moment he considered ceasing the struggle, and letting the dirt weigh him down as the sense of responsibility to himself, Mitchell, and the world now weighed him down, but he could not bring himself to surrender.

It wasn't in him, for he'd had to struggle to survive since the day he was born, and that was just the way things were.

The pup lifted his head, finding air, and sucked in snorting nosefuls of the precious stuff. He saw that he was still in the hole, broken pieces of blue stone that were no longer glowing beneath him.

He knew that he had done something quite wrong at the bottom of this hole and was overcome with the urge to fix it. Tensing his muscular legs beneath his bulky body, the pup sprang up to the edge of the hole, his front limbs catching the lip and giving him the opportunity to haul himself out from the hole.

Looking around, he saw that the mist still drifted across the ground, and he thought he saw the hint of movement beneath it.

The pup carefully advanced to where he thought he'd seen something moving and leaped quickly back as the smell of something horribly rotted invaded his snout, before it snapped at him.

Whatever it was, it was still partially concealed by the rolling fog, and patches of nighttime darkness, but the pup was ready.

Or at least he thought he was.

The top part of the raccoon hauled its upper half across the ground, dragging the remains of its innards behind it like some sort of tail.

I'm too late, the pup thought, continuing to back away as the raccoon crawled toward him, its yellowed teeth bared in a snarl, and ready to take a bite.

Remembering where he was, and that the hole was close-by, the pup continued to back away, the dead raccoon picking up speed as it came after him. Just as the dead beast lunged, the puppy sprang over the head of the raccoon and the momentum of the dead thing's thrust carried it over the edge of the hole, where it tumbled to the bottom.

The pup peered over the side at the horrible thing as it writhed around in the dirt, trying to drag itself up the side, but with little success.

"Try and bite me, will ya," he called down to the struggling creature.

There was another noise from behind, and the pup whirled toward it, surprised to see even more dead animals—now alive—emerging from the woods. There was a bird, more bones than feathers, a pack of squirrels, their wide, dead eyes glowing an eerie red, and a rabbit, its head a bare skull but its body still plump and fluffy.

Tempted to deal with these awful things as well, the pup curbed the urge, turning away to head back to the house.

Perhaps he was too late, but maybe there was something that he could still do to make things right.

Murphy's favorite blanket, with something now alive beneath it, pushed its way up from the center of the grave.

Murphy watched in horror as the shape squirmed and thrashed, gradually emerging in front of the boy.

The dead were returning to life all around him; long dead, and more recent. Skeletal remains of forest rodents dug themselves out from beneath dirt and leaves while an opossum, its belly swollen with the gases of decay, waddled out from beneath a bush where it had crawled away to die mere days ago. There were even things, their bodies decayed to dust, that swarmed in the air like clouds of gnats.

The boy's special talents were being enhanced by the forest spirit, and the ghost dog had to wonder how far they were able to reach. Murphy recalled the burial place of many humans not too far off where the boy's grandmother had been laid to rest not long ago, and imagined these terrible talents reaching beneath the ground to rouse the sleeping corpses there.

Multiple human dead climbing from their graves.

"And a darkness will spread across the land as the dead replace the living," the spirit joyously proclaimed, looming above the boy, hands of fog resting upon Mitchell's shoulders.

The boy dropped to his knees before the thrashing shape enwrapped in the filthy blanket, reaching down to tear away the deteriorating fabric of this birth sac, to set the thrashing corpse of the dog inside it free.

The ghostly hackles on Murphy's neck rose, the skin around his snout pulling back in a ferocious snarl as he beheld the abomination within.

Mitchell stood back, allowing the reanimated corpse to climb unsteadily to its feet. The boy stared in rapt attention at the thing that had appeared dead but was now very much alive.

All because of him.

"I told you, Mitchell," the spirit cooed. *"I told you I would help to bring your beloved friend back to you."*

Murphy surged toward the boy, and his own living corpse.

"No, Mitchell," Murphy said. "It's not me. Please listen."

The boy did not hear, instead reaching a trembling hand down to pet the dead animal's lowered head. The reanimated dog let out a sound that might have been a groan of pleasure, but could have also been the expulsion of gases caused by rot.

"Just think of all that we will be able to help," said the spirit voice. *"All those loved, and lost to the living, returned to life again. It will be . . . glorious."*

"Don't listen to him, Mitchell," Murphy begged. "It isn't right . . . it isn't natural, what you're doing."

The boy put his arms around the dampened neck of his best friend, hugging him to his chest, resting his head against the animal's face.

"I told you I'd bring you back," Mitchell said. "I told you."

The ghost dog watched, feeling his heart breaking. How he longed to feel his boy's arms around him again, but it just wasn't how it was anymore.

"It isn't me," Murphy said, now mere inches from Mitchell's ear.

And the boy seemed suddenly to stiffen, the hand that he had been using to stroke the dog in his arms suddenly leaving the animal's back. Mitchell stared at that hand. It was covered in fur that had fallen out, and the foul-smelling sweat of decay. The dog turned its milky gaze to the boy, blackened tongue lolling from its mouth, and whined pathetically.

"Your special friend loves you very much, Mitchell," said the forest spirit. *"Loves you even more than you could possibly imagine now that you've brought him back."*

Murphy watched as the boy took the dog's face into his hands, looking deeply into his eyes.

"And I love you, too," the boy said, his voice trembling with emotion. "But you're gone now."

"No, Mitchell," the voice proclaimed in the churning mist. *"No, he's right there . . . your best friend, returned by what you did . . . what we did together."*

"No," the boy said with a sad shake of his head. "No, Murphy's gone . . . he's dead . . . and that's just the way it is."

"*But it doesn't have to be.*" The voice in the churning fog was growing louder.

Mitchell sadly leaned forward, kissing the dog atop his blocky head, again saying his goodbyes.

"Yes, it does."

"*Mitchell, Mitchell, Mitchell,*" the spirit repeated angrily. "*We were so close.*"

Murphy heard the evil intent growing in the voice, leaping to his ghostly feet to bark wildly.

"Get out of there, Mitchell!" Murphy warned, knowing that something even worse was about to happen. "Go, Mitchell. Go!"

"*I think it's time that you let me take control,*" the spirit said as the mists began to roil and churn, and the things that had been returned to life from the dead started to converge upon the boy.

The corpse of the dog was now growling, blackened tongue sliding across yellow teeth as a pocket of insects hiding within the safety of one of its ears erupted, new life crawling out from beneath ears once soft as velvet, becoming a skittering swarm.

Mitchell screamed then, stumbling backward and falling over the putrefying body of an old tomcat that had crawled back there to die. He went down hard, stunned by the impact as the dead advanced upon him.

"Get up!" Murphy screamed, watching as the boy fumbled upon ground still slippery from the succession of rainstorms since the hurricane.

It was sheer torture having to watch what was happening and being unable to react, and the ghost dog tossed his head back, howling to the heavens, begging for someone—anybody, or anything—to help his special boy.

The puppy charged from the dark of the woods with a menacing growl, his compact and muscular body cutting through the still-drifting fog as he made his way toward the boy.

"*Insolent, pup,*" the voice boomed. "*What do you think you're doing?*"

The pup didn't slow down, barreling through the gathering of dead things. Murphy watched in awe as the little dog darted and wove through the clusters of dead animals that tried to nip at him, but the puppy was far faster than the dead, avoiding their attacks as he headed toward Mitchell.

"That will be enough, pup," the spirit warned.

A bird of bones and mottled feathers that had once been a mighty hawk exploded from the underbrush, its talons poised to take hold of the little dog.

The pup came to sudden halt, as the rotting hawk bore down upon him. Murphy saw fear in the little dog's eyes as the winged nightmare attacked.

"The boy needs you!" Murphy wailed, his ghostly form flowing over to scream in the puppy's overly large ears.

Startled to action, the pup darted quickly to one side, avoiding the bird's razor-sharp clutches as it swooped down.

Mitchell lay upon the ground, struggling with Murphy's corpse. The living-dead dog was trying to bite him, mouth snapping furiously as the boy fought to hold it back.

The pup struck Murphy's corpse as if fired from a cannon, knocking the dead dog from atop the boy's body.

"And here I was thinking that you and I would be friends," the spirit's voice said, dripping with malice.

Murphy urged the pup to get up, but the little dog lay upon his side, his breathing coming in short, strained gasps as he sucked in air through his flat face. The puppy was exhausted now, unable to catch his breath.

"Get up," Murphy warned, watching as his own corpse climbed stiffly to its feet and advanced upon the exhausted pup. "Get up! Get up! Get up!"

The pup leaped to his feet with a grunt and a growl, staring into the dead eyes of the corpse dog.

"When you are dead, I shall enjoy making your pathetic, runt-of-the-litter body dance," the evil proclaimed as the animated corpse of the dog tensed its rotting legs to spring.

But the attack did not come, as another voice filled the night.

"No more," Mitchell commanded with authority.

The boy had risen to his feet, the dead animals of the forest still advancing toward him, clouds of the beasts that were no more than dust swarming around his head like smoke.

But Mitchell didn't seem to notice, his eyes directed at a particular section of mist that swirled and seemed temporarily to solidify to reveal something hidden within.

"We're done here," the boy said.

"*Foolish boy, you haven't the strength,*" the spirit proclaimed. "*I am free and—*"

"I said we're done!" Mitchell's voice boomed, and the churning atmosphere of evil seemed to recoil from his powerful words.

"*You're making a terrible mistake,*" the thing in the mist warned.

"No," the boy said, looking around at the reanimated monstrosities that continued to make their way toward him. "I already made a mistake . . . and now I'm taking it back."

With those words the dead stopped in their tracks, dropping to the ground, ashen remains carried upon the night wind.

The dead, dead again.

The pup yelped, jumping back as Murphy's corpse pitched forward to the ground.

"*We could have done amazing things together,*" the voice in the mist rasped.

Murphy could see that the boy was ready, his fists clenched in preparation for what was to follow.

"I think we've already done enough," Mitchell said, eyes darting around in an attempt to locate the remaining threat.

"*This isn't over, boy,*" the spirit warned

But even in his ghostly form, Murphy could feel a change in the atmosphere, a lightness in the ether, signaling that the spirit had fled.

But to where?

That was a question for another time, the ghost dog knew, but for now . . .

The pup sniffed at the dog's corpse as Murphy's ghostly form approached.

"Are you all right, pup?" the ghost dog asked.

"Yeah, I'm fine," the puppy answered. "Is this . . . was this you?" he asked.

"Yes."

The pup and ghost were silent for a moment.

"You must've been a fine-looking dog," the pup said.

"Thanks," Murphy answered.

They both turned to see Mitchell coming over to them. The boy stood there, a grim look upon his face as he stared down at Murphy's body, once again devoid of life.

"He was my best friend," Mitchell said as he dropped down to his knees beside the body.

The pup and Murphy's ghost listened.

"You wouldn't believe how much it hurt when he wasn't with me anymore," the boy said sadly, laying a hand upon the dead dog's side.

"He isn't really gone," the pup tried to tell the boy, but he couldn't understand.

Mitchell looked at the pup, and Murphy saw something promising in the youth's eyes.

"Thanks for trying to save me," he said to the little dog. "You're pretty brave. That's something Murphy would've done."

He took the hand that he'd fondly laid upon his best friend's corpse and lovingly scratched behind one of the pup's pronounced ears.

"Brave and cute, that's a good combination."

"I think you're starting to grow on him," Murphy said into the pup's other ear. The little dog responded by licking the boy's hand.

"You don't even have a name yet," the boy told the young dog, still continuing to scratch.

"You could call me Jack," the pup told him.

"How about Jack?" Mitchell asked him. "Would you like that name?"

The pup licked the boy's hand again, coming closer to him and attempting to crawl up into his lap.

"Nobody will ever replace Murphy," Mitchell said, taking the puppy into his arms and holding him tightly.

"I wouldn't even try," the pup said, snuggling into the boy's warmth, as Murphy looked on, content with the permanent place he'd always hold in the boy's heart.

After

The pull of the afterlife was getting stronger.

Days had passed since the forest spirit's attempt, and things had returned pretty much to normal.

Murphy stood on his back legs in Mitchell's bedroom, gazing out the window at the yard beyond. He could see his grave, where his body had been reburied, and the two rabbits that now perched upon it.

"You can leave now," Murphy heard one of the rabbits say.

"Time to chase us all you want," said the other.

It was a pleasant thought, but the ghost dog turned his head from the window to gaze at his boy, sleeping in the bed, the little dog, now named Jack, snuggled up close beneath the covers beside him.

Mitchell and the pup had become fast friends over the days that followed the spirit incident, and it seemed as though the pup was going to work out just fine as the boy's new guardian.

If the spirit should attack again, the pair would be ready and waiting.

Yes, everything seemed to be as it should, the worries that he'd had since becoming a ghost dog finally put to rest.

Mitchell moaned softly in his sleep, rolling over onto his side, his arm draping across Jack's sleeping body, pulling the puppy closer.

The ghost dog turned his gaze to the window once more, to the rabbits that were still waiting there for him. The old man and the large black dog were out there now as well, waving him on, telling him that it was time to go.

Murphy dropped down from the windowsill and went to the rug on the floor beside the boy's bed.

"Not tonight," the ghost dog said aloud, not knowing if the rabbits and the old, black dog could even hear him. "I think I'll stay just a little bit longer."

Circling once, and then twice, the ghost dog lay down upon the rug with a contented sigh.

To watch over his pups while they slept.

TIC BOOM: A SLICE OF LOVE

Kurt Sutter

WE PEER THROUGH a dirty windshield. In the dying sunlight we can see a small city. Something caught in the middle of urban and quaint. Between the potholes and the lack of suspension, the ride on the old school bus is violent.

A thick red curtain separates the driver's seat from the rest of the massive vehicle. The driver, HORATIO BOOM, tall, lean, nods knowingly as if listening to someone. His scarred, ill-shaven face looks almost angelic in dusk's half-light. His years of life, 35. His years of experience, 335. He's seen some shit.

On the floor next to him, propped up on the step of the swinging door, is a MAN. He's dead. Evident by the fact that he has no head. Boom engages his topless friend—

Yeah, I know. This isn't what I wanted out of life either. Or death, in your case. None of us saw this coming. How could we?

Boom cocks his head in recognition, as if he hears the response—

That's real true. Man only knows as—

Suddenly Boom's face contorts and twitches, and in a strained, caustic voice, he blurts out—

MOTHERFUCK TIT CUNT ME!

Then as quickly as it erupted, the spasm fades and Boom continues his sentence with his previous level of control—

Only knows as much as he can see.

Boom turns, making a point to *see* his passenger as he listens—

Oh, yeah. I'm sorry. Get so caught up in the big-picture stuff, forget my manners. It's good to meet you, Ed. My name's Horatio Boom.

Boom smiles at the man's reply that clearly only he can hear—

Yeah, Boom. An unfortunate exchange at Ellis Island turned Philippe Garabune into Phil Gary Boom. My grandfather didn't like conflict. My friends call me Tic . . . for obvious reasons.

Boom pauses as he takes in his passenger's inquiry.

Oh . . . it's not all that interesting. I really want to talk about you.

Boom shrugs at the imaginary insistence—

Yeah, all right. I was born at 11:08 P.M., on Monday, December 8, 1980. Exactly two minutes after Chapman shot John Lennon four times in the back. My mother said my affliction was clearly a result of God's retribution, punishing the world for the devastation brought to one of his angels. Mom was a big Beatles fan. She was also certifiably insane.

Boom takes in the imaginary feedback, nods appreciatively—

She did the best she could. Not much was known about Tourette's Syndrome in the early eighties. Even after the doctors diagnosed me, my mother insisted my ailment was a divine correction. She refused to seek treatment, kept me sheltered. Caged like a spastic bird.

Boom gives his passenger an ironic glance—

Mom shunned science and embraced the absurdity of the religious arcane. Little did we know, she'd be right.

Boom can't help but offer a sad laugh. Then his friend asks a potent question that gets a pensive reply—

I remember all of it. Like it happened this morning.

As the bad memories flood his mind, his tone shifts. The weight of his recall lowers Boom's timber—

When the Devastation began, I watched the intelligentsia try to shed some light—a plague, a mutant gene, some kind of supervirus? They identified it as a Neurodegenerative Deficiency, but we all knew that meant nothing. All it did was give them a nickname, the NODS, but other than that, the science was all smoke. They had no idea what it was, what caused it, or how to stop it. Nothing made sense—

Again his face contorts, he blurts—

SUCK MY SHIT ASS!

Boom composes, offers a contrite nod, then returns to his conversation—

Politicians, police, the armies—they vowed to protect us, find a solution. Like most of their words, it was a promise they couldn't keep. It's not their fault. How do you stop it? How do you even go about explaining it? Suddenly, the dead just lingered, not alive, but animated. In death they were reborn into a world that shouldn't exist. Brains void of memory or logic, driven by primal fear. Trust me, I know what that feels like. Fear quickly becomes rage. Instincts control your actions. Soon you hunt and feed like any other animal. Survival.

Boom looks at the headless man. Sincerely—

I saved you from that. You know that, right?

Boom gets the response he wanted. Thanks the man with a glance. Listens. After a long, lost moment he continues—

As I watched the populous fall to the NODS, creating more dead . . . the Devastation exploded exponentially. It was like watching a bad horror movie in slow motion. Cities, states, countries . . . they fell in less than a year. By the time we all realized it was the Apocalypse, it was too late. We laughed at the religious freaks who claimed it was the End of Days. We knew man would live forever. We knew nothing. Our lust, greed, and condemnation of all things holy reached a breaking point. Evil outweighed good and God gave up on us. The punishment was in play.

Boom slows the bus to a stop, turns to the quiet torso, and with the conviction of a holy man he shares his truth—

And that's really why I need to talk to you. It's why I brought you here. You see, God spoke to me through a man who couldn't speak. I was lost, running in a blind panic like everyone else. Yet, somehow I stayed alive while those around me fell to their hunger. And then on a cold November morning, I found a man sitting outside my bus. Like you, his head was nowhere to be found. And yet, like you, he spoke to me in a clear, sweet voice. He told me I was God's shepherd. Me, a man of no faith, little ambition. A messy amalgamation of genetic and familial flaws. How could I—

Boom tics—

CUNT, CUNT! FUCK BLOOD ME!

He regains composure and continues, his passion rising—

How could I save souls? Then he explained it to me. The reason the scourge hadn't afflicted me was because of my disorder. This brutal syndrome that reduces me to vulgar rants somehow protected me from the dead. God gave me the repellent. So you see, my mother was right, my affliction was divine. But it wasn't retribution, it was a gift. I am the salvation of man. Me. Tic Boom. But now I need to know more. I need to know how I'm doing. So I ask you, are you another prophet? Can you tell me, am I making a difference?

Boom waits, then gets his response. His body relaxes, calmed by the weight of disappointment.

Okay. Okay, I understand. I'm sorry. . . . Thanks for listening. I appreciate it.

Boom smiles—

Yeah, me too. I'll see you at dinner.

Then Boom looks out the windshield, surveys the quiet hood, checks his watch. He stands, grabs a large leather satchel, slings it over his shoulder, and calls to the back—

I love you, sweetheart. Boys, keep an eye on your mom. Make sure you stay in the bus.

He leans into the curtain and hears a woman's voice—

We miss you already. Be safe.

The boys chime in—

See you later. Love you, Dad.

Boom smiles. He hops over the corpse, swings open the door, and exits the vehicle.

As he locks the bus door with a padlock, we see the side of the vehicle is covered in CROSSES and hastily painted sayings: GOD LOVES YOU. I AM THY SHEPHERD. THE LOST SHALL BE FOUND. Hitched to the back of the bus is a small trailer, on it, a road-worn 1968 Harley Shovelhead.

Boom rolls the bike off the trailer, kick-starts it, and roars into town.

Night arrives as Boom rides. The city is deserted. No lights, no people. It's as if someone scooped away the sweetness of humanity and left the empty cone as a reminder of how bland everything is without the flavor of man.

Boom stops in front of an alley, hops off his bike, and disappears into the shadows between the buildings. Moments later, he emerges with the end of a thick rope, which he tightly ties to an eye-hitch welded on the back of the Shovelhead. The rope is moving on its own. Something on the unseen end is pulling, twisting it like a thick hemp fish line. Boom hops on his bike. Bows his head—

Dear God. Give me the strength to follow your calling. To save the souls I can today. Knowing that one day when the saved outnumber the lost, the Devastation will end. And these poor creatures will have peace. Then mankind, like Adam and Eve, will be pure and free and live in blessed gratitude for this bountiful world you have provided. Amen.

Boom ends his prayer with a quick sign of the cross, then starts the bike and accelerates. As he does, the rope pulls out of the alley, revealing the source of its action—CATS. The rope is wired with thick hooks, fifteen feline victims are snagged at the head and mouth. Some hooks are free of catch, with the fish bait still attached. The cats SCREAM and YOWL as they are dragged through the street. Boom rides slowly down the main boulevard. The pavement ripping through mange leaving a trail of blood and fur.

Within moments, the NODS appear. Seemingly from thin air. Hiding in the shadows like frightened children, they stumble awkwardly into the moonlight. Their senses on fire with the smell of blood, they begin to follow the cat trail. They move slowly at first, but then as dozens amass, they take on a mob mentality. The lumbering picks up pace and turns to frenetic running. Boom throttles the old Harley, keeping the kitty bait just out of reach, but moving slowly enough to engage their anxious pursuit.

Soon Boom sees his destination ahead. A Chevron station. He speeds up, pulls away from the dead pack. Then quickly turns into the dark gas station, hops off his bike, and runs inside the gas mart. Inside, he throws a pump switch, grabs a few bags of Skittles, and exits.

The NODS approach quickly. Boom reaches inside his leather satchel and pulls out a well-honed garden machete. He cuts the rope from the back of the Shovelhead and pulls the gas nozzle from the pump. He hits Premium and jams the end of the thick rope into the nozzle trigger to engage the fuel. Gas begins to flow. Then Boom hops on the Harley and speeds away as the petrol pools around the raw cats.

The dead are on their prey. Twenty, maybe thirty of them begin to rip and claw at the feline feast. Some on their knees, some spinning in euphoric madness. It's an awful thing to witness.

But Boom does. He eats Skittles as he watches from across the street. The NODS congregate like crazed roaches in his self-serve trap. After he finishes his snack, Boom pulls a flare gun from his bag. He takes a deep breath, then fires at the Chevron. The obvious result. The fuel catches fire and explodes in a blinding whoosh. Then as the flames get drafted down into the underground tanks, they explode. Violently, one after the other, four tanks blow the station and its corner acreage apart. The dead are ripped to pieces. Some try to escape, but succumb to the flames, melting into the crumbling pavement. Boom is pleased—

There's another thirty-two for you, God.

The big bang and light show reveal other NODS. Most cower in their now-unshadowed crevices, staring at the flames. Mesmerized. Several of the dead spot Boom. Their senses alert with living flesh. They begin to move toward our hero. Boom, unfazed by their approach, hops off the Harley and walks fearlessly toward the oncoming pack. The sight of them triggers his malady, he contorts and blurts—

BITCH SUCK MY FUCK HARD!

The NODS stop in their tracks. Another fit—

233

CLIT MAKER DOUCHE PUSSY!

Now the dead begin to retreat, panicked by Boom. He chases them, quickly overtaking their broken coordination. With swift, calm waves of the machete, he lops off the heads of the devastated. It's over as quickly as it began.

Thirty-eight.

Boom wipes the ooze-glazed blade on the leg of a saved NOD. As he turns to walk back to his bike, he sees someone else approaching—an elderly WOMAN. Alive. She sizes up Boom and realizes—

You're human. You're alive. . . .

Boom takes in the desperate woman. He walks toward her, reassuring her as he does—

Yes. I'm alive.

The woman begins to weep with joy—

Oh my God. Thank you. Thank you. I knew I wasn't alone. I knew if I prayed hard enough, God would send help.

Boom embraces the woman, comforts her—

Yes, he did.

Then in a flash of steel, Boom slices off her head with the machete. It happens so fast, it takes time for her body to realize it has no top. Boom kneels, cradles the woman in his arms, seemingly unaware of the quarts of blood pumping from her arteries. He listens to her politely, then—

You're welcome.

Boom nods knowingly—

Yes, I know. My name's Horatio.

Boom waits for her introduction—

Very nice to meet you, Abigail. Do you mind if we ride? I'm so tired and the night wind wakes me up.

Boom listens—

Thank you.

He lays the headless woman across his gas tank like a cowboy would drape the wounded over a horse. He assures Abigail—

No. I won't let you fall.

Boom starts the Harley and rides off.

As the half-moon slides directly overhead, the Shovelhead pulls up next to the bus. It's still incredibly quiet. Boom throws the old woman over his shoulder and unlocks the padlock. He pushes open the door and gently drops the woman down next to the headless man, calls to the back—

Hey, baby, I'm home.

He slides open the heavy red curtain, grabs the man and woman by a leg, and drags them deeper into the bus—

I brought someone else home for dinner. I think you'll like her.

The bus has been converted into a makeshift RV. A simple kitchen, a couch, books, candles. Almost homey. Then we see iron mesh at the back of the vehicle and realize that it wasn't a school bus, it was a prison transport bus. The back three rows caged for dangerous criminals. As Boom approaches, we see three people in the cage. His family, MARTHA, ELLIOT, and PAUL. Martha, in a clean simple dress, his sons in neat khakis and sports jerseys. They'd be the ideal

American family if they weren't all dead. His wife and kids are NODS.

They smell living flesh and begin to move frenetically in the confined space. Bouncing off one another like angry monkeys. They rush to the face of the cage, snarling in fear-fueled rage. As Boom nears the cage door, he tics—

LICK COCK FUCKER MOW ME!

His family panics and backs away from the door as Boom unlocks it.

Here you go. Eat up. Boys, makes sure your mom gets her share.

Boom tosses in the two headless corpses and relocks the cage. Martha and the boys dig into their dinner.

Boom drops down on a bench near the thick curtain. He pulls the other bag of Skittles from his pocket and joins his family in a quick meal. He glances up and watches as the three people he loves the most rip and claw at human flesh.

After a moment, he reaches up, grabs an old PHONE-MESSAGE MACHINE off the counter, next to the red curtain. He hits the button and listens—

We miss you already. Be safe.

See you later. Love you, Dad.

Boom rewinds a bit and hits the button again—

See you later. Love you, Dad.

And again—

Love you, Dad.

And again.

JACK AND JILL

Jonathan Maberry

1

JACK PORTER WAS twelve going on never grow up.

He was one of the walking dead.

He knew it. Everyone knew it.

Remission was not a reprieve; it just put you in a longer line at the airport. Jack had seen what happened to his cousin Toby. Three remissions in three years. Hope pushed Toby into a corner and beat the shit out of him each time. Toby was a ghost in third grade, a skeleton in fourth grade, a withered thing in a bed by the end of fifth grade, and bones in a box before sixth grade even started. All that hope had accomplished was to make everyone more afraid.

Now it was Jack's turn.

Chemo, radiation. Bone marrow transplants. Even surgery.

Like they say in the movies, life sucks and then you die.

So, yeah, life sucked.

What there was of it.

What there was left.

Jack sat cross-legged on the edge of his bed, watching the weatherman on TV talk about the big storm that was about to hit. He kept going on and on about the dangers of floods and there was a continuous scroll across the bottom of the screen that listed the evacuation shelters.

Jack ate dry Honey Nut Cheerios out of a bowl and thought about floods. The east bend of the river was one hundred feet from the house. Uncle Roger liked to say that they were a football field away, back door to muddy banks. Twice the river had flooded enough for some small wavelets to lick at the bottom step of the porch. But there hadn't ever been a storm as bad as what they were predicting, at least not in Jack's lifetime. The last storm big enough to flood the whole farm had been in 1931. Jack knew that because they showed flood maps on TV. The weather guy was really into it. He seemed jazzed by the idea that a lot of Stebbins County could be flooded out.

Jack was kind of jazzed about it, too.

It beat the crap out of rotting away. Remission or not, Jack was certain that he could feel himself dying, cell by cell. He dreamed about that, thought about it. Wrote in his journal about it. Did everything but talk about it.

Not even to Jill. Jack and Jill had sworn an oath years ago to tell each other everything, no secrets. Not one. But that was before Jack got sick. That was back when they were two peas in a pod. Alike in everything, except that Jack was a boy and Jill was a girl. Back then, back when they'd made that pact, they were just kids. You could barely tell one from the other except in the bath.

Years ago. A lifetime ago, as Jack saw it.

The sickness changed everything. There were some secrets the dying were allowed to keep to themselves.

Jack watched the Doppler radar of the coming storm and smiled. He had an earbud nestled into one ear and was also listening to Magic Marti on the radio. She was hyped about the storm, too, sounding as excited as Jack felt.

"Despite heavy winds, the storm front is slowing down and looks like it's going to park right on the Maryland-Pennsylvania border, with Stebbins County taking the brunt of it. They're calling for torrential rains and strong winds, along with severe flooding. And here's a twist . . . even though this is a November storm, warm air masses from the south are bringing significant lightning, and so far there have been several serious strikes. Air traffic is being diverted around the storm."

Jack nodded along with her words as if it were music playing in his ear.

Big storm. Big flood?

He hoped so.

The levees along the river were half-assed, or at least that's how Dad always described them.

"Wouldn't take much more than a good piss to flood 'em out,"

Dad was fond of saying, and he said it every time they got a bad storm. The levees never flooded out, and Jack wondered if this was the sort of thing people said to prevent something bad from happening. Like telling an actor to break a leg.

On the TV they showed the levees, and a guy described as a civil engineer puffed out his chest and said that Pennsylvania levees were much better than the kind that had failed in Louisiana. Stronger, better maintained.

Jack wondered what Dad would say about that. Dad wasn't much for the kind of experts that news shows trotted out. "Bunch of pansy-ass know-nothings."

The news people seemed to agree, because after the segment with the engineer, the anchor with the plastic hair pretty much tore down everything the man had to say.

"Although the levees in Stebbins County are considered above average for the region, the latest computer models say that this storm is only going to get stronger."

Jack wasn't sure if that was a logical statement, but he liked its potential. The storm was getting bigger, and that was exciting.

But again he wondered what it would be like to have all that water—that great, heaving mass of coldness—come crashing in through all the windows and doors. Jack's bedroom was on the ground floor—a concession to how easily he got tired climbing steps. The house was 115 years old. It creaked in a light wind. No way it could stand up to a million gallons of water, Jack was positive of that.

If it happened, he wondered what he would do.

Stay here in his room and let the house fall down around him.

No, that sounded like it would hurt. Jack could deal with pain—he had to—but he didn't like it.

Maybe he could go into the living room and wait for it. On the couch, or on the floor in front of the TV. If the TV and the power were still on. Just sit there and wait for the black tide to come calling.

How quick would it be?

Would it hurt to drown?

Would he be scared?

Sure. Rotting was worse.

He munched a palmful of Cheerios and prayed that the river would come for him.

2

"MOM SAID I can't stay home today," grumped Jill as she came into Jack's room. She dropped her book bag on the floor and kicked it.

"Why not?"

"She said the weatherman's never right. She said the storm'll pass us."

"Magic Marti says it's going to kick our butts," said Jack.

As if to counterpoint his comment, there was a low rumble of thunder way off to the west.

Jill sighed and sat next to him on the edge of the bed. She no longer looked like his twin. She had a round face and was starting to grow boobs. Her hair was as black as crow's wings, and even though Mom didn't let her wear makeup—not until she was in junior high, and even then it was going to be an argument—Jill had pink cheeks, pink lips, and every boy in sixth grade was in love with her. Jill didn't seem to care much about that. She didn't try to dress like the other middle-school girls, or like Maddy Simpson, who was the same age but who had pretty big boobs and dressed like she was in an MTV rap video. Uncle Roger had a ten-dollar bet going that Maddy was going to be pregnant before she ever got within shooting distance of a diploma. Jack and Jill both agreed. Everyone did.

Jill dressed like a farm girl. Jeans and a sweatshirt, often the same kind of sweatshirt Jack wore. Today she had on an olive-drab U.S. Army shirt. Jack wore his with pajama bottoms. Aunt Linda had been in the army but she died in Afghanistan three years ago.

They sat together, staring blankly at the TV screen for a while. Jack cut her a sly sideways look and saw that her face was slack, eyes empty. He understood why, and it made him sad.

Jill wasn't dealing well with the cancer. He was afraid of what would happen to Jill after he died. And Jack had no illusions about whether the current remission was going to be the one that took. When he looked into his own future, either in dreams, prayers, or when lost in thought, there was an end to the road. It went on a bit further and then there was a big wall of black nothingness.

It sucked, sure, but he'd lived with it so long that he had found a kind of peace with it. Why go kicking and screaming into the dark if none of that would change anything?

Jill, on the other hand, was different. She had to live, she had to keep going. Jack watched TV a lot, he saw the episodes of *Dr. Phil* and other shows where they talked about death and dying. He knew that some people believed that the dying had an obligation to their loved ones who would survive them.

Jack didn't want Jill to suffer after he died, but he didn't know what he could do about it. He told her once about his dreams of the big black nothing.

"It's like a wave that comes and just sweeps me away," he'd told her.

"That sounds awful," she replied, tears springing into her eyes, but Jack assured her that it wasn't.

"No," he said, " 'cause once the nothing takes you, there's no more pain."

"But there's no more *you*!"

He grinned. "How do you know? No one knows what's on the other side of that wall." He shrugged. "Maybe it'll be something cool. Something nice."

"How could it be nice?" Jill had demanded.

This was right after the cancer had come back the last time, before the current remission. Jack was so frail that he barely made a dent in his hospital bed. He touched the wires and tubes that ran from his pencil-thin arm to the machines behind him. "It's got to be nicer than this."

Nicer than this.

That was the last time they'd had a real conversation about the sickness, or about death. That was nine months ago. Jack stopped talking to her about those things and instead did what he could to ease her down so that when the nothing took him she'd still be able to stand.

He nudged her and held out the bowl of cereal. Without even looking at it she took a handful and began eating them, one at a time, smashing them angrily between her teeth.

Eventually she said, "It's not fair."

"I know." As he knew that they were having two separate conversations at the same time. It was often that way with them.

They crunched and glared at the TV.

"If it gets bad," Jack said, "they'll let everyone go."

But she shook her head. "I want to stay home. I want to hang out here and watch it on TV."

"You'll be *in* it," he said.

"Not the same thing. It's better on TV."

Jack ate some Cheerios and nodded. Everything was more fun on TV. Real life didn't have commentary and it didn't have playback. Watching a storm beat standing in one while you waited for the school bus to splash water on you. It beat the smells of sixty soaking-wet kids on a crowded bus, and bumper-to-bumper traffic while waiting for your driveway.

As if in response to that thought, there was a muffled honk from outside.

"Bus," said Jack.

"Crap," said Jill. She stood up. "Text me. Let me know what's happening."

"Sure."

Jill began flouncing out of the room, but then she stopped in the doorway and looked back at him. She looked from him to the TV screen and back again. She wore a funny half-smile.

"What—?" he asked.

Jill studied him without answering long enough for the bus driver to get pissed and really lay on the horn.

"I mean it," she said. "Text me."

"I already said I would."

Jill chewed her lip, then turned and headed out of the house and up the winding drive to the road where the big yellow bus waited.

Jack wondered what that was all about.

3

MOM CAME INTO HIS ROOM in the middle of the morning, carrying a tray with two hot corn muffins smeared with butter and honey and a big glass of water.

"You hungry?" she asked, setting the tray down on the bed between them.

"Sure," said Jack, though he wasn't. His appetite was better than it had been all summer, and even though he was done with chemo for a while, he liked only to nibble. The Cheerios were perfect, and it was their crunch more than anything that he liked.

But he took a plate with one of the muffins, sniffed, pasted a smile on his mouth, and took a small bite. Jack knew from experience that Mom needed to see him eat. It was more important to her to make sure that he was eating than it was to see him eat much. He thought he understood that. Appetite was a sign of health, or remission. Cancer patients in the full burn of the disease didn't have much of an appetite. Jack knew that very well.

As he chewed, Mom tore open a couple of packs of vitamin C powder and poured them into his water glass.

"Tropical mix," she announced, but Jack had already smelled it. It wasn't as good as the tangerine, but it was okay. He accepted the glass, waited for the fizz to settle down, then took a sip to wash down the corn muffin.

Thunder rumbled again and rattled the windows.

"It's getting closer," said Jack. When his mother didn't comment, he asked, "Will Jilly be okay?"

Before Mom could reply, the first fat raindrops splatted on the glass. She picked up the remote to raise the volume. The regular weatherman was no longer giving the updates. Instead it was the anchorman, the guy from Pittsburgh with all the teeth and the plastic-looking hair.

"Mom—?" Jack asked again.

"Shhh, let me listen."

The newsman said, "Officials are urging residents to prepare for a powerful storm that slammed eastern Ohio yesterday, tore along the northern edge of West Virginia, and is currently grinding its way along the Maryland-Pennsylvania border."

There was a quick cutaway to a scientist-looking guy that Jack had seen a dozen times this morning. Dr. Gustus, a professor from some university. "The storm is unusually intense for this time of year, spinning up into what is clearly a high-precipitation supercell, which is an especially dangerous type of storm. Since the storm's mesocyclone is wrapped with heavy rains, it can hide a tornado from view until the funnel touches down. These supercells are also known for their tendency to produce more frequent cloud-to-ground and intra-cloud lightning than other types of storms. The system weakened briefly overnight, following computer models of similar storms in this region; however, what we are seeing now is an unfortunate combination of elements that could result in a major upgrade of this weather pattern."

The professor gave a bunch more technical information that Jack was pretty sure no one really understood, then the image cut back to the reporter with the plastic hair, who contrived to look grave and concerned. "This storm will produce flooding rains, high winds, downed trees—on houses, cars, power lines—and widespread power outages. Make sure you have plenty of candles and flashlights with fresh batteries because, folks, you're going to need 'em." He actually smiled when he said that.

Jack shivered.

Mom noticed it and wrapped her arm around his bony shoulders. "Hey, now . . . don't worry. We'll be safe here."

He made an agreeing noise but did not bother to correct her. He wasn't frightened of the storm's power. He was hoping it would become one of those category 5 things like they showed on Syfy. Or a bigger one. Big enough to blow the house down and let the waters of the river sweep him away from pain and sickness. The idea of being killed in a superstorm was so delightful that it made him shiver and raised goose bumps all along his arms. Lasting through the rain and wind so that he was back to where—and what—he was . . . that was far more frightening. Being suddenly dead was better than dying.

On the other hand . . .

"What about Jill?"

"She'll be fine," said Mom, though her tone was less than convincing.

"Mom . . . ?"

Mom was a thin, pretty woman whose black hair had started going gray around the time of the first diagnosis. Now it was more gray than black and there were dark circles under her eyes. Jill looked a little like Mom and would probably grow up to look a lot like her. Jack looked like her, too, right down to the dark circles under the eyes that looked out at him every morning from the bathroom mirror.

"Mom," Jack said tentatively, "Jill *is* going to be all right, isn't she?"

"She's in school. If it gets bad they'll bus the kids home."

"Shouldn't someone go get her?"

Mom looked at the open bedroom door. "Your dad and Uncle Roger are in town buying the pipes for the new irrigation system. They'll see how bad it is, and if they have to, they'll get her." She smiled and Jack thought that it was every bit as false as the smile he'd given her a minute ago. "Jill will be fine. Don't stress yourself out about it, you know it's not good for you."

"Okay," he said, resisting the urge to shake his head. He loved his mom, but she really didn't understand him at all.

"You should get some rest," she said. "After you finish your muffin why not take a little nap?"

Jeez-us, he thought. She was always saying stuff like that. Take a nap, get some rest. *I'm going to be dead for a long time. Let me be awake as much as I can for now.*

"Sure," he said. "Maybe in a bit."

Mom smiled brightly, as if they had sealed a deal. She kissed him on the head and went out of his room, closing the door three-quarters of the way. She never closed it all the way, so Jack got up and did that himself.

Jack nibbled another microbite of the muffin, sighed, and set it down. He broke it up on the plate so it looked like he'd really savaged it. Then he drank the vitamin water, set the glass down, and stretched out on his stomach to watch the news.

Rain drummed on the roof like nervous fingertips, and the wind was whistling through the trees. The storm was coming for sure. No way it was going to veer.

Jack lay there in the blue glow of the TV and the brown shadows of his thoughts. He'd been dying for so long that he could barely remember what living felt like. Only Jill's smile sometimes brought those memories back. Running together down the long lanes of cultivated crops. Waging war with broken ears of corn, and trying to juggle fist-size pumpkins. Jill was never any good at juggling, and she laughed so hard when Jack managed to get three pumpkins going that he started laughing, too, and dropped the gourds right on his head.

He sighed and it almost hitched into a sob.

He wanted to laugh again. Not careful laughs, like now, but real gut-busters like he used to. He wanted to run. God, how he wanted to run. That was something he hadn't been able to do for over a year now. Not since the last surgery. And never again. Best he could manage was a hobbling half-run like Gran used to do when the Millers' dog got into her herb garden.

Jack closed his eyes and thought about the storm. About a flood.

He really wanted Jill to come home. He loved his sister, and maybe today he'd open up and tell her what really went on in his head. Would she like that? Would she want to know?

Those were tricky questions, and he didn't have answers to them.

Nor did he have an answer to why he wanted Jill home *and* wanted the flood at the same time. That was stupid. That was selfish.

"I'm dying," he whispered to the shadows.

Dying people were supposed to get what they wanted, weren't they? Trips to Disney, a letter from a celebrity. All that Make-A-Wish stuff. He wanted to see his sister and then let the storm take him away. Without hurting her, of course. Or Mom, or Dad, or Uncle Roger.

He sighed again.

Wishes were stupid. They never came true.

4

JACK WAS DROWSING when he heard his mother cry out.

A single, strident "No!"

Jack scrambled out of bed and opened his door a careful inch to try to catch the conversation Mom was having on the phone. She was in the big room down the hall, the one she and Dad used as the farm office.

"Is she okay? God, Steve, tell me she's okay!"

Those words froze Jack to the spot.

He mouthed the name: *Jill . . .*

"Oh my god," cried Mom. "Does she need to go to the hospital? What? How can the hospital be closed? Steve . . . how can the damn hospital be—"

Mom stopped to listen, but Jack could see her body change, stiffening with fear and tension. She had the phone to her ear and her other hand at her throat.

"Oh, God, Steve," she said again, and even from where Jack stood he could see that Mom was pale as death. "What *happened*? Who did this? Oh, come on, Steve, that's ridiculous . . . Steve . . ."

Jack could hear Dad's voice but not his words. He was yelling. Almost screaming.

"Did you call the police?" Mom demanded. She listened for an answer, and whatever it was, it was clear to Jack that it shocked her. She staggered backward and sat down hard on a wooden chair. "*Shooting*? Who was shooting?"

More yelling, none of it clear.

Shooting? Jack stared at Mom as if he were peering into a different world than anything he knew. He tried to put the things he'd heard into some shape that made sense, but no picture formed.

"Jesus Christ!" shrieked Mom. "Steve . . . forget about, forget about everything. Just get my baby home. Get yourself home. I have a first-aid kit here and . . . oh, yes, God, Steve . . . I love you, too. Hurry!"

She lowered the phone and stared at it as if the device had done her some unspeakable harm. Her eyes were wide but she seemed not to be looking at anything.

"Mom . . . ?" Jack said softly, stepping out into the hall. "What's happening? What's wrong?"

As soon as she looked up, Mom's eyes filled with tears. She cried out his name and he rushed to her as she flew to him. Mom was always so careful with him, holding him as if he had bird bones that would snap with the slightest pressure, but right then she clutched him to her chest with all her strength. He could feel her trembling, could feel the heat of her panic through the cotton of her dress.

"It's Jilly," said Mom, and her voice broke into sobs. "There was a fight at the school. Someone *bit* her."

"Bit—?" asked Jack, not sure he'd really heard that.

Lightning flashed outside and thunder exploded overhead.

5

MOM RAN AROUND for a couple of minutes, grabbing first-aid stuff. There was always a lot of it on a farm, and Jack knew how to dress a wound and treat for shock. Then she fetched candles and matches, flashlights and a Coleman lantern. Big storms always knocked out the power in town and Mom was always ready.

The storm kept getting bigger, rattling the old bones of the house, making the window glass chatter like teeth.

"What's taking them so damn *long*?" Mom said, and she said it every couple of minutes.

Jack turned on the big TV in the living room.

"Mom!" he called. "They have it on the news."

She came running into the room with an armful of clean towels and stopped in the middle of the floor to watch. What they saw did not make much sense. The picture showed the Stebbins Little School, which was both the elementary school and the town's evacuation shelter. It was on high ground and it had been built during an era when Americans worried about nuclear bombs and Russian air raids. Stuff Jack barely even knew about.

In front of the school was a guest parking lot, which was also where the buses picked up and dropped off the kids. Usually there were lines of yellow buses standing in neat rows, or moving like a slow train as they pulled to the front, loaded or unloaded, then moved forward to catch up with the previous bus. There was nothing neat and orderly about the big yellow vehicles now.

The heavy downpour made everything vague and fuzzy, but Jack could nevertheless see that the buses stood in haphazard lines in the parking lot and in the street. Cars were slotted in everywhere to create a total gridlock. One of the buses lay on its side.

Two were burning.

All around, inside and out, were people. Running, staggering, laying sprawled, fighting.

Not even the thunder and the rain could drown out the sounds of screams.

And gunfire.

"Mom . . . ?" asked Jack. "What's happening?"

But Mom had nothing to say. The bundle of towels fell softly to the floor by her feet.

She ran to the table by the couch, snatched up the phone, and called 911. Jack stood so close that he could hear the rings.

Seven. Eight. On the ninth ring there was a clicking sound and then a thump, as if someone had picked up the phone and dropped it.

Mom said, "Hello—?"

The sounds from the other end were confused and Jack tried to make sense of them. The scuff of a shoe? A soft, heavy bump as if someone banged into a desk. And a sound like someone makes when he's asleep. Low and without any meaning.

"Flower," called Mom. Flower was the secretary and dispatcher at the police station. She'd gone to high school with Mom. "Flower—are you there? Can you hear me?"

If there was a response, Jack couldn't hear it.

"Flower—come on, girl, I need some help. There was some kind of problem at the school and Steve's bringing Jilly back with a bad bite. He tried to take her to the hospital but it was closed and there were barricades set up. We need an ambulance. . . ."

Flower finally replied.

It wasn't words, just a long, deep, aching moan that came crawling down the phone line. Mom jerked the handset away from her ear, staring at it with horror and fear. Jack heard that sound and it chilled him to the bone.

Not because it was so alien and unnatural . . . but because he recognized it. He knew that sound. He absolutely knew it.

He'd heard Toby make it a couple of times during those last days, when the cancer was so bad that they had to keep Toby down in a dark pool of drugs. Painkillers didn't really work at that level. The pain was everywhere. It was the whole universe because every single particle of your body knows that it's being consumed. The cancer is winning, it's devouring you, and you get to a point where it's so big and you're so small that you can't even yell at it anymore. You can curse at it or shout at it or tell it that you won't let it win. It already has won, and you know it. In those moments, those last crumbling moments, all you can do—all you can *say*—is throw noise at it. It's not meaningless, even though it sounds like that. When Jack first heard those sounds coming out of Toby he thought that it was just noise, just a grunt or a moan. But those sounds *do* have meaning. So much meaning. Too much meaning. They're filled with all the need in the world.

The need to live, even though the dark is everywhere, inside and out.

The need to survive, even though you know you can't.

The need to have just another hour, just another minute, but your clock is broken and all the time has leaked out.

The need not to be devoured.

Even though you already are.

The need.

Need.

That moan, the one Jack heard at Toby's bedside and the one he heard now over the phone line from Flower, was just that. Need.

It was the sound Jack sometimes made in his dreams. Practicing for when it would be the only sound he could make.

Mom said, "Flower . . . ?"

But this time her voice was small. Little-kid small.

There were no more sounds from the other end, and Mom replaced the handset as carefully as if it were something that could wake up and bite her.

She suddenly seemed to remember Jack was standing there and hoisted up as fake a smile as Jack had ever seen.

"It'll be okay," Mom said. "It's the storm causing trouble with the phone lines."

The lie was silly and weak, but they both accepted it because there was nothing else they could do.

Then Jack saw the headlights on the road, turning off River Road and onto their driveway.

"They're here!" he cried, and rushed for the door, but Mom pushed past him, jerked the door open, and ran out onto the porch.

"Stay back," she yelled as he began to follow.

Jack stopped in the doorway. Rain slashed at Mom as she stood on the top step, silhouetted by the headlights as Dad's big Dodge Durango splashed through the water that completely covered the road. His brights were on, and Jack had to shield his eyes behind his hands. The pickup raced all the way up the half-mile drive and slewed sideways to a stop that sent muddy rainwater onto the porch, slapping wet across Mom's legs. She didn't care, she was already running down the steps toward the car.

The doors flew open and Dad jumped out from behind the wheel and ran around the front of the truck. Uncle Roger had something in his arms. Something that was limp and wrapped in a blanket that looked like it was soaked with oil. Only it wasn't oil, and Jack knew it. Lightning flashed continually and in its stark glow the oily black became gleaming red.

Dad took the bundle from him and rushed through ankle-deep mud toward the porch. Mom reached him and tugged back the cloth. Jack saw the tattered sleeve of an olive-drab sweatshirt and one ice-pale hand streaked with crooked lines of red.

Mom screamed.

Jack did, too, even though he could not see what she saw. Mom said that she'd been bitten . . . but this couldn't be a bite. Not with this much blood. Not with Jill not moving.

"Jill!"

He ran out onto the porch and down the steps and into the teeth of the storm.

"Get back," screeched Mom as she and Dad bulled their way past him onto the porch and into the house. Nobody wiped his feet.

Roger caught up with him. He was bare-chested despite the cold and had his undershirt wrapped around his left arm. In the glare of the lightning his skin looked milk white.

"What is it? What's happening? What's wrong with Jill?" demanded Jack, but Uncle Roger grabbed him by the shoulder and shoved him toward the house.

"Get inside," he growled. *"Now."*

Jack staggered toward the steps and lost his balance. He dropped to his knees in the mud, but Uncle Roger caught him under the arms and hauled him roughly to his feet and pushed him up the steps. All the while, Uncle Roger kept looking over his shoulder. Jack twisted around to see what he was looking at. The bursts of lightning made everything look weird and for a moment he thought that there were people at the far end of the road, but when the next bolt forked through the sky, he saw that it was only cornstalks battered by the wind.

Only that.

"Get inside," urged Roger. "It's not safe out here."

Jack looked at him. Roger was soaked to the skin. His face was swollen, as if he'd been punched, and the shirt wrapped around his left arm was soaked through with blood.

It's not safe out here.

Jack knew for certain that his uncle was not referring to the weather.

The lightning flashed again, and the shadows in the corn seemed wrong.

All wrong.

6

JACK STOOD SILENT and unnoticed in the corner of the living room, like a ghost haunting his own family. No one spoke to him, no one looked in his direction. Not even Jill.

As soon as they'd come in, Dad had laid Jill down on the couch. No time even to put a sheet under her. Rainwater pooled under the couch in pink puddles. Uncle Roger stood behind the couch, looking down at Mom and Dad as they used rags soaked with fresh water and alcohol to sponge away mud and blood. Mom snipped away the sleeves of the torn and ragged army sweatshirt.

"It was like something off the news. It was like one of those riots you see on TV," said Roger. His eyes were glassy and his voice had a distant quality, as if his body and his thoughts were in separate rooms. "People just going apeshit crazy for no reason. Good people. People we know. I saw Dix Howard take a tire iron out of his car and lay into Joe Fielding, the baseball coach from the high school. Just laid into him, swinging on him like he was a total stranger. Beat the shit out of him, too. Joe's glasses went flying off his face and his nose just bursting with blood. Crazy shit."

". . . Give me the peroxide," said Mom, working furiously. "There's another little bite on her wrist."

"The big one's not that bad," Dad said, speaking over her rather than to her. "Looks like it missed the artery. But Jilly's always been a bleeder."

"It was like that when we drove up," said Uncle Roger, continuing his account even though he had no audience. Jack didn't think that his uncle was speaking to him. Or . . . to anyone. He was speaking because he needed to get it out of his head, as if that was going to help make sense of it. "With the rain and all, it was hard to tell what was going on. Not at first. Just buses and cars parked every which way and lots of people running and shouting. We thought there'd been an accident. You know people panic when there's an accident and kids are involved. They run around like chickens with their heads cut off, screaming and making a fuss instead of doing what needs to be done. So, Steve and I got out of the truck and started pushing our way into the crowd. To find Jill and to, you know, see if we could do something. To help."

Jack took a small step forward, trying to catch a peek at Jill. She was still unconscious, her face small and gray. Mom and Dad seemed to have eight hands each as they cleaned and swabbed and dabbed. The worst wound was the one on her forearm. It was ugly and it wasn't just one of those bites when someone squeezes his teeth on you; no, there was actual skin missing. Someone had taken a bite *out* of Jill, and that was a whole other thing. Jack could see that the edges of the ragged flesh were stained with something dark and gooey.

"What's all that black stuff?" asked Mom as she probed the bite. "Is that oil?"

"No," barked Dad, "it's coming out of her like pus. Christ, I don't know what it is. Some kind of infection. Don't get it on you. Give me the alcohol."

Jack kept staring at the black goo and he thought he could see something move inside it. Like tiny threadlike worms.

Uncle Roger kept talking, his voice level and detached. "We saw her teacher, Mrs. Grayson, lying on the ground and two kids were kneeling over her. I . . . I thought they were praying. Or . . . something. They had their heads bowed, but when I pulled one back to try and see if the teacher was okay . . ."

Roger stopped talking. He raised his injured left hand and stared at it as if it didn't belong to him, as if the memory of that injury couldn't belong to his experience. The bandage was red with blood, but Jack could see some of the black stuff on Uncle Roger, too. On the bandages and on his skin.

"Somebody bit you?" asked Jack, and Roger twitched and turned toward him. He stared down with huge eyes. "Is that what happened?"

Roger slowly nodded. "It was that girl who wears all that makeup. Maddy Simpson. She bared her teeth at me like she was some kind of fuckin' animal and she just . . . she just . . ."

He shook his head.

"Maddy?" murmured Jack. "What did you do?"

Roger's eyes slid away. "I . . . um . . . I made her let go. You know? She was acting all crazy and I had to make her let go. I had to . . ."

Jack did not ask what exactly Uncle Roger had done to free himself of Maddy Simpson's white teeth. His clothes and face were splashed with blood and the truth of it was in his eyes. It made Jack want to run and hide.

But he couldn't leave.

He had to know.

And he had to be there when Jill woke up.

Roger stumbled his way back into his story. "It wasn't just here. It was everybody. Everybody was going batshit crazy. People kept rushing at us. Nobody was making any sense and the rain would not stop battering us. You couldn't see, couldn't even think. We . . . we . . . we had to find Jill, you know?"

"But what *is* it?" asked Jack. "Is it rabies?"

Dad, Mom, and Roger all looked at him, then at one another.

"Rabies don't come on that fast," said Dad. "This was happening right away. I saw some people go down really hurt. Throat wounds and such. Thought they were dead, but then they got back up again and started attacking people. That's how fast this works." He shook his head. "Not any damn rabies."

"Maybe it's one of them terrorist things," said Roger.

Mom and Dad stiffened and stared at him, and Jack saw new doubt and fear blossom in their eyes.

"What kind of thing?" asked Dad.

Roger licked his lips. "Some kind of nerve gas, maybe? One of those—whaddya call 'em?—*weaponized* things. Like in the movies. Anthrax or ebola or something. Something that drives people nuts."

"It's not ebola," snapped Mom.

"Maybe it's a toxic spill or something," Roger ventured. It was clear to Jack that Roger really needed to have this be something ordinary enough to have a name.

So did Jack. If it had a name then maybe Jill would be okay.

Roger said, "Or maybe it's—"

Mom cut him off. "Put on the TV. Maybe there's something."

"I got it," said Jack, happy to have something to do. He snatched the remote off the coffee table and pressed the button. The TV had been on local news when they'd turned it off, but when the picture came on, all it showed was a stationary text page.

WE ARE EXPERIENCING
A TEMPORARY INTERRUPTION IN SERVICE.
PLEASE STAND BY

"Go to CNN," suggested Roger, but Jack was already surfing through the stations. They had Comcast cable. Eight hundred stations, including high-def.

The same text was on every single one.

"What the hell?" said Roger indignantly. "We have friggin' *digital*. How can all the station feeds be out?"

"Maybe it's the cable channel," said Jack. "Everything goes through them, right?"

"It's the storm," said Dad.

"No," said Mom, but she didn't explain. She bent over Jill and peered closer at the black goo around her wounds. "Oh my god, Steve, there's something in there. Some kind of—"

Jill suddenly opened her eyes.

Everyone froze.

Jill looked up at Mom and Dad, then at Uncle Roger, and then finally at Jack.

"Jack . . ." she said in a faint whisper, lifting her uninjured hand toward him. "I had the strangest dream."

"Jilly?" Jack murmured in a voice that had suddenly gone as dry as bones. He reached a tentative hand toward her. But as Jack's fingers lightly brushed his sister's, Dad smacked his hand away.

"Don't!" he warned.

Jill's eyes were all wrong. The green of her irises had darkened to a rusty hue and the whites had flushed to crimson. A black tear broke from the corner of her eye and wriggled its way down her cheek. Tiny white things twisted and squirmed in the goo.

Mom choked back a scream and actually recoiled from Jill.

Roger whispered, "God almighty . . . what *is* that shit? What's wrong with her?"

"Jack—?" called Jill. "You look all funny. Why are you wearing red makeup?"

Her voice had a dreamy, distant quality. Almost musical in its lilt, like the way people sometimes spoke in dreams. Jack absently touched his face, as if it were his skin and not her vision that was painted with blood.

"Steve," said Mom in an urgent whisper, "we have to get her to a doctor. Right now."

"We can't, honey, the storm—"

"We *have* to. Dammit, Steve, I can't lose both my babies."

She gasped at her own words and cut a look at Jack, reaching for him with hands that were covered in Jill's blood. "Oh, God . . . Jack . . . sweetie, I didn't mean—"

"No," said Jack, "it's okay. We *have* to save Jill. We have to."

Mom and Dad both looked at him for a few terrible seconds, and there was such pain in their eyes that Jack wanted to turn away. But he didn't. What Mom had said did not hurt him as much as it hurt her. She didn't know it, but Jack had heard her say those kinds of things before. Late at night when she and Dad sat together on the couch and cried and talked about what they were going to do after he was dead. He knew that they'd long ago given up real hope. Hope was fragile and cancer was a monster.

Fresh tears brimmed in Mom's eyes and Jack could almost feel something pass between them. Some understanding, some acceptance. There was an odd little flicker of relief, as if she grasped what Jack knew about his own future. And Jack wondered if, when Mom looked into her own dreams at the future of her only son, she also saw the great black wall of nothing that was just a little way down the road.

Jack knew that he could never put any of this into words. He was a very smart twelve-year-old, but this was something for philosophers. No one of that profession lived on their farm.

The moment, which was only a heartbeat long, stretched too far and broke. The brimming tears fell down Mom's cheeks and she turned back to Jill. Back to the child who maybe still had a future. Back to the child she could fight for.

Jack was completely okay with that.

He looked at his sister, at those crimson eyes. They were so alien that he could not find *her* in there. Then Jill gave him a small smile. A smile he knew so well. The smile that said, *This isn't so bad.* The smile they sometimes shared when they were both in trouble and getting yelled at rather than having their computers and Xboxes taken away.

Then her eyes drifted shut, and the smile lost its scaffolding and collapsed into a meaningless, slack-mouthed nothing.

There was an immediate panic as Mom and Dad both tried to take her pulse at the same time. Dad ignored the black ichor on her face and arm as he bent close to press his ear to her chest. Time froze around him, then he let out a breath with a sharp burst of relief.

"She's breathing. Christ, she's still breathing. I think she just passed out. Blood loss, I guess."

"She could be going into shock," said Roger, and Dad shot him a withering look. But it was too late, Mom was already being hammered by panic.

"Get some blankets," Mom snapped. "We'll bundle her up and take the truck."

"No," said Roger. "Like I said, we tried to take her to Wolverton ER but they had it blocked off."

"Then we'll take her to Bordentown, or Fayetteville or any damn place, but we have to take her somewhere!"

"I'm just saying," Roger said, but his voice had been beaten down into something tiny and powerless by Mom's anger. He was her younger brother and she'd always held power in their family.

"Roger," she said, "you stay here with Jack and—"

"I want to go, too," insisted Jack.

"No," snapped Mom. "You'll stay right here with your uncle and—"

"But Uncle Rog is hurt, too," he said. "He got bit and he has that black stuff, too."

Mom's head swiveled sharply around and she stared at Roger's arm. The lines around her mouth etched deeper. "Okay," she said. "Okay. Just don't touch that stuff. You hear me, Jack? Steve? Don't touch whatever that black stuff is. We don't know what's in it."

"Honey, I don't think we can make it to the highway," said Dad. "When we came up River Road the water was halfway up the wheels. It'll be worse now."

"Then we'll go across the fields, goddammit!" snarled Mom.

"On the TV, earlier," interrupted Jack, "they said that the National Guard was coming in to help because of the flooding and all. Won't they be near the river? Down by the levee?"

Dad nodded. "That's right. They'll be sandbagging along the roads. I'm surprised we didn't see them on the way here."

"Maybe they're the ones blocking the hospital," said Roger. "Maybe they took it over, made it some kind of emergency station."

"Good, good . . . that's our plan. We find the guard and they'll help us get Jill to a—"

That was as far as Dad got.

Lightning flashed as white-hot as the sun and in the same second there was a crack of thunder that was the loudest sound Jack had ever heard.

All the lights went out and the house was plunged into total darkness.

7

DAD'S VOICE SPOKE from the darkness: "That was the transformer up on the access road."

"Sounded like a direct hit," agreed Roger.

There was a scrape and a puff of sulfur and then Mom's face emerged from the darkness in a small pool of match light. She bent and lit a candle and then another. In the glow she fished for the Coleman, lit that, and the room was bright again.

"We have to go," she said.

Dad was already moving. He picked up several heavy blankets from the stack Mom had laid by and used them to wrap Jill. He was as gentle as he could be, but he moved fast and he made sure to stay away from the black muck on her face and arm. But he did not head immediately for the door.

"Stay here," he said, and crossed swiftly to the farm office. Jack trailed along and watched his father fish in his pocket for keys, fumble one out, and unlock a heavy oak cabinet mounted to the wall. A second key unlocked a restraining bar and then Dad was pulling guns out of racks. Two shotguns and three pistols. He caught

Jack watching him and his face hardened. "It's pretty wild out there, Jackie."

"Why? What's going on, Dad?"

Dad paused for a moment, breathed in and out through his nose, then opened a box of shotgun shells and began feeding buckshot cartridges into the guns.

"I don't know what's going on, kiddo."

It was the first time Jack could ever remember his father admitting that he had no answers. Dad knew everything. Dad was Dad.

Dad stood the shotguns against the wall and loaded the pistols. He had two 9-mm. Glocks. Jack knew a lot about guns. From living on the farm, from stories of the army his dad and uncle told. From the things Aunt Linda used to talk about when she was home on leave. Jack and Jill had both been taught to shoot and how to handle a gun safely. This was farm country and that was part of the life.

And Jack had logged a lot of hours on Medal of Honor and other first-person shooter games. In the virtual worlds he was a healthy, powerful, terrorist-killing engine of pure destruction.

Cancer wasn't a factor in video games.

The third pistol was a .32-caliber Smith & Wesson. Mom's gun, for times when Dad and Uncle Roger were away for a couple of days. Their farm was big and it was remote. If trouble came, you had to handle it on your own. That's what Dad always said.

Except now.

This trouble was too big. Too bad.

This was Jill, and she was hurt and maybe sick, too.

"Is Jill going to be okay?" asked Jack.

Dad stuffed extra shells into his pockets and locked the cabinet.

"Sure," he said.

Jack nodded, accepting the lie because it was the only answer his father could possibly give.

He trailed Dad back into the living room. Uncle Roger had Jill in his arms and she was so thoroughly wrapped in blankets that it looked like he was carrying laundry. Mom saw the guns in Dad's hands and her eyes flared for a moment, then Jack saw her mouth tighten into a hard line. He'd seen that expression before. Once, four years ago, when a vagrant had wandered onto the farm and sat on a stump, watching Jill and Jack as they played in their rubber pool. Mom had come out onto the porch with a baseball bat in her hand and that look on her face. She didn't actually have to say anything. The vagrant had gone hustling along the road and never come back.

The other time was when she went after Tony Magruder, a brute of a kid who'd been left back twice and loomed over the other sixth-graders like a Neanderthal. Tony had been making fun of Jack because he was so skinny and pantsed him in the school yard. Jill had gone after him—with her own version of that expression—and Tony had tried to pants her, too. Jack had managed to pull his pants up and drag Jill back into the school. They didn't tell Mom about it, but she found out somehow and next afternoon she showed up as everyone was getting out after last bell. Mom marched right up to Nick Magruder, who had come to pick up his son, and read him the riot act. She accused his son of being a pervert and a retard and a lot of other things. Mr. Magruder never managed to get a word in edge-wise, and when Mom threatened to have Tony arrested for sexual assault, the man grabbed his son and smacked him half uncon-scious, then shoved him into their truck. Jack never saw Tony again, but he'd heard that the boy was going to a special school over in Bordentown.

Jack kind of felt bad because he didn't like to see any kid get his ass kicked. Even a total jerk-off like Tony. On the other hand, Tony had almost hurt Jill, so maybe he got off lightly. From the look on Mom's face, she wanted to do more than smack the smile off his face.

That face was set against whatever was going on now. Whatever had hurt Jill. Whatever might be in the way of getting her to a hos-pital.

Despite the fear that gnawed at him, seeing that face made Jack feel ten feet tall. His mother was tougher than anyone, even the school bully and his dad. *And* she had a gun. So did Dad and Uncle Roger.

Jack almost smiled.

Almost.

He remembered the look in Jill's eyes. The color of her eyes.

No smile was able to take hold on his features as he pulled on his raincoat and boots and followed his family out into the dark and the storm.

8

THEY MADE IT all the way to the truck.

That was it.

9

THE WIND TRIED to rip the door out of Dad's hand as he pushed it open; it drove the rain so hard that it came sideways across the porch and hammered them like buckshot. Thunder shattered the sky above the yard like an artillery barrage and lightning flashed in every direction, knocking shadows all over the place.

Jack had to hunch into his coat and grab on to Dad's belt to keep from being blasted back into the house. The air was thick and wet and he started to cough before he was three steps onto the porch. His chest hitched and there was a gassy rasp in the back of his throat as he fought to breathe. Part of it was the insanity of the storm, which was worse than anything Jack had ever experienced. Worse than it looked on TV. Part of it was that there simply wasn't much of him. Even with the few pounds he'd put on since he'd gone into remission, he was a stick figure in baggy pajamas. His boots were big and clunky and he half walked out of them with every step.

Mom was up with Roger, running as fast as she could despite the wind, forcing her way through it to get to the truck and open the doors. Roger staggered, as if Jill were a burden, but it was just the wind, trying to bully him the way Tony Magruder had bullied Jill.

The whole yard was moving. It was a flowing, swirling pond that lapped up against the second porch step. Jack stared at it, entranced for a moment, and in that moment the pond seemed to rear up in front of him and become that big black wall of nothing that he saw so often in his dreams.

"Did the levee break?" he yelled. He had to yell it twice before Dad answered.

"No," Dad shouted back. "This is ground runoff. It's coming

from the fields. If the levee broke it'd come at us from River Road. We're okay. We'll be okay. The truck can handle this."

There was more doubt than conviction in Dad's words, though.

Together they fought their way off the porch and across five yards of open driveway to the truck.

Lightning flashed again and something moved in front of Jack. Between Mom and the truck. It was there and gone.

"Mom!" Jack called, but the wind stole his cry and drowned it in the rain.

She reached for the door handle and in the next flash of lightning Jack saw Jill's slender arm reach out from the bundle of blankets as if to touch Mom's face. Mom paused and looked at her hand and in the white glow of the lightning Jack saw Mom smile and saw her lips move as she said something to Jill.

Then something came out of the rain and grabbed Mom.

Hands, white as wax, reached out of the shadows beside the truck and grabbed Mom's hair and face and tore her out of Jack's sight. It was so *fast*, so abrupt that Mom was there and then she was gone.

Just . . . gone.

Jack screamed.

Dad must have seen it, too. He yelled and then there was a different kind of thunder as the black mouth of his shotgun blasted yellow fire into the darkness.

There was lightning almost every second and in the spaces between each flash everything in the yard seemed to shift and change. It was like a strobe light, like the kind they had at the Halloween hayride. Weird slices of images, and all of it happening too fast and too close.

Uncle Roger began to turn, Jill held tight in his arms.

Figures, pale-faced but streaked with mud. Moving like chess pieces. Suddenly closer. Closer still. More and more of them.

Dad firing right.

Firing left.

Firing and firing.

Mom screaming.

Jack heard that. A single fragment of a piercing shriek, shrill as a crow, that stabbed up into the night.

Then Roger was gone.

Jill with him.

"No!" cried Jack as he sloshed forward into the yard.

"Stay back!" screamed his father.

Not yelled. Screamed.

More shots.

Then Dad pulled the shotgun trigger and nothing happened. Nothing.

The pale figures moved and moved. It was hard to see them take their steps, but with each flash of lightning they were closer.

Always closer.

All around.

Dad screaming.

Roger screaming.

And . . . Jill.

Jill screaming.

Jack was running without remembering wanting to, or starting to. His boots splashed down hard and water geysered up around him. The mud tried to snatch his boots off his feet. Tried and then did, and suddenly he was running in bare feet. Moving faster, but the cold was like knife blades on his skin.

Something stepped out of shadows and rainfall right in front of him. A man Jack had never seen before. Wearing a business suit that was torn to rags, revealing a naked chest and . . .

And nothing. Below the man's chest was a gaping hole. No stomach. No skin. Nothing. In the flickering light Jack could see dripping strings of meat and . . .

And . . .

Was that the man's spine?

That was stupid. That was impossible.

The man reached for him.

There was a blur of movement and a smashed-melon crunch and then the man was falling away and Dad was there, holding the shotgun like a club. His eyes were completely wild.

"Jack—for Christ's sake, get back into the house."

Jack tried to say something, to ask one of the questions that burned like embers in his mind. Simple questions. Like, what was happening? Why did nothing make sense?

Where was Mom?

Where was Jill?

But Jack's mouth would not work.

Another figure came out of the rain. Mrs. Suzuki, the lady who owned the soy farm next door. She came over for Sunday dinners almost every week. Mrs. Suzuki was all naked.

Naked.

Jack had only ever seen naked people on the Internet, at sites where he wasn't allowed to go. Sites that Mom thought she'd blocked.

But Mrs. Suzuki was naked. Not a stitch on her.

She wasn't built like any of the women on the Internet. She had tiny breasts and a big scar on her stomach, and her pubic hair wasn't trimmed into a thin line. She wasn't pretty. She wasn't sexy.

She wasn't whole.

There were pieces of her missing. Big chunks of her arms and breasts and face. Mrs. Suzuki had black blood dripping from between her lips, and her eyes were as empty as holes.

She opened her mouth and spoke to him.

Not in words.

She uttered a moan of endless, shapeless need. Of hunger.

It was the moan Jack knew so well. It was the same sound Toby had made; the same sound that he knew he would make when the cancer pushed him all the way into the path of the rolling endless dark.

The moan rose from Mrs. Suzuki's mouth and joined with the moans of all the other staggering figures. All of them, making the same sound.

Then Mrs. Suzuki's teeth snapped together with a *clack* of porcelain.

Jack tried to scream, but his voice was hiding somewhere and he couldn't find it.

Dad swung the shotgun at her and her face seemed to come apart. Pieces of something hit Jack in the chest and he looked down to see teeth stuck to his raincoat by gobs of black stuff.

He thought something silly. He knew it was silly, but he thought it anyway because it was the only thought that would fit into his head.

But how will she eat her Sunday dinner without teeth?

He turned to see Dad struggling with two figures whose faces were as white as milk except for their dark eyes and dark mouths. One was a guy who worked for Mrs. Suzuki. José. Jack didn't know his last name. José something. The other was a big red-haired guy in a military uniform. Jack knew all the uniforms. This was a National Guard uniform. He had corporal's stripes on his arms. But he had only one arm. The other sleeve whipped and popped in the wind, but there was nothing in it.

Dad was slipping in the mud. He fell back against the rear fender of the Durango. The shotgun slipped from his hands and was swallowed up by the groundwater.

The groundwater.

The cold, cold groundwater.

Jack looked numbly down at where his legs vanished into the swirling water. It eddied around his shins, just below his knees. He couldn't feel his feet anymore.

Be careful, Mom said from the warmth of his memories, *or you'll catch your death.*

Catch your death.

Jack thought about that as Dad struggled with the two white-faced people. The wind pushed him around, made him sway like a stalk of green corn.

He saw Dad let go of one of the people so he could grab for the pistol tucked into his waistband.

No, Dad, thought Jack. *Don't do that. They'll get you if you do that.*

Dad grabbed the pistol, brought it up, jammed the barrel under José's chin. Fired. José's hair seemed to jump off his head and then he was falling, his fingers going instantly slack.

But the soldier.

He darted his head forward and clamped his teeth on Dad's wrist. On the gun wrist.

Dad screamed again. The pistol fired again, but the bullet went all the way up into the storm and disappeared.

Jack was utterly unable to move. Pale figures continued to come lumbering out of the rain. They came toward him, reached for him. . . .

But not one of them touched him.

Not one.

And there were so many.

Dad was surrounded now. He screamed and screamed, and fired his pistol. Three of the figures fell. Four. Two got back up again, the holes in their chests leaking black blood. The other two dropped backward, with parts of their heads missing.

Aim for the head, Dad, thought Jack. *It's what they do in the video games.*

Dad never played those games. He aimed center mass and fired. Fired.

And then the white-faced people dragged him down into the frothing water.

Jack knew that he should do something. At the same time, and with the kind of mature clarity that came with dying at his age, he knew that he was in shock. Held in place by it. Probably going to be killed by it. If not by these . . . whatever they were . . . then by the vicious cold that was chewing its way up his spindly legs.

He could not move if he was on fire, he knew that. He was going to stand there and watch the world go all the way crazy. Maybe this was the black wall of nothing that he imagined. This . . .

What was it?

A plague? Or, what did they call it? Mass hysteria?

No. People didn't eat one another during riots. Not even soccer riots.

This was different.

This was monster stuff.

This was stuff from TV and movies and video games.

Only the special effects didn't look as good. The blood wasn't bright enough. The wounds didn't look as disgusting. It was always better on TV.

Jack knew that his thoughts were crazy.

I'm in shock, duh.

He almost smiled.

And then he heard Jill.

Screaming.

10

JACK RAN.

He went from frozen immobility to full-tilt run so fast that he felt like he melted out of the moment and reappeared somewhere else. It was surreal. That was a word he knew from books he'd read. Surreal. Not entirely real.

That fit everything that was happening.

His feet were so cold it was like running on knives. He ran into the teeth of the wind as the white-faced people shambled and splashed toward him and then turned away with grunts of disgust.

I'm not what they want, he thought.

He knew that was true, and he thought he knew why.

It made him run faster.

He slogged around the end of the Durango and tripped on something lying half submerged by the rear wheel.

Something that twitched and jerked as white faces buried their mouths on it and pulled with bloody teeth. Pulled and wrenched, like dogs fighting over a beef bone.

Only it wasn't beef.

The bone that gleamed white in the lightning flash belonged to Uncle Roger. Bone was nearly all that was left of him as figures staggered away, clutching red lumps to their mouths.

Jack gagged and then vomited into the wind. The wind slapped his face with what little he'd eaten that day. He didn't care. Jill wouldn't care.

Jill screamed again and Jack skidded to a stop, turning, confused. The sound of her scream no longer came from the far side of the truck. It sounded closer than that, but it was a gurgling scream.

He cupped his hands around his mouth and screamed her name into the howling storm.

A hand closed around his ankle.

Under the water.

From under the back of the truck.

Jack screamed again, inarticulate and filled with panic as he tried to jerk his leg away. The hand holding him had no strength and his ankle popped free and Jack staggered back and then fell flat on his ass in the frigid water. It splashed up inside his raincoat and soaked every inch of him. Three of the white-faced things turned to glare at him, but their snarls of anger flickered and went out as they found nothing worth hunting.

"Jack—?"

Her voice seemed to come out of nowhere. Still wet and gurgling, drowned by rain and blown thin by the wind.

But so close.

Jack stared at the water that smacked against the truck. At the pale, thin, grasping hand that opened and closed on nothing but rainwater.

"Jack?"

"*Jill!*" he cried, and Jack struggled onto his knees and began pawing and slapping at the water, pawing at it as if he could dig a hole in it. He bent and saw a narrow gap between the surface of the water and the greasy metal underside of the truck. He saw two eyes, there and gone again in the lightning bursts. Dark eyes that he knew would be red.

"Jill!" he croaked at the same moment as she cried, "Jack!"

He grabbed her hands and pulled.

The mud and the surging water wanted to keep her, but not as much as he needed to pull her out. She came loose with a *glop*! They fell back together, sinking into the water, taking mouthfuls of it, choking, coughing, sputtering, gagging it out as they helped each other sit up.

The white things came toward them. Drawn to the splashing or drawn to the fever that burned in Jill's body. Jack could feel it from where he touched her. It was as if there were a coal furnace burning bright under her skin. Even with all this cold rain and runoff, she was hot. Steam curled up from her.

None curled up from Jack. His body felt even more shrunken than usual. Thinner, drawn into itself to kindle the last sparks of what he had left. He moaned in pain as he tried to stand. The creatures surrounding him moaned, too. Their cries sounded no different from his.

He forced himself to stand and wrapped his arm around Jill.

"Run!" he cried.

They cut between two of the figures, and the things turned awkwardly, pawing at them with dead fingers, but Jack and Jill ducked and slipped past. The porch was close but the water made it hard to run. The creatures with the white faces were clumsier and slower, and that helped.

Thunder battered the farm, deafening Jack and Jill as they collapsed onto the stairs and crawled like bugs onto the plank floor. The front door was wide open, the glow from the Coleman lantern showing the way.

"Jack . . ." Jill mumbled, slurring his name. "I feel sick."

The monsters in the rain kept coming, and Jack realized that they had ignored him time and again. These creatures were not chasing him now. They were coming for Jill. They wanted her.

Her. Not him.

Why?

Because they want life.

That's why they went after Mom and Dad and Uncle Roger.

That's why they want Jill.

Not him.

He wasn't sure how or why he knew that, but he was absolutely certain of it. The need for life was threaded through that awful moan. Toby had wanted more life. Jack wanted to be alive, but he'd reached the point where he was more dead than alive. Sliding down, down, down.

I'm already dead.

Jill crawled so slowly that she was barely halfway across the porch by the time one of *them* tottered to the top step. Jack felt it before he turned and looked. Water dripped from its body onto the backs of his legs.

The thing moaned.

Jack looked up at the terrible, terrible face.

"Mom . . . ?" he whispered.

Torn and ragged, things missing from her face and neck, red and black blood gurgling over her lips and down her chin. Bone-white hands reaching.

Past him.

Ignoring him.

Reaching for Jill.

"No," said Jack. He wanted to scream the word, to shout the kind of defiance that would prove that he was still alive, that he was still to be acknowledged. But all he could manage was a thin, breathless rasp of a word. Mom did not hear it. No one did. There was too much of everything else for it to be heard.

Jill didn't hear it.

Jill turned at the sound of the moan from the thing that took graceless steps toward her. Jill's glazed red eyes flared wide and she screamed the same word.

"*No!*"

Jill, sick as she was, screamed that word with all the heat and fear and sickness and life that was boiling inside her. It was louder than the rain and the thunder. Louder than the hungry moan that came from Mom's throat.

There was no reaction on Mom's face. Her mouth opened and closed like a fish.

No, not like a fish. Like someone practicing the act of eating a meal that was almost hers.

There was very little of Jack left, but he forced himself once more to get to his feet. To stand. To stagger over to Jill, to catch her under the arms, to pull, to drag. Jill thrashed against him, against what she saw on the porch.

She punched Jack, and scratched him. Tears like hot acid fell on Jack's face and throat.

He pulled her into the house. As he did so, Jack lost his grip and Jill fell past him into the living room.

Jack stood in the doorway for a moment, chest heaving, staring with bleak eyes at Mom. And then past her to the other figures that were slogging through the mud and water toward the house. At the rain hammering on the useless truck. At the farm road that led away toward the River Road. When the lightning flashed he could see all the way past the levee to the river, which was a great, black, swollen thing.

Tears, as cold as Jill's were hot, cut channels down his face.

Mom reached out.

Her hands brushed his face as she tried to reach past him.

A sob as painful as a punch broke in Jack's chest as he slammed the door.

11

HE TURNED and fell back against it, then slid all the way down to the floor.

Jill lay on her side, weeping into her palms.

Outside, the storm raged, mocking them both with its power. Its life.

"Jill . . ." said Jack softly.

The house creaked in the wind, each timber moaning its pain and weariness. The window glass trembled in the casements. Even the good china on the dining-room breakfront racks rattled nervously, as if aware of their own fragility.

Jack heard all this.

Jill crawled over to him and collapsed against him, burying her face against his chest. Her grief was so big that it, too, was voiceless. Her body shook and her tears fell on him like rain. Jack wrapped his arms around her and pulled her close.

He was so cold that her heat was the only warmth in his world.

Behind them there was a heavy thud on the door.

Soft and lazy, but heavy, like the fist of a sleepy drunk.

However, Jack knew that it was no drunk. He knew exactly who and what was pounding on the door. A few moments later there were other thuds. On the side windows and the back door. On the walls. At first just a few fists, then more.

Jill raised her head and looked up at him.

"I'm cold," she said, even though she was hot. Jack nodded; he understood fevers. Her eyes were like red coals.

"I'll keep you warm," he said, huddling closer to her.

"W-what's happening?" she asked. "Mom . . . ?"

He didn't answer. He rested the back of his head against the door, feeling the shocks and vibrations of each soft punch shudder through him. The cold was everywhere now. He could not feel his legs or his hands. He shivered as badly as she did, and all around them the storm raged and the dead beat on the house. He listened to his own heartbeat. It fluttered and twitched. Beneath his skin and in his veins and in his bones, the cancer screamed as it devoured the last of his heat.

He looked down at Jill. The bite on her arm was almost colorless, but radiating from it were black lines that ran like tattoos of vines up her arm. More of the black lines were etched on her throat and along the sides of her face. Black goo oozed from two or three smaller bites that Jack hadn't seen before. Were they from what had happened at the school, or from just now? No way to tell: the rain had washed away all the red, leaving wounds that opened obscenely and in which white grubs wriggled in the black wetness.

Her heart beat like the wings of a hummingbird. Too fast, too light.

Outside, Mom and the others moaned for them.

"Jack . . ." Jill said, and her voice was even smaller, farther away.

"Yeah?"

"Remember when you were in the hospital in January?"

"Yeah."

"You . . . you told me about your dream?" She still spoke in the dazed voice of a dreamer.

"Which dream?" he asked, though he thought he already knew.

"The one about . . . the big wave. The black wave."

"The black nothing," he corrected. "Yeah, I remember."

She sniffed but it didn't stop the tears from falling. "Is . . . is that what this is?"

Jack kissed her cheek. As they sat there, her skin had begun to change, the intense heat gradually giving way to a clammy coldness. Outside, the pounding, the moans, the rain, the wind, the thunder—it was all continuous.

"Yeah," he said quietly, "I think so."

They listened to the noise and Jack felt himself getting smaller inside his own body.

"Will it hurt?" she asked.

Jack had to think about that. He didn't want to lie but he wasn't sure of the truth.

The roar of noise was fading. Not getting smaller, but each separate sound was being consumed by a wordless moan that was greater than the sum of its parts.

"No," he said, "it won't hurt."

Jill's eyes drifted shut and there was just the faintest trace of a smile on her lips. There was no reason for it to be there, but it was there.

He held her until all the warmth was gone from her. He listened for the hummingbird flutter of her heart and heard nothing.

He touched his face. His tears had stopped with her heart. *That's okay,* he thought. *That's how it should be.*

Then Jack laid Jill down on the floor and stood up.

The moan of the darkness outside was so big now. Massive. Huge.

He bent close and peered out through the peephole.

The pounding on the door stopped. Mom and the others outside began to turn, one after the other, looking away from the house. Looking out into the yard.

Jack took a breath.

He opened the door.

12

THE LIGHTNING and the outspill of light from the lantern showed him the porch and the yard, the car and the road. There were at least fifty of the white-faced people there. None of them looked at him. Mom was right there, but she had her back to him. He saw Roger crawling through the water so he could see past the truck. He saw Dad rise awkwardly to his feet, his face gone but the pistol still dangling from his finger.

All of them were turned away, looking past the abandoned truck, facing the farm road.

Jack stood over Jill's body and watched as the wall of water from the shattered levee came surging up the road toward the house. It was so beautiful.

A big, black wall of nothing.

Jack looked at his mother, his father, his uncle, and then down at Jill.

He would not be going into the dark without them.

The dark was going to take them all.

Jack smiled.

TENDER AS TEETH

Stephanie Crawford and Duane Swierczynski

"IS IT TRUE that the cure made all of you vegetarians?" Carson asked.

Justine was staring at the road ahead, but could see him toying with his digital recorder in her peripheral vision. He was asking a flurry of questions, but at the same time avoiding The Big Question. She wished he'd just come out with it already.

"Why are you asking me?" she replied. "I'm not the mouthpiece for every single survivor."

Carson stammered a little before Justine glanced over and gave him a wide grin.

"Oh, yes, I referred to former zombies as 'survivors.' Make sure to include that. Your readers will love it."

As they drove across the desert the sun was pulling the sky from black to a gritty blue gray. The rented compact car held a thirty-three-year-old man named Carson with enough expensive camera equipment to crowd up the backseat, and Justine, a woman two years younger, who kept her own small shoulder bag between her feet.

The rest of her baggage was invisible.

Some said as far as apocalyptic plagues went, it could have been a lot worse.

The dead didn't crawl out of their graves. Society didn't crumble entirely. The infection didn't spread as easily as it did in the movies— you had either to really *try* to get infected or be genetically predisposed to it.

Justine happened to be one of the latter.

After work one night, Justine was nursing a Pabst at her local generic, suburban sports bar while half listening to the news about a virus that would probably quiet down like H1N1 and texting her friend Gina, who was late. She was just raising the bottle's mouth to her lips when a thick, dead weight fell against her and knocked her off her bar stool and onto the sticky, peanut-shell-covered floor. Too fucking enraged to wait for a good Samaritan to jump up and give a *hey, pal,* Justine started blindly kicking out her heels and thrusting out fists at the drunk bastard. That's how it played out until the drunk started gnawing at her fists until his incisors connected with the actual bones of her fingers while his mouth worked to slurp up and swallow the shredded meat of her knuckles.

After that, Justine remembered little until the cure hit her bloodstream.

That had been six months after the attack in the bar. And in the meantime . . .

Carson tried to look at Justine without full-on *staring* at her. Like much of the time he'd spent with her so far, he was fairly certain he was failing miserably. The miracle vaccine seemed to have left Justine with little more damage than a scarred face, a lean-muscled body that bordered on emaciation, and an entire planet filled with people who actively wanted her dead. That was called "being one of the lucky ones."

Keep her talking, he reminded himself. Carson asked, "I understand your mom paid for the cure?"

Justine kicked the glove compartment while crossing her legs. "Sadly, yes. I guess she meant well."

"Aren't you glad to be alive?"

"If you call this living."

"Better than being dead."

She turned to face him, squinting and twisting her lips into a pout. "Is it?"

Asking questions was the problem, Carson decided. He wasn't a real journalist. He'd only brought the digital recorder to please his editor, who couldn't afford to send both a photographer *and* a reporter.

Just keep her talking as much as possible, the editor had said. *We'll make sense of it later.*

But most important, his editor added, *we want her to talk about what it's like.*

What what *is like?* Carson had asked.

His editor had replied, *What it's like to go on living.*

A year ago today he'd been out in Las Vegas for one of the most inane reasons of all: a photo shoot for a celebrity cookbook. The celebrity in question was a borderline morbidly obese actor known for both his comedic roles and as his darker turns in mob flicks. Right before he'd left on that trip, the first outbreaks had been reported, but the virus seemed to be contained to certain parts of the country, and Carson thought he'd come to regret it if he turned down the assignment over the latest health scare. Especially if that would leave him stuck in his Brooklyn apartment for months on end while this thing ran its course. They were saying it could be as bad as the 1918 flu pandemic.

Oh, if he had only known.

The outbreak had happened midshoot. A pack of zombies had burst in just as the food stylist had finished with the chicken scarpariello. They weren't interested in the dish. They wanted the celebrity chef instead. Carson kept snapping photos before he quite realized what was happening. He escaped across Vegas, continuing to take photos as the city tore itself apart.

And then he saw Justine, though he didn't know her name then.

Back then, she was just . . .

Carson heard his editor's impatient reminder in his head: *Keep her talking.*

Yeah.

Not talking was the reason he'd become a photographer. He preferred to keep the lens between himself and the rest of the world, speaking to subjects only when he absolutely *had* to.

He was struggling to formulate a new inane question when she spoke up.

"Do you remember the exact place?"

Carson nodded.

"So where was it?" Justine asked.

That surprised him. He had assumed she would have just . . . known. Maybe not when she was in that state, because the former zombies—the *survivors*—were supposed to have blanked memories.

The photo, though . . . surely she had to have seen the photo at some point.

Or had she?

"Outside of Vegas. Almost near Henderson."

"Huh," Justine said. "Makes sense."

"Does it?"

"That's not far from where I used to live. So come on. Where did you . . . um, *encounter* me?"

Carson pulled onto the 5, which would take them out of the Valley and out through the desert. "I'm hoping I'll be able to find it again once we're out there," he said.

"Don't count on it, buddy boy," she said. "My mom tells me they've razed a lot of the old neighborhood. There's even been talk of abandoning Vegas altogether. Clear everyone out, then drop an H-bomb directly on it. Wipe the slate clean."

Carson, still fumbling, heard the question tumble out of his mouth before he could stop himself.

"Have you, um, *seen* the photo?"

Justine had woken up in the hospital, still spoiling for a fight. After about a minute her eyes registered that she was in a hospital bed, and she felt her mom squeezing her hand through layers of aching pain and a wooziness that could only be coming from the IV attached to her arm—so she'd assumed. So the bastard had actually put her in the hospital?

Justine's first lucid words were spent reassuring her mom, who herself looked like she'd been put through the ringer.

"Hey, Ma, it's all right . . . you should see the other guy."

That's what she attempted to say, at any rate. It came out sounding more like, "ACK-em, aight . . . shouldas . . . other guy." Her voice sounded cracked and enfeebled . . . almost as if her actual esophagus were bruised and coated in grime.

Her mother teared up and went in for the most delicate hug Justine could remember ever having experienced.

"Thank God . . . He finally showed up. Thank God you're back, and thank Him that you don't remember."

It was only then that Justine noticed that the doctors and nurses surrounding her had what could only be taken as unprofessional looks of pure, barely disguised disgust on their faces. All this for a fucking bar fight she hadn't even started?

Before Justine could ask what exactly was going on, her mom cupped her palm against her daughter's cheek; Justine couldn't help realizing how hollowed out it felt against her mom's warm hand.

"Sweetie . . . I have a lot I need to tell you. It's not when you think it is, and you're not exactly who you think you are anymore. The world got infected and wormed you worse than anyone. You're going to need to prepare yourself. Just know I love you, always."

And then her mom told her what the world had been up to.

Justine stared at the passing power lines with an interest they didn't exactly warrant. "Is this professional curiosity?"

"No," Carson said. "I'd really like to know."

Justine glanced over at Carson, who gave her a tight-lipped smile. She had done her research on him, and she was almost personally insulted by what she'd found. A small part of her was hoping she'd get a gonzo-journalist type that would end the interview with him trying to hunt her in a "most dangerous game" scenario. Carson was, at best, a midlevel photog—his writing credits adding up to captions under his glossy photos of celebrities she had never heard of. There were a few dashes of pretension, but he was clearly paying the bills.

Except for those unexpected, dramatic moments every photographer lives for. He had a few absorbing shots.

The main one starring her own self.

"My mom kept it from me for as long as possible. She acted a bit as if seeing it would trigger me, somehow. But . . . eh."

Justine started absently gnawing on a fingernail with more vigor than she realized.

"I'll see little thumbnails on Google and squint my eyes to blur it out. I've been told about it enough that my taste to see the actual money shot has long been sated."

Justine glanced over at Carson to see how that had landed. She was sleep deprived and barely knew the guy, but he somehow looked . . . puzzled.

Was she serious? How could she have *not* looked?

Carson knew he'd created that photo by pure accident. Even the framing and lighting and composition were a happy accident—a trifecta of the perfect conditions, snapped at exactly the right moment. He admitted it. He'd lucked into it. He couldn't even claim to have created that photo. He'd merely been the one holding the camera, his index finger twitching. That image had wanted to exist; he'd been simply the conduit.

The photo wasn't his fault, just like her . . . sickness . . . wasn't her fault. They were like two car-accident victims, thrown together by chance and left to deal with the wreckage.

He got all that.

Still . . . how could she *not* want to see? How could you ever hope to recover if you didn't confront it head-on?

"Pull over," she said suddenly.

"Are you okay?"

"Unless you want to clean chunks of puke out of this rental, pull over now. Please."

Carson was temporarily desert-blind. He couldn't tell where the edge of the broken road ended and the dead, dry earth began. Blinking his eyes, he slowly edged to the right as Justine's hands fumbled at the door handle. He saw—*felt*—her entire body jolt. He applied the brake, kicking up a huge plume of dust. Justine flew out of the passenger seat even before the car had come to a complete halt. She disappeared into the dust. Within seconds, Carson heard her heaving.

He knew this was what the cure did to you. It took away the zombie, but left you a very, very sick person.

Should he get out? Did she maybe want a little water, or her privacy? He didn't know. For a moment, Carson sat behind the wheel, watching the dust settle back down. There were a lot of dust storms out here, he'd read. The Southwest hadn't seen them this bad since the 1930s Dust Bowl days. Some people thought it was nature's way of trying to wipe the slate clean, one sharp grain of sand at a time.

All was quiet: she'd stopped heaving.

"Justine?" he called out. "You okay?"

He opened the door just as the truck pulled up behind them. Dammit. Probably a good Samaritan, thinking they needed help.

"Justine?"

Car doors slammed behind Carson. He turned off the ignition, pulled the keys from the steering column, pushed open the door with his foot, and stepped out into the hot, dry air. There were three people standing there. Carson was struck at first by how familiar they looked but couldn't immediately place them. Not until one of them said, "Where's the baby killer?"

Fuck me, he thought. It was the protesters.

They'd followed them out into the desert.

When Carson arrived at Justine's Burbank apartment just a few hours earlier, he was stunned to see them there, carrying placards and pacing up and down the front walkway. They must have been at it all night, and toward the end of some kind of "shift," because they looked tired, haggard, and vacant-eyed. Ironically enough, they kind of looked like you-know-whats.

Carson was equally stunned by the things coming out of their mouths, the sheer hate painted on their signs: AN ABOMINATION LIVES HERE; THAT BABY HAD A FUTURE; KILL YOURSELF JUSTINE.

Delusional people who had to seize on something, he supposed. There was a whole "disbelief in the cure movement" going on now, with a groundswell of people who brought out these pseudoscientists claiming that the cure was only temporary—that at any moment, thousands of people could revert to flesh-eating monsters again. There was not a lick of scientific evidence to back this up, mind you. But when has that stopped zealots before?

Carson had parked the car a block away, in the rubble of a lot in front of an old fifties-style motel that had promptly gone out of business a year ago during the chaos. He wiped the sweat from his brow—wasn't California supposed to be cooler at this time of year? At first he grabbed his small digital camera and locked everything else in the trunk, figuring that if he tried to run that gauntlet with his full gear there was a strong chance he'd be molested. Carson was prepared for anything, but wasn't in the mood to lose ten grand worth of gear that he *knew* the paper wouldn't replace.

But then again, when the going gets weird, the weird turn pro . . . wasn't that what Hunter S. Thompson said? Carson donned his vest (he hated it, but people associated it with being a pro, so . . .) and walked right up to the nut cases, smiling. *That's right*, he thought. *Just a happy photojournalist on assignment, here to take your picture.*

That's the thing: you don't ask. You keep your camera low and just start shooting. Ask, and there's a strong chance they'll think, *Hey, wait a minute, maybe I shouldn't agree to this.* But if you act like God Himself sent you down here to record the moments for posterity, most people will step out of your way and let you do His Holy Work. Carson snapped away from waist level. Sometimes you want that feeling of looking up from a child's POV, right up into the faces of these lunatics, the sun bouncing from their hand-painted signs. Carson was feeling good about the assignment when something hard slammed into the center of his back and he tumbled forward into someone's fist.

These things happen so fast—your ass getting kicked. In the movies there's always an explanation. Your antagonists go to great pains to tell you exactly *why* you're going to receive a brutal beating right before the beating actually happens. Not in reality. When a mob attacks you, and blood's filling your mouth, and someone's kicking you in the back and you can feel your internal organs convulsing . . . there are no explanations.

But Carson heard one thing. The most chilling thing he could possibly hear, actually. And that was his name.

They know who I am, he thought. *They know I'm the one who made Zombie Chick famous.*

Which was when said Zombie Chick saved Carson from hospitalization.

She didn't rush down and start growling at the crowd, asking for brains. She merely opened her window and stared down at them. Carson didn't notice it at first; all he sensed was that the kicks came slower, and then tapered off entirely.

The crowd backed away from Carson and focused on her, up in her window. Cursing at her. Gesturing at her. Spitting. Picking up tiny chunks of broken sidewalk and hurling them at her. Only then did she duck inside and slide the window shut.

Carson wanted to get the hell out of there . . . *pronto.* But then he imagined stepping into his boss's office empty-handed, without a single photo. That simply wasn't an option. Not if he wanted to eat. So he pushed himself, ribs and legs screaming, and took advantage of the temporary distraction, jogging right up through the center of the crowd, pushing his way past them, blasting through the front door of the apartment complex. By the time they noticed, it was too late—Carson had flipped the dead bolt behind him. As he scanned the mailboxes with the call buzzers he could hear them yelling, threatening to kill him for real. . . .

Looked like they wanted to make good on that promise now, out here in an empty stretch of desert, with no one to interrupt them.

Justine looked down at what she had evacuated, noting it was pretty much pure water. She started to straighten up but stopped herself when she noticed the long shadows stumble over themselves.

"Shit."

Justine stayed bent over, hands on her knees, mind racing. She heard muffled angry voices and some halfhearted pounding on a car. She figured it was road warriors, insanely persistent Latter-Day Saints missionaries, or they were being followed by her own personal Raincoat Brigade. Whoever it was, she was going to need a decent-size rock at the very least, and she needed to look as fucked up as possible. The latter was covered, and her eyes scanned quickly for the former.

Jackpot.

Eyes up. Take it slow.

Most of the brigade (*Biggest bunch of vultures this desert has ever produced,* Justine thought) was standing back from the car, attempting to look casual but barely pulling off "vaguely gassy." There were three men in their midforties actually on the car. One was playing the lean-against-the-windshield cop move, with the other two settling for leaning against the side.

Justine crouched in the warm dirt, obscured by a large grouping of banana yucca. If Carson had left the passenger seat unlocked she could probably jump in, and he could floor it and ride like hell until they got to a gas station.

Fake cop had just cocked some kind of gun. Seriously? Fuck this. Fuck all of it. She should never have agreed to this interview. She was probably going to be one of those survivors who ended up dead—for real this time—at the hands of a frightened mob.

Unless she could use their fear against them.

Justine stood up, stretched . . . and moaned. Moaned like some kind of unholy undead piece of hell would yawn after centuries of hungry slumber—or whatever these assholes believed.

"There she is!"

"Why didn't anyone see her get out?"

"Weren't you supposed to be watching that patch, Dana?"

"There's the baby-killer! I bet they don't prosecute in Nevada and he's smuggling her!"

But the crowd quickly lost interest in Carson and his compact car, and moved en masse toward Justine. Just a yard down was a van with a flat tire facing the road.

Clever dumb bastards, Justine thought. *That'll keep the passing cars moving.*

"I'd ask if you didn't have anything better to do," Justine called out. "But after watching you all for months out my window I know you don't."

Justine had found that bravado sometimes worked when the rocks weren't up to snuff.

One of the guys leaning against the car gave Justine a grimace that bordered on a grin.

"You have served no jail time for killing the most innocent of our Savior's creations. We just want to . . . talk to you about it. Maybe get you to turn yourself in. There's no reason for you to get your bowels in an uproar."

Some of the gang nodded in agreement, while others just eyed Justine as if she were about to leap out like a cat in a closet in a bad slasher movie. Fake Cop kept his fingers moving on his gun, which he was holding close to his thigh.

Justine glanced over to the car. Carson was standing there quietly. Now that their little "freak" was front and center, nobody bothered to keep an eye on him. He had his cell phone in his hand. He made eye contact and gave a short nod.

Please, Justine thought. *Don't come to my rescue, photo boy. From the looks of you, you've got the muscle strength of warm butter.*

Moving her eyes back to the group, Justine took a deep breath and tried to make eye contact with as many as possible.

"Look, I really understand. I hate myself, too," Justine said. "But I really, truly was not myself when that happened, and believe me they would have found out if I was. I'm cured now and my life is a living hell, so can you just leave me alone to fester it out, please? You guys will just go to jail and I'm really not worth it."

"Maybe we can just shoot 'er here," one of them said.

Another: "Shut up. Just shut up. You weren't even invited here, you dumb psycho."

Fake Cop and the one that had been talking had a tension between them that made Justine more nervous than the pure hatred that was being leveled at her.

The man turned back to her.

"I'm sorry, this was stupid. My name is Mike. How about you let your friend leave, and you come with us and we can talk to my brother—he's a police officer—and we can get you right—"

Mike stopped himself. Justine could see that he had just spotted the phone in Carson's hand.

"Well, shit, son," Mike said. "I really wish you hadn't done that."

Justine, strangely enough, wished the same thing.

For an awful moment there, Carson thought that Justine's "cure" hadn't fully taken.

His fevered imagination put together the sequence of events this way:

She's riding along, in the sun, next to a living human being. She doesn't get out much. She's not around people much. Something in her breaks down. She senses the flesh, the blood beating through his veins. It's all too much. It makes her sick. She thinks she has to puke. She asks him to pull over and she scrambles from the car when it hits her. She can't help it, can't control it. Suddenly she's acting like a zombie again. . . .

Because suddenly, she *was*.

A zombie again.

Forcing this unholy sound out of her throat, clawing at invisible enemies, eyes rolling up in the back of her head . . .

The protest mob jolted, taking a step away from one another, as if collectively hoping the crazy baby-killing zombie bitch would attack the person standing next to them. Carson jolted, too, from the shock of it, but also the thought that just a few minutes ago, he'd been inside a speeding car with this woman. *Thing.*

He instantly regretted that it was a cell phone in his hand and not his camera, which was still packed up in the backseat. He hated himself for even thinking it, but . . . c'mon! The impact of a photo would be seismic. Proof that the cure doesn't work! As shown by its most infamous poster child . . .

But those fantasies were dashed the moment he heard Justine scream, in perfect English:

"Carson—the car—*now*!"

The best Justine could hope for was not getting shot.

She dived into the crowd and just started shoving. There was no telling how many other guns were hiding in this group, but she was counting on the stark-raving-fear factor and the element of surprise to keep the men from using them. For a few seconds at least. Until fucking Carson got the car revved up . . .

"Carson, goddammit!"

She couldn't keep herself from picturing how, if Carson weren't here, she'd probably just have gone for it. Her anger and annoyance were burning so hot that she could easily have chosen this day as her last—as long as she took these assholes out along with her.

Baby-eating Zombie Desert Rampage; 8 Dead! Justine smiled at the imagined headline; she should have been the journalist.

But no, Justine felt oddly protective toward Carson. He wasn't much, but right at this moment he was the only one listening. One last blind elbow to what felt like a butt and Justine scrammed it to the passenger door.

"*Go go go!*" she screamed at Carson as she locked her door, screaming in laughter as Carson fishtailed it out of there with white knuckles. "All we need is some banjo chase music, compadre!"

Once they'd cleared the first quarter mile, Justine patted the shoulder of the poor, shaking Carson.

"The fuck," Carson sputtered. "The fuck was that?"

"The usual," Justine said.

"Are you okay? I mean . . . shit, did they . . ."

Justine looked behind them, seeing only a random semi truck. "I'm fine. Actually, no. I'm not fine. I'm hungry. *Starving* even."

Carson looked at her wide-eyed. Justine noticed the stare also contained a bit of apprehension. "What?"

"And in answer to your earlier question," she said, "no. I'm not a vegetarian."

Justice had Carson stop at a roadside barbecue joint a handful of miles outside Barstow. She assured him it was the best obscure, outdoor barbecue you could get in the Southwest; not to mention that she was pretty sure the owner was a Hell's Angel and therefore coated the area with a kind of grimy aura of protection.

Carson sat at a picnic table while Justine ordered them two orders of the works. She had put on a pair of large-frame glasses and affected an uneven Texan drawl, claiming it was a disguise, while Carson suspected it was mostly to amuse herself.

Roughly half an hour had passed since they were accosted, but in that short span of time Justine had seemed to come alive. Bouncing in her seat, looking behind them in her sun visor's mirror, and squeezing his shoulder every few minutes—she was as enthusiastic as he imagined she might have been on a regular road trip in her life before infection had made her somber and shifty-eyed. Her skin also seemed to take on what he could only be described as a glow, and her stone-gray eyes seemed to skew closer to silver.

"How much for one rib?"

Carson sat up straight and turned to see Justine laughing with the barbecue proprietor before shaking her head and walking to their table. She smiled at him before laying down a stack of white sandwich bread and two Styrofoam boxes in front of him.

"Is everything okay? Did you need more money?" Carson asked while he peeked under one of the lids.

"What? Are you not familiar with the comedic stylings of Chris Rock?" Justine was still putting on her weird drawl, which was toeing the line between cute and unsettling pretty aggressively. "*I'm Gonna Git You Sucka*? No? Boy, we need to hook you up with a movie marathon."

Justine took the bench across from Carson, popped open her lid, and proceeded to stare at the meat. The only motion she made was to follow in the tradition of countless customers before her in leisurely picking at the peeling red paint off the table with a fingernail. Carson couldn't help indulging himself in a mouthful of brisket before asking her if everything was okay.

Justine sighed. "No. Sure. Everything is fine. This is the first time I had even the desire to eat meat since you-know-what, let alone actually ate the stuff. Before that I was a stone-cold carnivore."

She never took her eyes off her meal, but had worked up to poking it around with her spork.

Carson raised his eyebrows and took a long sip of his lukewarm Mountain Dew. He became aware of a weird undercurrent that had seemed to sit itself at their table, but couldn't place it.

Justine stabbed at a piece of pork until the weak teeth of the spork finally speared it enough to lift. He eyed the meat and her mouth, wishing he had his camera out. She caught him staring. He flashed her a quick, reassuring half-smile when their eyes met. Justine saluted him with her spork full of pork, and took it in one bite.

She chewed. Carson took another mouthful of his meal in camaraderie. He waited until they both had swallowed and taken sips of their respective drinks before asking her how it was.

"Tastes good, but just that one bite already made my jaw ache."

"Does eating hurt?"

"Aren't you forward? But no: the little I eat just sits with me funny and makes my tongue feel coated in something like wax. I probably brush my teeth about ten times a day. I don't care enough about my check-ups with the therapist or doctor to find out if it's mostly in my head or if human veal just forever fucked up my stomach."

Carson coughed in surprise, choking a bit as Justine's words hit him. She gave him a sad shrug and continued eating the meat.

"This is good, though. No coated-tongue feeling, either."

"Maybe you just needed time. Just try to take it slow."

Carson took out his camera, nodded as if to ask, *Is this okay?* Justine paused for a moment before nodding in return. He snapped a few photos of her eating with the large, faded MOOSE'S BBQ sign behind her.

Suddenly he noticed a man moving at a leaden pace a few feet behind Justine. Carson lowered his camera. The man was gaunt, with gnarled hands reminiscent of arthritic joints and old tree branches. He worked his mouth around hungrily, almost like an infant eyeing a nipple just out of reach. Only when he noticed the old, slow-shambling man pull out a Black & Mild cigar and chomp it between his grinning teeth did he relax.

"I'll be right back," Justine said, and put a hand on his shoulder as she passed. Carson thought she might be feeling sick again, but when he glanced across the way a few minutes later he saw that she was on her cell phone.

They rode in mostly companionable silence for about ninety more minutes, until the suburban sprawl of Henderson appeared. Carson felt a thrumming work its way up his spine, plucking at his nerves until his skin physically itched. Here was the moment he'd been dreading: setting up a shot where you ask someone to hunker down in a place where she'd experienced the darkest moment of her life.

"You, uh, feeling okay?" Carson asked.

Justine rustled a bit in her seat, looking tiny and weird from the corner of Carson's eye.

"Yeah. Was worried about all that food I ate, but it's staying down."

Carson cleared his throat, and Justine hurried over the sound. "I know that's not what you're asking about, but I'm putting off any reaction to this as long as I can. Is that okay with you?"

Carson nodded as he squeezed his hands tighter around the wheel. Justine crammed some more gum into her mouth. She had told him that with her stomach's working with rarely any food in it, it had given her "death breath." He hadn't noticed any of it personally, but when she also divulged how often and obsessively she brushed her teeth, he understood that the situation went a little deeper than oral hygiene.

Carson fumbled at the radio dials until he heard Sam Cooke's voice. He told himself to stop feeling guilty. Everyone in this car was there by choice, right? Of course they were.

Except they really weren't.

Carson had been there by chance.

Justine had been there because of a fluke of a disease. She didn't know what she was doing, where she'd gone, whom she'd hurt.

And it was only because Carson happened to be there, with his camera, that Justine—and the rest of the world—knew that while she'd been a zombie, she had eaten an infant child.

The area had been cleaned up more than Carson expected. Imported palm trees stood perfectly distanced from one another, pretty and welcoming like well-trained showgirls. As they pulled into the parking lot of the grocery store, his memory replaced the newly built structures with the way he remembered the place looking the last time he'd been here—a looted-out, broken shell of a place crawling with cops, zombies, and "reporters" like himself. There was a rumor that the area was harboring a building full of people who had taken over a grocery store after raiding a gun store, but the virus had gotten in there with them. Carson had been unable to confirm any of this at the time. He was mostly walking around the area in a horrified daze, snapping photos to give himself a sense of purpose in all the chaos.

"So, where were you?" Justine asked.

Carson shook himself mentally into the present. "I was walking around the barricades at the back of the lot. I guess luckily nobody was paying much attention to me. My editor just told me to snap anything interesting or fucked up that might pop out."

Justine turned to him. "And then I popped out, all interesting and fucked up with bells on?"

Carson tried to smile. "Yeah."

Justine laughed in surprise but it quickly died in her throat.

They slowly pulled themselves out of the car, groaning and stretching as they squinted into the sun. A nervous and false jovial energy permeated the air between them, as if they had decided by an unspoken vote to act as if they were here to re-create a photo from a first date rather than an amnesiac murder.

Justine wandered the half-full parking lot while Carson started gathering and preparing his gear. Once he was fully kitted up, he inhaled deeply and started toward her.

Keeping her back to him, she said, "I thought maybe standing here there'd be . . . something. A fragment of memory. But no."

"In all honesty, it's almost hard to remember it happening myself. It happened so quickly and there was so much chaos. . . ."

"Did anyone try to stop me? Did you?"

Carson stopped fidgeting before answering.

"Stop? I mean . . . the cops tackled you. The thing is, I think the baby was already dead. I didn't hear crying."

"How did I get it?"

"Uh . . ." Carson wished for a cigarette more than he had wished for anything else in the entirety of his life. "There was a huge crush of people running out of the shopping center when the police smoked them out. They think the baby was inside, and got . . . trampled. There was a broken stroller nearby."

It was, in fact, in the photograph.

He heard Justine exhale shakily.

"Fuck me, fuck you, and fuck this. What's the point of us being here? I'd want me dead, too. Let's just get this done so I can crawl back to my hole."

Carson silently worked his mouth open and closed, platitudes at the ready on his tongue. They didn't want to come out, though; every fiber of his being fully agreed with her that being here was wrong. In for a penny, in for a pound, though. The texts he had been getting from his editor were becoming increasingly insistent.

"Yeah, all right."

The photojournalist considered the parking lot around them, trying to avoid looking at the photo again on his iPhone and going solely by memory.

"The pile of rubble . . . I'm pretty sure it was over there."

He pointed at a grouping of empty parking spaces, completely indistinguishable from any other in the world. Apparently not everything required a plaque.

They made their way over, the cloud of unease silencing them. Everything was so generic and bright around them that it gave the entire assignment the feel of some kind of ill-planned playacting. The only piece of reality that didn't seem a part of their make-believe was a small murder of crows nearby that was effectively edging any pigeons out of their territory.

It seemed easier just to mumble and gesture the whole thing. In the back of his mind Carson supposed he had hoped returning here might summon up at least an emotional memory for Justine, but it was clear that whatever breakthrough he had been hoping for was doomed to die the quiet death of simply going through the motions.

Carson pointed and shot, getting the majority of his pictures framing Justine in front of the rapidly setting sun. She crouched, stood, and even sat in a few, looking pensive and disconnected in each one. The stark contrast of a traumatized woman in a new parking lot made the whole thing feel a dust-in-the-blood kind of dirty to Carson. The look in her eyes, though . . .

"All right, I think we got it. We can go."

She didn't move.

"What's wrong?" Carson asked.

"Aren't you going to ask me?"

"Ask you what?"

"All this time together, and you're too timid to ask the question I know you want to ask. It's been all over your face since we met."

Carson opened his mouth, then closed it and shook his head.

"Go ahead," Justine said, hands on her hips. "Ask me, how can I possibly go on living after something like that? How can I make jokes and drop stupid pop-culture references and eat ribs and laugh and listen to music? Isn't that what you want to know? Isn't that what you've been dying to ask me this whole time?"

Carson didn't know how to respond, mainly because she was dead right. It was the question he'd wanted to ask ever since he'd heard the news a month ago that the Famous Baby Eater—the subject of a photo that had won him fame he didn't want and acclaim he didn't deserve—was still alive.

How *do* you go on living after something like that?

Justine sighed and walked past him, muttering, "Let's get to a hotel with a bar."

"Thanks for being less of a dick about this than I thought you'd be," she said.

They were sitting at the bar in some sports-themed joint on the ground floor of a chain hotel on the edge of Henderson, knees almost touching. Carson stared into his beer, already thinking about the new set of photos he'd just made. Wondering if it was going to do more harm than good. Of course, he'd sold it to Justine as a way to show the world that she wasn't a monster, that the cure *did* work. But now he wasn't so sure.

Justine laid her hand over his and gave a gentle squeeze. Her other hand fiddled with her cell phone on the bar top.

"Hey."

Carson met her gaze. Said nothing. What could he say? That he was about to ruin her life all over again?

The photo of Justine eating ribs alone . . . ugh. She had no idea what she'd agreed to.

"Look, I'm serious," Justine said. "You've been good to me, despite everything. Which is why I feel bad about doing this."

"Doing what?"

Without warning she leaned forward and pressed her lips to his.

To a passerby it would have looked like a couple doing a parody of a cover of an historical-romance novel, except with the man in the submissive stance. Right in the thick of it, however, was a demented sincerity. Justine used her tongue to pry open his lips. What the hell was she doing?

Justine didn't have "death breath." He could taste peppermint and beer; her lips were warm. But still, all he could think about was where her lips had been, and about the chunks of flesh her tongue had once licked away from her teeth. . . .

Before he could break the embrace he heard the sound of a fake camera shutter snapping closed.

Oh God, Carson thought as his eye popped open and saw the cell in her hand. *She's taken a photo of her own.*

"Wait," he said. "Please . . ."

But Justine's fingers were already working the keypad, and the photo was already on its way to a wireless-cell tower, and from there . . . who knew? She glanced up at him.

"Sorry, I grabbed your boss's number when you left your cell alone at the barbecue place. He's just one, though. I guess I could have sold this as an exclusive, but that felt a little tacky."

Carson pulled back from the table and just stared. His eyes felt feverish as they flitted from Justine's face to the phone, to the staring bar patrons surrounding them.

"You want to know what it was like, to have you worst moment broadcast to the world?" Justine asked. "Buddy, you're about to find out."

She smiled, and reached back to hold his shaking hand. "But at least we have each other, right?"

COUCH POTATO

Brian Keene

ADELE DIDN'T KNOW MUCH about the zombies until they interrupted *The Jerry Springer Show*. It happened during an episode about—well, Adele wasn't sure what it was about. She never paid that much attention to Jerry Springer. Her momma sure did, though. That was how Adele knew something was wrong. She'd been sitting on the floor, playing with her four Disney princess dolls—Belle, Cinderella, Ariel, and Sleeping Beauty, all purchased for her by their neighbor, Mrs. Withers, at the Goodwill store ("And ain't a one of them black," the older woman had complained)—when the audience chants of "Jerry! Jerry! Jerry!" were suddenly interrupted by a monotonous, urgent tone. Her mother groaned, muttered a curse, and reached for the remote control. Adele was quietly hopeful. Momma got upset when her television viewing was disturbed, but it was also the only time she tended to pay any attention to Adele.

The droning alarm continued, and letters scrolled across the bottom of the screen. Adele read them as they flashed past: E-M-E-R-G-E-N-C-Y . . . B-R-O-A-D-C-A-S-T . . . S-Y-S-T-E-M. She didn't know quite what that meant, but it sounded scary, whatever it was. Still muttering, Momma pointed the remote at the television.

"Wait, Momma. Maybe it's important."

Her mother turned toward her. The gesture was slow and exaggerated, as if she'd forgotten that Adele was in the room and was surprised to hear her voice. She didn't respond. Instead, she just stared at her daughter with a blank, indifferent expression, then turned back to the screen.

Jerry Springer was gone now, replaced by the local news. The ticker was still scrolling across the bottom of the screen, but the words were going by too fast for Adele to read them. Her mother began scanning through the channels, but all her favorite programs were gone, replaced instead by newscasts. Momma cursed. Adele listened.

And that was how she learned about zombies.

The people on television said it was a disease. Adele knew about diseases. Cancer, the thing that had taken her grandma away last year, was a disease. So was Momma's addiction to heroin, or at least that's what some people said. But she'd never heard of the disease that was turning people into zombies. It was called Hamelin's Revenge. Adele hadn't understood what the name meant. She heard a pretty newscaster say it had something to do with the story of the Pied Piper, but the only version of that story Adele was familiar with was from an old Looney Tunes cartoon that she'd seen on one of the rare occasions when her mother wasn't watching television.

Apparently, the disease came from rats—dead rats, crawling out of the sewers and subways in New York City and attacking people. The people who were bitten got sick and died, and then they came back as zombies. And it wasn't just people and rats, either. Dogs and cats could catch it, too. So could cows, bears, coyotes, goats, sheep, monkeys, and other animals. A few animals, like pigs and birds, were immune, and for that Adele was glad. There weren't any pigs in Baltimore that she knew of, but she saw birds every time she went outside. She hated to think what would happen if they all turned into zombies.

All the shows that Momma liked—the court programs and soap operas and talk shows—were preempted by twenty-four-hour news footage. She'd had no choice but to watch it, and as a result, Adele had watched it, too. Much of what she saw was confusing or scary, and in those first three days, it became a hodgepodge of horrific imagery. New York City was quarantined. National Guardsmen blockaded the bridges and tunnels and rail tracks, and fired on people trying to escape. Then the troops began fighting one another. The disease spread to other cities and then to other countries. More and more people became zombies. The news said that all it took was one bite, one drop of blood, pus from an open sore or cut—any exposure to infected bodily fluid. People who died normal deaths stayed dead, but those who came into direct contact with the disease became zombies. A law was passed requiring the dead to be burned, and the television showed pictures of bulldozers pushing bodies into big, smoking pits. Chicago and Phoenix burned to the ground. Zombies overran an airport in Miami. A nuclear reactor melted down in China.

More and more people died every day, and then came back as zombies. There were also regular people—still-living people—who were just as bad, if not worse, than the zombies. Adele knew all about bad people, of course. Her neighborhood was full of bad people (although there were some good ones, like Mrs. Withers next door, and her son, Michael). But there were more bad people than good, and more zombies than either. The only thing that hadn't changed was that the police still didn't show up when people called for help. Now, the bad people finally had the opportunity to do everything they'd ever dreamed of.

Not so for Adele. Her dreams didn't involve rape or murder or robbery. All she'd ever wanted was for her momma to pay attention to her. But that didn't happen, either. Not even when the power went out on the third night. It was off for an hour before it came back on. Adele lay there in bed, hoping her mother would come in and check on her.

She didn't. Instead, she called the electric and cable companies to complain about the outage. Outside, the streets echoed with more gunshots and screams than usual. Adele fell asleep listening to Momma complain on the phone.

When she woke up the next morning, the power was back on again, but several stations had gone off the air.

Although Adele was only nine years old, she knew what a normal, loving family was like. She'd seen plenty of examples on television. She'd seen plenty of the other kind, as well. Oftentimes, the people on the television used big words to refer to those bad relationships. One of the words was *dysfunctional*. Another was *neglectful*. In time, Adele came to understand that those words applied to her own home life, especially when compared against the lives of the kids on television. Those kids usually lived in nice houses, with one or two loving parents that took an interest in what they were doing, and talked to them, and played with them, and let them know that they were loved. Adele's mother didn't do those things. It wasn't that Momma was abusive. She was just neglectful.

Before the zombies had come, Momma's daily routine had been: wake up on the couch, fix, make coffee and light a cigarette, then sit back down on the couch again. She'd sit there all day and watch television between fixes. Occasionally, she'd make something to eat. Sometimes she'd even remember to make something for Adele to eat, as well, but Adele had become accustomed to making meals on her own. She liked school because she knew she'd get breakfast and lunch there. At home, she could never be sure. Adele put herself to bed most nights—bathed herself, put on her pajamas by herself, brushed her teeth, and read herself a bedtime story. She always told her momma good night. Occasionally, her mother would grunt in response. In rare moments, she might even spare a hug or a kiss on the cheek. But usually she just nodded, eyes glued to the television, cigarette smoldering between her fingers, discarded needle lying on the coffee table. Momma usually fell asleep on the couch at night. The television stayed on, even while they slept.

On the fourth day, Mrs. Withers sent Michael over to check on them. Momma didn't like the Withers family very much, on account of the time Mrs. Withers had threatened to call social services on her, but Adele liked the older woman and her son very much. They were always nice to her. Mrs. Withers always had a kind word and gave her hugs and smiles, and Michael could always make Adele laugh, and would talk to her about how school was going. Both took an interest in her, and for Adele, that meant everything.

When Michael knocked on the door, Momma's eyes barely flicked from the images on the television screen—footage of dead people and animals marauding through the streets of Camden. There was dried spit on Momma's cheek and she hadn't changed her clothes in days. Adele went to the door, peered through the peephole to verify that it wasn't a zombie, and smiled when she saw Michael.

So far, the worst part of the zombie apocalypse had been the loneliness and boredom. Staying cooped up inside the apartment, Adele missed her friends at school and the people she talked to on the block. She was no stranger to loneliness, of course. Living with Momma was a lot like living alone. But in the past, she'd been able to temper the loneliness with occasional interactions with others. Now, it was just her and Momma and the people on television, so seeing Michael made her happy.

He hurried inside and shut the door behind him, and advised them of the situation outside. Zombies were all over Baltimore, but it hadn't gotten as bad as some of the other cities yet. He'd heard that the National Guard and something called FEMA would have the situation under control soon. All they had to do was wait it out. Momma grunted in response to all this, and got mad and impatient when Michael reminded her to lock the door and barricade all the windows. Michael ended up doing it for them. Adele helped him as best she could, and when they were done, Michael slapped his forehead in mock surprise.

"I almost forgot!" He reached into his shirt pocket and pulled out a candy bar. Then he handed it to Adele. Smiling, she gave him a big hug.

"Thank you," she said.

"You're welcome." He hugged her back, and then sighed. "Adele, listen. Maybe you should come stay with me and my mom. I could talk to your momma about it. I don't think she'd mind."

Adele heard the tone in his voice, and her smile faltered. She knew what other people thought of Momma, and sometimes she felt that way, too, but still—it was her momma, and she loved her.

"I can't," she said. "I'd like to, but I guess I better stay here with Momma."

"Maybe we can convince her to come over, too. There's safety in numbers."

Adele shook her head. "You know Momma. She won't go."

"Then you should come."

"No," she repeated. "I need to stay here and take care of her."

Michael frowned. "Okay. But if you need anything, you come over. Check outside first. If you see anybody—zombie or otherwise—you stay inside. But if the coast is clear and you need us, you come hollering."

Adele nodded. "I will."

Michael gave Adele another hug and then left. Momma barely

acknowledged the young man when he said goodbye. He made Adele promise to remain quiet and keep away from the windows, and told her to lock and barricade the door behind him, and she did.

Later that night, after she'd eaten her candy bar, Adele wondered what they'd do if they ran out of food. She never got the chance to find out, because they ran out of heroin and cigarettes first.

Adele woke to the sound of gunfire. That in itself wasn't unusual, even before the zombies. But the gunshots were right outside their apartment, and they went on for a very long time, punctuated by screams. Adele couldn't tell if the shrieks belonged to a man or a woman. When the sounds finally faded, she got out of bed and crept to the window. Michael had nailed it shut and put a blanket over it, preventing anyone from seeing inside. Adele lifted a corner of the blanket and cautiously peered outside. Several bodies lay in the street. She couldn't tell if they'd been living or the living dead. Now, they were just old-school dead. Each one had been shot in the head.

Unable to sleep, Adele wandered into the living room. Even though Momma would most likely ignore her, she'd still get some comfort just from being in her mother's presence and not sitting there alone. The living room was lit only by the glow of the television. Momma had turned the sound low, so as not to attract attention from outside. Adele turned toward the couch and gasped. Her mother was gone. The blanket had been kicked to the floor and the pillow and couch cushions still held her impression. Adele glanced at the stained coffee table. It was littered with used needles, an overflowing ashtray, and empty, crumpled cigarette packs. Most telling was the television remote control sitting on the arm of the couch. Momma's lighter was gone, as were her shoes. Adele knelt down and reached under the couch, careful not to jab herself with any discarded needles that might be lurking in the darkness. She pulled out a slim cigar box that her mother used to hide her stash in. When she opened the box, there was a faint whiff of tobacco. The box was empty.

"Oh, Momma . . ."

She'd gone outside, in search of heroin or cigarettes, or more likely both.

Adele began to cry, not so much from sadness or fear. She felt those things, of course, but she felt another emotion, deep down beneath them, and it was that strange, unexpected emotion that caused the tears.

The emotion was relief.

Momma had left the door unlocked, so the first thing Adele did was lock it. She made herself a bowl of cereal. There was no milk in the fridge so she ate it dry. Then she did something she rarely had the opportunity to do—she picked up Momma's remote and changed the channel to something she wanted to watch. Two of the local Baltimore affiliates were off the air, and the third was showing news, but Cartoon Network was still on the air. She sat there, munching cereal and watching television, and was content.

She fell asleep in front of the television.

She woke to another noise outside. This time, it wasn't gunshots or screams. It was quieter—more discreet. At first, Adele thought she'd imagined it, but then the sound came again—a soft, subdued scratching at the door, followed by a thump. Wide-eyed, she pulled the blanket over her head. The fabric smelled like her mother. The noise came again, louder this time. Adele got up from the couch and padded across the room in her bare feet. Holding her breath, she glanced through the peephole.

It was Momma. She looked sick. Her eyes were glassy and drool leaked from the corner of her open mouth. As Adele watched, she raised one arm and scratched at the door again.

She must have found some, Adele thought. *She scored, and now she can't open the door. I'd better let her in and help her lie down.*

Adele's fingers fumbled with the lock. As it slid back, Momma pushed the door open so fast that Adele had to scurry backward to avoid being hit by it. Momma stumbled into the house, swaying unsteadily on her feet. Her lips were pale, and her eyes remained unfocused. She glanced at Adele, frowning in confusion, as if she wasn't sure who the girl was. That was when Adele noticed the bite on Momma's arm. There was an ugly, bloody, ragged hole where her biceps had been. The wound was white and red in the center, and bluish purple strands of tissue dangled from it.

"Momma, you're hurt! Lie down."

Her mother's lips pulled back in a snarl. She reached for Adele and moaned. Drool splattered onto the floor. Adele had time to realize that Momma was neither high nor hurt. She was dead. And then Momma lunged for her, finally paying the attention that her daughter had craved for so long.

Screaming, Adele ducked her mother's outstretched arms and ran down the hall. She fled into her bedroom and slammed the door. Her mother's slow footsteps plodded toward her, but then stopped. Adele shoved her toy box against the door and stood there panting, waiting for the blows and scratches that would surely follow, but they didn't. If Momma was on the other side of the door, she was being quiet. Adele wondered if it could be a trick. Maybe Momma was lurking, waiting for her to come out. The zombies on television hadn't seemed very smart, but this wasn't televison. This was real life. This was her mother.

Adele tiptoed over to the far corner and slumped down to the floor. She kept her gaze focused on the door, waiting for it to burst open, but it didn't. She began to cry again—this time, because that feeling of relief was gone. She didn't know what to do. She couldn't escape through the window, because Michael had nailed them all shut. But even if she could have gotten the window open, there would be no escape outside. She was safer in here with one zombie than she was out on the streets with hundreds.

If she could make it over to Mrs. Withers's apartment next door, she'd be okay. She was sure of it. Michael and Mrs. Withers could help her. But the only way to get there was through the front door, which meant going past Momma. Taking a deep breath, Adele crept to the door again and listened. The only sound from the rest of the apartment was the television, which was still tuned to the Cartoon Network.

"Momma?" Her voice, barely a whisper, was simultaneously hopeful and terrified.

Like she had when she was alive, Momma didn't answer.

Adele reached for the doorknob with one trembling hand and turned it. Then she slowly opened the door a crack, fully expecting her mother to barge into the room. When she didn't, Adele opened it wider and peeked into the hall. It was empty. She shut the door again and got dressed. She had a moment of panic when she realized that her shoes were in the living room, but then she found a pair of flip-flops in her closet. When she was finished, Adele quietly rummaged through her toy box and pulled out a small rubber ball. Then she opened the door again and rolled the ball down the hall. It bounced into the living room and vanished from sight. Still, there was no reaction.

Satisfied that her mother had left, Adele crept down the hall. The television grew louder as she neared the living room. When she rounded the corner, two things became immediately apparent. The front door was still hanging open . . .

. . . And Momma was sitting on the couch.

Adele stifled a shriek. Her mother sat slumped over on the sofa, her wound leaking onto the cushions. Flies flitted about the bite, landing on Momma's arm and then taking off again. Their droning buzz was noticeable beneath the noise from the television. If Momma noticed her, she gave no indication. The zombie's attention was focused instead on the remote control. Momma clutched it in one hand, and her thumb slid idly across the buttons, but she was holding it backward and nothing happened. As Adele watched, the thing that had been her mother moaned.

Adele looked out into the street and saw that it was empty. She was sure it wouldn't be for long. If she was going to flee next door, she had to do it now. Taking a deep breath, she dashed into the living room and raced past her mother. She glanced back over her shoulder as she ran through the open door.

Momma hadn't even noticed.

THE HAPPY BIRD AND OTHER TALES

Rio Youers

EVEN THE SKY IS SCARRED. Never blue but constantly ash-colored, and rent so that rain falls in narrow sheaves. Its belly is touched by the glow from campfires, where villagers huddle for warmth, damp blankets on their shoulders. Their eyes are open wounds. Nothing left in their hearts. They are the broken pieces of something that can never be fixed. Children play in the ruins of the school. Others make up games with stones and shapes drawn in the dirt. Their hands are cold and cracked.

Two years since Kosta Kojo was overthrown and executed for war crimes. The conflict is history, but the suffering continues.

The old woman glances at him and tries to smile but her lips only tremble weakly. She looks at the apple he has given her. It is pale green, bruised and nicked, but still her eyes mist with grateful tears. She clutches the piece of fruit as if someone might take it from her—as if, with callous nature, the wind would spirit it away.

"Thank you," she whispers.

"You feel gratitude." His voice is dull, as gray as the sky.

"Yes."

"Anything else?"

The old woman nods and a tear trickles, separates into the creases of her nose. "I am hungry. And scared."

"We are all scared," he replies.

Raif Cerić is twenty-seven years old but the lines on his face run deep and he walks crooked, supported by a steel cane he has fashioned from wreckage. His left leg is atrophied, his calf muscle a series of broken strings. A bullet from an M57 is lodged close to the bone. His body is a tapestry of scar tissue. Nose broken out of shape. Blind in his right eye from countless beatings.

"We are all scared," he says again.

Across the wastes of their village, stepping over rubble and broken glass and appliances stripped for parts. This building, with its blackened walls and collapsed roof, is where his best friend had lived, where they had laughed, guzzled rakia, and played belot until the numbers on the cards had blurred. Here is the shell of his brother's house, empty of everything, especially life. This section of wall is all that remains of Jasna Džihan's home. Jasna had been the village "grandmother," loved by all. She offered food to the hungry, blankets to the cold. The light in her eyes gave hope to the forlorn. Jasna had been raped and beaten in front of the entire village. Her dismembered corpse hung from the swing frame in the children's playground for six days.

Dust and ash thicken the air. You can taste it in your throat when you breathe. Weep, and even your tears are stained.

Raif wipes his sunken face and thinks, *What are you feeling?*

Through the allotment, where seeds are planted but few flourish, seeking nutrients in the soil, foliage pale. Past a row of shacks built from what materials they could salvage, and where they gather when it's cold. The river they sometimes bathe in. Crippled houses of worship where prayers have turned to lamentations. The cemetery: the only place you will find flowers. Onward, past ruin, stacked and delicate, like books in a library, telling many thousands of tales. To the west, the hospital's ghost shimmers through the dust. Its thirty-two beds had been filled with children when the Supreme Republic Army took to it with flamethrowers. The building had burned to the ground in less than three hours, but the screams can be heard to this day.

Raif continues to limp through the village, weaving through the rubble and woe, picking a route with the tip of his cane. He comes to the summit road, which leads through the mountains, down into the cities, and from there to the rest of the world. But Raif stops less than a kilometer from the village, at the agreed meeting point: the husk of a burned-out bus. He breathes unevenly and his blind eye weeps gritty tears. Hands on his thighs. Metallic pain seeping from his left leg into his pelvis, his gut.

He waits.

He reaches into his jacket pocket and takes out a photograph, damaged by time, by being constantly taken out, creased and folded. It shows a young family: a man, wife, and their son, who looks to be about five years old. The man's face is too faded to read. All that can be seen of his wife is a swirl of auburn hair. The boy sits on his father's lap. He is grinning, missing a front tooth but altogether handsome, clutching a book titled *The Happy Bird*. Raif touches the boy's face. Draws a circle around his head, like a halo.

"Cerić."

He jerks, startled, at the sound of his name. Drops the photo. Reaches down to retrieve it and the pain makes him groan. He pushes the photo back into his jacket pocket and straightens with another groan, pressure on his cane, body trembling. A figure steps toward him, broad in the shadows.

"I startled you, Cerić?"

"I didn't hear you approach."

"You should be more vigilant."

Raif nods and runs a hand through his hair. He steps to one side to see the man more clearly. Jergović. A small-time crook from the next village. There are two bulges beneath his jacket. One is the package. The other is a weapon of some description. A lead pipe. Maybe a machete. Insurance, Jergović calls it.

"You found it?" Raif asks.

Jergović nods and his heavy eyes flick down to the bulge in the right side of his jacket.

Raif licks his lips and his blind eye flutters. He feels something deep inside. He thinks it's hope, but it has been such a long time since he has felt this emotion that he cannot be sure. A gray line of sweat trickles from his brow.

"You have something for me?" Jergović asks.

"I do." And Raif shakes a knapsack from his back, made from sackcloth and string. He pulls it open and shows Jergović what is inside: apples, potatoes, peppers, tomatoes. Each fresh and ripe. Nothing like the pale, bruised apple he had given the old lady. Jergović plucks a potato from the top and bites into it. Juices dribble onto his chin.

"Good," he says. Dirt on his teeth.

"Of course," Raif replies. His healthy eye drifts to the bulge in

Jergović's jacket. He holds out one hand. Jergović grins, drops the potato into the sack, draws the strings tight. There is a moment where Raif thinks he is going to shoulder the goods and run without making the exchange. His heart ticks heavily; he knows he could never give chase. But Jergović opens his jacket and takes out the package, solid and thin, wrapped in old newspaper. Raif all but snatches it from his hand. Peels the wrapping away.

"Yes," he says, and feels like crying. He turns it over in his hands—can't remember having seen so much color, so much joy.

A moment later and he is out of Jergović's shadow and limping back toward the village. It is growing darker now and he can see the fires flickering, like bright wings, smoke lost in the low cloud. He limps past the phantom school and Jasna Džihan's home. Through the village square, where his people gather in sad flocks. The old lady is no longer there. She has stolen away, Raif thinks, to eat her apple in privacy. She will even eat the core, and perhaps weep guilty tears afterward. A villager notices him and calls out across the square, asks if he has any produce, and Raif lies with a heart like flint, tells him that the crops are effete. He limps on with his eyes down and doesn't look up until he is on the roadway to his farmhouse.

Before the war, he'd farmed sixteen acres. Maize and wheat, mostly, although his potatoes were regarded as the best in the district. Thirty head of cattle. Goats for dairy. Enough hens to supply the village with eggs. It was a small farm, but rewarding. Now it is—like everything else—a shattered reminder. Withered fields. Stripped machinery. A farmhouse burned to black, brittle sticks. The barn (where SRA soldiers drank, raped, sang noble war songs until their throats were raw) is still standing, filled with mildewed hay, thick with bugs. Raif has salvaged a patch of land where the soil is fertile enough for a few crops. He distributes most throughout the village, though he uses the occasional batch for currency.

He limps, now, into his barn, and to his secret. A place undiscovered by SRA troops during their assault. He brushes aside a thin covering of hay to reveal a trapdoor in the barn floor. Pulls it open. Canted steps lead into a cellar. Used for storing wood before the war. He takes a kerosene lamp from a hook on the wall, lights it, ventures down, closes the trapdoor behind him. The lamp flashes orange on concrete walls and old tools thick with rust, cobweb. The stink of rot and cold earth. A dripping sound. A scratching sound. Raif's healthy eye flickers in the lamplight. His hope is as brightly colored as the thing inside his jacket.

Across the dirt floor to the wretch in the corner, chained to the wall. Naked and wasted. Dead eyes staring into some pale place beyond words. Raif jabs him with the cane and he looks up, regards Raif without expression.

"What are you feeling?"

The wretch looks away and, as always, says nothing.

The world had been absorbed in crises. Global economic uncertainty. Civil unrest across the Middle East. War in Africa, Asia. Natural disasters in Chile, Greece, Japan, California. A North Korean despot with his finger on the trigger. Nobody noticed when General Kosta Kojo ascended to power. The world was blind to the anger in his smile. The hate in his eyes. This suited Kojo's cruel agenda. He declared all Jews and Muslims impure and divided the nation in a heartbeat. Skirmishes broke out in all major cities, and after a failed attempt to take his life, Kojo established the Supreme Republic Army and the ethnic cleansing began.

There was resistance but it amounted to nothing. Rebels and militant factions. Unfunded, largely unarmed. A threat of intervention from the West, as hollow as a bullet casing; the West had its own concerns, many of them fiscal, and with Allied forces scattered across the world, they had little to offer in the way of military support. Kojo tightened the screw. His army marched from the cities to the towns, to the villages. The destruction was absolute, apocalyptic. Inhumanity reigned. While women were raped and children murdered, the West existed in a haze of naïveté. It—as ever—flicked channels, from the news to *Monday Night Football*. It downloaded music and apps and looked at the world like it wasn't really happening. It clogged the interstates, railways, airports. It slept at night in a warmer bed.

They came to Raif's village like a new machine. A spinning saw blade that cut through families and homes, across roadways and through livelihoods. Severing hope, goodness. Cutting belief down at the knees. The villagers had no fight. Raif—a strong, young farmer—was made an example of: tied to a post in the square and beaten, tortured, while his family was forced to watch. It was then—looking into the unfeeling eyes of his enemy—that Raif realized the stories about the Dead Ones were true. He'd believed them a fallacy. Metaphor for heartlessness.

No.

Put a gun in a young man's hands and call him a soldier. Doesn't make him a killer. Sew a stripe on his arm, a ribbon on his chest. Doesn't make him soulless. The Supreme Republic Army was formed of patriots, eager to serve their country, their leader, often contrary to their own moral philosophy. For some, it was not easy to shoot a child in the face, to rape an elderly woman, burn babies in their cribs. They did as they were ordered, knowing the punishment for dereliction of duty. Still, there were rumors of SRA soldiers taking their own lives. The easy way out. Others turned to Synph.

Dr. Anfisa Muratova discovered Synphotryptic while researching the analgesic effects of various street drugs. Synph was a psychoactive substance that affected neurotransmitters in the limbic system; it literally crippled one's emotional response. Thus, a soldier could engage in acts of war, genocide, without qualm, without guilt. Synph was made available to the SRA before testing was complete, and many soldiers turned to it in order to desensitize themselves to the terrors they inflicted. In moderation, the effects would have worn off within hours. But when taken in excess, it rendered the soldiers permanently emotionless.

And without emotion, they died inside.

They became the Dead Ones.

To see them—these ragged-faced things, these once-men . . . armed with M77s, knives, apathy. Dressed in their dour fatigues and torturing without expression, killing without feeling. They didn't even wash the blood from their hands. They marched through the war, stained and silent, as deep as shadows. There were whispers among the living that they were cold to the touch, and that even their hearts had stopped beating.

Raif has no idea who saved him. Not Branka, his wife. She was long dead by that time. Perhaps Jasmila, his best friend's sister, though he will never be sure. A female, almost certainly, who dared the village square in the small hours and cut his binds with a piece of glass.

Raif staggered into the woods and hid beneath leaves for three days, venturing out only to drink rainwater from scoops of bark or to eat fungus and seeds.

He lost track of time. Could have been in the woods three days or three weeks. Once strong enough, he moved to the mountains and lived in a cave for another painful stretch of time. Ate dead wildlife while he watched fires rage through not only his but distant villages. Heard every scream and gunshot. Found strength in every new breath.

Healing brought with it a surge of anger. The unquenchable thirst for revenge. Everything he loved, and had worked for, had been taken from him. His wife and son had been murdered in front of his eyes. He had nothing left to lose.

And so he resolved to return to his village and kill as many SRA monsters—there was no other word for them—as he could. Maybe he'd find Jergović, if he was still alive, and barter for a firearm. Even a machete. He would attack at night, with the element of surprise, and would cut and bludgeon and kill until the last breath had been ripped from his lungs. One thousand monsters would not be enough. To see their pain. To have them feel—if only for a moment—a fraction of the suffering that they had inflicted.

Raif stayed another two days in the mountains, eating wildlife, berries, drinking spring water, trying to build his strength. He had been full of muscle once. Another shadow of what used to be, and never would be again. It took him a further two days to traverse the rocky slopes and journey through the woods to his village. Watchful. Always hurting. He returned to emptiness. The SRA had moved on, leaving skeleton buildings, still smoldering. Bodies in the streets. People Raif had known and loved. Hanging from trees and streetlights. Piled like wood. There were a few survivors scattered among the ruin. Most had gathered in the remains of the mosque, on their knees, their backs forming perfect domes. Raif passed them by. He had no desire for prayer. He staggered to the debris that used to be his farmhouse and saw one of his son's shoes among the ruin. Held it and wept. Then he heard the sounds from the barn.

Not all the SRA soldiers had moved on. Raif saw, approaching his barn, two long figures dressed in stained fatigues, methodically beating a naked girl. So involved in what they were doing that they didn't see or hear him. He entered via a side door hanging from one hinge. He thought his tools would have been destroyed, and most of them were, but he noticed on the wall a pitchfork with rusted tines and grabbed it. Shuffled toward the Dead Ones from behind. One of them turned as he approached and Raif saw nothing on his face. No expression of surprise or dread. Only glassy eyes and a flat, open mouth. All of Raif's anger—his taste for revenge—erupted. He cried out and drove forward with the pitchfork. One tine punctured the soldier's throat. The other popped through his skull just above the right eye. Still no expression. No pain. No fear. Raif pulled back on the pitchfork, drove forward again. The tines found the soldier's chest this time. Punched deep and pushed him backward. He staggered over the bleeding girl and fell hard but got up again.

The other Dead One had turned by this point. Equally blank eyes. A flop of dirty red hair. He pulled an M57 from his holster and took aim. Raif swiped at the gun with the pitchfork and it went off with a flash. The report shook dust from the loft and the bullet went astray, ricocheted, hit Raif in the lower leg. He screamed and dropped to one knee but managed to thrust forward with the pitchfork. It plunged into the soldier's stomach and he folded, dropped the gun. Raif picked it up and swiveled. The other Dead One moved toward him. Dark holes in his chest, in his throat and forehead. No blood. Still no emotion. Raif framed his vacant face in the M57's sights.

"For my family."

Pulled the trigger.

The bullet hit him just below the nose and tore through cartilage and bone and the altered material of his brain. Smashed through the back of his skull, wide as a fist. The soldier crumpled, twitched once, and was still.

Too much adrenaline to feel pain. Raif got to his feet and wheeled, gun ready, dragging his wounded leg. The Dead One with the flop of red hair lurched toward him, and Raif parked the M57's muzzle point-blank in the middle of his forehead.

"For my people."

His finger curled around the trigger and exerted pressure but not enough to discharge a round. He wiped a bloody tear from his blind eye and then his finger relaxed completely. Where was the satisfaction in taking this man's life while he remained emotionless? A void in his brain where feeling had been.

"What are you?" Raif asked, exhibiting enough emotion for them both. A storm of hurt and anger. Grief piled high, like the ruins of his farmhouse. Fear, solid inside him, something he could hold, like his son's empty shoe.

No response from the Dead One. Not a flicker in his eye.

"What are you feeling?"

Nothing.

Raif struck him with the butt of the gun and his head rocked sideways and his red hair flopped and when he turned his eyes back to Raif they were still expressionless.

"You have nothing inside."

To kill him now wouldn't be revenge, it would be mercy. So he lowered the M57's sights and put a bullet in the soldier's thigh. He dropped hard and tried to get back up but Raif was on top of him, knee between his shoulder blades. Raif pulled off his shirt and used the sleeves like a rope, wrapped around the soldier's throat. Dragged him across the barn floor to a trapdoor hidden by loose hay. Opened it and threw him down the steps to the mud floor below. Followed. And with his heart still raging and tears flowing from his eyes, he stripped the soldier naked and used his uniform to bind him.

It was while removing his clothing that the photograph fluttered out. Raif picked it up and looked at it. A man—the soldier—with his wife and son. The wife had a swirl of auburn hair. The son was grinning, tooth missing, holding a book.

"This is your family," Raif said. He held the photograph for the soldier to see but there was no sign of recognition. "Do you miss them? Do you wish to love your wife again? Feel her in your arms? Hold your son and read to him?"

The soldier said nothing. Eyes like stones.

Raif hit him hard and his hair flopped again, to the other side. He pushed the photograph into his face.

"Feel something," his hissed. "Something."

He could be just another block of wood. Or a leaf, fallen from the tree, retaining shape and color but severed from life.

Raif pocketed the photograph and struggled up the cellar steps. Bolted the trapdoor behind him. Concealed it with hay. Went to the girl. She shrieked and shied from him and tried to cover her nakedness.

"I won't hurt you."

He drew water from the well and cleaned her wounds. Wrapped her in a blanket he had taken from what used to be his bedroom. She wept and trembled and her emotion overwhelmed him. She was human, and he held her.

Raif's village lived, then, in a state of fear, flinching at every loud sound and hiding in the shadows, until the UN finally intervened and Kojo was removed from power. His statue toppled to yells of triumph. Fists striking the air. Flags high. His execution was secretly filmed with a Motorola cell phone. Went viral. A billion hits on YouTube.

The SRA faded into the very land they had burned. The Dead Ones drifted aimlessly. Most were disabled by UN peacekeepers.

Raif spent his days helping in the village. Clearing rubble. Digging graves. Nursing the sick. International aid was a long way off. Nothing they could depend on. The world was bereft and so many sought help. They salvaged what they could and tried to heal. Raif sectioned off a small plot of land and fertilized the soil and grew vegetables, plants with medicinal properties. He hunted wildlife and gathered berries and seeds from the woods. Every three or four days he would put together a package and distribute it among the villagers.

His nights were spent in the barn cellar.

"What are you feeling?"

The Dead One, chained to the wall, felt nothing. His wounds didn't bleed. He didn't eat. Didn't weep. Didn't die. Raif made it his goal—tried everything—to elicit some emotion. Showed him the photograph every night. Held it in front of his eyes until the lamp burned out. He put down food and water, just out of reach, but the Dead One made no move for it. Asked about his family, his home, his life before the war, hoping to trigger some memory.

Hoping for pain.

Tortured him. Took a stick to his body. Broke his fingers with a hammer. Pounded nails through his wrists and ankles and left them there until they corroded.

"What are you feeling?"

Two years. Twenty-six months, to be exact. The village looked from beneath its shadow and saw a cold gray emptiness but learned to breathe again. The world stretched into more crises and downloaded apps and watched "reality" TV and considered the side-effects of pharmaceutical drugs. A new war in Afghanistan. A newer, slimmer iPad. Genocide in West Africa. The new Chevy Silverado with its biggest payload yet. Flash floods in Mexico. A coke-addled sitcom star back in rehab. Avian flu in China, killing thousands.

The Dead One chained to the wall in Raif's cellar, feeling nothing. Nothing at all.

The lamplight flashes and presses deep orange flowers on the floor and walls. Raif sits opposite the Dead One, cross-legged, holding the photograph for him to see. Crisp and colorful when it had fluttered from his pocket. Now creased, peeling, faded. All is silent but for the wind hissing through the barn above. The rain chattering on its roof.

The Dead One sits head low and body cracked. His spine and rib cage resemble something partially uncovered at a dig site. Wrapped in a skin of dust. His mouth is as black and dry as a coal chute.

"She's beautiful," Raif says. "Your wife."

The Dead One blinks and shifts across the floor and his pelvic bones roll like something under water.

"And your son. Four, five years old?"

He draws his knees close and hangs his head again.

"Your eyes. Your jaw."

Stillness. Silence.

"I had a wife," Raif says. His chin dimples as he tries to keep his mouth from quivering. "She was beautiful, too. Not a day—not a *minute*—goes by when I don't think about her. The way her eyes would grow wide when she laughed. The shape of her hips. Her lisp, which she hated, but which I thought made her sound adorable. And my son. Five years old. The same age as your son, perhaps. So bright, and so happy. He wanted to learn everything—would always ask questions. 'Why is the sun so hot, Daddy? Why do trees have leaves? Why can ducks swim *and* fly?' I was certain he would grow up to be a great man. An academic, who would teach people and help make the world stronger."

The Dead One shifts again and the chain securing him to the wall clangs. The lamplight etches a warm tattoo on his skin.

"Yes, our life was good and rich. Simple. Loving. And then you came. Your . . . army." Raif stops. Wipes his eyes. He takes a deep breath that shudders in his chest as if it has edges. "Took everything away. Destroyed my village. My life. You made my wife and son watch while you tied me to a post and beat me like a dog. Then, as if that wasn't enough, you killed her in front of me. Butchered her and dragged her body through the dirt. Killed my son, too. Cut off his hands. His head. And I saw a million unanswered questions in his terrified eyes, each one beginning with the word *why*."

Raif turns the photograph around and looks at it. Touches the woman's hair. The boy's face.

"Why?"

Clang goes the chain.

Raif flips the photograph like a magician flipping a playing card and it spins through the air and lands, face up, at the Dead One's feet, where he can see it.

"Every day I hurt. The pain . . . the sorrow. It tears me apart. And the only thing that keeps me going—that has stopped me from suicide—is the promise of making you feel the same. After all, why should you, who have caused all this hurt, go without pain?"

The barn creaks above them, wind talking through the gaps in the boards in haunted sounds. Raif closes his eyes and thinks of nights spent with Branka, an open fire, the silhouettes of branches dancing in the windows. Naked with Branka. Her hair coiled in his hand as the fire pops and glows.

He lowers his head and weeps, and when he looks up, quite some time later, the Dead One still hasn't moved.

"I tried to find out more about you," Raif says, voice cracking. "I hoped to find your wife and son. Bring them here. I thought for sure they could unlock that missing part of your brain. But you carried no ID. Just a number stitched into your uniform. Like a prisoner."

Raif grabs his cane and stretches it across the floor. Taps the photograph.

"That is all I have. Everything I know about you is right there."

The Dead One's mouth opens and closes silently.

"So, if I cannot bring your family . . ." Raif unbuttons his jacket, reaches inside, and takes out the package he received from Jergović in exchange for two weeks' worth of fruit and vegetables. He unwraps the newspaper and the sound makes the Dead One look up but still his eyes are zeros. Raif tosses the wrapping to one side and holds up the object for the Dead One to see. The colors—burning reds, blues, and yellows—are instantly engaging, designed to draw a child's attention. Raif had hoped to see a shred of recognition in the Dead One's eyes but there is nothing at all.

"*The Happy Bird*," Raif says, reading the bouncy, oversize words on the cover. It is the same book the Dead One's son is clutching in the photograph. It has taken Jergović eleven months to find a copy. But here it is, at last, in Raif's hands. A thing of happiness. And, for the Dead One, of memory.

Yet, his zero eyes flick away and he shifts and his chain makes a dull sound.

"This is your son's favorite book, isn't it?" Raif opens the cover and flips through a few pages and they all bleed color. "I bet you read this to him over and over again. You'd reach the end and have to go right back to the beginning, wouldn't you? I know . . . I must have read *Šerif and the Magic Flower* to my son a thousand times. Every word is printed on my mind. Just like every word of *The Happy Bird* is printed on yours. I bet you could recite it to him without having to turn a single page. But your son liked the pictures, didn't he? This one . . . the bird singing as he flies over the bright red tractor. And this one . . . the squirrel waving. Look at his funny little teeth."

The Dead One glances at him. Not at the book—the picture of the squirrel with his funny little teeth—but at him.

"What are you feeling now?"

Away go the eyes again.

Raif's heart flashes like the lamplight and another tear runs from his eye. He is close to the end now, one way or another, and his emotion surges. He presses a knuckle to his mouth. Wipes his face. Flips to page one and begins reading.

The Happy Bird

It was another beautiful morning in Evergreen Wood. The sun was shining brightly, and all the trees and flowers swayed like they were dancing to music. Obrad the sparrow woke up early. He fluttered out of his nest, chirping happily, then swooped low and said hello to all his friends.

"Good morning, Obrad," said the bears and rabbits, blinking their sleepy eyes.

"Sing us a happy song, Obrad," said the squirrels, waving from the branches.

Obrad liked to sing. It was one of his favorite things.

"Cheep-cheep," he sang, and flew in a big, bright circle.

Afterward, Obrad decided to visit a different wood to see if the animals there were just as friendly. However, he hadn't flown far before realizing that not everywhere was as happy as Evergreen Wood. . . .

In the next field he spotted a little red tractor sitting all on its own. He fluttered down and landed on its steering wheel, and saw that the tractor was very sad indeed.

"Why are you so sad, Mr. Tractor?" Obrad asked.

"My engine is old and has stopped working," the tractor huffed and grumbled. "And the farmer doesn't use me anymore."

Obrad felt sad for the tractor, but he knew just what to do!

"I'll sing you a happy song," he said. "Cheep-cheep." And he flew in a big, bright circle.

The tractor smiled and tooted his horn. "Thank you, Obrad. I feel a little better now."

Next, Obrad flew over the playground, where he spotted a little girl with tears in her eyes. He fluttered down and landed on her shoulder.

"Why are you crying, little girl?" he asked.

The little girl wiped her bright blue eyes. "My best friend moved to a new town, and I've got nobody to play with."

Obrad didn't like to see the little girl so lonely, but he knew just what to do!

"Cheep-cheep," he sang, and flew in a big, bright circle.

The little girl laughed and danced with him. "Thank you, Obrad. Come play again soon."

Next, Obrad flew to Dusky Forest. He had never been there before, and was surprised to find it filled with lots of men with angry, buzzing machinery. Obrad watched as the men used the machines to cut down the trees! He whistled for them to stop, but their machines were so loud that they couldn't hear him.

Obrad flew deeper into the forest, where all the animals were huddled and scared.

"What's going on here?" he asked, fluttering his wings.

"The humans are cutting down our trees," said the squirrels.

"Our homes," added the woodpeckers.

"So that they can build a factory made of concrete and steel," snarled the wolves.

"But where will you live?" Obrad asked.

The animals looked at one another and shrugged. "We don't know," they said fearfully.

Obrad tried to cheer them up. He sang the happiest song he knew, and flew in the biggest, brightest circle. But the animals were still sad.

Obrad thought for a little while, and then he knew just what to do!

"Follow me," he tweeted. "Come and live in Evergreen Wood. It's the happiest place I know, and the animals are all so friendly."

Obrad cheeped another happy song, and although some of the animals didn't want to leave the woods they had grown up in, they all followed. Out of Dusky Forest, past the playground where the little girl danced and waved, past the farmer's field where the tractor tooted its horn, and into Evergreen Wood. The new animals were made to feel very welcome. They made lots of special friends and weren't afraid anymore.

Later that day, Obrad was sitting on his favorite branch, singing as always, when Sava the wise owl shuffled over to him.

"You did a good thing today, Obrad," Sava said, blinking his wide eyes. "You helped those who were sad, lonely, and afraid."

Obrad shook his feathers. "It's because I felt sad, lonely, and afraid for them."

Sava nodded wisely. "And that is a good thing. Remember, Obrad, it's what we feel that makes us truly alive."

And from that day on, Obrad would fly far and wide, helping those in need.

"Cheep-cheep," he would sing, flying in big, bright circles.

He would make them all feel better. And that, more than anything else, made him the Happy Bird.

Just over a year ago, Raif had been tearing up old newspapers for mulch when he came across an article about how the U.S. military was exploring a link between biosemiotics and suicide bombing. Subliminal messages can be relayed via signage and imagery, and a combination of sensory input can be powerful enough to trigger a biosemiotic cascade—communication at a cellular level, inspiring action, reaction, memory. The article suggested that suicide bombers had been brainwashed by key sensory stimuli, in a way similar to how a person can be made to feel thirsty with the sound of a soda can being opened.

Biosemiotics was also being used to aid those with brain damage. Raif read with interest how, for certain people, the right combination of sound and imagery could activate memory . . . emotion.

Feeling.

The photograph of the Dead One's family was not enough. Nor was the photograph and the book combined. But these two key visuals, coupled with the auditory stimulus of the story . . .

Raif notices something on the Dead One's cheek. It could be a trick of the lamplight. It could be a tear.

He reads *The Happy Bird* again.

And again.

The wind gusts through the barn and the rain laughs. The Dead One shifts, shoulders trembling. The framework of his rib cage, spine, rises and falls. Rises and falls.

Raif reads the book a fourth time. A fifth. Midway through the sixth reading, the Dead One makes an involuntary sound: a grunt; a sob. Raif lowers the book and his heart bangs as he watches the Dead One reach across the floor. Pick up the photograph. Look at it. His eyes aren't zeros anymore. He blinks and tears flash down his face. Raif continues reading and when he finishes he puts down the book and looks at the Dead One, who clutches the photograph to his chest, shakes his head, weeps openly.

Raif lets him cry. Lets him feel pain.

The lamplight dances like nothing has happened.

"What was his name?" Raif asks, pointing at the photograph covered by the Dead One's hands.

It takes him awhile to answer.

"Tihomir."

Raif nods and wipes away his own tears. "My son's name was Halid." He uses the cane to get to his feet. "They could have been friends."

Across the village, smoke rises from fires extinguished by the rain. The people gather close enough to taste one another's skin. To feel their bodies, like the walls of the houses they once lived in. They whisper assurances as the wind skates from the mountains and through the trees, ushering heavy bags of cloud across a sky that remains scarred.

In the cellar beneath Raif's barn, the soldier kisses the photograph and lowers his head.

Like so many before him, he feels.

And then he bleeds.

PARASITE

Daniel H. Wilson

I dreamed I was breathing.

Lark Iron Cloud

New War + 2 years, 8 months
When I was a boy, Lonnie Wayne Blanton lead me into the deep
dark woods and left me there. After I fought my way back out
he told me I was a man and I could feel that he was right. Six
months later, I led the soldiers of Gray Horse Army into the deep
dark woods to face the machines of the New War. We fought our
way out, but honest to god, I could not tell you what we have
become.

—Lark Iron Cloud MIL#GHA530

CARL IS ON HIS ASS. Whimpering and clawing and kicking his
way backward through the snow. My soldier won't look at me and
he won't take my hand and I can't for the life of me understand why
until I notice his eyes.

Not where he's looking. But where he *won't* look.

Something black crawling low and fast on too many legs. And
another one. Coming up from under the snow.

Too late.

I don't feel the pincers at first. Just this strong pressure on the
base of my neck. I'm in a hydraulic-powered bear hug. I spin around
in the slushy snow but there's nobody behind me.

Whatever it is has climbed up my back and gotten a good hold.
My knees sag with the lurching weight of it. Crooked black feelers
reach around my chest and my spine is suddenly on fire as the thing
decides to dig in, a bundle of squirming razor blades.

Shit shit shit—what is this that it hurts so *goddamn much.*

Carl's got his frost-plated rifle up, training it on me. The gun strap hangs stiff and crusty in the arctic breeze. Around us, the rest of my soldiers are screaming and dancing in tight, panicked circles. Some are running. But me and the engineer are having our own little moment here.

"Carl," I wheeze. "No."

My voice sounds hollow from the pain of whatever has gotten between my shoulder blades. Judging from Carl's blank face, I figure that I'm not in a very happy spot here. No, sir. That is a full-on nega*tory.*

Carl lets go of his rifle but the strap catches on his forearm. He stumbles away, gun dangling. Wipes his eyes with shaking fingers, tendons streaking the backs of his hands. His complicated engineering helmet falls off and thunks into the snow, an empty bowl.

He's crying. I could give a shit.

I'm being flayed alive, straining and groaning against black spider legs gripping my body, doing drunken pirouettes in the slush. Knotty black arms slice into the meat of my thighs, sprouting smaller feelers like vines. Others grip my biceps, elbows, forearms, and, goddammit, even my fingers.

I am in command but I am most definitely not in control. Some of my soldiers are still thrashing. Some aren't. The wounded are crawling and hobbling away fast as they can, coiled black shapes slicing toward them like scorpions.

Carl's gone now: hightailed it. Left his ostrich-legged tall-walker behind, collapsed awkwardly on its side. Left all of us unlucky dancers behind.

My legs are wrapped too tight now to struggle. A motor grinds as I push against it, reaching back with my arm. I feel a freezing fist-size plate of metal hunkered in the warm spot at the base of my neck. Not good.

The machine snaps my arm back into place.

Can't say I'm real sure of what happens next. I got a lot of experience breaking down Rob hardware for Gray Horse Army, though. After a while, you get a feel for how the machines think. How they use and reuse all those bits and pieces.

So, I imagine my guess is pretty accurate.

As I watch the vapor of my last breath evaporate, the parasite on my back jerks and severs my spinal column with a flat, sharpened piece of metal mounted to its head region. My arms and legs go numb, so much dead meat. But I don't fall because the machine's arms and legs are there to hold me up.

And I don't die.

Some kind of cap must fit over the nub of my spine, interfacing with the bundle of nerves there. This is a mobile surgery station leeched onto my neck. Humming and throbbing and exploring, it's clipping veins and nerves and whatever else. Keeping oxygen in my blood, circulating it.

I'm spitting cherry syrup into the snow.

Lonnie Wayne Blanton, my commander, says that this late in the war you can't let anything the enemy does surprise you. He says Big Rob cooks up a brand-new nightmare every day and he's one hell of a chef. Yet here I am. Surprised, again.

The machine is really digging in now. As it works, my eyes and ears start blurring and ringing and singing. I wonder if the scorpion can see what I see. Hear what I hear.

I'm hallucinating in the snow.

A god-size orange tendril of smoke roils across the pale sky. It's real pretty. Smaller streams fall from it, pouring down like water from drain spouts. Some of the streams disappear behind the trees, others are even farther away. But one of them twists down and drops straight at me. Into my head.

A line of communication.

Big Rob has got me. The thinking machine that calls itself Archos is driving the pulsing thing on my back. A few dozen clicks from here, the architect of the New War is crouched where that fat orange column of transmission ends. Pulling all the strings.

I watch as my dead arms unsling my rifle. Tendons in my neck creak as the machine twists my head, sweeps my vision across the clearing. I'm alone now, and I think I'm hunting.

In the growing twilight, I spot dozens of other orange umbilical cords just like mine. They fall out of the sky and into the dark woods around me. As I lurch forward out of the clearing, the other lines drift alongside me, keeping pace.

All of us are being dragged in the same direction.

We're a ragged front line of dark shapes, hundreds strong, shambling through the woods toward the scattered remnants of Gray Horse Army. My consciousness begins to fade in and out as my cooling body slogs among the trees. The last thing I remember thinking is that I hope Lonnie Wayne don't see me like this. And if he does, well, I hope he puts me down quick.

I don't hear the gunshot itself, just a dry echo in the trees. It's something, though. Enough to wake me up.

I dreamed I was breathing.

The impossible smoke in the sky is gone. All those evil thoughts disappeared. And the place where Archos lived is empty now. Big Rob must be dead. It's the only explanation.

The New War is over and we won and I'm still here. Still alive, somehow.

I focus on it and the wires of my parasite start to work my legs. Carry me in the direction of the gunshot. Over the charred earth of a weeks-old battlefield. I pass by a titanic spider tank leaning still and cold and heavy against a snow bank. It's armor is pocked with sooty craters, intention light shattered, joints cracked open like lobster claws. And bodies.

Frozen bodies melded with the snow. Stiff uniforms and frostbitten metal. The occasional alabaster patch of exposed frozen flesh. I recognize most of the corpses as Gray Horse Army, but pieces of some other army are here, too. Bodies of the ones who came and fought before we ever knew Archos existed.

Among the trees at the edge of the clearing, I see the others.

A cluster of a dozen or so walking corpses stand huddled, shoulder to shoulder. Silent. Some are still in full uniform, normal-looking save for the clinging clockwork parasites. Others are worse off: a woman is missing her leg, yet she stands steadily on the narrow black appendage of the parasite; one man is shirtless in the cold, skin windblasted to a marbled corpse sheen. All of them are riddled with puckered bullet holes. Cratered exit wounds flapping with icy skin and torn armor.

And I see another, freshly killed.

A still form lays in the snow. Its head is missing, pieces scattered.

A parasite lays on its back nearby, coated in rusty blood, slowly flexing its mouthpieces like a squashed bug.

So that gunshot served a purpose.

These survivors have one combat shotgun left among them. A big man, stooped over with his own size, has got the gun now. Most of his face is hidden in an overgrown beard but I can see his mouth is round and open, a rotten hole. He's moving slow because frostbite has taken all his fingers, but I figure out pretty quick where he's going with that barrel.

They're taking turns killing themselves.

"No," I try to shout, but it comes out a shapeless sob. "No, this is *wrong*."

I shuffle faster, weaving among shredded bodies trapped in permafrost like it was quick-set concrete. None of the survivors pays me much attention. They keep their faces aimed away from the big man, but stand close to grab the shotgun when it falls.

The bearded man has his eyes closed. So he doesn't understand what's happening when I shove the butt of the gun. His blackened nub of a thumb nudges the trigger and the gun thunders and leaps out of his hands. Pieces of bark and a puff of snow drift down from the trees overhead. The slug missed.

Those great black eyes open, mottled with frost, and understanding sets in. With an angry moan, the big man swings at me. His frozen forearm lands like an aluminum baseball bat, propelled by black robotic musculature. It chips off a piece of my elbow, knocks me off-balance. Only now do I realize that I'm missing half of my torso. My guts are gone and so is my center of balance. Guess I'm not the steadiest corpse alive.

I drop hard into the snow.

The guy lifts his leg, his long tendons snapping like frozen tree branches, and drops a boot into my stomach cavity. Rib fragments scatter in the snow among shreds of my clothing and flesh. The beard keeps stomping and moaning, destroying my already ruined body in a slow-motion rage.

And I can't feel a goddam thing.

Then another shot is fired. The booming echo skitters through the trees in unfamiliar lurches. An unidentified weapon.

The next stomping blow doesn't land.

I shove myself into a sitting position as something comes out from behind a cracked tree trunk. It is short and gray skinned, limping. The parasite on its back is blocky, not as graceful as the smoothly ridged humps the rest of us wear. And it's got on a strange uniform, long frozen to warped bone. This thing was a soldier, once.

Not one of ours. A Chinese soldier.

A familiar tendril of orange smoke rises from the new soldier's parasite. It's some kind of bad dream, something the parasite makes me see, yet it feels more real than the ice world around me. The tendril floats like a spider web on the wind. Closer and closer.

When it lands on my head, I hear a woman's voice.

"I am Chen Feng. Wandering lost in Dìyù, yet honor-bound to live. I greet you in solidarity, survivor," she says.

The soldier thing is a female. Exposed cheekbones dapple her shrunken face, polished by the weather. She has the grinning, toothy mouth of a corpse, yet her words expand into my head like warm medicine.

"Hello?" I ask, watching a flicker of radio communication intertwine with her light. Whoa. She's gone and taught me to speak. *"Where did you come from?"*

"I am the might of Manchuria. A spirit. No longer alive and not yet dead."

"Where are your people?"

"They are as dust. The Northeast Provinces foolishly marched alone. We sought glory and instead were devoured by the jīqì rén. Those consumed rose again into Dìyù. Forced to slaughter our brothers and sisters. The Siberian Russians arrived with vodka and boasts and we slew the Èluósī, too. You dark-skinned ones came on walking tanks, and we rose wearily once more."

"You were waiting for us."

"Your metal soldiers were too fast. The pànduàn cut through our frozen flesh. Raced into the west. And when the final pànduàn defied the great enemy, we heard its screams of rage. The foul deep light was extinguished, and I awoke from Dìyù into another nightmare."

Years. This soldier must have been out here in the cold for *years.* The enormity of her suffering fills my mind.

"We've got to leave here," I say.

Chen Feng doesn't respond. Neither do the others. A hopeless silence settles onto my shoulders like gravity. There is nowhere to go and we all know it. I turn to the horizon, avoiding their faces. And only now do I realize that I can see a kind of leftover orange haze beyond the trees.

It's the place where Archos must have made its final stand. And where I might still find Lonnie Wayne. The man saved my life and brought me into Gray Horse Army. I'm scared to let him see me like this but I've got hurt soldiers who need me.

"We reunite with Gray Horse Army," I say, and begin to limp away.

Our group walks for three days and nights. We don't tire and we don't change pace. The orange mist on the horizon always grows. Our sluggish steps never stop.

I don't notice when Chen Feng stops moving. I'm watching her back and thinking that you could almost mistake her for a human being. Somebody who has been tore up, sure, but a living person. Daydreaming, I walk right past her.

I'm almost killed before I can stop.

The slender silver machine named 902 is standing motionless in the snow. A seven-foot-tall humanoid robot with a scavenged rifle on the high ready. Its three eyes are on me, lenses dilating as it absorbs the fact of my existence. It hasn't shot me yet, so it must be trying to classify what it sees.

Am I a severely wounded human being? A broken war machine? Am I dead or alive or what the hell? Nine-o-two doesn't seem to know and neither do I.

Over the machine's shoulder, I see a little tent shivering in the wind. The structure is wrapped up tight and the interior is throbbing with that rotten orange glow. Some shard of Archos is inside, talking.

I take a step forward.

Nine-o-two bristles. Thin sheets of ice crack and fall from his joints as the barrel of his gun settles between my eyes.

Familiar smoke rises from the machine's forehead. A line of communication that settles over me. Nine-o-two points at the snow a few yards away.

"*Path blocked, acknowledge. Alternate route indicated. I wish you luck . . . creatures,*" it says.

All kinds of tracks are in the muddy ice. Regular old footprints, the neatly spaced mine shafts of high-stepping tall-walkers, and the flat-topped mesas left by spider tanks dragging their equipment-filled belly nets over high snow drifts.

Gray Horse Army passed this way.

There are no mirrors out here in the wilderness and I thank the Creator for that.

Without a mirror, it's up to my imagination to guess what Gray Horse Army sees when they look out at us. A shambling group of a dozen corpses following in their tracks, brain-dead and deaf and dumb. Luckily, my imagination isn't that good anymore.

The humans don't travel at night, which is why we catch up to them.

At dusk on the third day, we watch the spider tanks amble into covered-wagon formation. The legged metal giants squat into bunker configurations for the night, encircling the human camp. In the protected clearing, campfires glitter into existence. Soon, rifle scopes wink at us from the tops of the tanks.

Got to keep the zombies at bay.

But we keep a safe distance. Sway together numbly through the night, the wind cutting moaning tunnels between us. Gray Horse Army does not fire. The war is over, after all. I imagine we are just another one of the odd atrocities left behind in this new world. Not enemies, not yet.

At dawn, there is movement.

A tall-walker pulls up short and the rider watches for maybe half an hour. The rest of the camp is packing up. Groaning tanks stand, loaded with soldiers. A flock of tall-walker scouts sprints ahead. But before the army moves, two tanks part and a handful of men approach. As they get near, I recognize Lonnie Wayne.

He's shading his eyes and shaking his head in disbelief.

Lonnie shrugs off his battle rifle and tosses it to the man next to him. Unfastens the loop on his sidearm holster, lets the pistol hang low on his hip. Extra ammunition and a knife and a hand radio hang from his belt, flopping as he strides toward us, alone.

"Lark," he calls, voice breaking.

His boots crunch through the brittle morning snow.

I don't react because I can't. My every move is monstrous. To speak is to groan. To move my corpse's puppet arms is to make a mockery of the dead. I'm so ashamed of my injuries. All I can do is stand here, a monster swaying with the wind as the breaking sun turns the ice to light.

Lonnie ignores the others. Gets near enough to look into my face.

"Oh, Lark," he says. "Look what they did to you."

I send all my concentration into the foreign, black metal in my head. Push out a glowing wisp of contact that only I can see. Let it settle over Lonnie's hand radio like ghostly fingertips. It doesn't catch, though. He's got man-made equipment and it doesn't work like Rob-built hardware. My light slips right through.

The old man studies me, looks for some reaction. But I can give him nothing.

"I can't leave you like this," he says.

Lonnie draws his pistol, reluctant, eyes shining. Lifts it glinting into the air and extends his arm. My head wobbles as the barrel noses into my temple. This close to death and I can't scream for Lonnie to stop. All I can think of is how much I miss the feeling of my goddamn heart beating in my chest.

"Lark," he says. "I'm proud of you, kid. You did real good."

The old man pulls back the hammer with his thumb. Drops his index finger into the trigger guard. Wraps it around the cold, familiar steel.

"You were a son to me," he says, and he squeezes his mouth into a hard line. Looks away, keeping his blue eyes wide to stop the tears from falling out.

Then his radio squawks. Lonnie pauses, cocks his head. Static.

". . . *Alive,*" the radio says, in a hoarse whisper.

I see the word register on Lonnie Wayne's face like a ripple on a pond.

Real slow, he turns his head to face all of us, a dozen silent corpses standing mute in the dawn. Spirits who are not alive and not yet dead. Honor-bound to survive.

Lonnie lowers his pistol.

"*Still alive,*" hisses the radio. "*Still alive.*"

The old man blinks the low sunlight out of his eyes along with a couple of crystalline tears. Holsters his weapon with trembling hands. My skin can't feel it when he cups my ruined face in his palms. I can't smell him when he pushes his forehead against mine. Inside, though, my heart is stinging with a pure, eternal kind of sadness that never makes it to my face. Never will again.

"We'll get through this, son," he says, simply.

If I could cry, I guess I would do it about now.

Not for what happened to me and my soldiers, or for the bone-tired despair dragging down the bags under Lonnie's eyes. I would cry for something even worse. For the sick orange glow that's been spreading just over the horizon. For what I recognize as the birth of another Archos, its tendrils of control looping and roiling out of a growing evil haze. For the never-ending goddamn trials of living things.

If I could, I'd cry for what's to come.

ABOUT THE AUTHORS

AMBER BENSON is an actor, filmmaker, novelist, and amateur occultist who sings in the shower. Best known for her work as Tara Maclay on *Buffy the Vampire Slayer,* she is the author of the Calliope Reaper-Jones series and the middle-grade ghost story *Among The Ghosts.* She is also the codirector (with Adam Busch) of the feature film *Drones.* She can be stalked on her blog—www.amberbensonwrotethis.blogspot.com—and on Twitter and Facebook.

S. G. BROWNE is the author of the novels *Breathers*; *Fated*; and *Lucky Bastard,* as well as the e-book short-story collection *Shooting Monkeys in a Barrel.* His debut novel, *Breathers,* a dark comedy told from the point of view of a zombie, was optioned for film by Fox Searchlight Pictures and is currently in development. His short fiction can also be found in several anthologies and collections, including *The Living Dead 2*; *Zombies: Encounters with the Hungry Dead*; *Swallowed by the Cracks*; and *Amazing Stories of the Flying Spaghetti Monster.* His writing is inspired by his love of dark comedy, social satire, and the supernatural. You can visit him at www .sgbrowne.com.

KEN BRUEN
Author of twenty novels.
Ph.D. in metaphysics.
Current book, *Headstone.*

CHELSEA CAIN is the author of *The New York Times* bestselling thrillers *Evil at Heart*; *Sweetheart*; *Heartsick*; and *The Night Season.*

All take place in Portland, Oregon, and focus on Det. Archie Sheridan, rainbow-haired journalist Susan Ward, and Sheridan's lovely nemesis, the serial killer Gretchen Lowell. Cain's books have been published in more than twenty languages, recommended on *The Today Show,* appeared in episodes of HBO's *True Blood* and ABC's *Castle,* and named among Stephen King's top ten favorite books of the year. NPR included her book *Heartsick* in their list of the top one hundred thrillers ever written. Cain lives in Portland with her husband and remarkably well-adjusted five-year-old daughter.

ORSON SCOTT CARD, the author of *Ender's Game,* has also written stories and novels in the horror genre, like "Eumenides in the Fourth-Floor Lavatory"; *Lost Boys; Homebody;* and *Treasure Box.* He teaches at Southern Virginia University, served an LDS mission in Brazil in the 1970s, directs plays at every opportunity, and resides in Greensboro, North Carolina, with his wife and youngest daughter. See www.hatrack.com.

DAN CHAON's most recent book is the short-story collection *Stay Awake.* He is also the author of the national bestseller *Await Your Reply,* which was named one of the ten best books of 2009 by *Publisher's Weekly; Entertainment Weekly;* Janet Maslin of *The New York Times;* and Laura Miller of Salon.com, as well as having been named among the year's best fiction by the American Library Association and such newspapers as the *Washington Post* and the *Chicago Tribune.* Chaon's other books include the short-story collections *Fitting Ends* and *Among the Missing,* which was a finalist for the 2001 National Book Award, and the novel *You Remind Me of Me.* Dan's fiction has appeared in many journals and anthologies, including *Best American Short Stories; The Pushcart Prize;* and *The O. Henry Prize Stories.* He has been a finalist for the National Magazine Award in Fiction and was the recipient of the 2006 Academy Award in Literature from the American Academy of Arts and Letters. He teaches at Oberlin College, where he is the Pauline Delaney Professor of Creative Writing and Literature.

STEPHANIE CRAWFORD lives in Las Vegas where she may or may not be a showgirl assassin, but usually does odd jobs that in-

tasy Award. His most recently published or forthcoming work includes the official tie-in novel for zombie apocalypse computer game *Dead Island* for Transworld, a novelization of the 1971 Hammer movie *Vampire Circus* for Hammer/Arrow, several *Doctor Who* audio dramas for Big Finish Productions, a short-story collection *Long Shadows, Nightmare Light* for PS Publishing, and a follow-up volume to *Cinema Macabre* titled *Cinema Futura*.

JOHN SKIPP is best known as an award-winning and bestselling author and editor, whose twenty-three books have sold millions of copies worldwide and been published in nine languages. His early works (written with Craig Spector) were considered seminal to the "splatterpunk" style of modern horror fiction. A 1987 conversation between Skipp and George Romero led to Skipp and Spector's 1989 anthology *Book of the Dead,* which was the beginning of modern post-Romero zombie literature. Skipp's other zombie anthologies include *Still Dead* (1992), *Mondo Zombie* (which won the Bram Stoker Award for Best Anthology in 2006), and the seven-hundred-page "Greatest Hits" collection, *Zombies: Encounters With the Hungry Dead* (2009).

THOMAS E. SNIEGOSKI is the *New York Times* bestselling author of the young adult series The Fallen, as well as the popular urban-fantasy books featuring angel turned private investigator, Remy Chandler. *The Fallen: End of Days* is the latest in the Fallen series, and *In the House of the Wicked,* the next of the Remy Chandler books, was released in August. Sniegoski lives in Massachusetts with his long-suffering wife, LeeAnne, and their French bulldog, Kirby. Please visit him at www.sniegoski.com.

STEPHEN SUSCO has accumulated tremendous success and is renown in a profoundly dynamic career spectrum, including stints in such unique and daring fields as dynamic cryptopaleontology, dark-matter-waste recycling, and extraheliosphere meteor hijacking. In this particular slice of the metaverse, however, he's achieved a more modest reputation, having concocted slightly more than a few movie recipes—including *The Grudge*; *Red*; and the upcoming *Leatherface,* of which slightly less than a few have been half baked. And yet his "twins" in their respective parallel universes surely look on with envy at this, his first foray into the publishing world.

KURT SUTTER is a television and feature writer. He is very familiar with things that should be dead, but are not.

DUANE SWIERCZYNSKI is the author of several crime thrillers, including the Edgar–nominated and Anthony Award–winning *Expiration Date*, as well as *Fun & Games*, the first in a trilogy. He currently writes the DC Comics series *Birds of Prey* and has written about the Punisher, Cable, the Immortal Iron Fist, Werewolf By Night, Black Widow, and Deadpool for Marvel Comics. Duane has also collaborated with CSI creator Anthony E. Zuiker on a series of bestselling "digi-novel" thrillers, which includes *Level 26: Dark Origins; Dark Prophecy*; and the forthcoming *Dark Revelations*. He and his family live in Philadelphia, Pennsylvania. Visit him at www.secretdead.com or twitter.com/swierczy.

DANIEL H. WILSON is the *New York Times* bestselling author of *Robopocalypse,* as well as six other titles, including *How to Survive a Robot Uprising, Where's My Jetpack?* and *A Boy and His Bot.* He earned a Ph.D. in Robotics from Carnegie Mellon University, along with a Masters degree in Artificial Intelligence. His next novel, *Amped,* will be released by Doubleday on June 5th, 2012. Daniel lives in Portland, Oregon. You can learn more at www.danielhwilson .com.

RIO YOUERS is the British Fantasy Award–nominated author of *Old Man Scratch* and *Westlake Soul*. His short fiction has been published by, among others, Edge Science Fiction & Fantasy, IDW, and PS Publishing. Rio lives in southwestern Ontario with his wife, Emily, and their daughter, Lily Maye.

THESE ANTHOLOGIES FEATURING TODAY'S HOTTEST AUTHORS WILL SATISFY YOUR BLOODLUST

Mike Mignola, the creator of *Hellboy*, and Christopher Golden team up once again in this illustrated novel